# THE ROLLER BIRDS OF RAMPUR

# THE
# ROLLER
# BIRDS
# OF RAMPUR

## Indi Rana

THE BODLEY HEAD
LONDON

British Library Cataloguing in Publication Data
Rana, Indira Higham
The roller birds of Rampur
I. Title
823 [J]

ISBN 0–370–31315–1

First published in 1991 by
The Bodley Head Children's Books
An imprint of the Random Century Group Ltd
20 Vauxhall Bridge Road, London SW1V 2SA

Random Century Australia (Pty) Ltd
20 Alfred Street, Sydney, NSW 2061, Australia

Random Century New Zealand Ltd
PO Box 40–086, Glenfield, Auckland 10, New Zealand

Century Hutchinson South Africa (Pty) Ltd
PO Box 337, Bergvlei, 2012, South Africa

Photoset by Speedset Ltd, Ellesmere Port

Printed in Great Britain by
Cox & Wyman Ltd, Reading

# THE ROLLER BIRDS OF RAMPUR

# ACKNOWLEDGEMENTS

This book came out of my experience of living in England, the US and Canada as a young adult, and observing my many nieces and nephews struggle to find their place and identity through their childhood and adolescence. During the past few years I have had the opportunity also to interact with my cousins and nieces growing up in both urban and rural India. None of the characters in this book is a representation of any one of them, but the inspirations and influences are certainly from real life. Scenes and events at the Mehta Farm and villages around them are drawn from my family farm in Madhya Pradesh, but names, characters and events are fictionalized, as are those in New Delhi.

I owe grateful thanks to Dr Ramachandra Gandhi and Badrinath Chaturvedi who, in conversation, gave me many profound insights into the Mind of India to supplement and clarify my own reading; to Werner, who demonstrates so clearly that the search for dharm is no different in the western mind than it is in the Indian; to my nieces Rena and Seema Sodhi in London and Nonita Kalra in New Delhi; Dr Charanjit Singh of the School of Russian Studies at Jawaharlal Nehru University who commented on various chapters of the manuscript; to my mother, Jeet Tara, who gave me insights, explanations and stories, and space on the farm in which to write the first draft of this book; to P. N. Tiwari and P. N. Nair, who typed and retyped the manuscript; and not least to my editor, Ann- Janine Murtagh, who saw the potential of the manuscript and put in her willing and careful editorial energy, enabling me to pull it into shape.

*Indi Rana*
*New Delhi, 1991*

*For Mimi, Rena and Seema*

# 1

Ever since we came to England, whenever I thought of India, I thought of trains. I had this picture of the country criss-crossed with thousands of miles of gleaming, metal rails along which steam engines achha-chugged away like tiny, busy ants, joggling people around on their business. People, people, people. People bursting out of the bogeys, clinging to the sides like so many flies; a spider's-web of railroads with its enormous catch.

Another picture I had was of endless miles of ripening wheat, swinging green into the horizon, broken by clusters of huts and trees; flashes of red and purple, as women squatted in rows, weeding; and men in white, patiently, patiently followed their oxen at the ploughs.

There were clichés like the Taj Mahal; temples, ugly, crowded towns; factories belching smoke; sculptures, paintings; idiotic films, plaintive songs . . .

There was Mehta Farm, where Dad and Mum and Rachna, my sister, and I had lived until I was seven, and she, five, before we came to England.

Then there was this one picture I had, which seemed so like a fairy story, I never really believed it – of bandits. Bandits like those in the American Wild West, except in India they were called dacoits. It was a hazy picture, just bits and snatches of conversations, way back in my memory: Shanti, my ayah, nursemaid, saying: 'Now behave yourself, Sheila Bai, or the dacoits will come and get you!'

But I never connected India with *women* bandits: gun-toting, khaki-clad women driving jeeps from mountains, on missions of revenge. Yet it was a woman bandit called Bijli, which means 'lightning', who was a sort of turning point for me, not two years ago.

Not that I ever met her, although she was very close at one point, or that I even knew of her existence that spring, when I

I

was to take my A-levels and didn't, because I simply had to get back to India.

I'm telling all this back-to-front, as usual, so perhaps I'd best start over in some sort of sequence, to make a little bit of sense.

I can't *begin* to say what it was like that spring. It's hard to put it down in black and white; but then, that's what a story-teller is supposed to do, right?

Confused, depressed, anxious . . . no, these don't quite say enough. I think the right word is *annihilated*. I know it sounds a bit dramatic but that's really what it was like.

I'd wake up at about four in the morning, my heart going like a runaway engine, and my breath coming in short gasps. I'd thrash around for a bit, in a sort of panic. Then I'd pick up a book, start to read, put it down, turn on the radio, turn it off, rush to the bathroom to brush my teeth, down to the kitchen to make myself a cup of tea. Anything, anything to get away . . . From what? I didn't know.

It wasn't until Dr Able taught me to *look* at what was going on that I began to see what was really happening inside me. It's difficult to stand aside and watch yourself thrash about like that – but I began to see a crazy sequence. It would begin with a clenching in my diaphragm, like a stab with a long, thin knife, which spread like a hundred million pin-pricks through to my back, up to my neck, across my shoulders and down my arms. My forearms would tense, and my fists curl up like stones. My stomach would knot so I'd feel nauseous and the world would be coloured a bilious green.

I'd hear a babble in my head as though there were thirty people in a crowded room, yelling their heads off; some giving me instructions: Don't do this . . . Don't do that . . . Do this . . . Why don't you . . .? Others telling me I was no good at anything. There'd be children crying, and fleeting pictures of teachers at school.

Sometimes I'd hear a clear conversation between people in white overalls sitting in front of a computer console like in a space-ship being guided to a landing. Other times there'd be a sad, sad feeling as everybody got ready to die, because the nuclear missiles weren't as safe as people had thought they were, and all the anti-war demonstrators were hanging on crosses on a bare hill.

And once an army in white jackboots marched over me as I lay helpless on a wide empty road, watching them come.

This early morning confusion always left me wiped out, feeling suddenly washed away, or going sort of rigid, my mind going blank. It got so I couldn't concentrate on anything, much less on the thought of exams. I became nervy and jittery, fading into my head any old time of day, so Rachna would say: 'How is it, Sheels, that just sitting there you disappear?'

But what could I tell her? That suddenly I was in a world I didn't know? At the time I didn't even have the words to describe it. And truly, it took me ages to realize it was all happening *inside* me.

Soon the spasms and prickles turned into a dull, continuous pain in my stomach and back. And Dad, who is a doctor, prescribed antacids and aspirin!

But I must keep on track. So I must say, even though it's so difficult, what it was that made everything seemed too much to bear that spring, so that just living from day to day became intolerable.

Jimmy. My boyfriend.

And even now, nearly two years later, as I write this, I feel a dull ache and I hear a harsh, dry little voice in my head say: 'Ha, bloody ha.'

It wasn't dramatic or anything the way we . . . well it's hard to even say we met. I'd seen him around at school a lot – just like I'd seen all the other boys. He wasn't one of the people you noticed right away. In fact, at that time, I rather fancied Roger Thomas who was the school hunk. Very tall, very broad, captain of the school football team. Jimmy was stocky, and square, very capable-looking. We'd smiled at each other every now and then in the corridors, or as we filed into class. And then, one day, very casually, very naturally we got talking.

The subject was toads. He did brilliant drawings of their insides, and Mr Lacoste had passed his practical book around

3

for us to look at in the Biology Lab. My drawings weren't bad either, but Jimmy's were definitely better.

As we left the lab, I happened to go through the door at the same time as him, and I said: 'I think your toads are great!'

Jimmy went rather pink, and said stumblingly: 'Thanks. But I think your frogs are better.' He blinked and smiled nervously. I noticed he had beautiful hands, as he clutched his books against his chest: long, slender fingers with square ends, on square palms. Sensitive and sensible at the same time. And somehow, that did it. I sighed very dramatically, and said: 'Oh, I'm sure I couldn't compete with your earthworms.'

He replied, surprisingly: 'Ah! the earthworm lives in the apple, and the appleworm lives in the earth . . .'

So I said: 'And thus the worm turns.'

And he said: 'Oh, you worm the cockles of my heart . . .'

And we ended up giggling over cups of coffee at the café across the road.

It was ages before Jimmy actually asked me out. He was really quite shy about it. He wasn't a noisy, flash type, like some of the boys, and that's what I liked so much about him.


We went out together a whole year, Jimmy and I. I didn't think about what our families might think, or that I was Indian and he was English. All I thought, if I thought at all beyond the sheer excitement of being with Jimmy, was that Romance, wonderful Romance, had come into my life at last. I didn't realize how unusual it was for an English boy to be going with an Indian girl.

Actually, I never really saw myself as Indian in any special sense. Of course, Mum wears a sari, and Dad's name is Mehta; our house is chock-a-block with brass tables and sandalwood lampstands, folk paintings on cloth and pseudo-antique sculpture copied from Indian temples. We eat Indian food and listen to Indian music and Mum and Dad watch Indian movies on the video until it makes you ill. But Dad and Mum never played the heavy Indian parents with Rachna and I, not like my friend Sunaina's parents did. They never drummed into our heads our Indianness, our traditions, the dangers of going out with boys, the way they did in England. I didn't really realize that for Indian parents in England, Mum and Dad were a little unusual.

Besides, because we'd been in England since we were seven and five, Rach and I felt – you know – British. We didn't feel different, not really, from the others, except perhaps when we had relatives from India visiting.

We'd been invited out, of course, in groups ever since we were so high – from school and with kids in our neighbourhood. We went on picnics, and to cricket and football matches. As we got older Rachna and I started to go round with a group from school: Barb and Janey, Sam and Dave, Bob and Phil. We'd all been friends since the first year. We'd meet up on the common to talk, and sometimes go to a film or a concert. In fact, no one asked me out for almost a year after Barb and Janey started having special boyfriends. Mum didn't mind when they brought Bob and Phil to spend the evening with Rachna and me, just talking and listening to music, sprawled on cushions in the family room off the kitchen.

But I *had* began wondering when I'd find someone a bit special. So when Jimmy asked me out to a Sunday afternoon film, I suppose something way inside me heaved a sigh of relief: now I was just like the others! But it wasn't just that. The birds did sing more sweetly, the skies really were a clearer blue when Jimmy and I were together. I know it sounds slushy, but that's really how it felt.

James Baker. Sheila Mehta. The names sounded good together. And pretty soon Jim and Sheels became like one name and we were invited out everywhere together.

It all seemed so natural I didn't even question it. Though Barb's boyfriend Phil, who was a religious nut, did make some comment on when was I going to convert Jim into a Hindu. Phil was a real Bible-basher. He was always spouting the New Testament at us, philosophizing about his faith, or asking us daft questions like, 'What is God?' We laughed at it all, of course. No one wanted to get into heavy discussions – we were

5

too busy having a good time. Phil went to church every Sunday and tried to get us all to go. And no one would.

About three months after we'd started seeing each other, I invited Jimmy home. At first it was only when the others were there, but pretty soon after that, Jim became a regular feature at our house in Chigwell. It is a large, airy, spacious mock-Tudor house, so people don't fall over each other's feet. And what Jim liked to do most, anyway, was watch the telly!


One day we were having a drowsy Sunday morning in the family room. Dad was snoring away in a corner armchair, and Mum was rather mistily watching a video with some prat of an Indian actor, his jowls hanging to his collar-bone, his belly wobbling like pudding over his belt, chasing a buxom, big-eyed, flat-footed heroine through the flowers in some far mountain meadow in India.

Mum said rather wistfully: 'Raj and I had a love marriage, you know. In those days that was a very daring thing to do. Only two of us girls at the TTI in Allahabad had the guts to marry for love; the rest of the girls all had arranged marriages.' Mum's a geography teacher at the local comprehensive. She'd graduated from the Teacher Training Institute in Allahabad and had had to take exams and a special degree to be able to teach in London.

'I've never regretted it,' Mum went on, 'even though Ma threatened to lock me up in my room till I could get over this "stupid infatuation" I had for Raj. Raj's parents were much more liberal. . .'

On the TV, the heroine flung her veil around her breasts in an all-revealing gesture, as she made a pretence of covering them, and began to shriek out a plaintive love song.

Rachna giggled: 'Oh Mum! You don't mean Dad chased you around the trees like that when you were courting, do you?'

'Don't be silly! That's just movies,' Mum said, but her smile was a bit tight, and I wondered whether these ridiculous Indian films *had* affected Mum's generation after all. Rachna and I, and even Sunaina, whose family is much more conservative, thought Indian movies were the dopiest things in the world, though Sunaina thought Indian *film stars* were terrific. In Indian films, pretty well *all* of them, family honour was held aloft like a banner of righteousness, true love was almost always thwarted at the start and it took all of three hours and gallons of melodrama for everything to come up roses in the end.

'Raj and I used to meet at Kwality's in Allahabad whenever he came through from Delhi on his way to Rampur,' Mum went on. 'We used to drink cold coffee with ice-cream and hold hands.' She sniffed. 'It was very bold and modern in those days, I can tell you.'

'Oh Mum, how romantic!' Rachna whooped. But there was an edge to her voice which Mum caught, and she changed the subject.

Another time, Mum got me alone one evening as I was stacking the dinner dishes in the dishwasher, and brought the subject round to boyfriends again. 'I sometimes think Raj and I were very selfish coming to England, Sheila,' she said unhappily, as she swilled the dishes under the tap and handed them to me. 'We were looking for a better life, and we just didn't think how you girls would adjust. Finding a husband is going to be difficult for you here, and I must say I haven't any answers about that.'

When I said nothing she went on a bit awkwardly: 'You're going to have to find out by yourself, Sheila. You know I don't believe in arranged marriages: most of the people I know who had arranged marriages blame their parents or husbands, or wives, whenever anything goes wrong. They don't learn to be responsible for their choices or their lives and never become independent people. So, I'm not going to put down any rules for you about English boys or Indian boys, though I had hoped you would find an Indian boy.'

I rattled the cutlery tray hard, and banged some dishes against each other.

She sighed. 'I know how difficult that is, but . . .' She trailed off, then pulled herself together and said: 'The rules don't change, though. You let me know where you're going and what time you'll be home. And no late nights except on Saturday. Home by twelve, all right?' But she kept standing there, looking out of the window.

'Mum!' I said, feeling very self-conscious, 'I'm too young to think of husbands right now. Jimmy and I are just friends.'

'Maybe, maybe,' Mum said, 'but you'll soon be thinking of husbands. It's only natural.' She wiped her hands on the dish-cloth. 'I know you're a sensible girl and you'll be responsible. But if anything goes wrong just remember I'm here and I'll try to help you as much as I can.' She smiled a little nervously, and said: 'I know you young people don't think sex is so important – well, not the way we did . . . but Sheila . . . in spite of all this new and modern thinking, sex is very old-fashioned. Our bodies' responses are very conservative . . . So be careful, all right? Don't . . .'

'Oh *Mum!*' I said, embarrassed to death. Sex! Jimmy and I hadn't even talked about it. The most Jim had ever managed was a goodnight kiss and a 'Bye then, see you tomorrow.' Barb and Janey and I discussed it endlessly of course, and Barb swore she and Phil were having it off. But Janey and I doubted it. Barb was like that – always ahead of everyone else. And Phil really was too hung up on religion. I always wondered how they'd hit it off. As opposite as could be.

'No! I mean it,' Mum said, reddening. 'It matters . . . So stay . . .' she struggled for words,—'pure. It *does* matter.' And she hugged me quickly and went off to get ready for some party or other.

Dad was a little different. It wasn't sex he was concerned about (thank God)! He pinned me down one morning when we were having an early breakfast and Mum and Rachna were still upstairs. He cleared his throat a couple of times, looked quickly at me from under his eyebrows, and jumped right in with both feet going like paddles on a boat rushing upstream.

'I don't mind you finding your own . . . ah . . . boyfriend, Sheila,' he said, spreading vast blobs of butter on his toast, very fast, 'but . . . ah . . . be careful about Englishmen. East is East and West is West . . . You heard that song? It's true . . . they don't mix.'

I groaned inwardly and waited.

He was silent for a bit, munching away. Then he said: 'This Jimmy fellow. He seems like a steady, reliable type. He was telling me his father's a policeman. Is that so?'

I nodded wordlessly.

'I'm not narrow-minded, Sheila, or snobbish,' Dad said carefully, 'but just think . . . would you have married a policeman if you were in India?'

'I don't know, Dad,' I said, wishing I was on Mars some place. 'I couldn't know, could I? I'm not in India.'

'You wouldn't,' Dad said decisively. 'You wouldn't marry an ordinary constable anyway, though you might marry a DCP.'

'Oh?' I said, dry as could be.

'Deputy Commissioner of Police,' Dad said as though that explained everything.

'Why?' I said, getting a bit cross with him. 'What's the difference?'

And Dad said heavily, wiping his mouth on a paper napkin, and then passing it unthinkingly across his forehead: 'Because a DCP would be of your own background. From an educated family.'

Then I realized he was talking about class, and I really blew up, I can tell you. And I gave him a lecture on being narrow-minded and old-fashioned. I told him no one in their right minds thought about class these days.

Dad listened without arguing, frowning a little. Then as he got up and brushed the crumbs off his shirt with a pudgy hand, he smiled suddenly: 'Well, the young always know better, Sheila, I can tell you this from my own experience. I can't force you to do anything: it's *your* life, *your* responsibility. But. Be careful, I don't want you to get hurt.'

I felt awkward about it all for a while, but actually, all in all, I thought I had the most considerate parents in the world. They weren't pushing me one way or other; they'd given me

9

some of their opinions . . . but not so I'd be crushed by them, and they'd assumed I was a sensible, responsible person. I was free to choose what was best for me.

I didn't realize then that responsibility for one's own life was such a very difficult thing.


At first I didn't pay any attention to the fact that Jimmy never invited me over to his house. Dad and Mum are very sociable people and our house is always full of people coming and going. So for almost nine months it never occurred to me that I'd never met his parents. Sometimes I'd ask Jim questions about his mum and dad, but I didn't get much of a response. He just said: 'Uh, huh,' and closed up.


Jimmy, Jimmy, Jimmy. Solid, reliable, dependable Jimmy. Jimmy whom I'd begun to see, as Mum had said I would, sharing a future with me. Living out our hopes and dreams. Quiet Jimmy. Jimmy who was going to become a surgeon. Jimmy with the capable, sensitive hands. Stocky, solid Jimmy with a brush of freckles across his nose, sandy hair over his brow, eyes crinkling when he smiled.

Sensible Jimmy, Jimmy of the quiet, dry wit, Jimmy who never said what was not necessary.

Silent Jimmy. Ultimately, *English* Jimmy.

'Mum wants to meet you,' he said, finally, a whole year after we'd started going together, nine months after he'd been making himself comfortable in our kitchen, talking sensibly, dependably, reliably with Dad and Mum. And stupid, idiot me, stupidly and idiotically thrilled, going through my dresses, choosing shoes, doing my hair . . .

It was a little terraced house in Ilford, two up, two down, with lace curtains and ornaments in the window.

Mrs Baker opened the front door. And, before she could stop herself, her hand flew to her unhappy mouth, her pale eyes widened, and she said: 'Sheila? Oh! But . . . I thought Sheila was an *English* name!'

Then recovering herself, trying to sound as though she'd

never said it, running her fingers distractedly through her thin, brown hair: 'Oh Sheila! Yes, I've heard so much about you. Come in. Come in.'

And with those words hanging like silent accusations between us . . . an *English* name, an *English* name . . . we sat against those polite armchairs and sipped polite sips of tea . . .

The clenching in my gut began then, I think, the stabs and pin-pricks, as we went through the motions in a meaningless, empty box, resounding with silences. Jimmy's mum and I talked about school and my parents, about doctors and surgeons and policemen, while silences sought shadowy corners and questions waited to confuse, searching for insecurities on which to feed, uncertainties to fill empty spaces.

For Jimmy, dear solid, reliable, dependable Jimmy with whom I'd been going out with for a whole year, who was going to live out my dreams with me, and share my life, said nothing, nothing at all.

Then or later.

We went out together twice after that, but his smile was wooden, his eyes sort of glazed and far away. At first I said: 'What's the matter, Jimmy?' and 'Why don't you say something, Jimmy?' and 'Jimmy, have I done something wrong?' And I heard a peculiar whine in my voice.

The second time out I began to understand. And my pride took over . . . luckily . . . or perhaps not so luckily. I wouldn't plead, I wouldn't nag. I wouldn't ask for explanations. I wouldn't *beg*. I would NOT! I was Sheila Mehta! I was *Sheila*. And Sheila, as I cried in bed at night, and grit my teeth, was *not* an English name . . . an English name . . . an *English* name!

He started to avoid me at school, then. Stopped calling. And the silences grew, reliably, solidly, dependably.

# 2

Then there was Sunny. Sunaina Raghbans Singh. So soon after Jimmy . . . it's hard to talk about her too, almost as hard as it is to talk about Jimmy.

She was my best friend. Not like Janey and Barb. More special because she was so different. I was like Barb and Janey in my head, even though, if I'd worn a salwar-kameez, I would have looked more like Sunny. The way you dress tells you a lot about what your head's like inside. Rach and I wore dresses and tights and jeans, but Sunny always wore Indian clothes, even at school. Her parents wouldn't allow her anything else. And that she did what they wanted, said everything about her.

Once we'd been going through an Indian fashion magazine in my room. It had been published recently in London and looked like an Indian copy of *Vogue*. But the models were Indian, and the clothes were rich with embroidery and glitter.

'I really wish I could wear stuff like that,' I said enviously. 'But I'd look a right lump with all that glitz. You'd look just terrific in an outfit like that, Sun.'

And Sunny said, simply: 'I wish I could wear dresses.'

'Oh no, Sun, you wouldn't be *you* if you did,' I cried. 'I think Indian clothes are brilliant.'

She sighed, and now that I think about it, very forlornly, and said: 'That's only because you don't have to wear them.'

She was small and round, with long, thick, black hair and enormous heavy-lidded doe eyes, like something out of Indian sculptures. I envied her the way she looked, because she was so . . . yes, Indian. Unlike me: sort of medium-average all around, with a squarish jaw, ordinary brown eyes and a short bob which is easy to manage.

I felt very protective towards Sunny: I was always gentle with her. I couldn't remember ever having had a cross word with her. None of the sarcastic banter I got into with Barb and

Janey. And I kept them pretty well apart. Sunny didn't much care for them. I think I was her only real friend.

The Singhs ran a grocery store on Ilford High Street. They sent Sunny to a good school though, because they believed in educating their children well . . . boys more than girls of course, so Sunny'd dropped out after her GCSEs to help out in the store.

Before Mum and Dad moved to Chigwell, they'd lived in a small semi in Ilford down the road from the Singhs, and I'd known Sun since I was seven.

Mum still shopped at the Singhs' store, looking for spices and pickles she couldn't find at Sainsbury's. They always gave her a cold drink or a cup of tea when she went to their store, and they chatted for a while about news from India.

I'd meet Sunny at Ilford tube station on my way back from school, and we'd spend a little time together, at McDonald's or wandering around, window-shopping, before I took the bus home, and she went back to the store.

Sunaina was waiting as usual outside the station that afternoon about two weeks after I'd begun to realize Jimmy'd chucked me.

I didn't notice the expression on her face as I said: 'Here,' opening my bag and handing Sunaina back the copies of Indian film magazines she liked to lend me.

Sunaina put them in her shopping bag.

'And here, these are for Babloo from Rach.' I handed her some music magazines.

But Sunaina shook her head and started walking away. I ran two steps to catch up with her. 'Hey, Sunny. What's the matter?'

'Don't want them, do I?' she snapped.

'But you *asked* for . . .' I said, puzzled. This was an unusual display of bad temper from placid Sunny. I looked at her set face as she concentrated on the pavement. 'Here, Sunny. What is it? Have I done something?'

'No . . .'

'Well,' I said, attempting to lighten the air, 'magazines aren't known to bite. So what is it?'

She looked up, opened her mouth to say something, hesitated, then shut it again. 'Oh nothing,' she said.

'Of *course* there's something! Do you think I'm stupid?' A flicker of pin-pricks coursed through my arms. 'You don't *want* to tell me. Well, if you don't want to say anything, don't make such a big deal out of it.'

Three steps later Sunaina said flatly: 'We're going back to India.'

I stopped. 'Oh, you lucky thing! When are you going? What've you got on such a long face for? I'd be thrilled.' I paused. 'How long are you going for? Look. Take the mags. You can return them before you go.'

Sunaina looked at me with an angry, hurt, undecided expression I had never seen on her face before, then looked away at the kitchen fittings in a shop window.

'Oh for God's sake, Sunny. What's the mystery? All right, then don't take the magazines.' I stuffed them back into my bag. 'Did your mum catch Babloo with the last lot then?'

'Oh God!' Sunaina said in an odd, strangled voice. Then, with an effort she collected herself and said: 'It's not that, I'm sorry, Sheels. It's a little different this time: very different.'

'What could be different?' I said with a little laugh. 'Oh I know, this time you are going overland, by camel and bullock-cart, and you're scared to death!'

But there was no smile on Sunaina's face as she said: 'No. The difference is that this time we're going for good. Forever. And we're not coming back.'

'What?' A spasm caught my gut. 'What do you mean never coming back?' I stared at her, reaching for her hand.

'Just what I said,' Sunaina put her hands in her pockets.

'But what about your dad's shop?' I said foolishly.

'Nothing about my dad's shop is what about my dad's shop,' Sunaina said cuttingly. 'We're selling it.'

'Selling it?'

Sunaina swung around and started walking again. 'Stop repeating whatever I say. I just told you we're going back to India, for good. And we're selling the shop. And that's what's bothering me. So accept it, and just catch your bus, all right? I'm not in the mood for talking today.'

Again I had to run to catch up with her. I grabbed her arm. 'That's not good enough,' I said, a dead red heat flowing up my back. 'If you don't want to talk today you could have rung me up and I wouldn't have got off at Ilford. So there is something else. What about Teji and Babloo? They were going to take over your dad's shop, weren't they? That's what your dad's been working for since he came here, isn't it? How can he sell it, then, just like that?'

Sunaina shook her arm free. 'Well, as you see, they're selling it, "just like that", and that's all there is to it. Teji doesn't want to be a shopkeeper: he has "bigger ambitions",' her voice was bitter, 'and you know Babloo, all he can think of is house music and American football.'

We waited for the pedestrian signal to turn green, without saying anything. Me looking at Sunaina, Sunaina looking determinedly up the road.

We crossed the street.

'Well?' I said, on the other side.

'Well what?'

'Well, pardon me for breathing,' I snapped. 'Well, it doesn't make sense Sunny, so make it make sense. Explain it to me. What's going on? Why are you leaving?'

Sunaina sighed, a short exasperated sound: 'I wish I hadn't said anything now. I knew you'd pester me with questions. I should've just gone.'

'Just gone?' My breath caught. 'When are you going?'

'Next Thursday.'

'Next Thursday?' It was like a slap across the face. 'But that's only six days away. How can you get everything tied up by then?'

'Mum and I are going next Thursday, Dad and Babloo will follow later.' She was walking very fast now, hands in her pockets, head down. 'Teji's going off on his own to Bradford.'

'Sunny! This is crazy! What in God's name's happening? You're all behaving like a plague's hit Ilford,' I almost shouted. I couldn't believe it. Sunaina was like a stranger to me then. It was a repeat of Jimmy!

We reached Sunaina's bus stop and joined the queue. I saw my bus at the lights across the road. I waited.

15

'Look,' Sunaina said, looking at the road. 'It's really to do with us: Teji, Babloo and me. You know how traditional Mum and Dad are. They're disappointed: none of us speak Punjabi, they say they sometimes can't even understand what we say: we're interested in things they don't approve of; and now Teji wants to go off, away from the family, and they're . . . they're arranging my . . .'

She turned to me, her eyes wide, holding herself in. 'Oh, Sheels, they're going to get me married off!'

And she was holding my hand, her eyes pleading. 'Sheels, I don't know what to do!'

I held her hand tight, relief fighting fear: relief that Sunaina was my friend again, fear that I was going to lose her.

'Sunny,' I said, 'why don't you come over tomorrow in the afternoon and we'll talk then. Can you do that?'

Sunaina's face closed up again.

'No.'

The momentary relief vanished. 'Sunny!'

'I . . . can't. I've not got time.'

'Sunny, it's *me*, Sheila! You must have time for me!' It came out like a wail. 'We've been friends all our lives and I might never see you again. And you have no time for me?'

Sunaina shook her head, the miserable, shut look final.

Desperately I cried: 'Look, all right, you don't have time. I'll come to your place, all right?'

Again Sunaina shook her head.

'What?' I said, feeling the hot flush on my cheeks, the tension at the back of my head spreading to my shoulders. Then, with an explosion of anger, oblivious to the people at the bus stop, I grabbed Sunaina's shoulders and shook her hard.

'I. *Will*. Not. Have. This!' I said each word separately, almost shouting. 'I will not! I will not allow our friendship to end like this, with mysteries and insults. I will not believe I mean so little to you!' I knew there were tears in my eyes as I said through gritted teeth, 'Sun-ain-na! What. Is. It?'

'Stop it!' Sunaina cried. 'Stop it! What do you think my dad's friends would say if they saw us? Who do you think you are?' She put both her arms between mine and with a wrench, freed herself. 'My bus!'

I dropped her arms. 'You cow!' I yelled. 'You cow! Sod your bus. I missed mine, didn't I?'

Sunaina's bus drew up and the queue began to move.

I grabbed Sunaina's shopping bag. 'Tell me.'

Sunaina let her bag go. 'Take it, for God's sake. Let me be!' She was crying. I handed her bag back.

'Sunaina,' I said again desperately, 'Tell me!' Sunaina moved forward and stopped. People behind her got on. Then she said very fast: 'Well, you asked for it, Sheila. They don't want me to see *you* again. It's because of *you* we're going back. And we've been fighting at home. I didn't want to tell you. Because of *you*. Ever since I told them you're going out with Jimmy, they've been looking for a man for me. I've got to go to India and marry some bloke I don't even know, and it's all because of . . .' she looked at my face, and stopped.

'Are you getting on, miss?' the bus driver said.

'Yes,' she said and jumped on.

I opened my mouth. I wanted to cry: 'But there's no Jimmy, Sunny, there is no Jimmy any more!'

But the door had closed. The driver changed gears and the bus moved off.

The drone and thunder of Ilford High Street swirled around me, I looked at the pavement, and my shoes swam in the blur in front of my eyes. First Jimmy. Now Sunaina.

I felt my stomach churn, my back and arms burn, my face flush. I felt humiliated. Everything seemed so pointless. The world seemed a chaos of deliberate misunderstandings; hopelessly, stupidly, ignorantly short-sighted. Sunny was to be 'married off'. An arranged marriage! To a stranger. I felt sick as I thought of it. I clapped my hands over my mouth and ran into the nearest shop and asked for the loo.

No, I didn't throw up, but the next morning the nightmare pictures began, and I woke up, crying: 'Sunny, Sunny, Sunny! Why does it all have to be so *stupid* . . .!'

# 3

Trouble comes in threes, they say. First Jimmy, then Sunaina. And the next crisis was right at home: Rachna.

She came home one afternoon, her long hair completely cropped, and dyed orange. It can't have been more than an inch all over. I was stunned.

As she stood in the kitchen door I looked at a face I would have given anything to have had. Rachna has high cheek-bones, a small, straight nose, full, pretty lips, huge heavy-lidded brown eyes in an oval face. She's a slim, tall, attractive girl, my sister, and if we'd been living in India she'd have been considered a beauty. Silk saris in a couple of years, hair skimmied down from a central part over a lovely domed forehead and coiled behind her head.

Now she wore a cut-off black T-shirt, a short red skirt, black leggings and Doc Marten boots. Huge oxidized silver earrings pulled at her earlobes, silver and plastic bangles clinked and clanked in jangling profusion up her arms. There were at least seven huge silver rings on her fingers. Her eyes were lined with thick layers of kohl, her eyebrows arched satanically: there was an artificial beauty spot on her left cheek, under her eye; and her lips pouted in an unearthly, overpainted, bright pink Cupid's bow.

'Oh Rach!' I whispered. It was all I could find to say.

Her eyes widened and tears sprang into them immediately. 'Don't . . . don't you like it?' she whispered. She meant her hair of course. Her taste in clothes was already well-established.

I shook my head. 'It's not that, Rach . . .' I faltered and stopped.

'I know Mum's going to be mad,' she said, 'but I didn't think *you'd* look at me like that. It's going to be bad enough . . . Oh Sheels . . . don't *you* go criticizing me, taking her side.' She bit her lip, looking like a wounded puppy. 'I . . . I *want* it, see. I want . . .' and she trailed off too.

'I understand,' I said, 'I really do, but . . .' and I stopped again. 'Oh Rach . . .'

We looked at each other for a moment, then she flung her arms around me, hugging me hard. She smelled of hairdressers. 'Sheels, please. You'll back me up, won't you? Oh, say you will. Say you'll stand up for me.'

I hugged her back and said helplessly: 'Rach, I wish you'd told me . . .'

She drew back. 'And if I'd told you, what would you have done? Said: "Yes, Rach, go ahead, I think it's a great idea"? You'd have given me a hundred reasons not to,' she said bleakly.

She was right of course. I envied Rach her skittering thoughtlessness. I sometimes felt very dull in comparison to her. She was as trendy as they come, following every whiff of fashion, always first to try something new. It's not that I was really boring or anything, but because Dad and Mum had always reminded me I was the older sister, and had responsibilities as an example to Rachna, I felt I had to be sedate. I'd always felt overburdened by this role. In *that*, I realized now, looking at my sister, we *were* very Indian.

'You're right, Rach,' I said slowly. 'I'll back you up, but God knows what I'll say.'

Her face lit up instantly. I envied Rachna the way her moods snapped from gloom to delight in seconds. 'Just say you think I'm all right,' she said. 'That it's an adolescent phase I have to go through or something. You know, how kids have to go anti-establishment and all that.'

I turned away, flopped on the cushions on the floor, and switched on the TV. 'I don't know who's going to have the greater fit,' I said, 'Mum or Dad. It's the classic generation gap, isn't it?' I said. 'But it's more than that, it's a culture gap too . . .'

Rachna grinned. 'Hey, that's good,' she said delightedly, 'that's really good. Where'd you get that?'

'I don't know,' I said, 'maybe it came up in conversation with Sunny.' And I felt that awful pounding start up in my gut again, and the feeling of something, rising, rising, wanting to get out. Something screaming away inside. I swallowed and blinked and looked hard at the wildlife documentary on TV. 'We were talking about Babloo.'

Rachna pulled a packet of frozen chips from the fridge and slammed it into the microwave. 'He's a great dancer,' she said approvingly. Then: 'It's funny they went . . .'

I said nothing.

'No, really,' Rachna said, 'I mean, what good's his dancing going to be in India?'

'Oh I don't know,' I said, 'maybe he'll join the Bombay movies, in a chorus line, like they have in the night-club sequences. You know? Or become a watchamacallit, a bhangra disco pop star.' I'd seen a Sikh in a turban on the Indian programme on TV, belting out Punjabi rock!

'Yeucchh!' Rachna said. 'It's all phoney copycat stuff. They're trying to be funky, and they sound like cats wailing at night.'

'Oh Rach!' I said.

'Don't "Oh Rach" me,' she said, scraping back the kitchen chair. 'It isn't as though you don't think Babloo's going to hate it in India . . . It isn't as though *Jimmy's* Indian.' Her lips curved in a small secret smile. 'That's getting warm, innit? He proposed yet?'

*Warm*! I thought. Proposed! How could I tell her? How could I tell anyone?

'Haven't seen him around for a bit,' she went on blithely. 'What's he up to?'

Pain spread down my arms and I fought down the nausea. Carefully I said: 'He's gone up north – his grandmother died,' and hoped it sounded casual. 'Anyway, we're only friends, you know that.'

'Yeah, I bet,' Rachna said and put her head on her arms on the kitchen table with an extravagant flourish. 'Sheels, I haven't had *anyone* ask me out yet.' She looked up and said seriously: 'It's not that I'm desperate or anything . . . but . . . I'm sixteen, and . . . I can't see who I could possibly even go out with . . . you know? I mean the Indian boys are such wimps, and the English boys won't ask us out . . . except Jimmy. You're just lucky. It's scary, you know. It's just scary.'

Scary! She didn't know the half of it. Lucky! Oh God. Lucky!

Then she ruffled her spiky hair nonchantly. 'Well the thing is,' she said, 'some of us were talking at school the other day, and the way to look at it is we're all really blacks. The whites don't like us, so we've got to stick together, we blacks . . .'

I groaned right out loud. God, where did she get it all from? I just *knew* this would happen. 'Rach, is all this about Cleve . . .?'

She looked at me defensively.

Cleve was the singer in the reggae band at school. A cool Rastafarian, always spouting off against the establishment. Rachna was always hanging about the band, hoping that he'd notice her. Recently, I'd seen them both going off for coffee in the café across the road from the school.

God! I thought. It had been hard enough for Mum and Dad to accept Jim . . . but if Rach brought back a black guy . . . It didn't bear thinking about. Oh, I hated prejudice, but that's the way it was. Class, education, family and colour. That's what counted amongst Indians.

I'd heard Mum talk disparagingly about some of the people they knew. 'Raj,' she'd said one day, when they were getting ready to go to an Indian wedding, 'really, I can't bear one more evening listening to those women going on and on about how fair, tall and beautiful their daughter-in-law from India is going to be for her tall, fair and handsome son.' She'd done a great job of mimicking them, and I did know the type! 'Yes, ji. Of course, ji. We put an ad in *The Hindustan Times* since Bunny is ready to be married. It's better that the girls come from India, haena? The girls growing up here are not trained to be good wives, isn't it?' Dad had laughed. But I heard an edge of discomfort in his laughter. I realized later when I thought about it, that they were thinking about us then, Rach and I, who were obviously so wrong for the darling Indian sons being brought up in England.

Dad and Mum were broadminded. But . . . I was sure not broadminded enough for a black boyfriend for Rachna.

And then Rachna burst out with: 'At least you've got an

*English* name, Sheels. *Rachna*, for God's sake. What chance is there for me? The Indian boys are brainwashed by their mamas. The English won't ask us out. Why shouldn't I see Cleve – so *what* if he's black! At least *he* thinks I'm beautiful!'

'Rach, you're a mass of contradictions,' I said lamely.

'Well, I'm sixteen, and that's my privilege,' she snapped in reply. She took the chips out of the microwave and began wolfing them down as Mrs Baker's voice said falteringly in my ear: '. . . Oh! I thought Sheila was an *English* name . . .' and it echoed around and around and around in my head '. . . an *English* name . . . an *English* name . . . an *English* name . . .'

'I think,' Rachna said, going through her chips like a garbage disposal machine, 'it helps to have an English name at least. Those instinctive associations, you know . . .'


Rachna's hair was too much for someone even as liberal as Mum. She walked into the house half an hour later, calling: 'Sheila, Rachoo . . .' came into the kitchen, saw Rachna's hair and stopped short. Her lips came together and her eyes blinked rapidly twice. Then she turned silently and went upstairs and shut the door to her bedroom.

'Cor,' Rachna whispered. 'That's done it.'

'Never mind,' I said soothingly, lying, 'it'll pass. It'll take a while for her to adjust to the idea.'

The tension in the house was high by the time Dad came home. Mum hadn't come down and Rach and I were botching up the dinner.

He looked at Rachna, snorted, and burst out laughing.

'Rachoo, Rachoo,' he howled, slapping his thigh, 'are you going bald, like me, or have you decided to become a brahmin priest? Has your mother seen you? By God, you look funny!'

But after he'd wiped his eyes and gone upstairs, he stopped thinking it was quite so funny.

We heard Mum and Dad shouting at each other in the bedroom and Mum didn't come down to dinner.

Over the fish and chips Rach and I dished out, Dad said soberly: 'Your mother blames me for not disciplining you girls

22

properly.' He ran a nervous hand over his bald head and said; 'I'm not so sure about that, but I agree with her when she says everyone we know is going to wonder what kind of home we're making for you, what values we're teaching you.' He coughed and said then, characteristically, right on target, with entirely the wrong thing, 'Rachoo, you'd better buy a wig, before I get laughed out of London.' Dad was a founder member of several Indian organizations, and as a GP was doing quite well; he was a pillar of the Indian establishment.

And Rachna said tightly: 'Sorry, Dad. But I'm not going to do any such thing. My hair is the in-thing. And it's a statement, see, about *me*. About who I *am*. And I can't be bothered what some old fogey bunch of stupid Indian businessmen think.'

And everything went downhill after that.

Mum refused to speak to Rachna. Dad glowered silently over his newspapers, and early in the morning I'd wake up with images of Rachna with her cropped hair and her black leather jacket, arms in the air, dancing in front of the TV, singing along with 'Top of the Pops' as though she didn't care whether Mum talked to her or not. Then Rachna saying in a choking voice: 'Mum . . . say something for God's sake . . .' and a flash of Mum wrapping the end of her sari around her waist and tucking it in the way she did when she was really mad, saying in a tight voice, her lips in a thin, prim line: 'Well, what do you *expect* me to say, Rachna?'

There'd be Sunaina looking at me accusingly with those huge brown eyes of hers as she said: 'It's *your* fault. *Yours*. It's your fault we're going back to India . . . *You* . . . You did it . . . *You*, Sheila, *you*!'

But the most insistent voice of all was Mrs Baker's saying in that surprised, embarrassed way: 'Sheila?' And, clearly, as though it were a movie in front of my eyes, I'd see her lined, pinched pink face, her unkempt brown hair, as she said, faltering: 'But I thought Sheila was an *English* name!' And the words would echo – 'an *English* name . . . an *English* name . . . an *English* name . . .'

Things got from bad to worse . . . Rachna started staying

out late in the evenings without telling Mum. I told Dad my aches and pains were worse, and he prescribed a day in bed, which I stretched to four. I couldn't bear the thought of running into Jimmy at school, so after that I started cutting classes, wandering around on Ilford High Street, thinking about Sunny and Jimmy, and then Sunny again. Until the Head called Dad to find out if I were sick. Mum confronted me one day, and I told her that Sunaina's leaving had upset me. She couldn't understand why, and I couldn't tell her.

'Are you having problems with Jimmy?' Mum said, and my heart lurched.

I shook my head. 'No, Mum, he's just gone up north. His gran died.'

Mum said: 'I didn't think the English had such extended death ceremonies.' But I didn't rise to that. She looked at me speculatively, but let it go.

'It's growing pains,' Dad said, comfortably. 'Let Able handle it. He's familiar with this mind business.'


Strange that Dad and Dr Able were partners. Dad was conservative Western medicine all the way: he scoffed at anything even faintly smelling of the non-scientific; and Dr Able tried everything he could: yoga, Zen, meditation, homeopathy, Japanese Shiatsu massage, acupuncture, naturopathy, bio-energetics (which had a lot to do with kicking and yelling) and Rolfing massages which went deep into muscles and cartilages. He'd read acres of books on psychology, religion, philosophy and stuff. Not that he did everything together, but he knew enough about everything, was willing to find out about anything new, and tried to see what worked.

'Biology and psychology are two sides of the same coin, Raj,' he told Dad one evening after dinner at our house. 'The mind can't be detached from the body. You can't expect to treat the body, forget the mind and hope for a cure. Western medicine, like all Western sciences, divides and separates, but without the psychological and spiritual aspects taken into account, it's useless.'

Dad grunted tolerantly.

'Your own traditions,' Dr Able went on, tapping his pipe and tamping the tobacco in, 'are a lot more sensible in many ways and it's a shame you don't know more about them.'

And Dad, who'd spent so much time and energy learning medicine the Western way, said huffily, 'You mean to tell me Western science is bunkum?'

'No, no, not at all,' Dr Able said. 'But we must integrate the systems. The new term is 'holistic medicine', Raj, and we'd best keep up with the times.'

Dad just snorted and changed the subject. Mum called him the archetypal pill dispenser, and, gobbling aspirins and antacids, I began to think she was right.

I remembered this conversation for a long time after, though I didn't understand it then.

It's incredible their practice is as successful as it is, and they aren't at each other's throats a lot more. They both look alike, Dr Able and Dad, in a most peculiar way. They're both short and round and bald and pudgy, with more chins than they should have. But Dr Able's pink, and Dad's brown. Of course, there are other differences, like the shapes of their noses and paunches. But Rach and I call them Tweedledum and Tweedledee.

I went to see Dr Able at the surgery. He gave me a complete physical, and asked me a lot of questions, and I told him what I'd told Mum. Dr Able looked even more sceptical than Mum.

'You're holding back something important, some feeling or information, which if you continue to suppress will make you sick in both mind and body,' he said. He went on to tell me that the mind/body is like a piece of knitting; if you release a small thread of what's bothering you, really release it, act it out, rather than just talk about it, then the whole structure of problems gradually unravels. 'But,' he said, 'this is easier said than done, of course, because the mind guards its secrets very jealously. And these secrets are what we call the subconscious. We can try to ferret out these out by analysis, talking things through. Or we can try bringing them out through body exercises. What do you prefer?'

I said I preferred exercises absolutely. I shuddered at the thought of being referred to a psychologist, and spending long hours on a couch telling him or her all my problems. I thought exercises would be an easy way out.

So Dr Able taught me to lie still and observe what was going on in my body. That took some doing, believe me. And soon after this he taught me to see the pictures in my head. So, very quickly, I began to see what was going on every morning, and told him about the space-ships and jackboots and people hanging on crosses.

'It's your night consciousness asking to be heard,' he said. 'You have a day consciousness which keeps you active in the world, and a night consciousness which holds the key to your personality. Your night consciousness speaks to you in your dreams, and when this doesn't work, it breaks through into day when your resistance is weakest, about four in the morning.'

He taught me how to breathe. I know it sounds silly, but the fact is that most of us breathe all wrong. He taught me exercises to do early in the morning to quieten my quick, gaspy breathing and deepen it, and he gave me some slow stretching exercises. 'The slower and deeper you breathe,' he told me, 'the healthier you are and the longer you live. Especially if you learn to breathe from your stomach.'

Then he gave me a word to say over and over in my head when the gabble started, or my body got tense. 'The word is like a strap you hold on to in a crowded tube,' he said. 'It keeps you steady as the tube lurches about tearing around corners.'

It worked, in that after a while my body would calm down, and the mad-house in my head would ease up. But that didn't mean the same feeling didn't come right back the next morning, and the babble start up all over again. Dr Able said I'd just have to stick it out, that the pain and nausea and the creeping crawling sensations would go on until whatever was bothering me was resolved.

And one day, almost casually, Dr Able said: 'Sheila, you're going through a confusing time of your life. It's a time to leave your childhood behind, and grapple with the big bad world.

26

You've stopped growing physically, but you have a lot of emotional growing to do. Growing is always painful, and if you weaken in your resolve to see it through, you'll try to take the easy way out: sleeping pills, drugs, or alcohol. Don't do that, Sheila, whatever you do. It's a sure way downhill.'

Well, that certainly made a lot of sense to me. I was certainly confused! But, it didn't change much around the house. Dad seemed to have become a master paper rustler, when he was home, saying nothing much, sunk behind his newspaper. Mum became a clock watcher, and her lips became a tighter and thinner line. Rachna had become the Vanishing Princess, and I was sure I had a cloud of black gloom, perpetually around my head like a satanic halo. Our cheerful, airy, sunny home became a misery to be in.

Then, one day, about a month and a half after the melodramas began, I had a postcard from India. It was from Munnia, she was the first friend I could remember, the daughter of Ram Milan, the tractor driver on Grandpa's farm in Rampur, where we'd lived until I was seven. It was written in an almost illiterate childish scrawl in Hindi, and Mum read it out to me. Munnia was going to have her gauna next month, after the harvest festival, which meant she was leaving Mehta Farm, and going permanently to her husband's home. Munnia was just a little younger than I. She'd been married almost two years ago, at fifteen, and as was the custom, had remained with her father all this time.

The next morning I jerked awake, gasping, with Munnia's face in the front of my eyes, looking at me accusingly, saying: 'It's *your* fault, Sheila Bai, it's your fault that I have to go to my husband's home . . .' and there was Sunny sitting in the space-ship saying: 'I suppose I'll have to guide you to a landing, Sheels, after all.' Then Jimmy came down the road, wearing white jackboots and walked all over me, and behind him was an army of Jimmys in white jackboots. And there I was, hanging on a cross on a bare hill with the rest of the anti-war demonstrators, while a mushroom cloud grew like an evil premonition in the horizon.

And I was crying: 'Oh Jimmy, Jimmy, Jimmy! Why does it all have to be so stupid?'

And I knew, I'd have to go back to India. I couldn't live in England any more, and nothing made any sense at all.

# 4

Which is why I woke up one morning in March, not with voices babbling in my head, but with a gentle, soothing achha-chugga, achha-chugga thrumming in the air around me, and I was rocking, rocking safely in one of those wonderful Indian trains which criss-crossed the country on their thousands of miles of gleaming metal rails.

As I woke, the achha-chugga, achha-chugga changed to a slower rhythm: kachha – kachalugga – kachug, as the wheels rolled over points and the brakes caught. I began to feel the expectation I remembered, coming into an Indian railway station. But then, the prickles and pangs started up again, and the wheels started saying, in a low groan: 'Oh Sunny, Sunny, Sunny, why does it all have to be so stupid!'

Thin streaks of daylight crept through the shuttered windows. Above me, the dull green of the upper berth shuddered; all along the underside, stencilled yellow diamonds enclosed the initials, CR, Central Railways. Home!

I stretched slowly in my sleeping bag as Dr Able had taught me, concentrating on body, bit by bit, from my toes to my head and down to my hands, and felt better immediately.

Above the rattle of the train, cries of hawkers came in waves as the bogey passed them on the platform. 'Chayae! Chayae garam!' Tea, hot tea! 'Cigraet! paan-bidi-cigraet!' Then: 'Aamlaette, tost-aamlaette! Paap caarn!' Omelettes and pop corn! That was new from three years ago. The train shuddered to a halt, and the din grew.

The man on the upper berth across from me climbed down, put on his dressing gown, picked up a bundle wrapped in a towel and, opening the compartment door, went out into the corridor.

The jumble of bed-clothes on the lower berth opposite mine began to grunt and stretch.

Above, I heard Tinkoo turn.

God, I thought, how am I going to get dressed with all these men around? The night before I'd waited until they were all stretched on their berths before going to the bathroom to change into my pyjamas.

'Come on, Sheels!' I said impatiently to myself, 'this isn't the first time you've been on an Indian train with complete strangers.'

'But,' a petulant voice in my head said, 'this is the first time I've been without Mum and Dad.'

Another voice said: 'You've become bloody *English*, Sheila.' And then, again I heard Mrs Baker's voice saying: 'Sheila?' in that embarrassed way, 'I thought Sheila was an *English* name, an *English* name . . .'

I kicked inside my sleeping bag, in exasperation and banged my feet against the table at the foot of the berth.

'Ah! we've stopped!' Tinkoo's voice came from the berth above mine. His pale face appeared over the edge. 'Awake, Sheila? Want to put chai?' Tinkoo talked, what I thought was absolute gobbledegook! It had taken me two days in Delhi to begin to decode his language; 'put chai' was to drink tea. And somehow he always managed to make me feel that whatever I did was wrong. He'd taken a dislike to me almost the instant we'd met at Indira Ghandi Airport.

'What's the time?' I said as levelly as I could.

'Six ten,' he said shortly. 'Why don't you look at your own watch, yaa.' He sighed loudly. After a while he said again, sounding supremely bored: 'Well? Chai?'

'No, thanks,' I said, nettled. Then: 'Yes, yes, all right. I'll get up.'

He sighed dramatically. 'No, *please*!' he said *very* politely, 'I'll get it. *Please*, don't trouble yourself. You're the honoured guest, isn't it? What will my esteemed mother say if you told her I hadn't looked after your each and every wish!' He leaped nimbly off the berth, his bare feet hardly touching the fold-down foot-rest against the wall. He peered below my berth and found his chappals. Then reaching up, pulled a shawl down from the upper berth and flung it around his shoulders in an unconsciously graceful gesture. He wasn't so bad when he wasn't trying so hard! He grabbed his jhola off the hook and shrugged it on to his shoulder. It was a large open-mouth cloth bag he wouldn't be seen dead without. It was a symbol of his identity. It had a rather interesting design of patchwork and embroidery over it. And it was dead scruffy. He took a packet of bidis, cigarettes rolled in tobacco leaf, out of his jhola and slid open the compartment door. Lighting a bidi he said: 'I'll be just a sec,' and swung off down the corridor in his pyjamas, leaving the sharp, raw smell of bidi smoke behind him. Bidis were *very* downbeat, I'd realized these last two days! Munnia's face floated briefly in front of my face. Her house had the same smell. Her father, a tractor driver, smoked bidis too.

I turned to open the window behind my head. There was an inner shutter of wood and an outer window of glass. The catches were awkwardly placed and I had to twist my waist like a contortionist, leaning on one elbow for leverage. I yanked on the shutter . . . and hit my head on the reading-light in the corner! The shutter stuck half-way up. With a resigned sigh, I lay on my side, head in hand, to look out of the window, below the shutter.

Neon lights lit the platform and the garish cinema posters on the pillars at regular intervals. Indian film stars in lurid colours leered out of them, striking the most incredible macho postures.

The yellow-washed walls were decorated with red beetle-nut spittle. And what looked like a high-street full of people milled about the platform: vendors of books, magazines, tea, bidis, omelettes, coffee, popcorn, garish wooden toys.

Passengers in pyjamas got off the train for tea, or to brush their teeth at taps at the end of the platform. I had a sudden picture of similar scenes at railway stations all over the country. And felt peculiarly warmed by it. India at her early morning ritual. Such familiarity amongst strangers. None of the formal, cool reserve, the correct public behaviour I was used to in England.

There were peanut shells, empty cigarette packets, crunched up papers, bits of hay, and large puddles of water all over the platform. And I suddenly realized I was comforted by

31

the mess! This was new. The last time I'd been in India with Mum and Dad, the public messiness of India had infuriated me; I'd felt humiliated, longing for the starchy cleanliness of England.

There was a tap at the glass window; I could see Tinkoo's hands clutching an earthen pot of tea in each, he leaned down gesturing at me to open up. I propped myself up and reached for the catches, ready for battle. Instantly the glass window slid all the way up, past the shutter with a crash. A blast of cold air, several complex smells, and a babble of voices swirled into the compartment.

Tinkoo handed me a pot, under the shutter. 'We're at Maniktala. Here's your chai,' he said, 'why don't you open the shutter also?'

'Because it's stuck, isn't it?'

'Here,' he said disdainfully, hold my chai. *I'll* open it.'

He hauled at it, but it remained steadfastly jammed.

'Lucky it was shut last night,' he said dryly, covering his embarrassment, 'or the dacoits might have caught you around your throat when we went through the Chambal Valley.'

'Dacoits?' I said, momentarily blank.

'Yah, dacoits,' he said, still doubled over. 'Translated for our Memsahib into English, the language of the civilized world: robbers, highwaymen, bands of thugs, bandits.' And he straightened up, and his voice floated in – 'They've been known to stop trains and attack passengers.'

'Very funny,' I said thinly, stung as I'd been every time he referred to my Englishness. Stupid wally. I remembered Shanti, fleetingly, going on about dacoits coming to take me away. I sipped my tea. It was hot, flavourless and too sweet. But it had the familiar tang of the earthenware pot, which I remembered and liked. I'd be seeing Shanti too, soon; Munnia's mother, my one time ayah. I was warmed by that.

'I *told* you we should travel second class, yaa,' Tinkoo said, 'I had to go all the way down the platform to get the chai.' ('Yaa' was the short form of 'yaar', meaning 'friend'. The way it was said could mean affection or exasperation. Guess which one I got?)

32

'Why?' I asked.

'The chaiwallahs don't like to come to the first class. Too few people. Economics.' He slurped his tea noisily and said: 'Aah! I dig railway chai.'

Tinkoo tried so hard to be 'proletarian' as he called it! First class, he'd said in Delhi, was for the bourgeoisie, government officials and tourists. He wouldn't be caught dead going first class. I'd felt cheesed off that Nina Maasi, his mother, Mum's sister, had insisted he escort me, so I'd said huffily he'd better not come. But Nina Maasi'd won out all around. 'This is India, Sheila, not England. A young girl shouldn't travel alone. It's not safe.' Then, when Tinkoo wasn't listening, she'd said: 'Don't mind Tinkoo. He's our resident knee-jerk Marxist.' I loved it! Knowing that was my private weapon against Tinkoo, though I tried really hard not to answer him in the same tone he used with me.

He leaned against the bogey nonchalantly smoking his bidi now, very unconcernedly sipping his tea. And, of course, just then a chaiwallah went past, swinging his bucket, clutching his basket of earthen cups, yelling: 'Chayae! Garam Chayae!' Tinkoo's a wally! I thought, with his great theories of economics.

'Tinkoo!' I said, irritated, 'Come in. I want to shut the window: It's getting cold in here.'

He laughed, 'Zap me your kuller,' he said and held out his hand. I finally understood and passed him my pot. He dropped them on the rails between the platform and the bogey. 'Biodegradable,' he said surprisingly, and shooing the beggars away, sauntered towards the door of the train.

Now, of course, the glass window refused to come down, and in the struggle with it I thought: Oh why do I bother! Everything's so uncomfortable here. Nothing works.

And suddenly the window came down with a bang . . . and I had the greatest feeling of satisfaction: it was so easy to feel good in India.

Tinkoo glided into the compartment like a lithe, graceful ballet dancer. He was a year older than I and in his first year at Jawaharlal Nehru University in New Delhi, studying

Russian. He was, really, if one could be a little detached about it, remarkably good-looking. Like Rachna, he was tall, thin, brown, with large heavy-lidded eyes and enormous lashes. He had that fine, straight family nose but his mouth was petulant. His chin was a bit slim, his jaw, narrow. Straight, lank, black hair, short on the sides, very much in fashion, licked his forehead in floppy spikes. He had an almost feminine way of flicking it back with his hand, chin up, or tossing his head to get it off his face.

People said there was a family resemblance between Tinkoo and I, but I knew when they were being polite. I had no illusions about being more than average. I'm nowhere as tall as Tinkoo, nor anywhere as slim and graceful. My jaw is squarer, my eyes not as limpid, my nose ends in a snub. Rachna, if you could see past her hair and clothes, is much more like him.

But that's appearance. While Rachna and I were essentially on the same side, Tinkoo and I were like naughts and crosses: quite simply opposed. It was a pity, really, because Nina Maasi and Mum were very close. Even though Mum lived in London and Nina Maasi lived in New Delhi, they called each other on the phone at least once every two weeks. I'd known Tinkoo when we were young but hadn't met him for a long time now.

Tinkoo sat down with a flop at the end of my berth and crossed his legs under him, pushing his feet in place with his hands.

'So,' he said, very politely, as though he were doing an unpleasant duty, 'enjoying the train ride?' I just grunted in reply. Tinkoo looked directly at me quickly and looked away. 'Very monosyllabic, our Sheila Mem, isn't it?' he said, his tone taking on the familiar jeering note. 'What's the matter? Depressed by the filth on the platform?'

Here we go, I thought, and sighed loudly.

'Not clean enough for our Memsàhib, I suppose. Not like your clean and pretty England? So why come to our poor filthy land, yaa!'

'Oh Tinkoo!' I groaned. 'Why don't you just *shut* up about

your country, my country. It's too early in the morning to get into this.'

'Oh *sor-ry!*' Tinkoo said immediately, his eyebrows going up in a Rachna-like arch. 'Of *course*, I'd forgotten! How *uncouth* I am! A boorish prole, who doesn't know anything about uptight bourgeois manners, isn't it?'

I reached for my dressing gown. 'I'd best get dressed,' I said.

The man on the opposite berth sat up, yawned hugely and stretched. He crossed his legs on his blankets and, reaching up with both hands, pulled a tiny comb from behind his top-knot, ran it through his hair, re-tied it, and put the comb back in place. He was a large Sikh with a complacent paunch, and an enormous black beard which rippled down his chest like a wiry black waterfall.

Tinkoo sat next to him, on his bed-clothes, with a great show of friendliness, saying: 'We are running late, isn't, sardarji?'

'Late, yes,' the Sikh said, as though continuing an interesting conversation which had been only slightly interrupted by a few hours of sleep. 'Always late, our wonderful trains.' He looked at his watch, glinting gold on his hairy wrist. 'Barakoh coming? Yes, I think we are two hours behind time.'

'I thought so,' Tinkoo said, 'but it's a long time since I came this way, and they change the schedules all the time.'

The Sikh looked at me in my dressing gown, wash-bag in hand, a small towel on my arm, reaching for my skirt and top hanging on a hook on the wall.

'You are going for a wash, Miss Sheila?' he said in an easy, friendly way. 'Don't worry, your brother and I will guard your things.'

'He's not my brother,' I said irrelevantly, because I was suddenly very irritated. 'Just a cousin.'

'Cousin. Brother. What is the difference, ji,' the Sikh laughed expansively. 'It's all the same. He is looking after you, isn't it?' He slapped Tinkoo on the back heartily. 'That's a brother's job, isn't it? Do not worry, we will look after you, ji.'

'Thanks,' I muttered, not at all thankfully, and I supposed

35

it showed: as I stepped out into the corridor, I heard the Sikh say dubiously: 'Your sister, she has character. Very strong personality, I suppose.'

That's what they all say, I thought savagely, so why do they think I need protection? I don't bloody need protection, specially not by wimps like Tinkoo. If it comes to it, I'll bet *I'll* be the one scraping *him* off the floor!

The man from the bunk above the Sikh's, an army Major, was standing in the open doorway at the end of the corridor, in his dressing gown, a toothbrush in one hand, a glass of water in the other, spitting out into the countryside.

That, I thought with irritation rising like a forest fire, is what they think of their country . . . they damn well spit all over it.

'Ah!' the Major smiled foamily at me under his little black moustache.

I nodded bleakly in return.

Two children in pyjamas ran screaming and laughing down the corridor, bumping into me. A woman peered out of the compartment reserved for women and shouted: 'Babloo, Seema, come back here!' The little boy called Babloo, turned and pulled a face. The children ran on. The woman smiled at me and said: 'Children! They think there are devils in the toothpaste.'

I smiled politely and stepped into the bathroom.

Babloo . . . Sunny . . . I didn't even have their address. I would never run into them in this huge country. They were lost for ever!


When I got back to the compartment the three men had changed into their clothes.

Tinkoo was now in his dearly beloved imported Levis, with a long, embroidered cotton kurta hanging lankly over them, his feet in leather chappals, his shawl draped around his shoulders. He was reading the Sikh's copy of *India Today*.

'We will have egg sandwiches for breakfast,' the Major boomed. 'My wife made plenty.' His orderly began unwrapping sandwiches from a blue plastic bag; there were many more than one person needed: the Major's wife had provided for travelling companions. Tinkoo pulled out the packet of parathas Nina Maasi had made for us in Delhi. We'd had some for dinner the night before, but there were many left. The Sikh offered oranges, bananas and tea from his thermos.

We ate together, as we had the evening before, sharing everything round. They took up the last evening's conversation about the Prime Minister; 'Our young well-meaning, but inept, prematurely crowned princeling', as the Sikh described him; the Sikh demand for their own nation in the Punjab; the growing middle-class of consumers; the corruption rampant, it seemed, at all levels of society. Tinkoo waded right in with his arrogant righteousness and left-wing opinions.

They tried politely to draw me in: 'What are they saying in England, about our involvement in Sri Lanka, Miss Sheila? Do they think we're making the same mistakes as the Americans in Vietnam?' 'What do you think of our Indian writers? Have you read Dom Moraes? What do you think of Farrukh Dhondy in London, Salman Rushdie, hey?' 'What do you young people think about nuclear disarmament?' 'What do they say in England about America's foreign policy?' 'Do you think Gorbachev's Perestroika will work?' I excused myself saying, I'd heard, I'd read . . . but didn't feel too sure about anything. And really, I didn't know. They didn't mind: the important thing was to talk. I warmed at the image: Indians, Indians, Indians. Indians chattering and babbling all over the country.

Unlike Jimmy. How unlike Jimmy! Jimmy, solid, reliable, dependable Jimmy. . . silent Jimmy. . .


As I looked out of the window my most constant picture of India became real. The countryside revolved quick-slow outside, flashing backward close to the train, moving sluggishly with it in the distance. Under the peach glow of the rising sun, green-black fields swung into the horizon, broken by clusters of trees. Villages huddled together, mud and thatch huts of instinctively perfect line and grace. There were irrigation ditches, bald footpaths, pools of stagnant water, low scrubby hedges like occasional frayed tempers . . .

A congregation of slim, long, white birds whipped by, stretching long necks into watery fields. Crows – I recognized them – and some ordinary-looking brown birds, which were very familiar, but their name escaped me, sat on the telephone wires, dipping and rising as the train hurtled by.

Then, suddenly, there was a blinding flash of blue as a large bird rose heavily from the fields, I could hear its harsh cry over the thrum of the train. It glided away in a blaze of turquoise and ultramarine whipping past the train.

My breath caught. It was a stunning flash of colour, unexpected and sudden against the dark fields, the dawning sky. So . . . controlled, despite its wild and ungainly flight.

Then for an instant, as the sun rose whitely in the orange Indian sky, the English countryside rose like a mist in front of my eyes. Tidy rolling hills, carefully worked fields, neat streams bordered with familiar wild flowers, trim hedgerows of May. Postcard pretty villages, tamed forests of familiar trees. The hesitant sun, the low grey bank of clouds, the thin, steady drizzle which kept England so green.

Raw, I thought raggedly as I saw, again, the Indian countryside outside. Raw, that's what it was, this India of fields and villages and scarred patches of earth. Un-pretty, meagre and lush at the same time. It doesn't have the . . . finish . . . that was right, the finish of England, the look of extreme care. That was it! It was careless, this India, careless. It was not *preserved*. Although people had worked the fields probably longer than the English, they'd done it as though they weren't conscious of what they were doing. I stared at the fields, blinking back tears. You couldn't tell what the birds were here, what the wild plants were. It was nameless, India, it was . . . unlabelled. In England you could tell practically everything in the country: hedgerows, primroses, thistles, mushrooms, robins, jays, bullrushes. Everything had been written about, talked about, categorized. But what did they have here? I didn't know.

Then a voice in my head said fiercely: 'But it's mine, mine. This India, it's *mine*, for me to discover. That's *me* out here!'

Tinkoo was declaiming excitedly about something behind me. I turned. He was holding up the copy of *India Today* saying: 'They sit on the fence, that's what they do; they don't take sides, what's the good of that?'

The Sikh beamed tolerantly: 'But that is what is so good about it, isn't it? They are neutral. So we can trust what they say.'

Tinkoo snorted. 'Neutral!' he sneered. 'Neutral! What is there to be neutral about, these days? Eh? You tell me. You should read *The Patriot*, sardarji . . .'

'But that's communist –' the Major began.

'You bet, yaa,' Tinkoo said excitedly. 'That's the whole point.'

I watched their animated faces, Tinkoo, flushed; the Major, amused; the Sikh, tolerant. And it was as though I'd never seen Indians before; that all those Indians in England were a different people, somehow unreal. And again, I was covered with a peculiar pride. This, I thought, this is me. This India with its stumbling, bumbling mess, its wildness, its dirt. With its kindness and hospitality, its goodness to strangers, its everlasting din and gabble, *this* is me!

And, for a while my mind went blank as I rocked with the swaying train, comforted with a decision, a small island of certainty, in an absolute *sea* of doubts.

# 5

Inder Uncle was at Rampur Station to meet us. With him were
Hariram, the driver of the farm jeep, and a coolie whose arm
Inder Uncle had in a tight grip.

'Coolies are hard to get these days,' Inder Uncle said grimly
as he shoved the man into the compartment to pick up the
luggage. I'd suggested bringing our suitcases out to the bogey
door to make it easy to get them off, but Tinkoo, the great
proletariat, had said airly: 'Don't get so agi, yaa, Inder Chacha
will handle it.' Agi, of course, I'd learned by now was
'agitated'.

Now there was a mad scramble to get the luggage out, with
the Sikh, the Major, Tinkoo and Inder Uncle all shouting
instructions at the same time.

Inder Uncle embraced us then, saying: 'So, Sheilaji, at last
after so many years, eh beti?' and 'How are you, son?'

'Freaked out, man . . .' Tinkoo began, morosely, and then
hurriedly changed it to: 'Fine, just fine, Inder Chacha.'
Tinkoo wasn't directly related to Inder Uncle, but in India
cousins and uncles and in-laws twice removed all know each
other. 'Where's Bumpy?'

'At the government seed farm,' Inder Uncle said. 'He will
be back for lunch.' Inder Uncle, Dad's elder brother, ran
Grandpa's farm, with the help of his son, my cousin, Bumpy.
And this farm, simply called Mehta Farm, was the place Dad
and Mum considered home. They planned to come back here
when they retired. The farm was also Bumpy's home.

And mine. Yes, mine too. It must be! I thought, suddenly,
desperately, standing there on the Rampur Station platform,
amongst the piles of luggage.

'So, Sheilaji?' Inder Uncle was saying fondly, his arm
around my shoulder. 'You're looking well. And how are Raj
and Sushila?'

Inder Uncle was so polite. He added the respectful 'ji' when he addressed you even if you were younger. Sometimes it seemed a little too sweet, but that was Inder Uncle's way. He was tall, unlike Dad. He had a black moustache and a thick mop of hair. And his eyes were sad, with many wrinkles around them: Ritu Auntie, Bumpy's mother, had died when Bumpy was a child, and Inder Uncle hadn't re-married.

Tinkoo bashed Hariram on the back and shook his hand saying: 'Kyon, Hariram? Kaise ho, yaar? Theek?' So, Hariram? How are you, friend? All right?, in that peculiar way that men in India have – a hearty-close-divided-by-class-united-by-maleness manner. The 'yaa', I'd noticed, changed to the complete 'yaar' when talking to people who weren't of the same class. Bumpy and Hariram were childhood friends as were Hariram's sister, Munnia and I. Tinkoo knew Hariram from past visits to the farm. Hariram and Munnia were the children of Ram Milan, the tractor driver and general handyman around the farm.

Hariram greeted me with the correct deference of class; no hearty-close distance between us. No chance, not between male and female. And I smiled at him, correctly, a little distantly, although I'd known him since we were children.

Hariram helped the coolie balance the suitcases precariously one on top of the other on his head, and hang Tinkoo's bedding-roll by a strap over one shoulder, his bag over the other. The coolie seemed to sag a bit, but no one noticed.

'I can wheel my suitcase along,' I said, feeling sorry for the man and a little aggravated by everyone's unthinking acceptance of the situation, but I might as well have been talking to a wall.

Hariram, of course, in the elevated position of jeep driver could not be expected to carry anything heavy! He picked up the food hamper, Inder Uncle picked up my holdall, and stuck it to the coolie's hand, so he had only one hand with which to balance his head load.

We jostled through the crowds, in a crashing tide towards the exit gate, almost running to keep up with the coolie, who seemed to be involved in a race with demons.

The scene outside the station was chaotic. Hundreds of bicycle rickshaws were ranged in semi-circles, their thin, ragged drivers hurrying passengers to them; the few coolies there were, deposited their luggage, argued loudly and abusively about rates, and ran back for more customers. To complicate things, innumerable rickshaw drivers besieged us outside the ticket barriers, soliciting fares, and our coolie disappeared.

Half a dozen cars and jeeps in the forecourt were being piled with luggage, everyone shouting instructions. And people who seemed to have no purpose other than to stride around outside railway stations, strode about, talking, gesticulating, staring.

Off in the distance a clutch of sadhus, wandering monks, were bathing solemnly at a public tap, wrapping and un-wrapping their saffron robes, managing to keep a degree of modesty as they washed.

Inder Uncle found our coolie and hurried us over to a green jeep which was obviously new; the last time Mum, Dad, Rachna and I had come, he'd had a hump-backed rattling old Ambassador, one of the few cars they made in India. He sat me in the front by Hariram saying: 'It's less bumpy in the front,' and climbed in the back with Tinkoo and the suitcases. He paid the coolie who, it seemed, would always consider himself underpaid and shouted obscenities at us as we drove away.


It had been three years since I'd been in India and I'd forgotten, in the relative calm of London suburban streets and shopping centres, just what a small town in India can be like. Now, as we rattled, bumped and honked our way out of the station forecourt, down a narrow alley and turned left into the main thoroughfare of Rampur, it all came back in a familiar rush.

Although it was only nine-thirty in the morning, it was like being in a seething cauldron of humanity. People scurrying, flurried, scrambling; people walking, ambling, strolling; and everything in between. There was a continuous buzz and hum in the air, broken by shouts and the insistent trink-trink of rickshaw bells. Hariram kept up a clamour on the horn of the jeep, as we edged past cyclists, pedestrians, and trucks filled to overflowing with produce.

Along with both edges of the main street, which was pitted with innumerable potholes, were open-fronted shops: shacks of wood, with tin or shingle roofs literally held together with canvas and rope. Interspread with them were brick buildings painted pink, green, yellow, decorated unattractively with stripes, curlicues, swastikas, crumbling even before they were fully erected. Ugly, open drains ran along the front of the shops, spanned by concrete slabs to the entrances.

The shops sold everything imaginable: one specialized in buckets, ropes, brushes and cooking stoves; others did aluminium kitchen-ware; many sold cloth; several sold electrical goods; some, prints of gods and goddesses in kitchy frames. There were shops which sold toys; drug stores; general stores . . .

Lanes ran off the main thoroughfare. In some I could see, as we jolted slowly by, vegetable markets; in others, shops selling paints, motor parts.

Tinkoo leaned forward and said: 'I bet you think this is a hajaar despo scene. Just filth, eh Memsahib? Rubbish and dirt everywhere. Heavy, slum scene, isn't it? England's nothing like this – damn khufiya, clean I bet?'

'Oh, oh, oh, oh,' Inder Uncle said, 'What's going on here, Tinkoo?'

'Tinkoo's convinced I'm some sort of reactionary bourgeois thicko,' I said. 'He's been at it since I got out of customs, practically.'

'You should have seen the hajaar trouble she had getting her damn camera in,' Tinkoo snorted, his thin, pretty lips curling down.

Inder Uncle smiled and patted my arm draped across the back of the seats. 'It's the age, Sheilaji, it's the age. Don't worry about it.'

Tinkoo sneered: 'However old *this* dame gets, she's going to maintain a brain the size of a pea.'

Inder Uncle laughed. 'Now stop it, Tinkoo. Look!' He pointed out a store with a sign over the top reading 'Lekhni-Dekhni'. 'It's like saying "The Readery and Writery". He sells pens and spectacles. Enterprising, isn't it?'

We passed through the town which was small, turned right, past a surprisingly well-kept building, with flowers in green painted pots, yellow washed walls. It was the cleanest building I'd seen so far. 'That building,' Inder Uncle said, pointing to it, 'is the police station. You know how old it is? At least one hundred years. It was built by the British.' And my spirits sank some more. I would never be free of them! Even here, in this small town tucked away in the heart of India, were reminders of the British. And then, of course, I realized I was thinking in English . . . the language was part of me. It was in my veins and arteries! And I felt that familiar clenching in my gut.

Up the slope we went, to wait with rickshaws, scooters and trucks at a level-crossing, as the train we'd been on chugged by on its way to Jabalpur.

The gates rose, an enormous handle unlocked ceremoniously and hauled on manually by a railway employee. He was wearing a tattered vest and loose khaki shorts falling to his knees, threatening to leave the tenuous security of his hips. Inder Uncle pointed to him. 'In British days, this fellow would have been given the sack,' he said grimly. And my gut gave another wrench.

Then we were passing open ground: scrubby, patchy, grassy spaces haunted by excessively ugly black pigs snuffling and snorting in the earth.

'They're eating shit,' Tinkoo said nastily. 'That should delight you, Sheila Mem. Colourful, ethnic, romantic shit!'

I laughed. What else could you do with Tinkoo!

We entered the Samli Village, familiar, yet so far away.

'This,' Inder Uncle said imputably, pointing to small flat-roofed brick houses of surpassing ugliness, crowding both sides of the road, 'is the brahmin area of the village, do you remember, Sheilaji? And over there,' he pointed to the right, 'is the Muslim area. And up there, where the road divides, that is the school.'

'Divided we stand,' Tinkoo muttered incomprehensibly.

'It's a pity that brick houses mean wealth,' Inder Uncle went on. 'Mud huts are not only clean, but more suitable for the climate.'

The school was in an indescribably run-down brick building in a messy yard. A group of school children sat on the ground around a teacher in a chair, chanting tables with enormous inattention. Another group played some unknown ball game, dropping it to come and stare at us. They all wore, despite their obvious poverty, regulation blue shorts and skirts and white blouses.

'There are other schools,' Inder Uncle said, seeing the expression on my face, 'which aren't so bad. On the other side of Rampur, where the industries are. We are in the poorer section, don't forget, the agricultural.' Then almost defensively, he said: 'Rampur is not bad, you know, other towns in this region are much worse. There is a government college here, a technical training institute, a good hospital, a veterinary hospital, a pathological laboratory. You children have not lived here for any time, always off to boarding schools and foreign countries, how can you expect to know a place properly?'

Tinkoo said insolently: 'Our Memsahib, of course, is used to hajaar better places, yaa.'

I decided I'd ignore him. 'You're right, of course, Inder Uncle,' I said, 'I don't . . . uh . . . know my own country very well, that's . . . er . . . why I came . . .'

Inder Uncle softened immediately: 'Yes, I can understand that,' he said. 'It's not easy to be transplanted from your own home, however bad you think it is, isn't it?' And restored, he went on: 'To the left, there is the Ahiran-ka-tolla of Samli Village. Do you remember any of this, Sheila? "Ka-tolla" means "the place of". The ahirs are cow-herders. The whole clan lives in the tolla and everyone is related. They're Yadavs and claim they are descended directly from Lord Krishna.'

No, I hadn't known, Inder Uncle was right. I'd lived at the farm only the few years Mum and Dad were in India. Dad had had a job at the hospital in Rampur and a good practice in

45

town. Mum had taken us to Allahabad, the nearest large city to her parents' house, to go to primary school most of the year. Then Dad had decided to go to London on a scheme which allowed Indian doctors to go as locums. Later Dr Able had offered Dad a partnership in his practice in London and we'd followed Dad to England when I was seven. I'd been back to India only three times since then; when I was nine, eleven and fourteen. And then, I'd hardly been aware of the villages; the farm and family had been the focus. Dad and Mum, though, had been back practically every year.

'Beyond the Ahiran-ka-tolla,' Inder Uncle was saying, 'closer to the farm, is the Malahan-ka-tolla, the place of the malahars, the fishermen.'

The ahir and malahar parts of Samli Village, I thought, as I gazed at the low, tiled mud huts, narrower at the top, broader at the base, between tall trees, were very beautiful. There weren't too many square brick buildings there.

'There to the right, away from everyone else,' Inder Uncle said, 'is the Chamaran-ka-tolla, the place of the chamars or leather workers. They're still considered untouchable because they work with leather, which means slaughtered cows.' The chamars lived almost exclusively in brick houses!

'Filthy, backward country!' Tinkoo said under his breath, mimicking me.

'Over there, beyond the lake, do you see those white structures with roofs and no walls? Well, those are government constructions,' Inder Uncle said, pointing to a row of small empty hutlets, in a straight row, like any suburban development in England. 'The municipality puts up the foundations, the wall supports and the roofs and anyone who needs a home can have it for practically free.'

'And,' Tinkoo said drily, 'I bet no one takes them, because they all want to live all agarbagar, bunched together, not in a straight line. Not even the chamars want them, I bet.'

Inder Uncle laughed. 'No, not even the chamars,' he said. 'Straight lines are not friendly.'

Up ahead, the long, low lines of the Chhimaria Plateau loomed purple in the almost white sky. The sun was beginning to bake the earth so the sweater I'd put on in the train was uncomfortably warm.

Over to the left, beyond a pond in which cows and buffaloes wallowed comfortably, the long, low yellow wall of the barns of Mehta Farm stretched over a hundred meters on the scrubby earth.

The farm faced away from the village of Samli and the town of Rampur – alone, enclosed, splendid, rejecting the world around it. Dad had said once, during the rare times he talked seriously about anything, that Grandpa who'd been in the Railways under the British, and had retired while posted in Madhya Pradesh, had built the farm from nothing, buying land in bits and pieces from local farmers. We're Punjabis, not originally from Madhya Pradesh and Grandpa didn't feel he belonged there any more than he did anywhere else in India. He was born in a town called Kala, up north near Rawalpindi, in what is now Pakistan.

Once past the school the road had petered out into a rutted, rubble path, and now we got off it altogether on to the grassy earth to keep from being shaken to bits.

Tall, lanky plants with drooping leaves and purple bell-shaped flowers which looked a little like morning glory, bordered the path.

'What's that flower?' I asked Inder Uncle.

'No idea,' he said, without interest, 'some wild flower.'

'Uh-huh,' I said under my breath, 'I thought so.'

'What d'you mean?' Tinkoo said at once, '*uh-huh*, in that high and mighty voice?'

'I mean Indians don't know the details of their countryside as well as the British do,' I said, sinkingly, knowing I was treading firmly on Tinkoo's corns.

'Damned British tourist, Mem!' he said.

I opened my mouth to reply, but we had arrived at the farm.

# 6

All along the right enclosure wall, facing out over the scrubland towards the Malahan-ka-tolla, were the servants' quarters of the farm. As we drove past them, several children tumbled out, wearing grubby clothes and faces, screaming and laughing. A woman looked up from a cooking fire in her front yard. And, out of Ram Milan's quarters came a young woman draped in a bright orange printed sari. She looked at me as we passed and our eyes caught. I waved excitedly.

Munnia! In a sari!

Up ahead, the wrought iron gates were open. Over them the arching red, purple and white bougainvillea were in full bloom. Under the archway hung a wooden board, with the legendary MEHTA FARM in black letters on white. We swung on to a curving red gravel drive bordered with tall trees and trimmed firs, rubber plants, and palms on each side. Beyond it was a wide green lawn, edged with brick-bordered flowerbeds and rose bushes.

And there was the house; a pillared portico, a long deep verandah along the front, tall french windows heavily draped against the light. Bougainvillea and some purple flowered creeper clambered up the white-washed walls. The roof sloped, covered with yellow tiles. It was actually two houses, the main house where Grandpa, Grandma, Inder Uncle and Bumpy lived, and the second, smaller house, built right next to it, with one common wall. It had its own small verandah in front. This house belonged to Dad and Mum, and was now used only for extra guests.

We came to a stop in the covered portico. Up three steps was the polished red floor of the verandah reflecting white-painted cane furniture.

As we climbed out of the jeep two figures in white came out of the french windows, arms outstretched. Grandpa and Grandma.

'Oh, ho, ho, ho, Sheila beti, Tinkoo beta!' Grandpa bellowed, welcoming us exhuberantly.

His beard seemed whiter than before, flowing majestically down his chest, and his hair hung long and full to his shoulders, contrasting pleasantly with a square nut-brown face. Two small, dark eyes glimmered like pools of mischief under an overhang of white eyebrows. He was wearing a fine white cotton kurta, and white churidar pyjamas, wrinkling at his ankles. Now, for the first time he carried a cane, but used it only sparingly. He was short and tubby, shorter than Grandma, but held himself like a tall man.

Grandma looked older than she had when I last saw her, but she still stood tall, thin and straight in her pale grey sari.

'Oh *my*, you have grown!' she said, unwrapping me from her embrace and holding me away. 'Doesn't she look like Sushila?'

Grandpa said: 'Aha, the foreign miss has come home, eh? And what's this Grandma and Grandpa business? We're your Bibiji and Pitaji, you're not so foreign as all that, are you?'

Inder Uncle said: 'She calls me Inder Uncle, what happened to Inder Chacha?'

'She's English, yaa,' Tinkoo said, making a small attempt at a laugh, but his voice was harsh with hostility. 'Listen to the way she talks – like explosions! You can't expect her to know all the different types of uncles and aunts. Her fundas are all gol, yaa.' By which mysterious statement he meant my fundamentals were zero. I looked at him with real dislike. I'd had just about enough of him. But I was beginning to feel lighter, looking at Grandpa and Grandma, so cheerful and so peaceful.

A skinny female servant in a green sari, came out of the house, smiled shyly at me, and started unloading the luggage from the jeep. She put my things in the guest room to the right, off the verandah, and carried Tinkoo's into the house. Hariram and Tinkoo did nothing, and when I went forward to help, she waved me away with a flash of a thin arm, and a reproving look.

'Who's that?' I said. 'She's new, isn't she, Gran?'

'Her name is Laxmi,' Gran said.

'She's so skinny and weak-looking,' I said. 'Surely she shouldn't be carrying such heavy luggage. Why doesn't Hariram help her?'

Gran smiled: 'They all look weak and skinny, but they're not.' She called the woman: 'Here, Laxmi, come here and meet Sheila Bai.'

The woman came forward and smiled and put her palms together in a namasté. She was very pretty, only a little older than me, I thought, with huge eyes and a coy smile. 'Namasté, Baiji,' she said shyly.

'Sheila Bai!' a voice said behind me.

I turned. Munnia was standing on the red gravel drive, a garland of marigolds in her hand.

'Munnia!' I cried gladly, pictures of us running through the fields to the river, making mud-pies together, rolling imaginary chapatties in imaginary kitchens, tumbling behind my eyes. I moved towards her, arms outstretched to hug her. But she came up the steps slowly, the garland held in front of her like a defensive shield. Stopping in front of me, she placed the garland around my neck as though I were a visiting dignitary. Then she stepped back, saying in Hindi: 'Welcome home, Sheila Bai,' and dropped her eyes to gaze at the floor.

'Munnia?' I faltered, holding back that familiar wave of nausea. Something had changed, something I'd had an inkling of when Munnia's postcard had arrived in London.

I looked at her short, plump figure covered with a cheap cotton sari; when did Munnia start wearing a sari? She was still in a dress the last time I was here. Saris were a sign of having grown-up. But of course! Munnia was a married woman now! She was an adult already, where I was still a child wearing skirts. And I was six months older than her! I'm only seven years old still, I thought fleetingly as I stepped forward and grabbed her hands. 'Munnia, how are you?' I said awkwardly in Hindi. 'You look so pretty. See, though I couldn't come for your wedding, I came for your gauna.'

'Yes,' she said gravely, still looking down, 'I am so glad.' I watched for some expression of intimacy on her round, plain face. I looked at her broad lips, her flaring nostrils, through one of which hung a thin gold ring. Her brown skin was shining, almost sweating.

I thought: she's a stranger, really.

But then, she looked up, and a light broke in her eyes; she shrugged and giggled, her hand going up to the mouth, her head turning slightly sideways, and she was the Munnia I had always known.

'Can you imagine?' she said, smiling, shy, excited. 'I'm going to my husband's house after the jabbah. Remember how we used to talk about getting married? Now I will be properly married.' Then she looked directly at me. 'Are you going to get married too, Sheila Bai? Soon? Is that why you've come? You should; it's getting late, you know.'

Late! At seventeen!

But I didn't say it. I could feel the gulf between us: of birth, class, education, expectations. I swallowed, and blinked back hot tears which suddenly rose behind my lids. Munnia had been married at fifteen; I'd been shocked when Grandpa wrote and told us. 'But Munnia's just a girl yet,' I'd cried. Dad had explained fifteen was late by the standards of her people – girls were generally married off at eleven. She was now seventeen, and that she hadn't yet been sent to her husband's house was a sign of progress. Many girls in the area were mothers at fifteen. Ram Milan, her father, was an ahir from Thana, some miles away. He'd been with Grandpa twenty years, rising from his traditional occupation as buffalo boy to tractor driver when he'd shown an aptitude for machines. Ram Milan had chosen Munnia's husband, Ram Prasad, an ahir from a village called Jagalkond on the other side of Rampur. Ram Prasad was a night-watchman at one of the local industries, a steel factory which spewed regular belches of black smoke away in the distance.

'You will come and have tea with us?' Munnia was saying. 'I am going up to the bazaar this afternoon specially to buy ladoos and jalebis.'

I stared at her, dismayed at this formality. Why did she need to ask? I would have gone around anyway. Why tea and jalebis?

'Yes, yes, of course, you must go,' Gran said. 'But tomorrow. Today you must rest.'

Inder Uncle said dubiously: 'I don't think you should eat bazaar food.'

'These foreign ladies with their delicate stomachs, isn't it?' Tinkoo jeered from the portico where he was standing by the jeep, talking in that manly way with Hariram.

'Yes, of course,' I said. 'Tomorrow, Munnia. But no ladoos and jalebis, all right?'

Munnia looked at me as if to say: 'Don't be silly!' and turned away, satisfied.

Yes, yes, yes, Munnia, I thought bleakly, lucky you, it's all yes, yes, yes, for you, isn't it? There's not a 'maybe' or a 'perhaps' in your life.

'Now,' Gran said briskly, 'time for a bath and breakfast.'

Tinkoo said we'd had breakfast on the train.

'Then coffee at eleven, and lunch at one, all right?'

Gran, I remembered, had run her house as she had when Grandpa worked in the Railways under the British, as though she were a colonial housewife. For lunch we'd have Indian food, for dinner Western: cold cuts, salads and burnt sugar pudding. Mum, in contrast, living in London, ran her house like an Indian, filled with as much of India as she could cram into it: books, records, films, food, festivals, friends, paintings, rugs . . .

I went into the guest room, cleaned and made ready for me. The bed was made up, frills along the bottom, the counterpane turned down at one corner; a vase of flowers, a stack of paperbacks, a box of biscuits and a jug of water on the side table; lace doilies on the dressing table.

So English, so bloody *English*! Even here in India, everything was so English.

I felt suddenly—I can only call it a time-warp—as though moments, days, events, had left their orderly procession one behind the other, and were skittering like tin soldiers under attack, on a glassy surface, in complete disarray. It was as though some last foundation was being pulled from under me, and I was slip-sliding along without a thing to hold on to.

I lay down on the bed, my hands clenched, breathing in short gasps. I looked at the three-pronged fan rotating on the ceiling, moving the air in sluggish waves. Dumbly I watched a couple of house lizards chase each other across the walls, snapping at each other's tails, and this alien-familiar sight increased the feeling of being too many different places at the same time. The room began to tilt.

With an effort I began to say the word Dr Able had taught me. At first it kept slipping away, giving way to the jumble of pictures in my head. Then, as I began to concentrate, the word began to steady me.

Like a strap in a lurching underground train.

Was that all there was to hold on to? A word?

I began to feel desperate again. And a voice in my head said: 'In the beginning there was the word, and the word was God.'

I sat up, startled. What *was* happening to me? Where were these thoughts coming from? Had Phil said something like this? When he was going on about the Bible? 'The word was God,' I said aloud. 'What does it mean?' I'd have to ask him when I get back to London.

It didn't make sense, but I felt strangely comforted.

I was home again, where the beginning was. I'd been born in this house: perhaps this was the place for me.

It must be, it must be!

# 7

I woke to the scraping of chairs in the verandah, the tinkle of china, subdued murmurs. No pangs in my gut.

The curtains were pushed aside and Gran looked in. 'Awake, Sheila?' she said.

I sat up. 'Yes, Gran. Is it coffee time?'

Gran spoke in Punjabi, I replied in English. We both understood each other perfectly. While I understood both Punjabi and Hindi, I spoke them so badly I felt awkward and ashamed, when I did.

'Coffee?' Gran laughed. 'Child, it's teatime. You slept right through the day. I didn't want to wake you up. You were sleeping so soundly. I thought you must have had a bad night on the train.'

'Teatime?' I sprang off the bed. 'Oh, I'm *sorry*, Gran. What's the matter with me? I slept perfectly well on the train. And I haven't even had a bath. I feel like a pig.'

Gran came in and sat on the bed. Even in her sixties she was beautiful. There was a distinct resemblance between her and Rachna. They had the same high cheek-bones and slightly hooked nose. Rachna had taken the best from both families, because while Mum was okay to look at, Nina Maasi was a stunner. Dad and I and Grandpa, seemed to belong to the same bloodline. Gran's eyes were a light greenish brown, her hair white, pulled back and tied in a small knot behind her head. Small gold earstuds glowed dully in her ears, and four thin gold bangles twinkled on her left wrist. Unlike most people her age, she wore little jewellery.

'Don't worry, beti,' she said. 'Young people should sleep as much as they can. It is a blessing, this ability to sleep. You don't sleep so much when you get older.' She held my hand, drew me down on the bed to sit beside her and ran a hand affectionately over my head. 'Well, well, you are growing up, I can see that. And pretty too.' She was sweet to lie, but that was her way; to say the right thing, and mean it. 'So much like Sushila. And how is Rachoo? She didn't want to come?'

'She did, Gran,' I lied in my turn, 'but she has exams now, she has to study.' I couldn't begin to think *what* Gran would have said about Rachna's practically bald head if she'd come.

'And you? No exams?' Gran said.

'Well,' I said. 'Yes, I do have exams . . . or at least . . . but . . .' Now, what could I say? That I couldn't concentrate? That I'd stopped caring whether I passed or not? What had Mum told them? 'Well, my teachers thought that if I missed them in June I could take them later. I wanted to come for Munnia's gauna . . .'

Gran patted my hand. 'Yes, Sushila wrote and said you were a bright girl and could catch up easily. Your teachers have confidence in you. But . . .' she looked keenly at me, and gave a small sigh, 'I hope you find whatever it is you're looking for . . . at Munnia's gauna.'

I said nothing, I didn't want to start explaining myself. In any case I really didn't have the words, then, to put around what was happening to me. What could I have said: 'I came because my English boyfriend chucked me, Gran'? 'I came because I ache every morning, Gran'? 'I came because I don't know where I belong, Gran'? It sounded so melodramatic.

'Sushila wrote that you want to join Delhi University after you finish school?' Gran said. 'That you were going to make enquiries in Delhi about courses. Did you find out?'

'Not yet,' I said, relieved to change the subject. 'I'll get the brochures and things when I get back. But I've been talking to Ashok Uncle and Nina Maasi and Tinkoo about it. I'll have to apply as a foreign student. I'll apply for a place in the hostel too. If I don't get in, Nina Maasi said I could stay with her.'

'And have you decided what you want to study?' Gran said.

'I'm going to take Politics Honours,' I said brightly, breathing in all the enthusiasm I could, and felt a little jump of interest as I said that. 'Later I want to do a Masters in International Relations.' It had been a relief to have made the decision.

Gran's eyebrows went up slightly. 'Politics and International Relations? My goodness! What will you do with that?'

'Well . . .' I said, 'I . . . well, I'll begin to understand people . . . you know . . . why they behave as they do . . .' And right away, at the first glimmer of doubt, the entire fabric of reasons began to unravel. 'I . . . I want to see why people get along with each other, or rather why they don't . . .' I trailed off, sitting on the bed looking at my hands, beginning to feel confused and silly, the way I always did when I thought about the future. Then I said with an effort at determination, squaring my shoulders: 'Well . . . we've all got to do something useful in the world, Gran . . . and . . .' Again, I stopped.

There was a small silence. Then Gran said cheerfully: 'We'll talk about this later, there's plenty of time. Now you go and have a bath and get changed and come out for tea.'

Showers are a rarity in India; tubs take an age to fill. I bathed out of a bucket, using a mug to slosh water over myself, squatting inside a huge old clawfooted enamel bathtub. At Nina Maasi's in Delhi, there wasn't even a bathtub; you bathed on the floor. This was *fun*, I told myself resolutely. But there was a definite traitor inside me who preferred British plumbing!

I dressed in jeans and a shirt and went out into the verandah. They were all sitting around a cane coffee table sipping tea and munching biscuits: Grandpa, Gran, Inder Uncle, Bumpy and Tinkoo. They made such a peaceful picture that I stopped dead for a moment, blinking.

The white cane chairs reflected perfectly on the polished red floor. Around them, over the edges of the verandah, bougain-villea and that purple creeper – ah! I remembered it – passion flower, drooped off the roof. Potted plants clustered all around the edges of the verandah, hung from lintels.

Beyond the verandah and portico, the lawns stretched greenly, bordered by flowerbeds shrubs and trees, ending in a tall hedge of bougainvillea. And off, past the hedges, fields of ripened wheat stretched to the river and beyond in varying shades of yellow, ochre and gold; bald brown where it had been harvested.

Just behind the front hedge, a huge patch had been cleared,

56

and here piles of wheat were stacked around the threshing machine. In the distance I saw the red of the tractor on the outer bund, heard its chug and rumble.

A thatched hut stood in the middle of the fields, with a well in front. Clusters of trees spread their benign shade at intervals. Three black silhouettes of men stood on tall tables under umbrellas, at widely spaced distances in the yellow fields. Faintly I heard them call 'Heeyah! heeyah!' and rattle tin castanets to frighten off the birds. In India they could afford human scarecrows!

'Come, come, Sheilaji,' Inder Uncle said, pulling up a chair, 'the tea is still hot. And here's Bumpy.'

If I had a brother at all, it was surely Bumpy. His name was Brijendra, but because he'd been a clumsy child, he'd got the nickname Bumpy and it had stuck. We'd grown up together till I was seven and he, twelve. As I moved towards them saying: 'Hello, Bumpy . . . I . . .' a dog barked. Around the side of the house, and up the steps of the portico, a huge Alsatian bounded straight at Tinkoo. He leaped on Tinkoo's shoulders delightedly, slobbering and yelping, licking Tinkoo's face.

'Down, down, Raja. Boy! Enough!' Tinkoo laughed, putting his cup down hastily. He looked at me. 'Can you believe he's nearly three years old?'

The dog stopped pawing Tinkoo, and came towards me, growling suspiciously.

I stepped back hastily.

Inder Uncle got up immediately and put his arm around my shoulders. 'It's all right, Raja, all right,' he said in Hindi. 'See. Friend. All right now.' Inder Uncle turned to me, and said, apologetically: 'We got him after your last visit, Sheilaji.'

'We need protection here now, Sheels,' Bumpy said, and came over and hugged me and kissed me on both cheeks. Like Tinkoo, he wore jeans, a long kurta and sandals. But the effect on him was quite different. Where the outfit made Tinkoo look pretentious, on Bumpy they looked like working clothes, comfortable, hard-wearing. I couldn't imagine Bumpy casually lifting his kurta and very elaborately groping in his back pocket for coins so we could all gasp enviously at the designer label on his jeans. Bumpy has a broad squarish face, large eyes, a small nose and a wide, smiling mouth.

'Protection?' I said, sitting. 'From whom?'

'Local roughs,' Bumpy said. 'The dacoit gangs are back.'

'I told her about dacoits on the train, yaa,' Tinkoo said, 'but she didn't believe me.'

I laughed. Dacoits, bandits! In this peaceful idyllic scene! It was ridiculous. Unreal.

'Oh, yeah,' I said lightly, 'on horseback, handkerchief masks, pistols and yahoo!'

Inder Uncle said soberly: 'No, not on horseback. In jeeps. This is India in the twentieth century, you know. Horses are too slow.'

I accepted a cup of tea from Gran. 'I can't remember any of you talking about bandits the last time we came?'

'They are back,' Inder Uncle said shortly. 'Not operating out of the Chambal Valley any more, or out of caves in the plateaux. More like urban bandits now, in the slums and villages.'

Grandpa said: 'I heard there was a gang of roughs in Rampur yesterday, Bumpy. Do you know who they were? What happened?'

'There were three,' Bumpy said slowly, leaning back in his chair, cup in hand, an ankle across his knee. 'It seems they stopped their jeep outside Nathoo Mal's coffee shop. They marched in and demanded coffee. They were carrying rifles, and refused to pay. When Nathoo Mal protested, they hit him with rifle butts and threatened to wipe out his family if he didn't shape up. Then they left. Nathoo Mal was badly beaten up and everyone is terrified that they might come back.'

'Are you serious?' I burst out. 'Didn't the man go to the police?'

'Police?' Tinkoo sneered. 'You think the police will do anything? They are so scared I bet they pee in their pants when there's trouble.'

To my surprise, Bumpy nodded.

'You mean they can just walk into town like that and terrorize everyone?' I said disbelievingly.

Grandpa said: 'They don't usually come into the main market place. Their business is in the slums and villages.'

'They are,' Tinkoo said smugly, 'what we call proto-revolutionaries.'

Grandpa flashed him an amused look, and snorted. He reached for a biscuit and crunched on it, smiling, saying nothing.

'The original dacoits were farmers who were rooked by money lenders and landlords,' Inder Uncle said, 'and had no other way to get justice; our law enforcement machinery is corrupt, and in the hands of people with money and power. The farmers used to get beaten up and tortured in jail. So when they escaped, they became dacoits. There was no choice for them.'

'Most of them gave up their arms a few years ago when the government offered amnesty and rehabilitation,' Bumpy said, 'but the political and economic situation in the country makes things worse in rural areas. People think that just because only seventy per cent of our population is rural today whereas ten, fifteen years ago, it was over eighty per cent, we've made progress. But our development policies have only marginalized rural people even more. The slums in our small towns and cities are bulging with rural migrants who've been uprooted from their land. They're turning to crime, just to make ends meet.'

Tinkoo was nodding sleepily with a small smile on his face. 'Ripe for revolution,' he said, with satisfaction.

Grandpa shifted heavily in his chair. 'I don't know about revolution the way you mean it, son,' he said, 'but certainly ripe for some major calamity, like epidemics of cholera. Or unorganized, mindless bloodshed.'

'In rural areas,' Inder Uncle said soberly, 'power is in the hands of a mafia made up of rich landlords and local politicians, who swallow up development money meant for farmers. They control the police, and use them for their own benefit.'

Tinkoo sat up. 'But the farmers will rise!' he said excitedly. 'The oppressed always rise. The Naxalites are already doing hajaar good work amongst the tribals. We'll go communist I tell you. Just you wait and see. We'll have a khufiya Marxist revolution here, just as they had in Russia and China.'

Grandpa guffawed. '*This* I would like to see,' he said, slapping his thigh. 'I know a thing or two about communism in India, beta, you can believe me. And communism in Russia and Europe isn't holding up too well from what I read. If there is anything which will unite the world, bring it lasting peace, it will be revolution of the spirit.' He became serious for a moment. 'And I don't mean reactionary religion, beta. I mean, when the true meaning of religion becomes available to everyone. *Then* we'll have a real revolution. And India, I think, is the *one* country in the world, where this is possible. The Indian mind is very ethical at its roots, although we've lost the link.'

I didn't understand him at all at this point, but I felt a faint, very faint stirring far away inside me. He puzzled me, and I frowned.

Tinkoo was almost hopping in his chair by the time Grandpa finished his little speech.

'Pitaji,' he said, almost croaking with excitement, 'you are hajaar idealistic . . . with due respect . . . your understanding of revolutionary issues is outdated . . . you're a back-slid Marxist, Pitaji, sorry to say . . .'

Grandpa sat back, his stomach wobbling with laughter. 'I suppose you think my fundas are gol!' he said. 'You sound just like I did when I was your age.' He leaned forward and patted Tinkoo's knee.

Tinkoo flinched away, his face red. 'Don't be so condescending, Pitaji . . .!' he began.

Gran raised one hand admonishing Tinkoo and handed me the plate of biscuits with the other. 'Now, enough,' she said, firmly. 'This is Sheila's first day here. Let's talk of pleasant things. Tell us what Sushila and Raj are doing in London.' She turned to Grandpa, 'We must go there again, soon, Channi, we have been so involved in the farm.' They'd come to

London about six years ago, after we'd moved to Chigwell.

Grandpa grunted: 'Next year maybe.'

Gran tutted: 'Always next year!' But she smiled. For Gran, Grandpa could do no wrong. 'When are they coming, Sheila? Isn't it time?'

'This winter, I think,' I said, 'they were talking about it.'

So we shifted the topic, and talked about life in London, and I managed to keep from telling them about Rachna's problems and mine, and the tension in the house.

When Laxmi cleared away the tea things, Bumpy suggested Tinkoo and I walked down to the river with him. But I found I was tired again. I selected an Agatha Christie from the living room bookshelves: they were *stacked* with really old books . . . and read for a while, lying on my bed.

When dinner was announced I was asleep.


Dinner was served at eight in the panelled dining room. It was all very correct and proper. And all very English. Laxmi, in a white sari, served from the left. I began to feel strange again. Mum's service in London was a hodge-podge compared to this. We usually ate in the kitchen, Rach and I helping out. We used the dining room only when we had company. We never had English food when Mum cooked, though Rach and I regularly turned up our 'monster foods' as Dad called hamburgers and fish fingers.

Inder Uncle, Bumpy and Tinkoo fit right in. But none of them seemed to be conscious that so much of them was so British. They seemed quite solidly Indian. While they did speak English, it was with a singsong intonation, and very accented, and they threw in a mixture of Hindi and Punjabi, using the words and expressions most convenient at the time. They dressed completely Indian, even though Tinkoo and Bumpy wore jeans, but it was with kurta and shawl which made it Indian. Inder Uncle seldom wore a business suit.

But the house looked mostly English, the way they ate was a mixture of English and Indian, although they could no longer

61

afford the number of household servants Grandpa once had working in the Railways.

It was as though a part of them was stuck in the past, and they weren't even aware of it!

The conversation at dinner was generally about the government controlled price of wheat that year which put a strain on farmers, the problems with auctioneers of fruit and vegetables in the market, and inevitably, politics. Everywhere, I thought, politics, politics, politics! India seemed to *breathe* politics!

After dinner, Grandpa said: 'Bridge, Sheila? Have you learned yet? Would you like a rubber?'

'No, thanks,' I said, 'I don't play, but I'll watch.'

'You can watch TV if you want,' Inder Uncle said anxiously, 'they have just installed an antenna at Rampur, so the reception's not bad.'

'The programmes are hopeless, though,' Tinkoo said, the know-it-all. 'All government propaganda. Even the news is hajaar biased.'

They paired off and drew chairs up around the coffee table in the living room. I slumped in an armchair by the unlit fire listening to Three hearts, No bid, Four clubs, like a lullaby in the background and looked sleepily around the living room.

Over the fireplace an old moth-eaten tigerskin hung, tail up, head down, its open mouth frozen in an eternal fangless snarl. Grandpa had shot it when he was young and tigershooting was still allowed. It must have been at least forty years dead now, poor thing. It used to be on the floor in front of the fireplace when we were little, and Bumpy, Rach and I rode it, shouting: 'Giddap, giddap, giddap!' clutching its head and banging it on the ground, till its teeth fell out.

A standard lamp threw a rosy warm, comforting glow on the faded, scruffy, well-used, homely room.

Then Tinkoo's voice came through the daze in my head. 'Well, partner, that was a hajaar stupid play!'

I sat up. 'If you'll excuse me,' I said, 'I'm for bed.' It was only nine-thirty.

'No one sleeps as much as you do,' Tinkoo said, unkindly,

still smarting from having lost his game. 'You're a heavy *avoid* scene, yaa.'

'You better sleep all you can tonight, Sheels,' Bumpy said. 'We start threshing tomorrow and we go nearly through the night.'

'Do you want a cup of hot milk?' Gran asked.

'No, no thanks,' I said. ''Night all.'

Gran put her arms out. I bent down and she kissed me on the forehead. When had Mum last done that? Did Mrs Baker ever kiss her darling Jimmy goodnight? I went to bed thinking no English mum could possibly be as warm and wonderful as my Indian gran. My bibiji.

# 8

The cacophony in my head was going full blast at four the next morning. I woke with my heart fluttering unevenly like wings on a wounded bird. There was a thumping in my gut, my breath came in gasps, as spacemen, nuclear fallout, Rachna dancing, Jimmy's mother frowning, followed each other, like pictures in a video recording gone mad.

I covered my head with my sheet, trying to shut out the babble before I realized it was all firmly inside my head. With that came despair: I'd come thousands of miles across continents and oceans . . . but I hadn't left the voices and pictures behind.

'The worm lives in the apple,' Dr Able's voice said in my head. 'And where the apple goes, the worm goes with it.' And I had a sudden flash of Jimmy saying: 'The earthworm lives in the apple, and the appleworm lives in the earth.' And me saying: 'Oh, so the worm turns . . .' and the futility of it overwhelmed me. I began to beat the mattress with my hands in pathetic little thumps.

'Why, why, why?' said a little voice somewhere inside my head. 'Why me? Poor me.'

Then, almost automatically, because Dr Able had taught me so well, and I'd done it so often, I raised my legs straight up in the air, soles flattened, and held them there until they began to tremble. My breathing deepened. I brought one leg straight down, slap! on to the mattress, and with it, the opposite arm. Then switched my arm and leg and brought them down, bang! Then, systematically, bang! bang! with rising intensity, I beat the mattress with legs and arms alternating.

A hundred times, a hundred and fifty. Gradually the despair changed to a slow, rising anger, and my legs and arms came down with real force. 'No! No! No!'

Then, for the first time since I'd started the exercise under Dr Able's guidance, I realized the pictures in my head and what I was feeling, were connected. I was ANGRY! I was angry with Mrs Baker; I was angry with Jimmy. Who did they think they were! Who the bloody hell did they think they were!

I was angry with Mum and Dad! Really! I was angry with Mum and Dad for taking me away from my home where I'd been safe. For not asking me whether I wanted to go.

I hadn't been consulted! I hadn't given my permission! I was angry! Angry! Angry!

Three hundred. I stopped, and lay flat, breathing deeply my heart slowing, my gut beginning to untangle. The anger receded. But then, I realized Mum and Dad probably hadn't thought children had valid opinions at the age of seven. And I became enraged again.

I stretched myself slowly, bit by bit from head to toe, sat up, crossed my legs and began to say the word Dr Able had given me, over and over in my head.

Involuntarily, my spine began to straighten, my knees and shoulders dropped, my chin came up. The anger faded away. And I began to hear sounds from the world outside.

Far in the distance, a steam engine wailed, the sound flowing like golden honey over the dark fields. With it, filling the air with busy officious grumbles, came a friendly achha-chugga, achha-chugga, far away, growing louder, receding.

The first birds began to twitter. I heard the call of a bird, melodious, mournful and insistent: koo-hoo, koo-hoo . . . and I felt a sharp sting of recognition; it was a koel . . . it was a sound I remembered from when we used to live here as steady and accepted, as taken for granted as the achha-chugga of trains. It resonated through me: koo-hoo, koo-hoo . . . I suddenly realized I didn't know its English name.

A dog barked.

Then, gliding over the thatched roofs of the villages, scudding over the open scrubby wasteland behind the house, came a single male voice.

'Allah ho Akhbar . . . Allah ho Akhbar . . . Allah ho Akhbar . . .'

The tone changed, the voice dropped a few notes, words I couldn't catch, then: 'Allah ho Akhbar . . .'

I found myself listening intently, as I saw before my eyes the muezzin in his turret calling the faithful to prayer.

The voice floated away over the black fields towards the plateau and there was silence.

More birds sang. A man called in a long, ululating cry: 'Aho Nathania-a-a-a!' and a female voice answered: 'Ah hoiyo!'

Then a rivulet of notes trilled an octave, each note flowing nasally into the other: a harmonium. Three male voices began to sing. I strained to understand, and caught the word 'Nanak'. I listened, trying to understand this harsh-soft song and gradually it fell into place. It was in Punjabi, a hymn.

It flowed around me, tinny over loudspeakers. I sat listening, eyes closed, cross-legged, and felt calmer.

Before the song ended, temple bells began to toll, the deep notes trembling in the lightening skies. An insistent male voice began chanting in three monotonous notes in a minor key. Smaller bells kept an uneven beat to the chant. The Hindus had joined the chorus of dawn.

I felt tears behind my closed lids. Then, below the growing sense of peace, I became aware of a great empty space.

'I'm lonely,' a feeble little voice said plaintively in my head. 'I'm lonely.'

But for what?

Jimmy? Perhaps. It still hurt thinking about him. But he didn't seem like reason enough.

For London? No. London, really, wasn't important enough.

For Mum? I was too old for that.

For Sunaina? Could friends make you feel this much?

I didn't think so.

'Remember it's a film you're watching,' Dr Able's voice said in my ear, 'and you're not in it.'

Not in it? But I was, I was! The feelings were all mine; this chaos in my head was all mine. This disproportionate ache for some great loss which I couldn't remember experiencing . . . it was all mine. How glib Dr Able's words sounded that morning.

I uncrossed my legs, fell over on my side and wept until I was exhausted.

Gran woke me at ten.

She shook my shoulder gently. 'Sheila, beti, enough sleeping now,' she said.

I sat up rubbing my eyes.

Gran sat down on my bed and took my hand. She was wearing her usual pastel sari. 'You've been crying,' she said. It was a flat, matter-of-fact statement without sympathy. And I was grateful for that.

I shook my head. 'No . . . I mean, perhaps . . . maybe in my sleep.'

'Bad dreams?' Gran said.

'Bad dreams,' I agreed. It was easiest.

She patted my hand and ruffled my hair. 'Well, now it's daytime. Time to be up and about. Would you like breakfast?'

I shook my head.

'Then have a glass of milk, all right? I'll send you one. What are you going to do today? Munnia has been here asking if you'd like to go for a walk to the river.'

Again I shook my head. I felt weak. 'No, Gran. Not now. Later. Maybe this evening after I've had tea with her. I just want to lie in bed and read today. Is that all right?'

Gran looked at my face intently. 'All right,' she said. 'Just today because you've come after a long journey, and you're tired. But from tomorrow no lying around. We begin threshing this evening.' She looked out of the window. 'At six when it's not so hot, and it will go on till twelve. Then tomorrow we begin again at four in the morning.'

'Yuk,' I said.

'Hanh, you'll find it a little difficult to sleep, I think, at first, but you'll get used to it. At harvest time we do the threshing for many of the smaller farmers, so we work long hours.'

Gran left, and Laxmi brought me a cup of hot milk. I washed and brushed my teeth, and climbed back into bed in my pyjamas, reading and listening to the sounds of the farm outside my window: the throb of the tractor, the calls of the workers, Grandpa's voice as he talked to the supervisor, Gran talking to the gardener. Raja barking. Children laughing.


Inder Uncle, Bumpy and Tinkoo weren't there for lunch, they'd taken a buffalo to the vet. Over dal, chapattis and vegetable curry, I said, 'Grandpa, did you hear the prayers in the village this morning?'

For a moment he looked blank.

'You know, Grandpa, the songs. The first one was Mohammedan, the muezzin calling, I'm pretty sure. Then there was some Punjabi singing . . .'

'Aha!' Grandpa said, his face brightening. 'Yes, yes. I see. You mean you were up so early?'

I nodded.

'I don't hear them any more,' he said, 'I've got used to all the noise around here, I suppose. Yes, the muezzin calls first . . . Allah ho Akhbar . . .'

He paused, with his hand half-way to his mouth. We ate Indian food with our fingers, Western food with knives and forks. He chewed thoughtfully for a bit, and said: 'Let me see if I can remember the rest. Yes. What he says is "Aiyya allaf fallah, aiyya allas salat . . ." which means: "Come all brothers, come to the house of the lord." *Allah ho Akhbar* means "the name of God is one".' He looked pleased he'd remembered.

'And the second one, was that Punjabi? It came over loudspeakers.'

'Yes, from the gurudwara. At that time of morning they sing the "Asa di-war".'

Gran said, crossly: 'We have to get them to stop using loudspeakers. It's all right if they want to pray, but do they have to announce their prayers to the whole world? Hindus, Muslims, Sikhs, all in competition with each other early in the morning.'

'But, Gran, it's beautiful,' I protested. 'I think it's great, you know? That all the religions express themselves together . . .' I stopped and felt my face redden. The morning prayers had seemed to say that here in this huge, overcrowded, uncomfortable land, there was enough space for everyone.

Gran said: 'Hmmpfh!' and called Laxmi to clear away the dishes. 'Papayas from our orchard for dessert,' she said. 'There are so many we can't sell them all in the market.'

I said to Grandpa who was wiping his plate with a chapatti and looking guiltily at Gran from under his eyebrows: 'The third one, Grandpa . . .'

'Pitaji,' he said.

'Gramps,' I grinned and he laughed and shook his head resignedly. 'The temple bells and chanting? Hindu, is it?'

'Yes, Hindu,' he said. 'Yes, I suppose you could say that.'

Laxmi brought the papaya sitting majestically green and yellow on a platter.

'I love the chanting,' I said. 'It's so soothing.'

Grandpa licked his fingers, and Gran frowned. 'It's Vedic,' he said, 'very old. The ancients found a combination of three notes which soothes the nervous system. It's very clever. Like "Om Shanti". The "Aummm" sound has a good effect on the nerves. Just close your eyes, put your fingers in your ears and go "Hmmmmm", it feels good.' Then he leaned back on his chair and said, drily: 'You give the masses sounds which calm their nerves, call it a prayer, and claim special dispensation from God because you're a brahmin . . .'

I looked at him, surprised at the change of tone. His hands were folded over his stomach, a frown on his forehead and a slight smile creasing what was visible of his cheeks above his beard.

'Your pitaji has a love-hate relationship with religion,' Gran said, carving the huge papaya on the plate in front of her. 'He was a Marxist in his youth, you know, and worked full-time for the Communist party before he settled down to earning a living and facing his responsibilities.'

She glanced at him and smiled maternally as though indulging a boyish prank.

'So I gathered,' I said, teasing, 'and now you're a *back-slid* Marxist!'

Grandpa raised his eyebrows and beamed. 'Tinkoo is my twin,' he said.

'You know what Nina Maasi calls Tinkoo?' I said and paused dramatically, 'a knee-jerk Marxist!'

Grandpa simply howled. He threw back his head and guffawed. 'Dead right!' he cried, his eyes streaming. 'Right on target!' He wiped his eyes with his napkin.

'But you were a real communist, weren't you, Gramps?'

'Yes,' Grandpa said, calming down. 'I was a very idealistic young man. I was looking for utopia, for answers to the world's problems, for justice, for a system that worked. We wanted to get the British out of India, and there were many different ideas with which we were trying to replace Victorian Imperialism.'

'Really, Gramps!' I said, impressed.

'I wasn't interested in what religion had done to our country,' Grandpa went on, 'I thought religion had stunted us, so we hadn't made "progress", and had allowed ourselves to be enslaved by another country.' He paused. 'But that was before I realized there is religion and there is religion, and the word "progress" is the most misunderstood word in the world.'

'What do you mean?' I said, puzzled.

And Grandpa said: 'Well, my darling daughter, what is progress? Does it mean material wealth and a high standard of living? Or does it mean a thing of the spirit, an inner evolution?'

'Oh,' I said, stumped.

'Or does it perhaps mean a balance of the two?'

'Oh,' I said again, putting down my spoon.

'And what is religion?' Grandpa went on, seriously putting both elbows on the table and leaning forward. 'Is it rituals which are housed in large edifices, misinterpreted for the ignorant by high-priests, to give them beliefs to help them escape from the responsibility of thinking for themselves? Or is it a personal philosophy, an inner code of conduct which has little to do with groups and communities and nations and beliefs?'

70

He accepted a third piece of papaya from Gran. 'True religion, beti, has to do with your relationship with yourself, self-knowledge, self-acceptance. Being responsible for yourself and your life.' He raised the whole slice of papaya to his face and said from behind it: 'Of course, you have to define what your "self" is, first.' He bit into his papaya, raising an eyebrow quizzically as he ate. 'And that in itself is an interesting problem, isn't it?'

At the time, all of this sort of passed me by. As far as I was concerned Grandpa was talking double-dutch. But after a bit, I said: 'I see.'

'Do you?' Grandpa said, 'Really?' He was smiling. 'It took *me* a whole lifetime to see.'

Gran tcchaed and clucked and shook her head reprovingly: 'Stop teasing, Channi, 'you're taking advantage of your white hairs.'

And Grandpa chuckled: 'All right, all right, let's leave it. But you go on and think about it, beti.'

'Aren't you really Marxist any more, Gramps?' I said to change the subject from religion. I wanted to see him standing on a soap box at Hyde Park . . . or some Indian equivalent, harranguing the crowds. It was a thrilling, romantic image. 'I thought once a Marxist, always a Marxist.'

Grandpa nodded amiably. 'True, but I realized as I got older that people have the ability to turn any good idea into an "ism"; and distort its essential truths. They set up organizations around it and suffocate it with misinterpretations. Marxism isn't any different to religion; it's suffered the same fate. It's become a system of beliefs propped up by organizations and high-priests.'

How confusing Grandpa was! And that confused me even more. What I'd studied about Marxism in school made a sort of sense to me. And it didn't sound like a religion at all. Religion meant the sounds I'd heard that morning. Marxism was a lot of yelling about the rights of the common people and about the rich being capitalist swine.

We aren't a religious family. We seldom went to any religious festivals or ceremonies back in London . . . except, of course, the Indian weddings which meant nothing to me, though interesting to look at. This morning I'd felt we'd missed out, not having had a religious upbringing.

'Grandpa,' I said, 'why don't we have any religion? We're Hindus, aren't we? Mum never does any pujas and things at home.'

'That's because I didn't bring Raj and Inder up to be religious,' Grandpa said. 'I told you: religion as it's generally understood is rubbish.'

'But, Grandpa,' I insisted, 'the songs this morning. I thought they were beautiful. I . . . felt good listening to them . . . I . . .' I stopped, embarrassed, and looked at the papaya pips on my plate, my face flushed.

Gran said quietly: 'Have you been missing the religious songs, Sheila beti, or have you been missing the sounds of India?'

I thought again. 'Ah! Yes. I suppose really the sounds.' I thought of the sound of the train, the sounds on the railway platform, in Rampur. India was mainly sound to me. But this morning there had been more than just sound. 'Yes, the sounds, yes,' I said, feeling a veil lift from my eyes. 'But more, Gran. I think, really, I have missed religion. It gives you, well,' I stumbled, 'it's like you *know* who you are when you follow a religion . . . You feel . . . you well, belong. You know, you feel . . . safe . . .'

Grandpa raised his eyebrows and cleared his throat after this, but he said quite neutrally, 'Yes, child, rituals and traditions are important if you take them in the proper context. There's been a lot of powerful thinking behind every ritual in every religion in the world. Some of it's useful, like the mantras, which soothe your nerves.'

'Mantras?' I said.

'Words you repeat to yourself, like "Om Shanti",' Grandpa said.

'Words you repeat to yourself?' I said. 'Are they secret?'

Grandpa laughed. 'More ritual. But yes, people like to keep them secret, they say it gives them more meaning . . . so they seem to work . . .'

'Oh,' I said.

'Why, what is it?' Gran said.

'Nothing,' I said. So what Dr Able had given me was a mantra! He'd said it was a secret I wasn't to tell anyone else.

'Even the solemn hymns in churches are meant to soothe your nerves. But most rituals are absolute nonsense to my way of thinking,' Grandpa said, 'just means of collecting money for the priesthood, a way of providing some illusion of safety, of keeping the ignorant and stupid on line.'

'But the morning songs *are* useful,' I said stubbornly. '*I* liked hearing them, so they're useful.'

'If you like,' Grandpa said, 'if you enjoyed them, that's good. But they aren't a . . . what do you call it . . . a panacea. There's no real safety in rituals and tradition. There is no substitute to thinking for yourself, you know, for finding your own code of conduct, your own feeling of self-worth in the world. For being responsible for your own life.'

There it was again. 'Responsible for your own life.' Mum's words, Dad's words. I started feeling sick again.

Words, words, words. *How* could I be responsible for my life when I got no help from my parents?

Did Sunaina's parents expect her to be solely responsible for her life? No. They assumed they had to help her make the important choices in her life.

Did Munnia's parents expect her to be responsible for her life all by herself? Not at all. Why was it *I* was expected to? What made it so different for me?

'What's the matter, Sheila?' Gran said, 'aren't you well? Did the dal disagree with you? You look pale.'

'Oh nothing, Gran,' I said, 'nothing, I'm just a bit . . . under the weather . . . you know . . . I'll just go and rest.'

'I'm glad you're interested in religion,' Grandpa said, scraping his chair back, 'it's a topic you can discuss endlessly. Now, time for my afternoon nap.'

'Mine too,' I said, grateful to be able to escape.

# 9

At four, I put on my jeans and shirt and slipped out of the house before the tea-on-the-verandah ritual began. I didn't want to talk to anyone.

It was still hot, and out in the fields I could see splashes of red and blue, the farm labour at work. The tractor rumbled in the distance, a great red beast with a hump of gold.

Suddenly, with an unexpected clarity, I saw my trainers on the red of the gravel below my feet; my hands as they pushed open the small, black wrought iron gate in the wall; the grainy texture of the yellow-washed wall; the tall, slim ashoka trees, leaves drooping, bordering the wall; the wide umbrella of the jacaranda above – and a surge of such inexplicable joy as I hadn't felt since I'd fallen in love with Jimmy, washed through me. It was a clean, sharp feeling I hadn't had for more than a year – in another world, a dream. I seemed to melt, to open up and become part of everything around me.

How peculiar, I thought, I feel like I'm in love without actually being in love! But almost before I could draw a second breath, the feeling vanished, leaving me perplexed and apprehensive; feeling again, that emptiness of being so far away from everything. What was happening to me? How I felt seemed independent of what was going on outside me!

As the gate squeaked open, Munnia grasped my hand, the smile on her face so wide her face seemed split in two.

'Come on, Sheila Bai,' she beamed and drew me to the courtyard in the front of her father's quarters. Her mother, Shanti, my one time ayah, was squatting on her haunches next to a small iron cooking container, a coal cigri. On it a pan of tea-leaves, milk, sugar, water, all simmered lingeringly together. Shanti stood as I came up, and joined her palms together, grinning: 'Namasté, namasté, Sheila Bai. Come. Come. Kaisé ho, Sheila Bai?' Her broad lips strained over poorly spaced, betel-stained teeth.

'Very well, Shanti,' I replied, 'and you?'

'I am well, I am well,' Shanti said, 'by God's mercy.' The warmth and welcome flowed out of her like a tidal wave. I remembered, suddenly, poor old Shanti chasing Rach and I around our bedroom: 'Heeyah heeyah! you bad girls. Time to go to bed. Come here and put on your pyjamas.' And Rach and I just giggling and screaming and pulling faces until Shanti gave up and sat on the floor, head in hands, wailing: 'Hey Mahadev! What devils these children are!'

'It has been so long since you came, Sheila Bai,' she now said, grabbing my hands, beaming.

'Too long,' Munnia murmured, 'too long. This is your home; you shouldn't stay away so long.'

I said quickly, to evade the pang in my gut Munnia's words caused: 'How pretty the drawings are.' I pointed to the white lines and swastikas painted along the tiny ankle-high wall around the mud and cowdung smeared courtyard.

'We did it yesterday in your honour,' Shanti said proudly.

And I remembered helping Shanti and Munnia smear the courtyard when I was little, and Mum, who'd been brought up in the city, fussing and clucking about the cowdung, and Gran saying she shouldn't be so concerned: cowdung, mud and lime made a very germ-proof mix and village wisdom was very ancient and well proven.

'Now, come, sit, sit,' Munnia said, drawing up a rickety old wooden chair with its raffia seat almost worn through.

I went to squat on the earth floor with Shanti. But this was met with indignant protests: 'No, no, Sheila Bai, it would not be seemly. You must sit on the chair.'

I sat on the chair. Munnia and Shanti squatted comfortably on the earth floor. The rules of class were unbreakable. They smiled at me, their eyes never leaving my face. Not saying anything, they stayed in just that position for long moments without embarrassment, until I began to feel uncomfortable and my smile began to feel forced.

I looked at the festive array of ladoos, samosas, jalebis, laid out on cracked china plates. Munnia's little brother sat grinning, perched on the edge of the charpai – a string cot –

waving a raffia fan over the feast to keep the flies off.

A few children from the neighbouring quarters gathered around, whispering and shoving. Munnia introduced me to Laxmi's four daughters, the orchard-keeper's sons, a couple of children from the Malahan-ka-tolla across the scrubby wasteland. They shrugged, putting hands to their mouths, giggling, nudging each other. They were all shabbily dressed in torn frocks and pants, barefoot and straggly-haired. They were thin, with scruffy knees and sooty faces. But they were . . . complete. Right *here*, as though made of the very earth below them; not flying about, like me, partly here, partly in England. I envied them. Yes, I really did envy them.

They hung around waiting for the sweets which they knew they would get after I'd had my share.

I looked around, feeling uncomfortable. A round-bottomed mud pot stood rocking slightly in one corner of the courtyard, a few stalks of wheat growing out of its mouth.

'What's that?' I asked.

'It's for the jabbah,' Munnia said. 'We all will take our pots with us to the Sharda Devi temple after the festival, and leave them as an offering to the goddess. We are all going together in a procession.' She looked at me with sudden enthusiasm: 'Will you come with us, Sheila Bai? Oh, do please come with us. It'll be such fun!'

'When is this?' I said.

'After the harvest,' Munnia said. 'We will have a celebration in the Ahiran-ka-tolla. There will be singing and dancing, and a Kali Mai will come.' Her eyes gleamed in anticipation. 'Then in the evening we girls will carry our jabbah pots and all of us will walk to the Sharda Devi temple in Maini. We will sing and dance all night.' She warmed to the picture. 'Then there will be prayers in the temple and there will be a funfair all day. Such a big mela it will be! All the villagers from everywhere will come. There will be merry-go-rounds and swings and jugglers and dancers and food.' She was already on the top of the ferris wheel, whooshing down. 'We will come back in the evening, by bus.'

I liked the picture of the noise and bustle and colour and

smells and people, people . . . The people of India . . . real people . . . people with traditions, history, rituals, *my* people . . . I warmed at the thought.

'You will come with us?' Munnia was saying.

'Yes,' I said, suddenly. 'Yes, I will.'

'But you must ask, Baiji,' Shanti said severely, remembering her one-time role as my ayah. She meant Gran.

'I will,' I said agreeably, 'but I'm old enough to make up my own mind, Shanti.'

Munnia giggled as though I'd said something funny. 'You must ask anyway,' she said, 'you mustn't come without asking.'

'It's the last year Munnia can carry the jabbah pot,' Shanti said importantly.

'Why?'

'Next year I'll be a properly married woman,' Munnia said. 'Only virgins can carry a jabbah pot.' And she put her hand over her mouth, turned her head aside in parody of coyness and shrugged, her eyes dancing. I looked at Munnia with something approaching jealousy. There was an air of smugness about her, a sort of bustling private importance as though she had arrived at her destined place, and it was to her satisfaction. She had reason to feel happy; she was safe. Her family, her traditions, everything told her what to do. Her choices were made for her; all she had to do was follow. There was no place for doubts, no place for this sickening feeling I had of being in a boat without moorings.

Then Shanti placed both hands on either side of her head, elbows supported by her knees. She opened her eyes wide. 'Baiji!' she whispered dramatically, 'So many young girls these days who aren't virgins. Hare Ram! The world is becoming very bad.' She ran her hand over Munnia's head. 'But my daughter is. She's a good girl. Eh?'

Munnia tossed her head and snorted. 'And *that's* a big thing, hey?'

Shanti said: 'Yes, child, it's a big thing.' She sounded just like Mum.

'Hmmf!' Munnia said. And I had a fleeting picture of Rachna saying, 'Hmmf' the same way.

Munnia's life was a series of certainties, I thought enviously: you're born to a particular family in a particular village, in a particular caste; tradition dictated you study if your parents could afford it; after a while, you're married to someone chosen for you, like you in background, education and expectations, and when your families agree it's the right time, you begin to live together; and soon, there are babies, and your life becomes a business of wet bottoms, cooking pots and making ends meet. Then the cycle starts over. Simple.

Shanti began wailing: 'But next year my daughter will be a married woman. Hai! Hai! next year my daughter will be gone!' She rocked on her heels and moaned, her head in her hands: 'Gone from her mother's home. Gone, gone, gone. Out into the big world . . .' Tears gathered in her eyes. She looked up at me like a stricken she-buffalo. Munnia and I exchanged a fast look: Shanti's histrionics were an old joke.

Munnia said roughly: 'Now Ma, stop it! All girls have to leave home and go to their husbands'. You've said it yourself a thousand times. Sheila Bai didn't come here to listen to your moaning. She came for tea. Now stop it!'

'My little girl, my angel, my baby! Gone!' Shanti whispered, and rocked some more, subsiding gradually under her daughter's glare.

'Now you have some tea,' Munnia said, and began bustling about pouring the over-cooked umber liquid into a cracked mug, placing a plate on my lap, handing me plates of ladoos and samosas.

I took one piece of each, and sipped my tea: thick, sweet and syruppy. Munnia and Shanti wouldn't eat with me. It would not be seemly. They would eat later. They watched as I ate, chattering about Munnia's coming gauna, forcing more sweets on my plate, more tea in my mug.

What was the *point* of looking for something 'better', I thought as I ate, as Dad had when he'd gone to England? He'd felt suffocated in Rampur, and thought he could give us all a 'better' life, 'better' opportunities. What had better opportunities brought me? A Jimmy who'd sat shifty-eyed, saying nothing while his mother as much as told me I wasn't good enough for her son. Because I had a darker skin?

And, I thought then, looking at Munnia looking at me, perhaps she was right at that. Perhaps it was best to stick to your own kind. Perhaps Sunaina was the fortunate one, after all, to have an arranged marriage.

'It will be wonderful,' Shanti was saying primly. 'We have collected a good dowry for our child. There is a proper wooden bed, with blankets and sheets, like Baiji has. There are seven saris, and blouses with petticoats.' She beamed as she counted her riches. 'And silver jewellery. We are giving Ram Prasad's mother and sister saris, and his father pants and shirts.' The generosity of all this giving made her eyes gleam. 'We are giving Ram Prasad a bicycle and a transistor radio. It was all arranged by the match-maker. It's a good match. It's a good family.' And she rubbed her knees with the palms of her hands, very satisfied. The world for Shanti was exactly the way it should be.

A dowry! I wondered if Mum had had a dowry when she'd married Dad. I doubted it, Grandpa wouldn't have allowed it to begin with. Would Sunaina have a dowry?

Wasn't giving a dowry to your daughter like selling her, paying a man's family to take her away? Giving them gifts so they wouldn't mistreat her? I wondered what Janey and Barb would think of it. Janey was always going on about feminism. She'd blow her top! Yet her sister had got married last year, and her father had paid for a swanky wedding. It wasn't quite like a dowry, though. Didn't they have dowries, though, in Europe at one time? Here it was still a custom coming down generations. Ram Milan's ability to give his daughter a substantial dowry proclaimed his status. They had been saving for this for a lifetime.

'Ram Prasad's family will come in a baraat with a band,' Shanti glowed at the thought of the procession, the cacophony of musicians. 'The whole family, and many relatives. We are hiring a truck for them. Can you imagine that? A truck! We will have lights, all different colours, which go on and off.' She twinkled like the lights which went on and off. 'We will make seven arches under which the baraat will come. There will be flowers and leaves and lights over all the arches. We will all exchange garlands.' She raised her arms, exchanging garlands. 'Then we will have a feast. We are feeding fifty people. Can you imagine that?'

Munnia said importantly: 'My father is a big man, now he drives a tractor. We are grateful to Babuji for making my father such a big man.' Babuji is a term of respect, like 'sir'; they called both Grandpa and Inder Uncle, Babuji. But Bumpy was 'Bhaiyyaji' – brother.

'We have to shop for food two days in advance,' Shanti said, already off on her shopping spree. 'Some women from the Ahiran-ka-tolla will come to help me to make the food. Baiji said we can use the garage for cooking. Your people are so kind.'

'They will stay the night. Baiji said they can sleep in the garage,' Munnia said.

'And the next morning,' Shanti's eyes began to fill again, as she whispered, 'they will take my daughter away in a doli . . . A palanquin.'

Munnia said disgustedly: 'Oh Ma!'

They chattered on until I'd finished eating. Then they distributed sweets to the lurking children, keeping some for themselves. Munnia's little brother had been surreptitiously popping sweets in his mouth through tea; now he looked a little green.

'We shall walk to the river?' Munnia said.

I agreed.

'Like old times,' Munnia said.

'Like old times,' I said, feeling that nothing was like old times. Nothing. On the surface it looked as though it might be. But underneath it was all different.


We walked down the left of the fields, under the ashoka and jacaranda trees, beside the barbed wire, on the bund. Tiny violet and pink and white flowers grew on miniscule spreading bushes on the mud walk under our feet and I stopped to pick some up and look at them. The white ones were bell-shaped, the others like miniature daisies.

'What are these called, Munnia?'

Munnia looked at me, surprised. 'They are only wild plants. And they're so small and useless. Why should I know their names? They don't have names,' she said.

I didn't answer. But I thought: Surely someone, somewhere has given them names. Why don't I know them? I know the names of thistles and nettles and heather and gorse, but I don't know anything here.

I pointed at a bush of pungent rough-surfaced leaves with tiny orange and yellow flowers clambering up the barbed wire.

'What about that? That's big enough, isn't it? Does that have a name?'

Munnia shrugged. 'I don't know.'

I picked a leaf and sniffed it. It had a familiar smell, a fragrance I remembered. But it had no name.

No name, Sheila? Oh but I thought Sheila was *English* name . . . an *English* name . . . an *English* name . . .

I felt a rush of red-hot prickles up my back. I'd spent my childhood reading Enid Blyton and the Brothers Grimm, Mother Goose and Winnie the Pooh. At school I studied England and Europe. My mind dwelt in the countryside of England, not here, in my own country where I didn't know the names of simple things. Yes, I knew jacaranda and gulmohur and bougainvillea and passion flower. It was like knowing crows and sparrows and pigeons. How stupid!

Oh Sunny, Sunny, Sunny . . . why does it all have to be so stupid?

'Munnia?' I said as we walked towards the river. 'Aren't you afraid to leave your parents' home? You'll have to go to your husband's home now. Aren't you afraid?'

'Afraid?' she said, genuinely surprised. 'Why should I be afraid? It's what we all must do.'

'I mean,' I said, faltering, 'you don't really know Ram Prasad, do you? He's a stranger.'

Munnia snorted. '*He's* no stranger to me!' She would not

say his name. '*He's* my husband!'

'But he was, wasn't he? He was a stranger when you were married? Weren't you afraid then?'

She thought about that a bit, and then said: 'I must have been I suppose. But I was so young. My parents decided everything. One day they said: 'You have to be married and we've picked the boy.' And the next week we were married. That's all.' She shrugged. 'Everyone does it. It's the way things are.'

They'd been married two years, she reminded me, and in this time they'd been allowed to meet. She'd gone, chaperoned, to his house for several days, and slowly she'd become accustomed to his family and his way of life, which was, in any event, so close to her own, that it would hardly take any adjustment on her part.

It was *I* who'd found the stranger, who'd thought I knew him in one year, and realized he was, after all, a stranger, and would always be. What a failure I felt, confronted with Munnia's content voice.

I said, a little enviously: 'You're lucky, Munnia. He could have turned out to be a drunk or a gambler, and you would have no choice, but to have remained married to him.'

'Yes, I'm lucky,' she agreed. 'He's a good man. Steady. He earns a good salary. He'll be a good husband. Yes, I'm lucky.' Then she said soberly, 'But who knows what will happen in ten years? Maybe he'll start drinking then . . . who can know about these things? It's all in our luck, our destiny.' Then breathlessly, her eyes sparkling, she said: 'But, Sheila Bai! I cannot think about ten years from now. I can only think of now. And now I am so happy. I cannot *wait* for after the jabbah, Sheila Bai. He's so wonderful! I want to be with him properly . . . you know . . .' she blushed, her dark skin turning a brownish purple. 'Two years is too long. He also, wants me to be with him. Oh we shall be so happy together, Sheila Bai!' She grabbed my hand and swung it with a fierce joy. 'Oh you too must be married soon. Are they arranging it for you in your new land? Your mother and father in your new land?' Have they found a boy for you?'

Arranging my marriage? Mum and Dad! Fat chance!

Munnia was prattling on: 'It is so wonderful to feel this way for a man!'

I said reprovingly: 'Munnia, you've been watching too many movies!'

'Oh no,' she said, 'I've seen some, but they're so foolish. The boy and girl run around with each other before they are married. They moan and sigh about love. But *that's* not love. It's craziness. That's why they get into so much trouble.'

What could I say to that?

I said: 'Look, there's Pandit, let's go and watch the cutting.'

We'd reached the bottom part of Grandpa's property. A line of women were squatting in the field, cutting the ripe wheat at the base with quick, sure strokes of their scythes. They laid the stalks in neat bundles in rows and moved forward on their haunches, their silver bracelets and anklets clanking. They wore coarse cotton saris in primary colours: red, green and blue. Their heads were covered, and part of the sari folded between their legs, tucking in at the back in the waist, leaving plenty of space for leg movements. They were all thin, dark brown, gleaming, strong and sinewy. They had huge eyes, fine noses, well-shaped mouths. They were lovely.

Amongst them were young girls in dresses, a few young boys in short pants.

Standing over them was the skinny supervisor, in white pants. He had a degree from a local agricultural college and was a brahmin. This ensured him complete deference from the labouring women, despite his age. He was only twenty-five.

There was a chorus of 'Sheila Bai!' 'Oh Sheila Bai, kaisé ho?' 'Namasté, Sheila Bai,' and all work came to a stop. Some women stood up and stretched.

'Do you remember me, Sheila Bai? Rani?'

'Going for a walk to the river, Sheila Bai?'

'Found your old friend, Sheila Bai?'

'She is going to her home after the jabbah, you know?'

'When are *you* getting married, Sheila Bai?'

And giggles, nudges, grins. I was surrounded again with warmth and friendliness.

They spoke in the local dialect of Hindi, with a strong Sanskrit root. I understood most of it, my ears straining to catch remembered syllables. But of course, the Hindi I spoke was of the city, and that too, now after many years in London, halting, awkward, coming out like a parody of a British Memsahib.

I recognized some of the women. All of them seemed to know me.

One said: 'Sheila Bai, you'll never find a husband if you go around dressed as a boy.'

Munnia said: 'You mustn't go to the bazaar wearing jeans. The boys will make rude remarks about you.'

Eventually, I said goodbye, and Munnia and I started off again, over the barbed wire fence towards Grandpa's orchard near the river.

Little black birds with long, sharp, pointed tails flitted between the stalks of wheat, dived to the ground to pick up an insect, shrilled at each other. Long white birds stalked the fields. Two large eagles wheeled overhead.

Then, suddenly, there it was again, a flash of blue. A large bird rose out of the wheat and streaked away, calling loudly, raucously, to the top of a tree with a quick roll and rustle of wings. Its wings had two distinct shades of blue: turquoise and ultramarine, but when it settled on the trees, the wings folded in and it was lost in a smudge of brown.

I knew crows and sparrows and pigeons. I'd seen wood-peckers and eagles. The small black birds, the long thin white ones – well they seemed somehow innocuous, steadily, always there. But this majesty of blue . . . it was special somehow. So sudden. So loud and colourful and large. Appearing and disappearing in its own colouring.

'What's that bird, Munnia?' I said, pointing to the blue bird now brown and almost invisible, but for a streak of blue in its tail, a splash on its head. She couldn't see it. Then it flew down again, brilliant turquoise and ultramarine, calling, rolling, sweeping away. 'There!' I said excitedly.

'Neelkanth,' she said simply. And of course the name meant nothing to me.

I'd look it up in a book I thought, if I could find one on Indian birds.

We reached the orchard, surrounded by a hedge of bougainvillea and hibiscus flowers. Munnia pushed open a small gate, and we were in what I can only call a little paradise. Guava, mango, papaya and banana trees covered the entire orchard. Below them, in clearer patches, vegetables grew on raised rows. We walked through the orchard, greeting Ramnath, the orchard-keeper, towards the gate which led to the path to the river.

Small trees and large bushes threatened to overwhelm the slight path to the river. I saw several dried-looking mushrooms in the undergrowth and felt gladdened that they were there. I found myself wishing I could see fairies dancing around them . . . and realized that the fairies in my mind were English. I couldn't even imagine what Indian fairies might look like. Would Indian fairies dance in a circle of mushrooms? My heart fell.

I pointed at a small, ordinary sparrow-like bird chirping and twittering in a tree. 'What's that called?' I said.

'Oh that!' Munnia giggled. 'That's a munia. Don't you remember? You used to tease me about being a tiny bird.' She frowned then. 'Once you even told me I was just ordinary – just like a dull, stupid, ordinary munia bird.'

I looked at her quickly, not remembering the incident. 'We were children, Munnia. Children fight. You must have said something too.'

Munnia smiled. 'Yes. I said you were like a monkey, always jumping around. Couldn't stay still. You kept going to Allahabad . . . to school . . .'

And suddenly, I remembered. Munnia'd been jealous. I was better educated. Went away to school. She went . . . where? To that ugly little school in Samli Village? I didn't even know. I'd never cared!

'There's nothing ordinary about you, Munnia,' I said slowly, meaning it. 'You're a very lucky girl. I . . . think . . . it's better to be a munia than . . . a monkey.'

As we turned and walked back, Munnia prattled on about

the last time the river had flooded. I realized suddenly that I hadn't really thought much about Munnia since we'd gone to England. I hadn't come rushing to India for her marriage . . . in fact, until her scrawled postcard which had come just after the problems with Jimmy and Sunaina and Rachna, I'd hardly even remembered her. Janey and Barb and Sunaina had been much, much, more important to me all these years.

'. . . and a dead cow floated all the way up to the house,' Munnia was saying, 'can you imagine that?'

Life's funny, I thought, glancing sideways at her. She really is a munia, a very ordinary bird . . . A very dull and brown person. There must be millions like her in India – around the world. She doesn't have an interesting life. She doesn't know very much about the world. But she's *safe*. She's lucky. Her life makes such sense.

We really belong to such different worlds, I thought, we never did belong to the same world at all. Now, we're saying goodbye. We never really were very important to each other. Never will be.

But I was mistaken. In a way I would never have expected, Munnia's life was to be very important to mine.

# 10

Inder Uncle didn't like the idea at all.

'Sheilaji, you cannot go off with peasants carrying jabbah pots, walking all through the night,' he said at dinner when I told them what I'd planned with Munnia. 'Are you mad? What are you thinking of?'

I looked at Gran for support. At Grandpa. And didn't see much enthusiasm there either.

Tinkoo said sarcastically: 'Why don't you take your precious camera also? Then you can get hajaar pics of exotic India and fulfil your life's mission as a tourist.'

'Tinkoo!' I cried, unable to stop myself, 'that's not fair. I'm *not* a tourist.' And hearing my North London accent, I was suddenly aware that I sounded just like one.

'Then what is it, yaa?' Tinkoo said, mixing his rice and stew together, angrily. 'You aren't malahar or ahir. You can't pretend you belong, so you're an outsider. Just watching them like animals in a zoo. Isn't it? A tourist. So take your pics. Then you can show your wonderful firang friends all about exotic India.'

'Enough, Tinkoo,' Grandpa said, raising his voice a little. 'Let's hear Sheila's reasons.' He turned to me. 'Do you understand what it involves, Sheila? Going to the village and watching the jabbah festival is all right. Tinkoo can go with you.'

'Not pos,' Tinkoo said immediately. 'I'm zapping back to Delhi day after.'

'Are you?' Inder Uncle frowned, 'you didn't tell me.'

'I have to get back to the Univ,' Tinkoo said, his mouth thin on his slim-jawed face. 'I have hajaar rato to do for the tension scene, or I'll just flunk. I can't spend all my time escorting some la-dee-dah female from England . . .'

Grandpa frowned and looked questioningly at Bumpy.

Bumpy said, smiling a little: 'He means he has to study for

his exams, Pitaji. I'll take Sheila to Delhi when she has to go.'

'I'm quite capable of getting back to Delhi by myself,' I flared. 'I don't need all this chaperoning around, for God's sake. I get from Chigwell to Wimbledon on my own. And I got all the way to Delhi from London on my own, didn't I?'

'Travelling in England and travelling by air are very different from travelling in a train in India, Sheilaji,' Inder Uncle said, sounding like Nina Maasi. 'And certainly, walking all night with peasants to another town, and staying for the mela is absolutely not something we will allow you to do.'

Gran looked at my face becoming stony, and said concilliatingly: 'Bumpy, you go with her to the festival in the village.'

I shook my head. 'No,' I said. 'The village isn't two minutes from here, and I refuse to be escorted like some fragile bit of china. I know I'm different to everyone here. But . . . but . . .' I stopped, fighting back the bitter tears at the back of my throat. 'But I'm a *human being*, aren't I? For God's sake. I can communicate with Munnia and Rani and Shanti. I'm human just like them, and,' the words came in a rush, surprising me; I hadn't thought about what I was saying: 'I'm fed up of always living as though I'm somehow different from everyone else. I'm *not*. I may be different in the way I speak and dress . . . and . . . in the colour of my skin . . . and in the way I've been educated, and where I live, and in some of the things I think are important. But underneath all that I'm *human* just like anyone else, and I *want* to *behave* just like those I want to be with, not *unlike* . . . not *different* . . .' I stopped, blinking hard to keep from crying, swallowing back the bile.

There was a silence as Laxmi cleared the dishes and brought on the bread pudding.

Then Grandpa said slowly, looking closely at me: 'All right, you can go to the festival in the village by yourself. But as for walking all night with Munnia and Shanti to the Sharda Devi temple, I am afraid we cannot allow that.'

I stabbed angrily at the table-cloth with a spoon, set my mouth and said nothing.

There was a long, uncomfortable silence. Then Grandpa

grunted and turning to Bumpy, said: 'I think you'll have to go with her.' Then sternly to me: 'Yes, I'll allow you to go to the Sharda Devi temple. But you will stay with Bumpy. And only with him. You will not wander amongst the ahirs spreading your rays of benevolence and friendship on everyone. And in the morning, Inder will go to Maini in the jeep and fetch you back.'

'But I want to stay with Munnia for the mela,' I said ungratefully.

Gran put her hand on my arm. 'The evening festivities and the pujas at night and in the early morning are fine,' she said, 'but after the holy times, the unholy times always begin and I don't think it is a sensible thing for you to be at the mela during the day when the rowdyism starts. Just be glad, beti, that you can go at all.'

I looked at her kind, serious face and nodded. 'All right,' I said. 'Agreed.' Bumpy in any event, would be better than Tinkoo.

'Thanks, Gramps,' I said, trying to lighten the gloom. I really was grateful. I thought he did understand why I wanted to go with the villagers. But he was frowning into his bread pudding looking very much the family patriarch.

Tinkoo scraped his plate glumly, and glowered.

Inder Uncle said unhappily: 'Sheilaji, you don't understand what it is like out there. Bad things are happening.'

'What bad things?' I asked drily, now I'd got my way.

'Listen, I'm serious,' Inder Uncle said. 'Don't go thinking that the bad elements won't touch you. There are bad elements of all kinds everywhere. Small-time goondas, petty thieves, dacoits. It all looks peaceful here, where we live, but we have heard that this woman Bijli has gathered together a bunch of dacoits and has been on a campaign of revenge. And dacoits often strike during large gatherings.'

I suddenly became conscious of three prints of Degas' ballerinas hanging one below the other in the corner of the dining room near the door. Degas' ballerinas and dacoits!

'*What!*' I said unbelievingly, 'Inder Uncle, what are you talking about! It sounds crazy!'

'Not so crazy,' Tinkoo said, mimicking me. 'This is India, remember.'

'And that's the most stupid remark I've heard in a long time,' I said. 'What's being India got to do with anything?'

Grandpa said heavily: 'It's got everything to do with it, Sheila. This is a land of extreme contrasts, very little real law and order, in the way the modern world understands it, and anything can happen any time. It is not like England at all.'

'But you've been here out in the sticks for years,' I said, 'and nothing has happened to you. It's been so peaceful . . .' My eyes went back to the Degas prints. They looked surrealistic in this environment with talk of bandits.

'My dear Sheila,' Grandpa said patiently, 'we don't belong here. We're Punjabis living in Madhya Pradesh. We're urban people living in a rural environment. We live in a sort of vacuum, a little island. We keep a low profile, we pay our labourers better than the going rate. We don't mix with local politicians. We pay our taxes and give medication to those around us who need it. We live quietly, so we're left alone.' He frowned and said: 'But all the villagers here are involved in histories of family feuds, of gambling debts, debts to money-lenders, encounters with the police. And this is especially true of the ahirs. They are always in some kind of trouble.'

'But Ram Milan and Munnia are ahirs,' I said, 'and they're in no trouble.' I knew I sounded stubborn and petulant.

'They are ahirs who've been uprooted from their own village,' Bumpy said, breaking in, 'so they're insecure and cling to us for protection. They've already changed greatly. They don't practise their traditional trade for instance, herding cows and selling cowdung cakes for profit . . .'

'And besides,' Inder Uncle said, 'there are always exceptions to the rule. Only last week some of the ahirs from the Ahiran-ka-tolla, only "two minutes away", as you say, Sheilaji, raided our orchard. We heard the commotion and Bumpy had to let off a few volleys from our rifle in the air to frighten them away. They had tied Ramnath to a tree and had already pulled down all the ripe papayas. And it's only recently, after I shot a few pigs and caught some cows and sent them to the municipal pen, that they have stopped letting their pigs and cows into our gates and under our fences at night to graze on our wheat.'

Everyone looked so stern and serious and unyielding, all of them ranged against me!

I said lightly: 'Look people, I only want to go on a religious festival. I can't imagine a riot on a religious festival, I'm not exactly going to be trampled underfoot.'

'Well,' Inder Uncle said soberly, putting his napkin by his plate and pushing back his chair, 'obviously we are unable to persuade you otherwise. Now come on, Bumpy, Tinkoo, let's go and have a look at the threshing.'

Chairs scraped back and everybody rose. 'Hajaar pseudo-ethnic chic . . .' Tinkoo muttered as he left.

The next morning I decided to drag myself out of bed early and behave, at least outwardly, like I was half-human. After an early breakfast I wandered about the garden and watched the labourers at work.

A skinny old man in a white dhoti and shirt, a turban around his head was sifting rubble through a huge sieve on the gravel path near the rose garden. He worked with absolute concentration, stopping only to push his heavy, lopsided spectacles up his nose, and on he went.

He paused as he saw me, grinned and said: 'Ram Ram, Baiji,' and went back to work.

I watched him for a long time, but he didn't look up again.

I went around the back and watched the silos being filled with grain and made friends with Raja who was tied up on the verandah.

Tinkoo was in the buffalo shed behind the house, looking at the buffalo he, Bumpy and Inder Uncle had taken to the vet the day before. He didn't look in the least happy to see me. He glanced up at me as I stepped in through the door and then back at the buffalo.

'So, you landed up,' he said sourly.

'How's the buffalo?' I said politely.

91

'Okay,' he said, 'no thanks to the vet. Damn ignorant dope.'

I wanted to even things up between us. But couldn't find anything to say.

'I bet you think this is a hajaar filthy, smelly place,' he said after a small pause.

'Oh I don't know,' I said, 'I sort of like it. Very raw, real, earthy, you know . . .'

He snorted. 'You and your wonderful, rural, ethnic chic, yaa. So romantic, isn't it? Just get off your cloud, and look at this.' He waved a small stick around the cowshed. 'Smell it. Have you seen cowsheds in England? I've seen like, pics of them . . . Proper sanitation. Clean. Milking by machines. Here it's hajaar primitive, like the dark ages. Every morning that female,' he pointed to a thin, brown woman with laughing eyes, wrapped in a soaking sari, washing down a buffalo, 'washes the dung off the buffaloes and cleans out the shed with about a ton of water. That's her job: wash, clean and feed the buffaloes. That's all she does. It's the pits, yaa.' He walked out of the door and I followed him.

'It will be better for the common people after the revolution,' he said righteously. 'Pitaji will have to take less profit and pay the people more, you can bet. He'll have to give all his labourers better working conditions.'

Oh! there he went again! I could see the poverty all around the farm, but the woman washing the buffaloes grinning at me, seemed to be just the happiest person around. But I didn't want to antagonize Tinkoo any more, so I said: 'Well, you have a point there, Tinkoo. There's a lot to be said for equality. You're quite right.'

He brightened immediately. This was something Dr Able had talked about. 'There's not much in the world beyond right and wrong,' he'd said. 'Underneath it all we want to be right. Most of our worries come from feeling somehow that what we think and do is wrong.' And here were the magic words, 'You're right', transforming the worst of grouches into a beam of sunshine.

'After I get my BA I'm going to Moscow to study,' Tinkoo said, suddenly expansive.

'What will you study then?' I said willingly, feeling relieved I could relax with him a bit.

He whistled tunelessly for a bit, looking at the garden. 'I'm taking Russian at JNU,' he said, 'so that I can study Marx and Lenin at Moscow University. I'm going to find out everything about communism, till I get to know it inside out.'

'That sounds very . . . committed,' I murmured.

'I want to read *Das Kapital* in the original,' Tinkoo said solemnly, standing there outside Grandpa's buffalo shed. 'Best to read important ideas in the original to get the fundas straight. Isn't it?'

I held myself well in check then, I'm proud to say. I didn't even snort. Even a dumb bourgeois like me knew that Karl Marx was German, and that *Das Kapital* was originally written in German. But it was more than my life was worth to point that out to Tinkoo right then.

'Really, I want to travel around,' Tinkoo said a little dreamily. 'I need to zap out of India and see the world. Only then can you get an ulti on your own country.' He began walking towards the rose garden. 'Maybe I'll even zap over to England,' he went on condescendingly. 'I never wanted to have a dekho at the decadent capitalistic West . . . but recently I have realized you have to see everything first hand.'

I nodded.

'You have to know the strengths and weaknesses of every system, isn't it?' Tinkoo went on conversationally. 'What do you think of the British system?'

I thought about Jimmy and Mrs Baker. Of Sunaina and Rachna. About race riots; about Southall, and Brixton and Bradford. I thought about council houses and the National Health Service, and dole queues. About Maggie Thatcher and the House of Commons and Princess Di and the Queen's Christmas message. 'I don't know,' I said, 'I really don't know.'

He looked at me curiously. 'You don't know much, do you?' he said smugly. 'Too comfortable in your comfortable middle-class London suburb, yaa.'

I sighed inwardly: He-e-e-re's Tinkoo!

93

'I haven't asked you this before,' he went on. 'But why do you want to come to India to study? Most of the kids at JNU and DU are all so despo to get out . . . not me of course . . .' he added hurriedly, 'but you want to come here. Why?'

I shrugged. I didn't want to explain myself to him. We were having a fairly good conversation for a change, and I didn't want to say anything on which he could throw cold water.

'Tinkoo,' I said, 'tell me about this woman bandit, this Bijli, whatever. I can't believe she's real.'

Tinkoo's eyebrows went up, and his mouth went down. 'Natch yaa, you can't. Coming from Chigwell, how could you imagine how despo people can get so they become bandits. You live such a cushy life. What you need is some shaking up of your fundas.'

I groaned. 'Please, Tinkoo. Would you stop lecturing me. Just tell me about her.'

And Tinkoo whipped the head off a rose with his stick. 'Bijli,' he said pompously, 'represents all that's wrong with our country. The anti-people developmental policies which our precapitalistic neo-monarchist feudocratic government zaps on us. And as you know, Sheila*ji*,' he emphasized 'ji' derisively, 'women are always at the bottom of the heap.'

What *could* one say to a jerk like Tinkoo!

'She's a revolutionary,' Tinkoo said. 'A primitive rebel, like all primitive rebels she will be sacrificed before the real revolution can take place. *That's* what Bijli is. And if you weren't so hazaar igno you'd know what I am saying.'

'Thanks for the explanation, Tinkoo dearest,' I snapped, trying hard not to be sarcastic, and failing completely. 'That really, really helps.'

Tinkoo said nastily, 'Now *there's* a career for you, Sheila *Bai*, if you can't become a pseudo-intel scholar of international politics – you can become a bandit woman, isn't it?'

'Oh, Tinkoo,' I groaned. 'Sometimes you can be a real prat.'

'Only sometimes?' Tinkoo said roughly, glaring at me through his huge lashes, his jaw aggressively thrust forward, a peculiar hurt look to his mouth. 'I thought I didn't match up to your requirements at any time, Madam High and Mighty!'

And with that he turned and went off towards the fields.

I stood looking at him for a while, thinking: *Now* what have I said? and feeling depressed. He seemed to swing around without warning. For the first time we'd had a decent conversation then suddenly, he started being aggressive again.

Boys! Sod the lot of them!

I turned and went back to the house.

# 11

Gran was getting ready to go to the market when I got back to the house. She had two plastic baskets in her hands.

'I'm going to buy vegetables,' she said, 'I don't like to allow Laxmi to do all the shopping all the time. Do you want to come? I am going by rickshaw, Inder has taken the jeep to the government farm.'

'Great, Gran,' I said. I didn't want to be around when Tinkoo came back from the fields. Remembering what the women in the fields had said, I changed from my jeans into a dress. Something long, and respectable!

We went out of the side gate towards the servants' quarters. Munnia's little brother was yanking the family goat around on a rope on their courtyard. He waved and grinned.

Gran climbed on the rickety old cycle rickshaw waiting outside the gate. Gran isn't fat; nor am I, but our bums together were a tight squeeze in the seat. The rickshaw driver was skinny, shabbily dressed, and as strong as a bull. His sinewy leg muscles tightened and relaxed as he pedalled on over the ruts in the road. I felt guilty sitting there, well-fed and well-dressed, going shopping for vegetables, while he huffed and pulled and strained. I said as much to Gran.

Gran said: 'We cannot be responsible for the world, now, can we, beti? I will pay him enough, and we are lighter than his usual load. What more can we do?'

We bumped along, jolting painfully on the seat, my hip grazing the wooden sides.

I pointed to the morning glory type mauve flower with the tall lanky stems and large leaves I'd seen when I first came, bordering the path.

'What are they called, Gran?' I asked Inder Uncle when we came, but he didn't know.'

'Oh, that!' Gran chuckled, 'we call it *besharam*, which

means "without shame", because it grows everywhere, quite shamelessly.'

I laughed. I liked it. I liked it. It warmed me to know this little titbit about the Indian countryside.

We were passing the Malahan-ka-tolla and the Ahiran-ka-tolla on the right, and the Chamaran-ka-tolla on the left, past the lake.

'Most of the people who come to work on the farm are from these villages, aren't they, Gran?' I said.

'The casual labour, yes, but the people we employ regularly, like Ram Milan and his family, Ramnath and his family, Pandit, the cook, Laxmi, they all come from elsewhere. It's very difficult to get people to work in the house, especially for washing clothes and dishes – it goes against their caste. And the local people are too proud to want regular paid work in anyone else's house.'

'Most of the field labour are ahirs and malahars, aren't they?'

'Yes,' Gran said, 'but we do employ chamars. We're the few people who do. That old man, Baredi, you saw him shifting the rubble? The one with glasses? He's our best worker. Regular, reliable. He is a chamar. But if you notice the women won't go near him or touch him. But because he is such a good man, they will tolerate working around him. Usually we cannot employ chamars to work with the other classes, because if even a chamar's shadow falls on them, they will go home to have a bath!'

'That's crazy!' I said.

Gran sighed: 'Yes. Quite often we'll get a labourer who says: "Employ me, I work well; you see, I'm a brahmin". And you know something? It's true. The brahmins are usually better workers.'

'Gran!' I protested. 'That sounds like prejudice.'

'It's not,' Gran said. 'It's true. You see what happens is that the lower castes are reminded all the time of how worthless they are. They lose self-confidence and self-respect.'

Yes, well, I thought fuzzily, you could say that of *anyone*!

'People tend to live up or down to the expectations of those around them,' Gran went on, 'so, the malahars are good workers; the ahirs are all right too, when they work. Generally the chamars are poor workers . . . but then you have the exceptions like Baredi . . . to look at him work you would think what he does is not work, it's worship. He's a lesson to us all.'

'It must be wonderful,' I said, 'to be able to concentrate like that.'

'It's the only way,' Gran said, 'when you concentrate so much, it's like saying a mantra. It soothes your nerves and gives you energy.'

'I'd like to see him in his village. Gran, I'd like to go to the village and wander around, will that be all right?'

'In the daytime, yes, I think there will be no problem,' Gran said. 'It will be a nice gesture on your part. Take your camera and take pictures of the families and send them copies, they'll enjoy that.'

We bumped our way slowly past the school where the children stared at us, past the brahmin part of Samli Village with its ugly brick houses, past the cross-roads, over the railway track, and into the incredible din and smell of Rampur market. The rickshaw wallah pedalled serenely between jeeps, tractors, trucks, bulls and people, tringing his bell continuously. Gran stopped the rickshaw near the vegetable market and began selecting vegetables. She bargained enthusiastically over the price of each.

A child hurried by clutching a tiny kid goat in her thin arms. I wondered what important rendezvous she was hurrying to with such an intense, worried look on her face.

A great humped black bull strolled majestically down the road and stopped to pull some leaves off a fruit cart. The fruit seller shoved him off, almost laconically.

A bunch of men across the road were cleaning huge mounds of raw cotton on a long instrument made with bamboo and catgut on which they twanged the fluff.

A motorcycle throbbed past, sending up a splash of mud as the man braked.

A woman went by balancing three brass pots on her head, her arms hanging gracefully at her sides.

And someone led a tall, disdainful camel through the roaring jeeps and trucks on the road.

I loved it. I peered at everything, sucking in the row of tailors against a wall, waiting for customers, behind their ancient pedal-pushed sewing machines; the carts selling food in front of the stores; the plastic shine on buckets, the texture of rope and tin, the display of sweets at the general merchant's; the people squatting along the roads selling bangles, flowers, underwear and frosted clay figures of gods.

I did see, of course, the wandering goats nibbling at heaps of rubbish, the wretched mistreated dogs, the bulls swaggering down the middle of the road, the flies, the dirt . . . but they didn't matter a bit. What was completely absorbing was the darkness of everything, the duskiness of the complexions, the shine on the brown faces.

What was most important, I realized after a while, was that there were no white faces . . . and that brought me up with a start.

No white faces!

I looked around the sea of brown humanity, and I felt a most incredible sense of exhilaration! Free! I was free of English faces. I was free of Jimmy. I was free of white jackboots walking all over me!

And I suddenly realized what my morning nightmare was all about. My spirits sank. This was a kind of racism too, I thought guiltily. And I was sobered by the thought.

Then, Gran and I hopped on the rickshaw with the vegetable baskets and trundled back to Samli Village, slowly, majestically, jolting with every bump on the road, watching the world go by in thick, liquid slow motion.

Grandma indicated the girls in the yard in front of the Government Girls College, in their salwar-kameezes, long plaits down their backs, and said: 'Maybe it's better if you wear a salwar-kameez, not a frock when you go out.'

'Why?' I said.

'You're blind, child, every man looked at you as though you were a heroine fallen out of the movie screen.'

'Me?' I said, amazed.

'Yes,' Gran said. 'You're pretty, you know, and you're young. But most of all it's the skirt. Our men are very narrow in their horizons. Any woman showing her legs must be a . . .' she searched for the Punjabi equivalent, '. . . a vamp.'

I laughed at the thought.

'You know there are only two kinds of women in the popular consciousness,' Gran went on, 'the good woman who becomes a wife, loyal and true, the long-suffering mother; and the vamp. The good women are modest and decorous in their dress.'

'Oh,' I said in a small, flat voice.

'Recently our heroines have become quite vampish!' Gran said, twinkling a little, 'but they live in the imagination only, they're not real. So when someone dresses like an Indian movie heroine, the men's fantasies are inflamed. It's all a little . . . primitive . . . here in small towns. It's only because you were with me that there were no catcalls. They venerate age.' She turned towards me, patted my hand and smiled. 'Age has its benefits too. It wasn't until I was a good fifty years old that men stopped staring at me. Some women seem to think it's necessary for their identity that they get attention from men. I've always thought it a nuisance.'

I said: 'I didn't even notice it. I suppose I must be thick. But . . . I wore jeans in Delhi, and there weren't any problems.'

'Delhi and Rampur are quite different worlds, Sheila,' Gran said. 'So what will you wear when you go for the jabbah festival?'

'Maybe I can borrow a sari from you, Gran?'

She patted my hand: 'Yes, of course. But will you be able to carry it? Have you worn one before?'

I shook my head.

'Then I'll lend you a salwar-kameez; it'll be easier.'


The next morning, after seeing to it that the harvesting and threshing, grain storage and tractor hire were all under control, Inder Uncle left Bumpy in charge and took Grandpa and me out to the Chhimaria plateau.

Gran packed us a lunch and we set off in the jeep around eleven, Hariram driving, Grandpa sitting in front, Inder Uncle and I behind. We jolted through the town, and out to the east, past ramshackle, closely packed slums. The road was empty after we left the town, but for the odd truck and local bus, all rattling and thundering and belching black diesel fumes.

It was a pleasant, shady road bordered with jacaranda, gulmohar, mango and eucalyptus trees.

'We'll just go to the foot of the plateau,' Inder Uncle said, 'to that pretty old ruined chhatri there, by the pond. You remember it, Sheilaji? There's a stream coming down the plateau, and we can have lunch there. If you like, we'll take a walk to the top of the plateau and down before lunch.'

I remembered. As though someone else had been there and told me about it. 'What does chhatri mean?' I asked.

'Just what it says – an umbrella,' Grandpa said.

'They were built to cremate the Rajas of Rampur, a long time ago, and stand as cenotaphs in their memory.'

'There are some excavations going on some miles south, past the Chhimaria plateau,' Inder Uncle said. 'An archaeological dig: they've found some old pre-Mughal city, I believe.'

'This place is full of history,' Grandpa said. 'Do you know part of the Ramayana is said to have taken place in Madhya Pradesh?'

'The Ramayana?' I said. 'You mean the epic? Like the story of Ram and Sita?'

'You know the story?' Inder Uncle said, pleased.

I nodded. We'd read a short version in our language readers, part of the new multi-ethnic curriculum! 'But I didn't realize it took place right *here*!'

'Well Ayodhya, Ram's capital, is in Uttar Pradesh just north of Madhya Pradesh. But when Ram and Sita were exiled from Ayodhya, they lived in a place called Ramvan not far from here,' Grandpa said.

Inder Uncle said enthusiastically: 'One day we'll take you to Ramvan, Sheilaji. There's a huge statue of Hanuman, the monkey king who helped Ram rescue Sita from the demon king Ravana.' He stroked his moustache bumpily in rhythm with the jeep. 'The story of the Ramayana is painted all around the temple walls there.'

'That's why practically every male in Madhya Pradesh has "Ram" attached to his name,' Grandpa said. 'Ram Milan means "the one who has met Ram", Ram Khilavan, means "the one who played with Ram", Hari and Ram are the names of Krishna and Ram, both reincarnations of the god Vishnu. "Ram Prasad" is the "offering to Ram". Even the Raja of Rampur is called Vinay Ramkaran Singh.'

'Raja?' I said. 'I didn't know there was a Raja of Rampur?'

Inder Uncle laughed. 'Oh he is a very *minor* Raja, Sheilaji.'

Grandpa said: 'Inder goes to play rummy with him some evenings.' He sounded very amused. 'And Bumpy is a friend of Vinay's brother.'

'Wow!' I said. 'Friends in high places, our Bumps.'

Grandpa snorted: 'Hardly high places, beti. You should go and meet our Raja Sahib some day.'

'Madhya Pradesh is the heartland of Indian culture,' Inder Uncle said, changing the subject. He sounded very proud of it. 'But both Raj and I were born outside Madhya Pradesh, so we are not Madhya Pradeshis. I was born in Assam and Raj in UP, where Pitaji was posted in the Railways. It's like being born in France and Italy.'

*That* jolted me a bit I must say. 'Incredible!' I said softly.

'Why incredible?' Inder Uncle smiled.

'Because I'd never thought of it quite like that,' I said. 'But of course, each of India's states is as large as any European country!'

'Certainly true,' Inder Uncle said, 'and India has held together as one country for over forty years, whereas Europe is only just beginning to come together under the EEC.'

'Incredible!' I said again.

Grandpa grunted and turned right around. 'But you see, Inder, I believe Europe *will* hold together as one unit now because each country has had the chance to assert its own identity. Here we're pulling apart because we were put together as a nation by the British, and since independence the Central Government has dominated the states, and tried to keep power centralized like the British Raj or the Mughal Empire. Each state has a distinct cultural and economic identity. They're actually like separate nations – which haven't had sufficient self-expression. Until each is allowed relative independence, India as a nation won't work.'

Well, I had nothing to say to that. Nor had Inder Uncle.

'Centralized power is not natural to our fundamental psyche,' Grandpa went on. 'It's unnatural. It's against human biology.'

We fell silent.

'You like it in Madhya Pradesh, don't you, Inder Uncle?' I asked after a bit.

'Hmmm,' he said, looking straight ahead past Hariram's shoulder. 'Yes, I do.'

Grandpa said: 'Don't get too attached to it, Inder. You know the time is going to come when Madhya Pradeshis are going to say: "Madhya Pradesh for Madhya Pradeshis", and OUT with the Punjabis and Rajputs and UPites and so on. Just as the Assamese are saying: "Assam for the Assamese", and the Punjabis and saying "Punjab for the Punjabis".'

Inder Uncle said: 'But Pitaji, I *am* Madhya Pradeshi. I've lived here nearly all my life. Bumpy was born here. Where would we go now? This is my life. And Bumpy's. We would fight for it.'

He sounded just like all those Indians and Afro-Caribbeans born in England. They were British. They were fighting for their right to be British, brown and black but British . . .

I know Grandpa didn't think of himself as Madhya Pradeshi, but Inder Uncle, and more than him, Bumpy, considered Madhya Pradesh their home. Just as Salima and Bano and the other Indians I knew in London considered themselves British. Even Sunaina was British – she'd been born in London . . . And as I realised that, I thought perhaps Sunny wasn't so lucky after all, being brought back to India.

Grandpa sighed: 'Yes, you would fight. I believe it. More stupidity. Stupidity piled on stupidity.'

Grandpa had a way of making mysterious statements so both Inder Uncle and I let that one pass.

The chhatri below the plateau was in ruins. Small boys splashed in the pond below, like whippy little seals, and leaped out to look at the jeep. They watched big-eyed as we began to climb the path curving up the plateau side.

Inder Uncle and I wanted to climb up to the top. Grandpa decided he'd rest by the stream until we got back, and Inder Uncle and I left him there with the tea thermos. Hariram waited by the jeep with the lunch.

It was a good brisk climb to the top of the plateau and we made it in half an hour with some sweat. The view north was lovely: green gold on all sides, dotted with villages. Golden fields interspread with square patches of earth where the grain had been harvested, clusters of trees on the banks of the river. I could see Mehta Farm. Very peaceful, very serene.

The view south was different: bare, scrubby, rocky plateaux as far as we could see, dropping off to the east and west. Deep shadows where there were ravines. Conical hills sprouted up beyond the Chhimaria plateau. Other plateaux rose up beyond.

Grandpa was dozing against a rock by the stream when we got back. He started awake as we came up to him.

'One of those little boys came up and asked me if I were a dacoit,' he grinned.

Inder Uncle frowned.

'Why would he think that?' I said.

'It's the jeep,' Grandpa said. 'Dacoits come in jeeps. They must have seen some movies in town too.'

I laughed lightly.

'It's not funny,' Inder Uncle said morosely.

We drank tea from the thermos flask. Hariram came up with the lunch basket and we ate egg sandwiches, parathas and bananas.

'We must take you to Govindgarh,' Inder Uncle said, 'the MP tourism people have really made that old fort look good.

They've planted bougainvillea, made walks, you can take boat rides on the lake.'

'And maybe one day we can go to Bandhavgarh forest,' Grandpa said. 'They've made it into a game sanctuary now, to preserve the wildlife . . . I believe the tiger population has gone up recently. Or else,' he went on *very* casually, 'you might like to go and see the Panna diamond mines. They're the only diamond mines in India, and quite close to here.'

'There's also Khajuraho,' Inder Uncle said, sounding like a tourist guide, 'with all those beautiful statues on the temple walls. Now you're old enough you might find them interesting.' He sounded as though he were selling succulent wares.

'We can stay overnight at one of the hotels. There are wonderful hotels there now. Four, even five star,' Grandpa said enthusiastically. Too enthusiastically?

Suddenly I heard, really heard them, oh so casual, and oh so concerned that I enjoy my holiday.

'Hang on a minute, you two,' I said, grabbing Inder Uncle's arm and shaking it, 'I have the feeling I'm being steam-rolled into doing everything *but* go on this jabbah procession. Right?'

Inder Uncle coughed, and smiled a little and looked away.

Grandpa looked unconcernedly up at the sky and said mildly: 'Well, there *are* many other interesting things to do and see, Sheila.'

Inder Uncle muttered: 'I cannot see why you want to go off with the villagers on this festival.'

I stood up and brushed the seat of my jeans. 'Oh come on,' I said, 'we already agreed, didn't we? So please no more tourist sales lectures. All right?'

Grandpa laughed and slapped his thigh. 'My little granddaughter is learning how to handle men, eh? I feel about twenty years old right now. Here, give a young man a heave up.' He put out his hand and I hauled him up.

Inder Uncle said: 'This girl is too clever for me. All right. let's go, let's go!'

And we skittered down the hill arm in arm, Inder Uncle on

one side of me, Grandpa on the other, laughing and shouting just like a bunch of kids out on a picnic in London.

It had been a perfectly wonderful afternoon. A sort of pilgrimage to a known shrine, for we had often climbed the Chhimaria plateau when I was a child, and every time we came back here from London. Yet this time it was as though I was doing something I'd never done before. This time it was more real than it had ever been. All previous times were like an echo. An echo, even of me.

On the way back Grandpa and Inder Uncle got into a discussion on farm produce, and I started thinking about Europe and India. Of being Madhya Pradeshi or Punjabi, Indian in India, or Indian in England.

Dad and Mum kept saying they were in England for a while only. They never really felt British at all. But Rach and I did, just as Inder Uncle felt he was Madhya Pradeshi. It didn't seem to bother him that he was Punjabi as well.

But neither Rach or I had really resolved the problem of being Indian as well. I suddenly realized, rattling along in that jeep, that Rach actually *resented* being Indian. She wanted to be just like all the other girls, who were playing at being pseudo-black. Black chic, really. I smiled as I realized I was using one of Tinkoo's expressions: pseudo-radical chic.

And *I* certainly hadn't resolved a *thing*. I'd just floated along dreaming up a cosy English future with Jimmy, while I had a war going on inside me. I had to be British, or Indian. Either-or-either-or. Why couldn't it be 'and'? I thought suddenly. Why can't I be both British *and* Indian?

'I'm both British and Indian,' I said tentatively to myself. And just then, dear old Mrs Baker's voice came floating at me again: 'Oh! I thought Sheila was an *English* name . . . an *English* name . . .'

# 12

Tinkoo left for Delhi the next evening in a flurry of suitcases, bags and bedding-rolls. Bumpy and I went to see him off at the station. The din in Rampur in the evening was, if anything, greater than it was during the day. Neon greens and blues just flickering on, bathed the rush and stumble of people in a stagey glare, giving the town an unreal, theatrical appearance.

As we stood around on the platform, with the crowds, waiting for the train, I watched the steam engines shunting in the yard, thankful that diesel and electric trains hadn't taken over completely here, making the world faster, more efficient, more anonymous. After a bit I sauntered over to the Wheeler bookstore while Bumpy and Tinkoo stood at the coffee counter drinking espresso coffees. We'd just had tea, but it seemed a visit to a railway station wasn't complete without a couple of cups of espresso.

The books in English were British and American detective stories and international best sellers. But the magazines were all Indian and there were an amazing variety, quite as glossy, glamorous and gossipy as any in England. I leafed through a few.

Tinkoo came up behind me. 'India's great magazine boom is kaput,' he said over my shoulder. 'TV has taken over all the advertizing.'

I frowned and glanced back at him. 'Is that all magazines are to you? An outlet for ads?'

'Sure, man,' Tinkoo said. 'They wrap a little news or beauty or a few film stars around the ads so the product is acceptable. Otherwise . . . it's all ads. Can't you see? Count the ad pages, yaa.'

I began to feel aggravated. 'Aren't you the cynical one,' I snorted.

'And aren't you the dreamer!' he mimicked me. 'Head and both feet in the clouds.'

Bumpy came over. 'What's up, Tinkoo,' he said, 'not fighting again?' Tinkoo repeated the gist of our conversation.

'The boom is over as Tinkoo said,' Bumpy nodded. 'But I think new magazines will continue to be published. TV and magazines have different markets. Do fewer people listen to radio since TV came in? Everything finds its own slot. Magazines will just become more specialized.'

'TV and magazines are for the rich, yaa,' Tinkoo said doubtfully. 'Radio's different. Transistors are cheap now. You find one in every dhaaba.' Tea Stall.

'Oh! TV will spread to villages too, don't worry,' Bumpy said. 'It's like a disease. People will want TV before they want clean water and toilets.'

'Yah!' Tinkoo snorted. 'Great vehicle for government propaganda. They'll make the whole country into idiots.'

'Well, when your revolution comes, Tinkoo,' Bumpy said drily, 'you'll have a ready-made loudspeaker system.'

I felt exhilarated and depressed simultaneously listening to them, but I didn't understand why, until later: it was exhilarating to listen to people talking knowledgeably about trends in India – and depressing because I wasn't part of them.

'What's TV like in England?' Bumpy turned to me. 'I hear British TV's quite good. We've been watching "Yes Minister". And we get some of your programmes on video. I hear you can't watch American or Japanese TV because there are so many ads, but British TV's not so bad.'

I nodded. 'Most of the programmes are quite good – there are lots of soaps, like EastEnders or Neighbours. There are no ads on BBC,' I said. 'ITV has ads though, so does Channel 4.'

'What's a soap?' Bumpy said.

'Well, it's a long-running drama. They're usually on a couple of times a week.'

'Oh, like our serials. And Channel 4,' Tinkoo said, 'what's that?'

'It's the name of the TV station,' I explained. 'BBC 1 and 2. ITV and Channel 4.'

'Why 4? Why not 6, 7, or 8?' he said.

'Because it's the fourth station, I suppose,' I said.

'Oh,' Tinkoo said flatly.

My depression grew: there were so many reference points which seemed to drop into a vacuum between us. So much to explain.

I turned and looked at the tracks. 'How long for the train?'

'Not too long. It's always late,' Bumpy said.

We stood around silently feeling awkward. The crowd on the platform had grown. People in groups, gossiping.

Then there was a shout and two guys about Bumpy's age walked up and wrapped their arms around Bumpy and Tinkoo, pounded their backs, grabbed their hands and held on to them.

'Hey yaar! How come?'

'Hey Tinkoo, going back already, yaar?'

Yaar, not yaa!

They sounded so delighted to see each other . . . as though they hadn't met for years and this was a wonderful surprise. They studiously avoided looking at me.

The four of them chatted on; the railway station was obviously a bit of a social club in Rampur, where friends met and drank espresso coffee together. Seeing friends and family off was also a bit of a social occasion.

Then Bumpy said a little uncomfortably, introducing me: 'This is my cousin, Sheila, from England. She's staying with us for a while. This is Harish and this is Sunil.'

The boys shuffled their feet and looked at me awkwardly. 'Hello,' one said, then. The other grinned inanely.

Harish was tall and thin, with straight hair and a cowlick over his forehead. He was dressed in a police uniform, very smart, very khaki, very properly creased. Sunil was wearing grey trousers and navy blazer with a badge embroidered on it.

'What's the badge?' I said, trying to be friendly, leaning forward to look at it, hoping to break the tension.

Sunil stepped back hastily: 'Oh nothing, it's nothing. I . . . I mean it's my college badge,' he said confusedly.

No good, I thought, I may as well be talking to a stuffed toy. I turned to Harish. 'Are you a policeman?' I said brightly.

'Yes,' he said with an embarrassed smile. He actually almost blushed. Bumpy looked steadfastly away. Tinkoo looked on grinning, a sly, satisfied look on his face.

'Bit young, aren't you?' I said, 'to be a policeman. What's your rank?'

'I'm Inspector,' Harish said, not quite so uncertainly.

'Really!' I said, 'an Inspector!' I wasn't being sarcastic; I was genuinely surprised. 'Is that as senior as a DCP?'

'Oh no!' Harish said. 'DCP is very senior.'

So, I thought drily, *this* was obviously not what Dad had in mind for me.

Tinkoo broke in. 'Some salary he earns, but,' he said with mock enthusiasm, 'some payoff being Inspector, hey yaar?'

'Arré, cut it, yaar,' Harish said uncomfortably.

'No, tell her,' Tinkoo insisted. 'Tell her what happens in the police. Tell her what you have to pay your superior to hold your job,' he said.

'What!' I said, astonished. 'Pay a superior to hold a job?'

'No, yaar,' Harish said. 'Come on!'

'It's common knowledge,' Tinkoo said. 'Everybody knows, so why be shy? Besides, yaar, I think our Sheila Bai needs a few lessons in reality. Tell her.' He was enjoying himself.

'Tell me what?' I said. 'I don't want to know what he earns, for God's sake!'

'Oh, in India we tell each other these things, don't worry,' Tinkoo said snidely. He'd asked one time what Dad made in London and I'd said a bit frostily that we didn't discuss such things; it wasn't polite.

'Enough, Tinkoo!' Bumpy said.

But Tinkoo said: 'Speak up, Harish, my chumma yaar.' He meant, special, dear and good friend. He held Harish's arm and shook it encouragingly.

'Well . . .' Harish said, looking at me a little defiantly. 'I pay my boss one thousand, five hundred rupees every month to hold my job.' And he passed a hand through his cowlick pushing it back, his chin jutting aggressively.

I looked at him blankly.

'Now tell her what you *paid* to get the job,' Tinkoo said.

Harish coughed. 'Er . . . I paid fifty thousand rupees too

'. . . I mean my father paid . . .' he stopped, looked around as though for an escape route, then giving up, grinned at me.

'What?' I said, giving Tinkoo, I knew, just the response he was looking for. 'That's awful!'

'Now tell her, how much you *earn*, yaar,' Tinkoo said delightedly.

Harish's face reddened a little but he kept his eyes on me and a smile on his face: 'I earn one thousand, five hundred rupees a month.'

Tinkoo turned to me triumphantly. 'Well, Sheila*ji*,' he said, emphasizing the *ji* very, very sarcastically, 'what do you make of that?'

'I don't understand it,' I said, looking at Harish. 'It really doesn't make sense. I don't see why anyone should take a job in which he earns the same as he has to give his boss. In fact,' I said, unable to contain my disgust, 'I don't see why anyone would allow themselves to be caught in such a system.' I knew I sounded preachy.

'Ah . . . I didn't tell you,' Harish said, with a note of bravado creeping into his voice, '. . . ah, what I *make* each month.'

'Make?' I said stupidly.

'Sure. I *make* six thousand rupees a month at least. Sometimes more.'

I shook my head. '*What* are you talking about?'

'I have eight policemen under me, you see, and each one of them earns seven hundred and fifty rupees a month. That's six thousand rupees.'

'Oh God!' I said, the penny finally dropping with a hollow, crushed sort of sound. 'But how do they . . .?'

'Use your imagination, Sheila*ji*,' Tinkoo crowed.

'You mean the policemen make *their* money . . .'

'. . . from the public, yes,' Tinkoo said. 'And sometimes even what *they* make go into Harish's pocket, and part of it gets passed on to Harish's superior.' He snorted. 'Those rich enough to pay taxes – that is maybe about fifteen per cent of the population – support the police system twice. And those who don't pay taxes – the majority of the country – they have to do their share too. A very superior and sensible system, isn't it, Sheilaji?' He beamed. 'Rough and ready justice right there at the grass-roots. Pay up, or get flogged. So simple, isn't it?'

'It's awful,' I mumbled and a picture of the average British policeman . . . Jimmy's father perhaps, whom I'd never met, floated towards me between the crowds on the platform of Rampur station. I'd always thought the English policeman fair when I was a child, someone to turn to for protection. Reports about the way they treated blacks and Asians had upset me. But I was sure they weren't party to this elaborate structure of what I could only see as bribery and corruption. The British policeman preying on blacks and Asians, somehow didn't seem as dreadful as Indian policemen preying on Indians. But then, I thought, what's the difference, really? It didn't seem like Indians thought of themselves as Indians anyway. More like Madhya Pradeshis and Punjabis. They even differentiated between villages. Look at the ahirs and malahars and chamars. All so separate from each other – like completely different people. My gut began to pound again and the prickles ran up my arms and back.

'Ah, the green light!' Bumpy said, sounding thankful.

A bell clanged. There was a general rustling thump and scrape on the platform as squatting people lifted luggage bundles, bed-rolls, tiffin carriers, water pots, and began to move towards the edge of the platform.

The train thundered in, pulled by a diesel engine.

'Stay by the bookstore,' Bumpy said to me. 'I'll get Tinkoo on and come back for you.' He hurried off to find the conductor to check Tinkoo's booking and berth.

''Bye, Sheila*ji*!' Tinkoo cried with malicious glee. 'See you in Delhi, a sadder but wiser dame, I bet!' And he disappeared into the swirling, milling, jostling crowd.


On the way back in the jeep Bumpy, hands on the wheel, said roughly: 'Next time you come to Rampur wear a salwar-kameez. Not a dress.'

'Oh God!' I groaned.

'I mean it,' he said.

I sighed loudly and looked out at Rampur.

'And, also, don't go getting so close to the men.'

Astonished, I turned to look at him: 'What *are* you talking about?'

Bumpy glowered. 'When you were looking at Sunil's badge, you leaned over, close to him. You know what he said to me when you weren't listening? He said: "Your sister's pretty fast, yaar!" That's what he said,' Bumpy was almost snarling.

I sat up, shocked. 'Are you all crazy or something?' I demanded. 'Paranoid, or what?'

'Look,' Bumpy said, 'I know *you* didn't mean anything. But when in Rome . . .'

'Aaah!' I said disgustedly, and turned back to the neon-lit streets and jostling crowds.

As we rattled and bumped and honked our way out of Rampur, I began to feel unclean. Really unclean. As though I'd been brushed by some filthy, smelly broom. What was *wrong* with these boys? Couldn't they behave normally with girls? Weren't we also people? Did the fact of my having a female body have to make such a difference? School in London, I thought, was *healthy* compared to *this*! So, all right, the fact that I was Indian had become a barrier for Jimmy, but before that came up, we'd been as normal with each other as . . . well, Phil and Barb and Bob and Janey. Just friends at first. Real friends. Boy and girl *after* that. Here bodies came first, and got in the way of people being people.

Was that why Tinkoo was such a wally? But then why not Bumpy? *He* treated me normally.

'Bumpy,' I said in the darkness, 'what do you think of me? Really?'

'Think of you?' Bumpy sounded startled. 'What do you mean? What should I think of you? You're my sister.'

I was silent.

'Why do you ask?' he said.

'It seems so complicated,' I said. 'I'm your sister, all right. But am I your friend?'

He was silent for a bit. 'I suppose you are,' he said slowly, 'but I never thought about it. It's enough that you're my sister.'

'Girls can't be friends with boys, right?'

I saw him purse his lips in the dim light from the dashboard. 'Yah, I suppose that's possible. I haven't really had friends who were girls. Except you, when we were kids.'

'So it's possible for us to be friends because we grew up together in the same family?'

'Ye-e-es,' Bumpy said. 'So?'

'Do you notice how rotten Tinkoo is to me? Why? It started almost as soon as we met at the airport. The moment I opened my mouth.'

Bumpy threw back his head and laughed delightedly. 'Well, I must tell you it's really something when an Indian face opens its mouth and out comes this incredible toon–toon, taen–taen English accent,' he said. 'Here it's old fogeys left over from the British Raj who speak like that and we think they're quite nuts.' And he did a really quite good take off of the landed gentry, country esquire, jolly-good-what-ho-hawrh-hawrh-hawrh-marbles-in-the-mouth variety of British English. He had me in stitches, almost crying with laughter. 'Where did you learn that?' I howled when he'd finished.

'All those old British films we saw in school and college,' he smiled.

'But I *don't* speak like that, Bumpy,' I wailed through my tears. 'My accent's quite ordinary, really. North London ordinary.'

'It's all the same to us out in the backwaters,' Bumpy said. 'We don't care to remember the British experience, although we're stuck with their language. And you speak British English. You don't speak like us. That's enough.'

'Hah,' I said emphatically. 'Tinkoo speaks a foreign language too, you know.'

'Yup,' Bumpy said agreeably. 'But that's a futcha phenomenon.'

I groaned. 'What's *that*, for God's sake, Bumpy?'

He grinned: 'First year college. Freshman. The "in-thing". You begin to pick it up in the first year, fling it around in the

114

second, and outgrow it by the time you start thinking about serious things, like real work and real life.'

'I think it's stupid,' I said sourly.

'But I'm used to it. And I suppose I'm used to the way you speak, since we've met about every two, three years. How long since you met Tinkoo?'

I tried to remember. Not the last time I came with Mum, Dad and Rach. He'd been away somewhere – to his grand-parents or something. 'Oh I don't know. Maybe seven, nine years?'

'So, there's your answer,' Bumpy said. 'He doesn't know you at all. You're a challenge to him.'

'A challenge?'

Bumpy said gently: 'It's his age, Sheels. I can remember feeling the same a few years ago. You get competitive with the opposite sex. It's a knee-jerk reaction. Fear and need all in one.' He paused. 'It's not so bad in Delhi – but here, in the country it's dreadful. Fear and need I mean. It's why we get married so early. It's the only way to be half-way sane.'

We were threading through Samli Village now. Dim lights filtered out of the brahmin houses lining the street. They had a warm, comfortable glow.

'How old are you, Bumpy?'

'Twenty-three . . . What is it, six, nearly seven years older than you?'

'Are you going to be married soon?'

He sighed and his hands tightened on the wheel. 'Yes,' he said shortly. Then: 'I'd *better*!'

'Who's the lucky girl?'

He glanced at me and smiled wryly: 'There isn't one yet.'

'When?'

'Well, Nina Auntie's looking. Bhanti Chachi's looking. Rano Maasi's looking . . .'

I leaned forward and put my head in my hands, shaking it and groaning exaggeratedly.

'What's the matter?' Bumpy said, a little coolly. 'You don't approve?'

I sat up and shook my head: 'No, it's not that. It's just that . . .'

We hit a huge pothole just then and the jeep juddered. Bumpy swore as he struggled with the wheel. The headlights picked up a buffalo sitting in the middle of the road, placidly looking at us . . . Like an arranged marriage, I thought hysterically, before my head hit the roof.

'Watch out, Bumpy!' I shrieked, grabbing the dashboard. Bumpy swerved wildly, and for a moment it looked as though we might make a lasting impression on a brahmin wall in Samli Village. When he'd got us under control, Bumpy said shakily: 'Well, that's another country adventure to take back with you to London, Sheels.'

'That's all I need,' I wobbled weakly, rubbing my head.

We drove along in silence for a bit, then Bumpy said: 'Well, Sheels. Before you get judgemental about it, where would I meet a girl of my own class and background here in this backwoods? Not in the Government Girls High School for sure.'

'Didn't you meet anyone at college?' I said.

'What! At Indore Agricultural College?' he replied disbelievingly. 'There were precisely six girls there.'

'Don't you go to Delhi?' I tried again.

'Sure, I met some of Tinkoo's empty-headed radical chic friends. All spouting revolution while their daddies make their crores running industry, or satelliting politicians. They'll all settle down to their papa's choice some day. Daughter of industrialist to son of movie moghul, or cabinet minister. Join together all their ill-gotten wealth . . .' He shook his head. 'We're a feudal society, Sheels. Slow, rigid and hierarchical. Not much freedom. Socially or politically. You only have to look at our films to see how little freedom there really is.'

'Bumpy,' I said unhappily. 'You sound very cynical.'

'Sheels, you saw how Harish and Sunil reacted to you. Don't expect very much different in Delhi, underneath it all. Even though on the surface it might look different. Now here we are, back home. *Just* in time so all your illusions are not totally destroyed.'

And he pulled up at the gate of Mehta Farm.

# 13

Inder Uncle's campaign to distract me from joining the jabbah procession continued . . . very subtly.

'I need a break from all this harvesting,' he said at dinner a couple of nights later. 'What do you say, Sheilaji, you want to see the diamond mines? I have a friend there I haven't seen for a long time.'

Another day Grandpa, Grandma and I drove over ninety kilometers to Khajuraho where temples with lovely sculptures built by the Chandella Rajas in the tenth century stand in greeny velvet parks decorated with huge swathes of bougainvillea.

And one day Bumpy took Gran and me to the Bandhavgarh Game Sanctuary, a hundred and twenty kilometers in the other direction. 'Go see tigers,' Inder Uncle said encouragingly. 'They are safer than humans.'

We saw deer, pheasants, nilgai, huge wild bison, the occasional wild boar, as we drove through the forest, which lay in a valley surrounding the old ruined Bandhavgarh fort high above the trees, but no tigers. We had tea at the dak-bungalow, the government rest-house where several huge elephants were waiting to take tourists around the sanctuary. I wanted to get on one . . . but I thought of Tinkoo getting to know of it and doing his bloody nut over my being a tourist. So I said nothing, and we set off again in the jeep, listening to the whoosh of the afternoon wind, the call of a peacock, and mostly to the over-powering, awesome sounds of silence.

On the way back through the forest in the evening, Bumpy stopped the jeep suddenly.

'Look!' he whispered. 'Over there to your right. There! Near the trees.'

It wasn't immediately visible against the trees. A magnificent, long, striped, majestic tiger, crouching across an open space as it watched us.

Bumpy revved the engine.

The tiger growled in answer. It was a chilling sound: hollow, echoing, rolling thunder. There was a dead silence around us as the thunder rose thinning into the air. Then Bumpy revved the jeep's engine again.

The tiger bared its teeth and thundered again, ending in an ugly snapping snarl. It loped sideways, along the trees, still watching suspiciously.

Gran said quietly: 'Enough, Bumpy. It can be on us in two leaps.'

Bumpy laughed: 'Bibiji, you're scared! The tigers are too well-fed these days. They have enough game. They're protected, they can't be bothered with us. Anyway it is a myth that tigers just leap at you. If they sense you don't mean them harm you can get up really close. Bandhavgarh is *meant* for tiger watching.'

We drove on. The tiger raced parallel with us for a while, and then disappeared into the trees.

I was thrilled. But I didn't want to seem like a tourist, so I didn't say anything.

We swung around a corner on the forest road, and Bumpy swore: 'Somebody's left a bloody log in the middle of the road!' and slammed on the brake, throwing Gran violently forward against the windscreen, and me sideways against the front seat.

But it wasn't a log, it was an enormous tiger! At least three metres long, lying there, indolently watching a herd of spotted deer behind the trees.

We stopped just a metre short of it.

Gran gasped.

I could feel the blood in my veins turn ice-cold with fright. It sounds like a cliché, but, I tell you, at moments like this it really is true!

Bumpy looked completely disconcerted. He didn't, perhaps couldn't, back off.

We waited, stunned into immobility.

The tiger had turned his head casually as we came at him. Now he got up slowly, looked at us with infinite disdain, twitched his tail, and sauntered into the surrounding undergrowth.

He didn't even bother to growl!

But we three humans couldn't move.

Gran said in a small voice after a while: 'I think we go home now, Bumpy.'

Bumpy simply let in the clutch and we drove on. It was a long time before any of us said anything.

Bumpy laughed shakily: 'You were scared?'

Gran flashed a quick look at him, and said: 'Hmmpf!' There was a small silence and after a bit, I said drily: 'Just about as much as *you* were, Bumps.' Bumpy caught my tone. He said: 'Now *Tinkoo*, of course, would have leapt out and grabbed the tiger around the neck!' And we all laughed together; the tension broke. But I was sad, really, that the tigers were this tame.

At dinner we exchanged tiger stories. Grandpa told us again of the time he'd shot the tiger, whose skin now adorned the living room wall. Gran told us about the time she'd almost walked straight into one at the bottom of the garden in Assam, late one evening.

Inder Uncle said: 'Haven't you had enough excitement now, Sheilaji? *Must* you go on the jabbah?'

'We agreed,' I said stubbornly.

And they all looked at each other and sighed.


The next day, Bumpy and I drove over to visit the Raja of Rampur.

It wasn't far, just south of Rampur.

'Tigers and Rajas,' Inder Uncle said. 'Yes, yes, Sheila should see the real India, Bumpy. Give my regards to Vinay Ji!'

'The *real* India,' Bumpy snorted. But I was excited. A real Raja! Wouldn't Barb and Janey just die with envy! We drove off the main road, climbed steadily up a hill, and went through a small village, which reminded me of . . . a miniature Edinburgh! All the mud and brick houses clustered together alongside a winding lane so the village managed to look pretty despite its squalor. And at the top of the hill was this old crumbling, ruined fortress! It was made of enormous hunks of grey and brown stone, and had towers and crenellations and narrow windows with helmets hewed on above.

'It's so medieval, Bumps!' I said, really and truly entranced.

'It is,' Bumpy said matter-of-factly. 'It's called Ramgarh. The village too. It's been here longer than Rampur. Rampur is a British town built around the railway line.'

He parked outside massive wooden gates, with huge slats and rusted iron studs. There was a small door let into the gates, for people to enter through.

And inside was an absolute wilderness! The open spaces were overgrown with weeds. Little trees sprouted from cracks in the wall.

The wooden stairs were crumbling dangerously. We tiptoed up to the main door, skipping over broken slats, jumping at every creak. Bumpy knocked on the door and called: 'Raja Sahib, Raja Sahib!'

'*This* is royalty, Bumps?' I said.

'You haven't seen anything yet!' Bumpy replied, enjoying himself.

After a while, a creaking old woman in a tattered white sari opened the door, smiled at Bumpy and ushered us into a vast empty hall, absolutely shrouded with dust. There was one small Persian carpet, old and mouldering, lying in the middle of the hall, looking very forlorn. No furniture! There were portraits of the family in worn old gilt frames glaring down at us. The old woman asked us to sit, and shuffled off. We squatted on the dusty carpet.

I looked around. Dreary, was the word. Rats scuttled in the corners. Sunlight came bleakly in through narrow windows high up on the outer wall only to be obscured by the dust.

Bumpy said: 'They only have a couple of hundred acres of land now. And the Raja doesn't even bother to farm that!'

'How do they live then?' I said.

Bumpy waved a hand around the hall. 'Poorly,' he said. 'I think he has some money stashed away somewhere. I know he took tourists tiger shooting one time, before the laws against tiger shooting were enforced.'

'But he could farm his lands. Why doesn't he?'

Bumpy snorted. 'Rajas don't do their own farming, Sheels. They live off rents and produce!'

'But . . .' I started.

'He hasn't made the transition,' Bumpy said flatly. 'He lives in the past. You'll see.'

Just then a tall, cadaverous man came down the stairs leading off one side of the hall. He was wearing faded trousers, an open-necked shirt, and a French beret perched between enormous jug ears. His eyes crinkled as he cried: 'Brijendra old boy! So good of you to come.' His accent was right fruity!

Bumpy scrambled up, said: 'Namasté, Raja Sahib,' in differential tones, and introduced me. I did a namasté too, feeling awkward in my dress.

'Well, well, from London, eh?' the Raja said. And he sounded just like Bumpy doing his marbles-in-the-mouth-jolly-good-what-ho act. 'That makes you very interesting, little lady. Come on, let's sit comfortably in my study, shall we?' And then he added: 'Such as it is.'

He put an arm around Bumpy's shoulder affectionately and led us out of the room, up the stairs, past an open space where the old woman was cooking over the kind of mud stove Shanti had in the corner of her courtyard, into his study.

Comfortable? It had several broken straight-backed chairs, a ratty, scratched, unpolished table and a worn old bookshelf with a few dusty books. Not even *one* armchair. We sat perched on the edges of the wooden chairs so our bums wouldn't go through the broken nylon cane work!

The Raja had been working at papers strewn over his desk.

'It's bloody murder the time I spend writing to Government to restore our lands,' he said wanly. He launched into reminiscences about the good old days when tiger shooting was allowed and European tourists came in droves and he took them around on elephants and jeeps. He rattled on about all the famous people who'd been to Ramgarh as his guests. It sounded a bit like a 'Who's Who' of the French Riviera. He even broke into bits of French every now and then. He looked out of the window a good deal as he talked; the panes were broken and those that were left were filthy. He was 'ebsolutlah enchanted m'gel' that I lived in London. Frowned a bit at my rather common accent, and shook his head doubtfully when I told him I was going to apply to study at Delhi U.

He enquired about the family, sent his respects through Bumpy and asked that Inder Uncle visit him soon. 'The only bloody decent fella around, what!' he said. He talked about his brother Vijay studying in England, and said he'd enjoyed his own stint at Oxford, but had had to drop out for lack of funds.

'I'm not as smart as Vijay,' he said wryly. 'I couldn't get a scholarship, so in the end they said: "Piss orf erl chep!" so I pissed orf!'

It was all I could do not to snort right out loud. I glanced at Bumpy, who looked very studiously at the Raja. All attention.

The old woman served tea in cracked china cups. It was really unbelievable. There wasn't a *thing* that wasn't falling to bits. I noticed that even the seams in the Raja's trousers had come apart and had been sewn together with white thread, clumsily by hand.

After tea, he introduced me to his mother, the Dowager Rani. And to his wife the Rani of Rampur. His upper-class British accent dropped away completely when he talked to his mother! The Dowager was lying sighing and groaning on a rickety old bed in her bedroom. At every turn, the bed sighed and groaned in unison. The Rani, wearing a faded blue sari with rusted silver threads in it, sat beside her, empty handed, as though she had nothing else in the world to do! They seemed very happy to have visitors to break the monotony of lying around groaning and creaking all day, sitting around empty handed. And after the first few polite sentences both of them began moaning about their fate, their ancestry and modern India.

Apparently, the Dowager Rani had had a falling out with her brother-in-law, the present Raja's uncle after the old Raja died, and the brother had cleaned the castle of all the furniture and furnishings, and had grabbed most of the land, and sold it. He hadn't wanted reminders of his ancestors so he'd left the portraits! It was as though their *job* was to moan and grumble about their fate. They went on for what seemed like hours. And the Raja sat nodding intelligently *all* the time, as though they were saying something of great importance to which they had given a great deal of thought.

It was really difficult getting away.

'Whooey!' I said, when we were back in the jeep, after Bumpy had managed an incredible Houdini of good manners escape for us. 'How did you run into *this* lot then?'

'Dad found them,' Bumpy said, 'he needed friends he could talk to . . . and after all, they do have wide horizons. And he doesn't have to sit with the Dowager Rani each time!'


I didn't much feel like going anywhere for a while after that. Instead I pulled out my camera, and shot film of the harvesting of the wheat. And one day, I went on my own to the villages behind the farm.

I wandered through the Malahan-ka-tolla, the fishermen's village, first, past the lovely huts with their red tiled roofs and lime and dung washed walls. The huts huddled together around a large central banyan tree. The courtyards of each hut were thoroughly clean. The little lanes between the huts too were swept. They were a tidy and clean people the malahars.

They welcomed me and showed me around eagerly, asking neighbourly questions about Grandpa and Gran, whom they held in great esteem. I watched a young woman wearing a sari in the city style talking to a group of village women in one courtyard. I was told she was an anganbadi worker from the Integrated Child Development Service in Rampur. She was talking about personal hygiene, sanitation and environmental cleanliness. About immunizing children and good nutrition.

'They're trying to get us to build toilets right next to our houses,' one of the malahar women said at my elbow. 'Filthy idea!'

I glanced at her, surprised. But I didn't know what to say.

She showed me around inside her house which was as clean and neat as a pin.

The malahars decorate their doors and windows with bas-reliefs of birds and flowers. They fashion these every year while washing down their walls with mud and dung and lime. The white on white is very subtle, very attractive.

A small temple stood to one side of the village, behind an iron gate. A Hanuman idol painted orange, looked sleepily at the flowers and incense placed before him.

The Ahiran-ka-tolla was larger, more formal, wealthier and less friendly. There were more brick buildings, less huddled together. And the village wasn't as clean here. I didn't feel quite as welcome, until Lilavati, one of the women who worked shifts on the farm, saw me and took me around. She owned two huts, a brick house and several buffaloes of her own. She proudly showed me her stacks of cow dung cakes which the ahirs make and sell for fuel.

I took endless pictures of family groups, who, giggling and shoving, ranged themselves for the solemn occasion. And everywhere I went I was followed by giggling, shoving children like mice behind the Pied Piper of Hamelin.

When I told Lilavati I was going next to the chamar village she was genuinely aghast. 'Why?' she said. 'What do you want with chamars? They're unclean.'

'Rubbish,' I said, and then, feeling very wicked, I said: 'We're chamars too, you know. Yet you come and work for us.'

Lilavati stopped dead, her face going pale. Then she laughed: 'Oh you are making fun of me. You cannot be chamars.'

'Why not?' I said.

'Your karma is too good. You have too much money.'

People seemed to think that money wherever you were equalled luck.

I visited Baredi's family in the Chamaran-ka-tolla, which had even more brick buildings than the Ahiran-ka-tolla.

Just like the brahmins! I was taken by the idea that the highest and lowest castes lived in identically ugly houses.

Baredi's old, very old mother, the village midwife, showed me around the rather largish ugly brick house, cackling with glee. 'My grandson is a motor mechanic, Baiji, he earns good money in Rampur. He built this house,' she said proudly.

There was a bore-hole toilet outside, bricked up, one wall common to the house. It was clean and didn't even smell much. Baredi's mother pointed out the toilet with special emphasis, saying: 'We learned from your family, Baiji, how to be clean! Now we're cleaner than all the others. *They* don't want their own toilets.'


That evening, sitting on the verandah with Grandpa and Raja, watching the threshing, I said: 'Grandpa, what's karma? Is it the same as luck?'

Grandpa's chair creaked as he leaned back on it. 'Well, if you stretch the meaning very broadly, you could say it is. But commonly understood, it's your destiny,' he said. 'It's what's predetermined for you in this life as a consequence of your past lives.'

'Oh,' I said, losing interest.

'Why do you ask?' I could hear the smile in his voice.

'Lilavati, over at the ahir village said today our karma is good – we have money – so we can't be chamars.'

Grandpa snorted.

I giggled. 'She didn't think I should go and see Baredi's family because they were unclean, so I told her we were chamars.'

'Hmmph!' he said, twinkling. 'Good! And how did she respond?'

'She went white, then she said that about our karma.'

Grandpa laughed delightedly.

'What's our caste, Grandpa?' I said idly.

'We don't *have* a caste, Sheila,' Grandpa replied a little severely. 'Remember you're talking to a one-time Marxist, and our socialist ideas never fade!' Then he relented. 'Caste is really a very simple concept, beti. It is the work you do. If you're a potter – that's your caste: kumhar; if you're a blacksmith, that's your caste: lohar; if you're a cow-herder, your caste is ahir. Originally caste lines weren't so rigid, you could move from one to another, like changing jobs. Caste actually was ecologically sound. Such and such a caste could

126

hunt deer using arrows in such and such a territory. Others could only trap rabbits in this area, or use x kind of materials for making tools. A large part of caste was made up of ethical behaviour, a bit like the professional ethics of doctors etc.' He grunted. 'But like everything else, a sound idea got perverted to make some people right and others wrong. Some good and some bad. Some superior and some inferior.'

'I see,' I said, not too interested any more. Then, to tease him a little, I said: 'Grandpa, for a one-time Marxist you don't do too badly. The way you live out here, you're like an old country squire!'

He harrumphed with embarrassment and scratched Raja behind his ears. 'That's nonsense! I own only the legal limit of thirty acres. Your father owns thirty, Inder owns thirty and Bumpy owns thirty. That's only one hundred and twenty acres. It's not so wonderful. We employ ten people full time, the rest seasonally, and we pay the going rate. In fact a little above. There's nothing country squirish or anything feudal about that. We don't own villages,' Grandpa glowered at me under his eyes, 'and nobody owes us any loyalties. Our farm labour just goes for the highest wages.'

'But come on, you have a much better lifestyle than the people who work for you, Gramps,' I said.

Grandpa said nothing for a bit, then he said heavily: 'I thought of going cooperative in the beginning but it didn't work. The caste lines are too strong. The people would not believe me. They refused to work. They quarrelled over every decision. The difference in our world views, our horizons and depths of understanding, was too great. If I had to do it over, I think I wouldn't make such a white elephant of a house though.' And he stopped, looking off over the fields. Then he said meditatively: 'One person on his own does not a revolution make, Sheila. In fact we found, in India, even many people together would not make a revolution. Not the socialist kind anyway. The weight of religion is too heavy.'

Well, *that* made no sense to me, so I said: 'Lots of young people in London are Marxist. Especially in the black community.'

'And you?' Grandpa said, raising those bushes that hung over his eyes, 'Are you a Marxist? And are you one of the blacks?'

Slowly, I shook my head.

'No,' I said, 'I can't say I'm anything really.'

'Have you ever signed a petition?' Grandpa said, 'anti-war, against nuclear weapons, for the environment? Joined a protest movement? Or worked for local government?'

I shook my head again: 'No, Grandpa, I haven't done anything like that. Well, I *did* sign a petition recently on the environment at school . . . But I suppose I didn't really know enough.' I sighed unhappily feeling I was very boring, very dull. 'I can't . . . see myself joining in marches and rioting and that. I suppose I don't, well, get het up enough.'

'You're just too comfortable,' Grandpa said.

Yes, I thought, I was, until this business with Jimmy. Then all the questions had started. And all the anxieties. I didn't really know enough about anything. I was a simpleton being run over by the world. Was that why I wanted to take Politics Honours? Would Politics Honours teach me about people? About the world and why it was the way it was? *Would* it get me worked up enough to become 'black' like Rachna? Marxist like Tinkoo? It certainly sounded a stupid enough reason to take Politics Honours just then, sitting comfortably on the verandah at Mehta Farm with Grandpa, the back-slid Marxist!

# 14

The days went by at an even jog and I drifted into something like a routine. I'd wake to the thunk and throb of the threshing machine, the laughing calls of the field labour at work since three in the morning and go through my morning exercises. Soon I began to realize my gut wasn't heaving and clenching as much, and my back and arms weren't always on fire. I'd bathe in the old claw-footed bathtub and go out into the fields, to look at the sunrise over the trees and the huts of Samli Village. And then at the harvesting and threshing of the wheat.

Bumpy complained incessantly of labour problems. 'They raise their rates at harvest time, they slack off because they're paid daily, and they spend their time just flirting with each other.'

Inder Uncle said: 'Next year we don't take that Mulloo, that Ram Milan's brother. He appears from God-knows-where during the harvest. All he does is romance the girls. He thinks he's a movie hero or something. He spends hours just combing that filthy greasy hair of his!'

I found Mulloo quite entertaining. He was truly ugly, with a pock-marked face and broad, coarse features. But he fascinated the women. He wore bright yellow flared pants and flower printed shirts. He sang continuously, loudly, off-key, the most banal Hindi movie songs. He was always cheerful, always willing to lend a hand . . . if it was to a woman – helping her jump off the wheat stacks, carry a basket, climb a ladder. He so obviously, blatantly, whole-heartedly fancied himself, you couldn't help liking him.


It rapidly became too hot to go out during the day, and I began helping out Gran in the kitchen, assisted by the solemn, skinny, big-eyed Laxmi.

'Poor girl,' Gran said one day, 'she's of these early marriage tragedies. Her parents got her married off at eleven. To be safe. And at fifteen she had her first baby, a girl. She's twenty-four now and has four daughters and her old mother to support. Her father died, her husband went off with another woman.' Gran shook her head ruefully, breaking eggs into a bowl. 'They're thakurs. They think quite a lot of themselves. I suppose her husband couldn't accept the fact that they had four daughters and no son,' she sighed, 'so he said the girls weren't his!'

Laxmi, at the sink, washing dishes, glanced up briefly at Gran. She obviously understood what Gran was saying: Punjabi and Hindi are very alike.

'You know how little they care here for daughters,' Gran went on, 'they're considered a liability. They have to be given dowries when they're married.' She beat the eggs with a fork, hard. 'Sons! Sons is what they want! Sons to work and bring them money. Sons who will marry and bring in a dowry and a drudge to work in the home! Sons who will support them in their old age.' She stopped and spooned butter and flour into the eggs. 'In many places they even kill off the girls at birth,' she said angrily, folding the mix with a rubber spatula. 'Isn't that stupid? As though the human race could go on without women!'

She washed her hands in the sink and dried them on a spotless towel. It was such a large kitchen, unlike Nina Maasi's which was almost squalid in comparison. 'Such fairy tales!' she said. 'Such fairy tales this culture breeds.' She rummaged in the cupboards for nuts and raisins. 'If you look at what is really happening, you see the sons are spoiled by doting mothers, taught to be little princes. You see very few really properly employed men here, specially in the agricultural castes. It's the women who work in the fields, cook the food. The men just gamble and drink and run around with other women. So few men actually look after their parents in spite of their traditions.'

'Aren't there exceptions, Gran?' I said, almost defensively. 'I mean, Baredi. His son built him a house.'

Gran nodded. 'Yes, beti, there are exceptions. Baredi

130

deserves the best. He must be a very evolved spirit. His is a karmayogi. His work is pure dharma.'

'Dharma, Gran?'

'Yes, his work is worship.'

'Oh,' I said, as usual flummoxed by all these Hindu words. 'Laxmi,' I said, as I helped Gran butter the cake tins and scoop the mixture in. 'Do you mind my asking you? Why did your husband run away?'

Laxmi smiled coyly, her eyes sliding at me sideways, like those of an Indian movie star, and adjusted her sari over her breasts tucking the end into her waist. 'Baiji, I come from a better family than he does. When I married him, he couldn't even write his name. I taught him how to write.' There was a flicker of disdain in her eyes. 'I taught him to wear pants instead of a dhoti.' She wiped her forehead with an arm. 'He was a boar. So coarse. He didn't want to send our daughters to school. I wanted them to study. Then he said they were not his daughters . . .' She paused. 'The liar!' she hissed. 'And now he is running around with some loose woman.' She stopped and then said angrily, 'It was *my* father who got him a job in the electricity board. But when he started making good money, he decided he didn't need me any more. He doesn't even pay for looking after our daughters!'

She wiped her hands on her sari. Then she went on to stacking dishes. I thought she'd have looked utterly miserable by now, but she smiled again and her eyes slid around coyly at me again.

'I've tried to get her to bring him to court,' Gran said, 'but she's too frightened.'

'If I take him to court he will come at night and beat me,' Laxmi said flatly.

'I've told her I'll get her a government lawyer. The Mahila Samiti will pay,' Gran said. She worked at a local women's organization, running schools, teachers' training courses and discussion groups. 'But she still won't agree.'

Laxmi snorted derisively: 'Government lawyer!' she said, gathering the forks and spoons, clashing them loudly together. 'And when my husband comes at night to beat me where will the government lawyer be?'

'The police . . .' Gran started and stopped.

Laxmi's eyes flashed at her. 'Police!' she said with contempt.

And Gran nodded, not saying anything.

'God is not kind,' Laxmi said in a low voice, beginning to wipe down the counter with hard, long swipes. 'I come from a better family than he does. I am better educated. But I have to work in a kitchen and make three hundred rupees a month and look after the children. And,' she said bitterly, 'because he's a man he makes nine hundred rupees a month and runs around with loose women!'

Gran sat down on the kitchen chair and said slowly: 'I really sometimes don't know what is right. Men do fear educated women it seems.' She looked ruefully then, at me. 'Even I gave up my studies, you know. I passed school before your grandfather and I were married. I tried doing my BA later, but . . .' she said, sounding a little weary, '. . . there were the children, Channi's job, running a home.'

'Oh Gran!' I said, 'Grandpa wouldn't have stopped you studying!'

'No, of course not,' Gran said. 'He encouraged me. He wanted me to be his partner in his work for the Party. But traditions *do* have such a hold on us. I never questioned the fact that the woman's primary role was to have children . . .'

And I groaned loudly, slammed open the oven and practically kicked the cake-tin in.

'Oh! I'll fix him,' Laxmi said in a low voice. 'I'll fix him good. In my own way, Baiji.'

And looking at pretty, tiny, coy, tough little Laxmi, I wondered fleetingly if her husband hadn't perhaps left her, not so much because she was educated, but because he got fed up of being told he was inferior.


When I talked to Munnia about Laxmi later, Munnia said: 'It's right that women should not be better educated than men.

You see what happens when the are? I will never make *him* (meaning Ram Prasad, her husband) feel inferior to me.' And with a starry smile she went on, 'I *couldn't*, he is so wonderful! He really is superior to me in every way.'

'Munnia!' I began indignantly. But then I stopped dead. What could I say? Part of me was boiling mad about poor Laxmi, but a part of me envied Munnia. Part of me was sorry for Sunaina being 'married off' like that. And part of me was so angry with myself for not having foreseen what happened with Jimmy, with Mum and Dad for not being firmer – stopping me!

Then I began to see my life was even more complicated than I'd thought. I had to get to grips with four parallel problems. I was female; I was educated and I would go *on* being as educated as my brain could handle; I was Indian living in England; *and* I had no traditions which told me what to do.

I think I've never felt as desperate as I did that moment when I said, 'Munnia,' and couldn't go on.


One evening I was out past the village in a neighbouring harvested field, sitting under a tree watching the sun blaze down into the west in a spectacular sunset of orange and purple and pink. The sky above me was bright blue with swatches of white clouds arching across it, edged with orange binding.

Far in the distance a voice called. I could hear the thresher and the tractor on the farm. A platoon of egrets flew in strict military formation overhead, necks out, legs stiff, heading south.

It was a quiet, still moment. There was even a quiet in my gut. No spasms. No prickles.

Then that beautiful blue bird flapped up from the fields, calling, turning from dull brown to brilliant turquoise to dull brown again as it settled in a tree.

And I seemed to melt into the world in one of those rare moments of peace and serenity, just as I had when opening the side gate to visit Munnia. Everything seemed still and peaceful and good.

Then across the field to my left, came a boy's piping voice, in local dialect Hindi calling out: 'Ahiyo, you old whore! Come on, walk! You mother of a sow!'

Serene! Did I say serene? It was like a two thousand volt shock from a high tension cable, in that peaceful landscape.

A scrawny young boy came through the tall grasses, beating his ambling, unconcerned buffalo ineffectively with a thin, long, hard stick. How could such a sweet-faced boy use such awful language, as though it were normal everyday conversation!

I called him over.

He came willingly, grinning.

'What's your name?' I said.

'Ram Mohan,' he said promptly in a friendly way, leaning his chin on his hands, his hands on his stick, legs apart, looking at me intently.

'Where do you live?'

'In the Ahiran-ka-tolla.' He answered in a neutral, matter-of-fact voice.

'What do your parents do?'

'They're buffalo keepers. My mother takes care of Babuji's buffaloes.' He pointed at our farm.

'Aha,' I said, remembering the laughing-eyed, good-humoured woman slathered with buffalo dung that morning Tinkoo'd yapped at me. 'Who taught you these wonderful names you call your buffalo?'

He looked surprised. 'What names?'

' "Whore", I said, "Mother of a sow". Where did you learn these names?'

He shrugged: 'It's what we call the buffaloes,' he said simply. He had a round face, very sweet, very innocent. His hands, arms, legs and feet were grubby. His pants hung almost in tatters to his knees.

A train went by in the horizon. Achha-chugga, achha-chugga, Whoo-a-whoo!

'Do you go to school?' I asked.

'No.'

'Do you want to?'

'No.'

'You *don't* want to go to school?' I said, surprised.

'No.'

'Don't you want to learn to read?'

'No.'

'What do you want to be when you grow up?' I asked him a little exasperated.

'A buffalo boy,' came the prompt response.

'But you are one already,' I said. 'Don't you want to be anything else?'

He looked at me as though I were mad. 'Why?' he said. 'I like being a buffalo boy.'

'Don't you want to . . . well maybe become an engine driver in that train.' I pointed to the train whooing away mournfully, 'and go to far-off lands?'

'No,' he said, puzzled. 'Why should I? I am a buffalo boy.' Then he said laconically: 'Main hoon so hoon.' I am what I am.

And with that he picked up a stone and threw it at his buffalo, chewing unconcernedly on the grass of the bund.

'Ahaiyyo, you old whore,' he said, 'get on with you!'

And together they ambled off.

I thought of the way Rach and I had been brought up: dolls to play with so we'd learn to be mothers; nurses' uniforms, doctors' stethoscopes; a toy typewriter so we might learn office work; Meccano sets in case we had engineering abilities tucked away; Lego to build fantasy space-craft. And always the question: What shall I be when I grow up?

The blue bird flew down just then, calling harshly, dipped into the fields and whirred away to the west.

What shall I do?

When I grow up?

A political scientist? A politician? A . . . a . . . my gut wrenched.

The question didn't even arise for this buffalo boy. Poor thing. But I felt peculiarly uncomfortable with the thought.


I told Grandpa that night, at our now usual half hour on the verandah after dinner, about meeting the buffalo boy and what he'd said. 'Grandpa,' I said indignantly, 'why doesn't that little boy go to school? Then he'd know what other opportunities there are for him.'

Grandpa said: 'Don't think we haven't tried. But he isn't the only boy we can't seem to move at all. There are many like him. And they're not stupid, either.' Then to my astonishment he said a little musingly: 'I don't know though, perhaps the boy is right, not trying to become what he's not. Perhaps he's living his life with dharm. He'll have less trouble between being and becoming.'

I opened my mouth and then shut it. Being and becoming! That sounded like some dark tome by some heavy German philosopher. It sounded dreary and involved and complex.

'What's dharma?' I said, instead; Gran had used the word too.

Grandpa harrumphed and shifted in his chair: 'That's not easy to explain,' he said. 'The English language has no word for it. Perhaps the best one can say is that it's, uh . . . the attitude with which you must live out your karm. Possibly . . . "right behaviour".'

'Oh that!' I said, immediately bored.

# 15

Grandma's salwar-kameez fit me like a bag. It was made of pale patterned cotton, and I looked dowdy in it. But I thought that was all right: it was best not to look too well-dressed amongst the villagers. I let the chunni loop modestly down the front and flung the ends around my shoulders.

I looked at myself in the long mirror on the cupboard: I looked like a stick. I sighed. For all my efforts I'd still look different: the locals didn't wear salwar-kameez. Salwar-kameez is a northern Punjabi dress, the local women wore their saris like pantaloons, but I couldn't possibly have dressed like that: I'd have felt fake, almost indecent with the cloth pulled tight between my bums. But I didn't feel indecent in my jeans. How strange clothes were!

Munnia came to fetch me at five. She was in a white sari with a red border worn straight, like a city woman. Her face was scrubbed. Her eyes were ringed with kohl. She wore flowers in her hair, and large silver earrings. Silver and glass bracelets and bangles tinkled on her wrists. Around her ankles were large, fat, silver anklets. She wore her wealth on her body; safer than safety-deposit boxes in banks, so she thought.

I got up from my chair on the verandah.

Bumpy got up too. 'I'm going with you,' he said.

I stared at him. 'But Bumpy!' I said in exasperation, 'we agreed you'd only join us for the procession to Maini, later.'

'I've changed my mind,' Bumpy said. 'These people go a bit crazy right here in the village before they set off.'

And he would hear no more argument. 'Don't take your handbag,' he said. 'I'll carry whatever we need. We don't want to encourage someone to snatch your purse.'

'Well, why don't you take Raja along to protect us, then,' I snapped. Although he said we were friends he really wasn't able to get over the fact that I was his little sister. Emphasis on *little*!

Gran called out: 'Now don't eat any rubbish. Bumpy's bringing tea in a thermos, and sandwiches.'

I turned and said: 'But Gran, the villagers have been fasting all day. Surely Bumpy and I can go without one meal.'

Bumpy said crossly: 'Oh for God's sake, Sheila. Grow up!' and thumped heavily into the house.

I didn't wait for him; I stormed off with Munnia.

Munnia picked up her jabbah pot from the courtyard of their house, and slung it on one hip, like a baby.

Shanti said: 'Baiji, take care of Munnia.'

'Aren't you coming?' I said, surprised.

'No, but *he* will go,' she replied, meaning Ram Milan, 'I'm getting too old and lazy.' She giggled.

There was a huge crowd gathered in the centre of Ahiran-ka-tolla, near the Krishna temple. Despite their festival finery, the villagers were a shabby-looking lot and I was glad I was dressed down, rather than up. They greeted me with deference, made some polite talk, and generally acted very gratified that I was there.

Mulloo swaggered by with a grin. Most of the men wore white pyjamas or dhotis, and white shirts; Mulloo was dressed like a peacock, with bright orange trousers and a pink striped shirt, the colour of which closely matched what should have been the whites of his eyes. He grinned and nodded and stood off inspecting the village girls clustered together in one corner, all in white, with their jabbah pots.

Then a drummer with a double-sided drum hanging by a strap around his neck, beat out a tattoo, both hands flying like dextrous flamenco feet. He began to dance, knees pumping sideways and up, feet hitting the floor, flat. He whooped two or three times and began to trot around in a circle, his head rolling, the drum swinging in arabesques. Gradually the crowd closed around in a circle three and four deep.

The drummer set up a thunderous crescendo: *dhug dhugi dhug dhug; dhug dhugi dhug dha, dhug dhugi dhug, dhug dhugi dhug, dhug dhugi dhug dha*.

People started clapping in time. The rhythm became intense. I felt my blood begin to respond.

Suddenly there was a howl. A man leaped from the ring of spectators. He fell on his knees, put his palms on the ground and began swaying his head in time to the drums. He moaned, flung his head back and began to roll his eyes. He howled again: 'Eee! Yaah, Heiyaah!'

I stepped back fearfully and bumped into Bumpy . . . and Grandpa! There was a general rustle and murmur as people realized Grandpa had come, and made space for him. Bumpy was wearing a white pyjama kurta and carrying a cotton sling-bag, a jhola, on one shoulder. The lips on his square face were set in a straight, grim line. Grandpa said wickedly into my ear: 'You bring out the *worst* in me, beti. I haven't been in the village for ten years. But my curiosity to see your reaction to this got the better of me.' I grinned at him. The man howled again.

'What's the matter with the man?' I said, glad in spite of myself, to see Bumpy and Grandpa.

'Nothing much,' Bumpy said caustically, 'this fellow's decided he's got the devil in him. Now he'll become holy for a while. After he's finished yelling and rolling around, people will start asking him questions and he'll foretell their futures.'

'And will he really be able to do that?'

'Probably not,' Grandpa said, 'but you can rationalize anything. If he's wrong, they'll think up some excuse to explain it away. As long as they can hold on to their beliefs.'

Bumpy grinned mirthlessly. The man rolled around on the ground as though he were having convulsions. Sweat dripped down his face. His eyes rolled up, so only the whites showed.

'Maybe he's just drunk,' I said, beginning to feel uneasy.

'Maybe,' Bumpy said.

'I think he needs a doctor,' I said, becoming anxious.

Grandpa said: 'They have their own way of dealing with these things, don't worry.'

Now the man began licking the dust on the ground.

'That's terrible,' I wailed, despite myself. And immediately stopped. I was behaving like a tourist!

And Grandpa said: 'You can't stop beliefs and rituals of this kind.' He tcchaed impatiently. 'Perhaps, somewhere, there's some sensible explanation like the worship of mother Earth – or Nature – but *this* is what it's become out of ignorance.'

Just then a woman began to howl. She fell on the ground inside the circle and began to beat her head with her hands.

'Now what!' I said, beginning to feel this was all too much.

Munnia beside me said: 'She's going into a trance.'

The woman went rigid and her eyes glazed. She began to speak in a high, keening whine.

After a while I asked Munnia what she was saying.

'She is saying she has been abused by her husband,' Munnia said. 'He beats her, he beats their children. He has stolen her dowry. Her mother-in-law works her like a slave. She says she is going to complain to Sharda Devi about her bad luck. She says she will cut off her tongue and offer it to Sharda Devi, and when her tongue grows back, she will know Sharda Devi will take revenge on her husband and mother-in-law.'

'Munnia!' I gasped, 'that's horrible!'

Grandpa said drily: '*There*'s your ritual and tradition, Sheila.'

The man had stopped rolling on the ground, licking the dirt. He was sitting wearily on the plinth below a tree, people crowding around him.

The woman wailed on and soon people stopped listening. There was a general restlessness in the crowd. The children drifted off in little groups. The girls in white began to gossip. Someone led the wailing woman away.

'What are we waiting for?' I said.

'Kali Mai,' Munnia replied.

'Some fellow from Rampur's been paid to dress up as Kali Mai,' Bumpy said. 'He's late. A priest will come with her, or rather him. There'll be prayers then the procession will start.'

We waited but no Kali Mai came.

A couple of men greeted Grandpa and began talking respectfully to him.

'Let's go home,' Bumpy said, impatient at the delay.

'You go,' I said rudely, 'I'm going to wait for Kali Mai.'

Bumpy sighed: 'These things are one big bore, Sheila,' he

said. 'They drag on and on. Munnia can call us if the Kali Mai turns up.'

I said: 'No,' and sat down on the plinth under the tree. I felt, suddenly, very distant from what was going on, and I found myself wishing I didn't feel such a stranger. Wishing I was another Lilavati or Munnia. Wishing I belonged to something. *Anything.*

Fifteen minutes later the drummer took up his drum, people drifted back and the singing and clapping began again.

And this time Mulloo fell into trance!

Bumpy said glumly: 'It's a guarantee he's going to be even more popular with the women tomorrow!'

Mulloo jigged around the circular space made by the ring of villagers, like a bandy-legged rooster, moving elaborately in time to the drums. He flapped his arms wildly and rolled his eyes; his tongue hung out of his mouth – he looked like a great ugly black fish out of water gasping desperately for air.

He yelled and staggered about, but he didn't fall down on the dirt: even in a trance he wouldn't dirty his pink striped shirt and orange trousers!

It was great entertainment. He was popular and everyone encouraged him heartily.

I felt queasy watching him. What would Barb and Janey think of all this? Perhaps Barb would enjoy it. But Janey would be embarrassed. She'd probably say: 'It's vulgar, really. Making a scene and showing off like that!' And I giggled at the thought. Phil would probably say, righteously, that this was the kind of heathen behaviour which was best converted to Christianity! And I felt a flicker of anger.

But after a while I whispered to Bumpy: 'I have to admit it's really a bit much.'

Surprisingly Bumpy said: 'Think of it as a purge, Sheels. It's an opportunity for people to air their grievances. People who do this are usually mentally healthier the rest of the year.' He sounded a bit like a psychology professor. 'Those who are unable to vent themselves like this, do it by proxy,' he paused, and said, 'so to speak.'

I looked at Bumpy, a little taken aback. It was an interesting explanation.

'Everyone needs to let go sometimes,' he went on again, 'move their arms and legs about like babies thrashing in a cot. Usually we so-called civilized, urban people turn this need for letting go into organized games and dances. These people go into trances. It's like Catholic confessions or psychological therapy taken to extremes. You could look at it like that.'

I thought of the exercises Dr Able had given me to deal with my anxieties. They too were a kind of 'thrashing of arms and legs like a baby in a cot'.

I looked around me at the villagers, thinking of Bumpy's explanation, and feeling a sort of bond with them. Under our veneers of culture, education, civilization – we really had the same bodies, the same nervous systems, the same anxieties and hostilities, the same needs.

I whispered to Bumpy a little uncomfortably: 'You'd have to be very . . . ah . . . brave to do this sort of thing publicly. You have to . . . er . . . admit your weaknesses . . . ah . . . I suppose you have to be willing to put up with what other people think about you.'

Bumpy said: 'Could you do it, Sheels?'

I countered it with: 'Could you?'

And for a brief minute we looked at each other like conspirators and laughed.

'Just imagine what people must be thinking about Mulloo,' I said. 'I couldn't take people seeing me as such a fool.'

Bumpy said: 'Perhaps they're not seeing Mulloo as a fool. Perhaps they're sympathizing with him. This kind of thing actually, I think, makes us all equal.'

I fell silent. I hadn't expected so much understanding from Bumpy. His resistance to my coming to the festival had made me think he wasn't even remotely interested in the people, but he'd been thinking away inside, exploring, understanding.

I looked at him from the corners of my eyes. We were of a kind, he and I, really. We *were*, after all, family.

At the height of Mulloo's trance, when he'd started shouting obscenities, the Kali Mai arrived.

She (he) was painted black from head to toe. White circles ringed her eyes, a red cardboard tongue pasted on to the lower lip, hung down to her chin. The mouth itself was painted into a hideous grimace. Two long white cardboard fangs dangled from the upper lip. This Kali Mai wasn't going to do much yelling! She was dressed in a long red skirt and blouse decorated with amazing gold and silver tinsel. Sticks painted white to resemble bones, and cardboard skulls painted white dangled from her neck and waist. Horns and a tinsel crown topped a wig of wildly disarranged hair. She carried silver-painted cardboard daggers and painted human heads in the throes of hideous death, with blood running down their faces, in extra cardboard hands at the ends of extra cardboard arms attached to her back like the wings of a nursery school angel. Glass bangles and brass anklets jingled and jangled as she moved.

A truly incredible sight!

With her came a paunchy priest in saffron robes with the regulation marks on his forehead, a smug expression on his face.

The crowd surged towards them, and poor Mulloo was quite forgotten.

The Kali Mai was bowed to and graciously led to a chair next to the Krishna temple. The priest sat down cross-legged on a mat in front of the temple. A small fire blazed in a charcoal brazier in front of him. Incense smoke coiled upward.

A bell was rung. A conch-shell blown. The priest began to chant. Every now and then he threw rice, flowers or sweet-meats into the fire. The villagers squatted around him, repeating stanzas.

Money piled up in front of the priest as people came to get his blessings. Grandpa, who'd joined us again, snorted: 'Easy money for the brahmins.'

The chanting went endlessly on. The Kali Mai forgot to look fierce. She began to doze.

Bumpy said: 'He must have been at a couple of other ceremonies before this. He looks a little ragged, isn't it?'

After a half hour, the priest stood up and the chanting rose in volume, as though someone had moved the setting on a hi-fi amplifier. The Kali Mai woke up with a start. The priest finished his prayers, collected his money, tucked it into a pouch, tucked the pouch into a belt under his shirt and waddled off, back to Rampur. Dazedly the Kali Mai got up to follow him. But the villagers held him/her back; they would get their money's worth!

She was shoved into the centre of a circle of people; a song was begun and the Kali Mai began to dance desultorily around, rattling a tin castanet, shaking the bones around her waist and neck. Occasionally she snarled and growled . . . the sounds coming out muffled behind the cardboard tongue and fangs.

Grandpa said: 'Did you know Kali Mai is the other face of Durga?'

'Who's Durga?' I said.

'Durga is another aspect of Parvati,' Grandpa said with a twinkle.

'And who is Parvati?' I said, falling right into it.

'The consort of Shiva . . .' Grandpa grinned.

I shook my head, dazed. 'And who's Shiva?'

Grandpa laughed aloud. 'Shiva's the other face of Vishnu.'

I glared at him. 'No, I'm not going to ask,' I said.

'It is quite complicated,' Bumpy said. 'I've never figured out what it all means.'

But I didn't care about the meanings. I was simply enjoying it all. I loved the fact that the villagers took all this so seriously.

'Soon Kali Mai will bless us,' Munnia said at my elbow, 'then we will start on the procession.'

The village girls were gathered together and shoved into the circle with Kali Mai. They placed their jabbah pots on their heads. The Kali Mai waved a spear over them to drive away all evil spirits. The drummer stopped beating his drum. The singing trailed away. And the Kali Mai sloped off towards Rampur.

'He's off to another ceremony,' Bumpy said. 'I hope his

cardboard tongue lasts through the evening. He'll probably make his entire year's living today.'

Ram Milan appeared, to escort Munnia on the procession.

People began to gather around, preparing for the procession.

And Grandpa said severely: 'Now, you stay with Bumpy, Sheila,' and went off home.

# 16

The crowds milled around; people shouted; some ran back to their huts to fetch things they'd forgotten; those who weren't going gave advice to those who were.

The men grouped in front, carrying kerosene lanterns, the flares glowing dully behind fat-bellied glass containers. The women in their festival finery followed. The village girls with their jabbah pots formed a giggling gaggle behind the women, and another group of men also carrying lanterns, brought up the rear like a protective rear-guard.

Bumpy and I fell in between the village girls and the rear-guard.

The voice of a lone woman, high and nasal, rose above the murmur of the group:

'Jai, jai mata, Kali maiyya, Durga maiyya, Sharda maiyya . . .'

Other female voices joined in. People started clapping and stamping their feet. Glass and silver bracelets and anklets jangled. The procession finally began to move at nine-thirty at night!

A high, clear, harvest moon hung in the black sky. The stars were out in a blanket of splendour. The hot, dry daytime winds which ripened the wheat had fallen, and a warm night breeze gently sifted through the huts.

We walked through Samli Village, turned right past the police station in Rampur on the road towards the Chhimaria plateau. Soon the outlying slums were behind us and we were on the open macadam road, heading east and south.

The women sang on.

'What are they singing?' I asked Munnia who was walking a little ahead of Bumpy and me with the village girls. I understood some of the words, but lost most.

'Praises to Sharda Devi, praises to Durga Mata, praises to

Kali Mai. Thanks for the beautiful harvest. Prayers for peaceful life,' Munnia said.

I turned to Bumpy: 'It's female goddess time, harvest, isn't it?'

Bumpy said generously: 'Well, I've read that agriculture was developed by women while men were out hunting, so – why not?' He was in a better mood, now.

'Do you think agriculture is really a woman's occupation?' I said, to provoke him a little. 'Is that why the men around here tend to be such layabouts? Because they can't get jobs doing other things?'

But Bumpy replied seriously: 'Probably. Our society is in transition – a gradual movement away from agriculture. But there's not yet enough of more industrial occupations to absorb the men. Not only that, the men aren't yet trained for other occupations.'

I thought of Ram Milan who felt so lucky he'd been trained from buffalo boy to tractor driver.

'But,' Bumpy went on, 'I think the kind of industrialization that's happening is all wrong for the country. We're a *very* agricultural people. And there's too many of us. There's one kind of economist who says population will be controlled only when the standard of living goes up. Which will happen when we become eighty per cent urban and twenty per cent rural, like America or Europe. But our ecosystems won't take the kind of industrialization which goes to make a high standard of living: we'll destroy our environment completely trying to do that. We've already destroyed our cities.'

'How's that?' I said, 'I thought Delhi was really pretty.'

Bumpy grunted: 'That's because you see only the better parts of Delhi. Delhi's over sixty per cent slums you know, made up of migrants from rural areas who are being pushed off their lands by large dams, huge factories, power stations.' He paused. 'Moneylenders, criminal politicians, rapacious land-lords . . . But you're right, Delhi's not so bad. You should see Bombay and Calcutta!'

I felt so stupid, hearing Bumpy talk so knowledgeably. I

seemed to know so little about India. I didn't say anything more.

We walked in silence for a while, listening to the villagers singing. Hundreds of crickets and frogs called from the grass verges of the road; a night bird flew overhead screeching; far off a dog howled; and in the distance, again, came the achha-chugga, achha-chugga, achha-chugga, of a train carrying its burden of humanity to the far corners of the country.

Then Bumpy said: 'A lot of us are beginning to think Mahatma Gandhi's way was the right way for India. More in tune with the rural psyche which is what most of India is. More conserving of the environment. Ecologically and spiritually sound. There's a strong environmental movement in the country now.'

To which I could only say vaguely: 'Oh, good.'

Talking to Bumpy and Grandpa made me feel truly ignorant, while talking to Tinkoo made me feel I was really, pretty intelligent.

Then, under the dark, spreading gulmohar trees lining the sides of the road, the village girls began a slow dance as they moved in circles and forward. It was a simple two step forward, one back and one to the side, their arms linked, their jabbah pots balanced securely on their heads on rings made of cotton and rope.

Mulloo, now recovered from his trance, fell back to encourage the girls. Those walking ahead of the girls turned and walked backward, singing and clapping. For a while all attention was on the girls.

The dance ended and Munnia fell in step with me, her face flushed, her eyes eager. Bumpy moved slightly off.

'*He* will be at the Sharda Devi temple,' she said secretively, meaning her husband Ram Prasad. 'He's coming with the procession from Jagalkond.'

'Do people come from all the villages in the area?' I asked.

'Yes,' she said happily. 'Not just from the villages. But also from the towns, some rich people also come from the cities. Sharda Devi grants many wishes.'

Lilavati, who seemed to be a friend of Munnia's, turned

148

around and said: 'They come also from the forests and the plateaux. Also from the Chambal Valley.'

'What do you mean?' I said.

'They say that at festival time even the dacoits come to the temples to pray and ask forgiveness for their sins,' Lilavati said.

I looked quickly around to see if Bumpy was listening. If she meant what she'd said, that would be the end of my little adventure. Bumpy would turn around and head us right back home, even though bandits were most certainly in the realm of fairy tales, like Sharda Devi granting wishes. But Bumpy was engrossed in a conversation with one of the men in the group behind us.

'And,' Munnia added, 'the priests welcome them and bless them.'

Lilavati said tartly: 'The dacoits leave a lot of money for the priests.'

'Are there still dacoits?' I said. 'I thought they'd all been rounded up.'

'There will always be dacoits,' Lilavati said simply, 'because there will always be injustice.'

We walked all night, sometimes singing, sometimes dancing. Sometimes resting on stones and parapets and sometimes running to catch up.

We met other groups at cross-roads. All groups carried lanterns and there were rows of little lights bunched together sporadically along all the roads in the flat landscape, dancing between trees or behind the occasional ruined chhatri. The night air was filled with the sound of songs and laughter and murmurous talk.

I have to admit I drank all the tea Bumpy had brought and ate all the sandwiches. Bumpy went without. And he stuck close by me, all the time, especially when Mulloo came to pay his respects.

'Ram Ram, Baiji,' he smiled greasily, falling into step with me.

'Ram Ram, Mulloo,' I said distantly.

'You're looking pretty fine dressed in girls' clothes, Baiji.'

'Thank you, Mulloo.'

'You should wear girls' clothes more often. There are enough men to wear pants in the world.'

'Thank you, Mulloo, I will remember that.'

'Are you enjoying the jabbah, Baiji?'

'Very much.'

'Do you have jabbah where you are living, in your foreign land?'

'No. No, we don't.'

'Aah! Baiji, what you are missing!' he shook his head sadly, grinning and clucking like a hen.

'Quite right, Mulloo,' I said, wanting him to vanish.

'Baiji,' Mulloo said, smarming atrociously, his wide, broad-lipped grin baring broken, uneven teeth smeared with beetle juice, 'why don't you take me with you, I will be your gardener. I will mend your fences. I am good at electricity.'

'Oh Mulloo!' I laughed, 'don't be stupid.'

'But Baiji,' he persisted, 'I can make a lot of money there. They say in foreign countries people become very rich.'

At which point Bumpy said: 'Enough Mulloo, you know very well Sheila Bai can't take you to England.'

'But Bhaiyyaji,' Mulloo insisted, 'I have to make money.'

'Why? So you can lose it all at satta?' Bumpy said drily.

'No, no. So I can get married!'

Bumpy snorted.

'What's satta?' I said.

'It's a numbers gambling ring, controlled from Bombay in relays by telephone. The whole country is hooked into it. It's the way most farmers lose their money – that is, if they haven't lost it to moneylenders, alcohol, the police or dacoits,' Bumpy replied bleakly.

Bumpy finally got rid of Mulloo. '. . . and you thought you could come on your own!' he said with an amused, almost superior look in his eyes.


It was close to four in the morning when we straggled through the streets of Maini.

My feet in my trainers were swollen and I was thirsty again. The sky was just beginning to hint at day over to the east. The temple was on top of a hill south of the town. Four hundred steps led to it, straight up the side of the hill. An incredible mass of people was gathered at the foot of the steps.

Traders were doing a smart business in garlands of marigolds and sweetmeats to offer the diety, beads and images of the Devi to take home. Great vats of tea were bubbling on stoves. Jalebis, pakoras, samosas were sizzling in huge pans of hot oil. People who'd been up to the temple were breaking their fast with gusto.

Behind the traders I could just make out the outlines of the funfair: wooden merry-go-rounds and roundabouts; donkeys, camels and an elephant which would carry children around on rides later in the day.

'Had enough?' Bumpy said.

'What do you mean?'

'I mean, do you really want to climb all those steps in this crowd?'

'Yes, of course! Why do you think I came all this way?' I said, piqued.

Bumpy sighed.

Munnia was looking anxiously around. 'I don't see him,' she whispered.

'Did you really expect to?' I whispered back.

'Well . . . no . . .' she said, 'we agreed to meet behind the temple, up there, after praying. But I thought, maybe . . .'

I punched her arm.

'Silly twit,' I said in English.

'What are you whispering about,' Bumpy said.

'Oh nothing,' I replied.

We started up.

The crowd jammed up the stairs in a more or less orderly way, but we were packed tight, moving slowly, jostled endlessly. Policemen at regular intervals along the steps kept one stream moving up, the other moving down.

The priest's voice came over the loudspeaker, chanting Sanskrit stanzas in a three-tone drone. The temple bells clanged at irregular intervals. It wasn't long before we were huffing like over-filled kettles.

'Who's this Sharda Devi?' I puffed at Bumpy, to keep from concentrating too much on the shoving.

'I believe she was the wife of a saint. She was also a holy lady, so when she died people gave her an aspect of Kali.'

'Why Kali?' I said.

'Why not?' Bumpy replied. 'It's as good as any.'

'Really, Bumpy,' I huffed. 'That's too confusing for words!'

We finally got to the top, all steamed up despite the fact dawn was only just breaking.

The stairs ended on a strip of raw earth which ran around the temple on the sides.

Beyond the strip of earth in front, four steps led up to a cement plinth. In the middle of this plinth stood a modest little temple, painted pink and green and blue. It followed the domes of the great temples of Khajuraho, vaguely in design, staggering up in receding layers like a small gold-plated wedding cake, but it was a poor thing considering the fuss made over it around the countryside.

Others straggled off to the flat ground behind the temple where, Munnia said, barbers would ritually shave the men and pierce the ears and nostrils of little girls.

Munnia was to meet her Ram Prasad under the old mango tree which leaned out over the hill back there.

'You don't really want to go into the temple,' Bumpy said resignedly.

'Yes, I do,' I said.

'Well, I'll wait here then,' he said, and he stopped below the plinth, to the right, and we left our shoes with him.

Munnia and I were shoved and pushed to the top of the plinth and towards the opening of the small temple. A priest's helper reached for Munnia's jabbah pot to heap it up with the others all around outside the temple on the plinth, but she jerked it away. 'I'll show it to Sharda Devi myself,' she sniffed. Many of the other girls just handed the pot up, not even climbing up to the temple; simply touching their fingers to the plinth and then their foreheads and turning away.

The image of Sharda Devi, what I saw of it in the hurry scurry, hustle and push, wasn't what one might call a thing of beauty. A block of wood or stone painted black with huge almond-shaped eyes on it, painted white, red cheeks and lips, draped in a red cloth lined with tinsel. That was all.

Heaps of flowers, money, offerings of sweets lay at her feet, curls of incense smoke snaked up in front of her. And on her right, wedged into the small space left by the Devi, a portly priest, chanted importantly into a microphone. His stomach bulged in sleek, well-fed folds over his saffron dhoti, a sacred thread slanted across his bare chest. He threw tiny bits of coloured powder, water and flowers towards the Devi, and with the other hand occasionally rang a little bell. Even the bell had a self-important sound to it.

Two policemen and two priests had the devotees moving in and out of the temple at a smart clip. Munnia just had time to ring the bell above her and wave the jabbah pot in front of the Devi before it was taken from her and we were hustled unceremoniously off the plinth, practically into our shoes below!

'Well?' Bumpy said, his lips twitching a little.

'Charming!' I said flatly.

But I was really enjoying myself. I was feeling connected, part of the process of village life. I was in love with these people! They had beliefs, traditions, rituals . . . They had certainty, they had the calm nerves and relaxed muscles which went with not having spasms of anxiety, doubts about the rights and wrongs of life. They had peaceful, positive thoughts – it was important to them to put mud pots with stalks of wheat in them in front of a black stub of wood on top of a hill in a temple which looked like burnt sugar pudding, to reach which you had to battle up four hundred steps!

I knew I couldn't become a villager like Munnia, but I could at least live in India. I could go to Delhi University and study . . . Politics . . . Social Science . . . And suddenly I was sure it was to be Social Science! I could then become a village social worker. Yes! That's what I would be, a social worker! I'd keep in touch with the real India, village India.

'Let's go,' Bumpy said.

'Where?'

'Down.'

'Oh no! I'm going with Munnia to the back,' I said.

'Why?'

'Oh, just to see,' I said. I couldn't tell him Munnia wanted to meet Ram Prasad.

'What?' Bumpy said, exasperated.

'The barbers and that,' I said irritably. 'As long as I'm here, I may as well do everything.'

Bumpy groaned: 'Let's go!' he said.

So we began to push our way to the ground behind the temple.

We reached the rows of barbers hard at work with old-fashioned razors on several stubby beards, and began to move towards the huge mango tree leaning over the hillside. Then, again, suddenly, there in that awful crowd of people all jammed up together, I felt that same lifting in my body I'd felt that evening as I went to Munnia's for tea . . . as I'd felt sitting under the tree in the field when the little boy came cursing his buffalo . . . as I'd felt when I'd first fallen in love with Jimmy. I floated out of myself. I became the temple, the people, the sounds, the hill. It was really peculiar – there seemed to be no pattern to this feeling that I could see.

'I think he's over there,' Munnia cried happily, pointing towards the mango tree. The feeling of lightness and union vanished.

'Who?' Bumpy said.

'No one,' I said quickly.

I was actually thinking about that passing feeling, thinking about social work, thinking I'd made the right decision when, over the clang of the temple-bell, the drone of the chanted hymns, the murmur of several hundred voices . . . clearly, came the sound of gunshots!

# 17

There were three distinct cracks. At first I thought a branch of the mango tree had fallen under the weight of people up it. For a moment no one else seemed to have noticed anything: the priest chanted on; the people shoved along; the barbers scraped chins.

Then someone ahead of us screamed. This was followed by several loud shouts and the sounds of a scuffle.

'They *shot* them!' someone yelled clearly, disbelievingly, in Hindi. And I felt a jolt below my ribs, as though I'd been hit.

There was the sound of rocks rolling down the side of the hill. People stood up and began to move towards the mango tree. Someone yelled: 'Stay back!' Another voice shouted: 'There! Down there!'

A harsh whisper jumped from person to person below the yells and screams and shouts, a name I couldn't catch. The back of my neck clenched, and I felt a spasm in my stomach. It was, for a moment, more terrifying than waking up on the worst morning.

With amazing alacrity Bumpy pushed his way forward and people jammed together immediately behind him. The crush of bodies began to sway. The movement of the crowd brought Munnia and me right to the edge of the flat top of the hill. We clutched each other to keep from being pushed over the side.

'Careful, Sheila Bai,' Munnia hissed. 'Hold on to me.'

'Munnia!' I cried. 'Hold on to me. Watch out. Push back!'

And for a moment we forgot everything but the need to keep our footing. I looked down apprehensively to gauge our chances if we were pushed down the slope.

Down below, dimly I could see four figures slither down the hillside. They were turbaned, dressed in dhotis and khaki shirts. They were headed towards a jeep parked on the path below. As I watched, the men reached the jeep, threw in something, that caught the early morning light and glinted.

The jeep was started. Faintly I could hear the engine rumble. Then, stumbling out of the cover of a clump of trees came a woman in a red sari. She put a foot against the side of the jeep, pulling her sari up above her knees, and held out a hand. A man reached out and pulled her in. The jeep roared off south on the dusty road, towards the plateau in the distance.

'Sheila! Where are you?' Bumpy's frantic voice came over the crowd.

'Here!' I yelled.

Bumpy came pushing and shoving back towards us. His face white, set in hard lines. 'Listen, I think there's going to be a riot. You'd better get on the plinth and sit near the entrance of the temple. Come on!' He grabbed my arm. I grabbed Munnia's. He pushed his way towards the plinth.

'Can you climb up?'

'Yes,' I said and hauled myself up on my palms. I pulled Munnia up by her arms while Bumpy gave her a shove from behind.

'Baiji!' It was Lilavati. I hauled her up.

'Stay in front,' Bumpy said, 'by the temple door where I can find you. Don't whatever you do, join the crowd! Don't try to get down the steps.'

'What's happened?' I said.

'Never mind. Go!' he yelled, and turning pushed his way towards the mango tree.

We could see over the heads of people by the mango tree but couldn't make out what they were crowding around. 'Let's go!' I said and grabbed Munnia and Lilavati by an arm each and pushed them towards the front of the temple.

Suddenly someone yelled clearly, loudly: 'My God! It was revenge!'

'Revenge!' The crowd took it up. People begun to turn and push and shove towards the front of the temple.

Someone screamed: 'He's dead!'

And in a moment there was a full-scale panic: people yelling, shoving, screaming.

Munnia turned back, pulling away from me: 'Who?'

'Never mind, who, Munnia! Come on! Do what Bhaiyya wants.'

We got to the front of the temple and I pulled Munnia and Lilavati down with me near the door, between the jabbah pots.

There weren't too many people on the plinth and those in front of the temple were beginning to join the frantic exodus down the steps.

People coming from the back of the temple surged past below the plinth in full flight, down the steps.

Shouting, jostling, shoving, inevitably people fell, and were trampled. Children cried. Women screamed. The din rose to a terrifying crescendo.

'Murder!'

'Revenge!'

'Run!'

'Dacoits!'

Lilavati sucked her breath in sharply: 'Dacoits!'

I could see the policemen struggling like flotsam in a mountain stream, their heads and arms bobbing as they tried to control the crowd.

Munnia clutched my arm, her eyes wide: 'Let's get away from here!'

'Are you mad?' I said. 'Do you want to be hurled down four hundred steps? We stay here.'

'But, Baiji,' Lilavati said fearfully, 'maybe the dacoits will come and shoot us also.'

'Don't be stupid!' I said impatiently. 'Don't get hysterical!' I wondered fleetingly whether I wasn't really talking to myself. I, too, just wanted to run.

Mulloo reached us, struggling through the crowd below the plinth. 'Baiji,' he shouted, the screen hero in his moment of glory. 'The dacoits are still behind the temple! Let's go!'

'No,' I said, wavering. 'Don't panic! Stay here with us.' I patted the plinth below me.

'Haré Ram!' he screamed, his eyes popping. He stood for a moment undecided, and then he disappeared into the thrashing, shrieking crowd. I saw him sidestep the stairs and begin to slither down the side of the hill.

Munnia and Lilavati had stood up when Mulloo appeared. I pulled them down. 'Sit,' I said sternly, pulling rank for the first time. But it was an act. Every cell in my body wanted to join that mad rush down the steps.

Now the chanting and bell ringing stopped. The priest came out of the temple and hurried around the plinth to the back.

The frenzied rush down the hill had thinned when Bumpy came around the side of the temple, drained. 'We'll leave in a minute,' he said, watching the crowds.

'What happened, Bumpy?' I said, in English.

'Three men shot,' he replied briefly, very upset.

I staggered up. 'Three men? Really shot? Are they dead?' He nodded.

'D . . . d . . . do you know who did it?' I stammered.

'Bijli and her men. They came up the other side of the hill and were waiting behind the rocks,' Bumpy said flatly.

Munnia caught the name. 'Bijli!' she whispered fearfully.

'Bijli?' I said. Bijli? The bandit woman we'd been talking about just the other day? I couldn't believe it. This sort of thing didn't happen in real life! It was a fairy tale!

'What happened, Sheila Bai?' Munnia said. She was pale. 'What is Bhaiyyaji saying?'

'He's saying it was Bijli who shot some people,' I said, still feeling the whole thing was unreal.

'Haré Ram!' Lilavati said.

'Bijli!' Munnia said softly.

'Some of the men saw her,' Bumpy said.

'But . . . but . . . that's crazy!' I said to Bumpy. 'Why would this bandit woman wait behind a temple to kill off a few men?'

'They say she's still looking for the man who betrayed Bhanupati Ram,' Bumpy said irritably.

'Who's that?' I said stupidly.

Bumpy looked at me, exasperated. 'Never mind,' he said. 'I'll tell you later. But it seems she came to pay her respects to Sharda Devi,' he was almost sneering with anger. He stopped for a moment, caught his breath and calmed down. 'She came up the back way. She was dressed in a sari and wasn't carrying

158

a gun, because the police were here, but she kept her men hidden in the bushes in case there was trouble.' He drew a long wavering breath. 'Evidently, she saw some ahirs loitering around at the back,' he went on, 'and began questioning them. One of them recognized Bijli, and started to shout. And her men shot three of them.'

I shook my head slowly. 'Bumpy, I can't *believe* this!'

Bumpy said heavily: 'You may not want to believe it, Sheila, but I saw Bijli and her men get in a jeep below the hill and make off.'

I turned on him, astounded. 'You *saw* them, Bumpy?'

I felt really jolted. I'd seen several men and a woman running towards a jeep below the hill. If he had seen them, had I seen them too?

Bumpy said, beginning to get angry, again: 'Sheila, I didn't see them this close. But they certainly were running like hell from something. I *did* see a woman amongst them. I *did* see rifles. They *did* go off in a jeep. There *was* shooting and there *are* three men dead back there.'

He looked around at the last of the crowds. 'Okay, now let's go,' he said.

But I clutched his arm. 'You mean they really were bandits? And the woman was Bijli?' The world was really beginning to seem mad . . . like some clichéd Hindi film full of co-incidences, melodrama and gaudy characters.

Bumpy tcchaed impatiently.

Just then, the priest came trotting back. 'You are wearing shoes,' he said, flickering a look downward, and disappeared into the temple. He came out with a brass pot and incense, muttering: '*Om svahah, Om svahah,*' and shaking his round head worriedly. He went down the steps and around the back of the temple below the plinth.

Just then Ram Milan came around the other side of the temple. He looked shell-shocked.

'Bhaiyyaji,' he croaked, 'please come here.'

'Wait here,' Bumpy said and went around the side of the temple with Ram Milan.

I sat down again.

'Are they dead?' Lilavati said.

'I believe so,' I said.

'Who were they?' Munnia said, her voice very low.

'No one knows,' I said.

We sat in silence for a while. Munnia kept staring at me, her eyes huge. Bumpy came back around the corner.

'Sheila,' he said oddly, 'just come here.'

I got up.

'Where are you going?' Munnia said, suddenly grabbing my hand, with a look of abject pleading on her face.

'Nowhere,' I said. 'Just wait. I'll be back. Bhaiyya wants me.'

'No!' Munnia cried. She was looking unnaturally pale.

'Munnia!' I said impatiently. 'Stop acting like a baby. I'll be right back.' I shook my hand free. 'Here, Lilavati, stay with her.' I went around the corner.

Ram Milan was squatting on his haunches, his back against the temple wall, sobbing, trying to keep his voice down, with the end of his shirt up against his face.

'What's the matter?' I said.

Bumpy said softly: 'It's Ram Prasad. He was one of the men killed.'

For a moment the name didn't register. Then: 'God! Munnia's husband?' I groped for the wall, feeling I'd been hit in the stomach. 'Are you sure?'

He nodded.

'Oh God!' I whispered again, and stared at the floor.

'You'll . . . er . . . you'll have to tell Munnia,' Bumpy said hesitantly.

'Oh God!' I said again.

We stood silently. Bumpy staring into the glowing eastern sky where a new day was breaking in sheets of orange.

Then Munnia came slowly around the corner.

'What is it?' she whispered, looking fearfully at us. She took in Ram Milan crouching on the ground, weeping, Bumpy's face, my drooping shoulders.

'What is it, Bhaiyya?' she repeated.

'Munnia . . .' I said, and stopped.

'No!' The scream seemed to rise from her bowels and tear, jerking and jangling right through her. She began to run frantically towards the back of the temple.

Bumpy grabbed her arm. 'No, Munnia, it's no good, don't go.'

'It's *him*, isn't it? He's been hurt . . .' Munnia cried, struggling to free herself. 'Please, Bhaiyya, he's been hurt . . .'

Bumpy shook his head, holding her now by both arms. 'No,' he said.

'I was going to meet him . . .' she whispered.

'It's no good,' Bumpy said roughly.

Then a look of terrible pleading came over her face. 'Bhaiyya!' she screamed. 'What are you saying?'

I stepped forward: 'Munnia . . .' I said.

She whipped around: 'Bhaiyya, *what is* it?'

I found it hard to make the words come: 'Munnia, he's . . . Bijli . . .'

'No! no! no!' she shook her head wildly, struggling. Ram Milan got up to help Bumpy hold her. Munnia looked at her father's face. She stopped struggling and whispered: 'He's dead?' She sounded like a child looking wonderingly at a very strange and beautiful flower. Then, without a word she collapsed.

Ram Milan and Bumpy lowered her to the ground and I sat down quickly and took her head in my lap.

'She's unconscious,' I said stupidly.

'Then leave her,' Bumpy said wearily. 'I'll go down and see if Papaji . . . We'll go and take the body . . .' He set off at a run around the temple.

The priest came from the front of the temple and saw the tableau.

'A relative?' he said.

I nodded dully: 'Her husband.'

He squatted down and stroked Munnia's head. 'Poor child, poor child,' he said, 'what bad karma.'

I stared at his pudgy, greasy face, and suddenly as though from some fearful depth, through the confusion which surrounded me, I was screaming: 'Karma? Is that all you can say? Her husband's been killed and all you can say is it's her karma?' My broken Hindi with its ridiculous North London accent rang obscenely in my ears.

The priest clucked: 'Beti, beti, don't be so upset. The body dies but the spirit is eternal,' he said gently.

And all the calm enforced during the crisis gave way completely and I screamed. All the passion and pent-up anger building inside me for all these months, took over uncontrollably: 'Get away from here, you stupid . . . bloody . . . fool! Don't give me that stupid religious Hindu horseshit! Get out! You . . . you . . . Shut up! Shut up! Shut up!' I reverted to English under pressure and the priest didn't seem to understand. Fortunately . . . I suppose. I calmed down after a while, still shaking and said: 'Jao, jao, jao. Bus. Humko chodo.' Leave. Enough. Let us be.

The priest stood up ponderously, sighing: 'Hari Om, Hari Om, Hari Om,' and waddled off.

Lilavati who had come around the corner when Munnia began to scream, sat down beside us. 'She knew it, I think, when you went,' she said quietly. Then she bit her lip, sobbing quietly: 'Haré Ram, Haré Ram, Haré Ram.'

Ram Milan now got himself under control and took Munnia's head from me. I got up and walked shakily to the back of the temple. There was a small knot of people and two policemen around the three bodies which had been covered by saris or sheets . . . or someone's dhotis . . .

I went back to Munnia. She had recovered consciousness, but was sitting propped up against the temple wall, her eyes glazed, staring at nothing.

I squatted next to her and took her hand.

'Munnia,' I said.

She didn't move or look at me. She seemed to be in deep shock.

Lilavati said: 'Leave her be, Baiji.'

The ahirs from Samli Village had come back up the hill. The word had already spread. They began to arrive at the side of the temple. They squatted around us on the plinth. Others sat below. They murmured and clucked for a while, then some of the older women started wailing. One or two others joined her. They cried, long and expressively. They bewailed Munnia's fate, decried Ram Prasad's passing. They began pulling their hair, rocking back and forth, squatting on their haunches. It was, I realized later, an attempt to de-freeze Munnia, to get her to cry, to bring up the grief and express it. Another ritual like the trances at the village. But at the time I only felt sick. I could feel spasms grip my arm and clench my diaphragm. I couldn't take this public expression of feeling. I couldn't accept it. I knew I was, in this, very English. Sheila . . . and English name . . .

I got up and stumbled to the front of the temple to wait for Bumpy. The lines of devotees had formed again, though sparser than before. News of Bijli's retreat had spread. Inside the temple, the priest was warbling placidly away. The bell clanged overhead, the jabbah pots were blessed and placed against the outer wall. Now people walked to the side to pause, look at Munnia, cluck sympathetically, shake their heads and move on to the back of the temple and repeat the process over the bodies. Relatives of the dead men, the police and ahirs from Samli kept the people moving along. But no one made any effort to keep anyone away. Participation to its fullest in all aspects of life was the way here.

The greatest soggy maw of fatalism and resignation was covering the event! The tragedy had made as much of a ripple as a pebble dropped into a vast scummy lake, causing small concentric circles, widening to join, and disappearing into, the generalized ache of living.

I rubbed my arm and shivered, despite the fact that the morning sun had gone from about ten minutes of dawn glory to fiery white-hot in a pale blue sky.

Fate! Destiny! Fatalism! Karma! I *couldn't*, I *wouldn't* accept it!

Bitterness flooded through me. I couldn't be that Indian. I couldn't, I just couldn't. I *wasn't* that *Indian*!

# 18

I woke just before tea. For a moment I couldn't focus on anything. Then I heard the subdued murmur of voices on the verandah and realized I was in my room. Everything came back in a heavy rush. I still jangled from the instinctive howl, like that of a lone wolf, that Shanti had set up when she saw Ram Milan help Munnia off the jeep, this morning. Like an absolute coward, I'd simply bolted then, locked myself in my room and 'gone unconscious' as Dr Able called it.

Inder Uncle and Bumpy must be back from Jagalkond, I thought drearily, and dragged myself out to the verandah.

Nobody said much at tea. Inder Uncle and Bumpy had gone back to Maini after bringing us back to the farm. It had taken them all their power and persuasion and all the clout they could muster to get the local Inspector of Police to release the body to them, in order to get it to Jagalkond before it rotted in the heat. The families of the other two men had had to use the Maini cremation grounds.

'What did you have to pay the police for the body?' I said bitterly.

Inder Uncle and Bumpy just glanced at each other and said nothing.

'And now I suppose the police are going all out to hunt down the killers,' I went on, astonished at my capacity for sarcasm.

Bumpy shrugged. 'You met Harish,' he said. 'That's the police.'

'Now, now, *beta*,' Inder Uncle said wearily, unenthusiastically. 'Not all the police are corrupt.'

Bumpy didn't even bother to reply.

'Would you walk with me, Bumpy?' I said, after a silent, unhappy tea. He agreed, and we started out towards the tractor path on the right side of the fields.

But I couldn't say anything.

'You're not blaming yourself, Sheila?' Bumpy said gently

after a little while. 'It would have happened whether you were there or not, isn't it?'

I nodded, blinking back tears.

'As it was, it was a good thing we were there,' he said.

I nodded again.

'So what's on your mind?'

I swallowed a couple of times. 'T-t-tell me about Bijli,' I said finally. 'I asked Tinkoo and he gave me a lecture on the revolution.' I smiled wanly.

'So it's Bijli that's bothering you?' Bumpy said.

'Yes,' I said, and shook my head. 'Why . . . why would . . .'

'I know,' Bumpy said, hunching his shoulders, 'I know.' Then after a bit: 'Well, I'll try to give you some sense of what happens to make people do this.' He gathered his thoughts some more. 'Bijli means "electricity" . . . no, really it means "lightning" because she's so quick. Her real name is Bhagmati. She's Mangal Bai's sister. Mangal Bai didn't manage to find the man who informed on Bhanupati Ram, so Bijli's completing her vendetta . . .'

I tcchaed irritably. 'Hang on, a minute,' I said. 'Slow down, Bumpy. Who's this Mangal Bai? Start at the beginning. I'm confused.'

Bumpy grinned lopsidedly. 'I keep forgetting you have such gaps, Sheila. So, from the beginning.' He hunched his shoulders again. 'Mangal Bai's real name is Phoolvati. They're ahirs from UP, north of us. She was married off at eleven, as they usually are.

'It's the usual sad, stupid story: the parents marry off daughters to get rid of them, yet hoping they'll be secure for the rest of their lives, and it works out just the opposite.

'Phoolvati's husband was twenty years older than her, and a small-time crook. He was involved in some trouble or other, and got on the wrong side of this Bhanupati Ram, who was a well-known dacoit.

'Well, Bhanupati Ram killed Phoolvati's husband and kidnapped her. She was only fourteen or so at that time. She became Bhanupati's . . . er . . . mistress. They lived in the Chambal Valley and she cooked for him and . . . ah . . . all that.

'Then some other dacoit killed Bhanupati. Revenge for something or other. For a while people thought Bhanupati's gang would fall apart. But to everyone's surprise, Phoolvati took over. She changed her name to Mangal Bai, because Bhanupati was killed on a Tuesday. Mangal means Tuesday.' He paused. 'It also means fun, joy, celebrations and laughter,' he said drily, and went on: 'She caught the rival gang in their hideout and shot them all as they slept. In cold blood. They didn't have a chance.' He sounded queerly satisfied.

'Then she went after the man who'd betrayed Bhanupati. She killed off quite a few men whom she suspected of being the informer, wiping out all the men in several villages, often ahirs. Caste ties didn't seem to matter at all. But then there was this government offer, and many dacoits gave themselves up. And, eventually, Mangal Bai was cornered. Her men surrendered . . . And she's still in the lock-up waiting trial, which keeps getting delayed – Indian style,' he said bleakly. 'Then recently she was, ah, gang-raped in her cell by the police . . .'

I stopped and stared at him.

'Oh Bumpy!' I felt I was shrivelling up inside, tears of desperation starting up in my eyes. Is it always so . . . horrible? Is nothing ever fair?'

And Bumpy put his arm around my shoulders. 'Poor Sheila,' he said, 'poor Sheels.' We stood there on the bund like that for a few moments. Then he said: 'Good things do also happen, Sheels. But this is a very *raw* country, with terrible disparities.'

He dropped his arm and we walked in silence. After a bit, I said: 'Go on.'

'They say that Bhagvati, that's Bijli, Mangal Bai's sister, went crazy when she heard her sister had been er . . . in the lock-up,' Bumpy said. 'She collected a gang of dissatisfied youths. Mostly from slums around small towns, and formed a gang. Mangal Bai's a sort of legend, you see. And people believe in the bonds of blood, and family honour and revenge. Bijli's gang have torched three police stations, murdered several policemen. I believe she got the men who raped her sister . . . *and* their sons. And now she's looking for the fellow who betrayed Mangal Bai's lover, Bhanupati Ram. And that's what she was doing at the Sharda Devi temple.' He smiled crookedly and raised his hands, palms up and shrugged. 'And that's the story,' he said.


At dinner Gran said: 'Munnia's still in shock. She hasn't said a word all day. I'm worried about her.'

'Did you tell the women not to start their wailing until Munnia's ready?' Grandpa said.

Gran nodded.

I have to admit, that while Gran had suggested that I not go and see Munnia just yet, I really didn't want to either. I didn't think I could stand it. I felt stretched out on a thin wire myself: what use would I be?


The next evening, Munnia began to scream.

I hadn't had the nerve to see her all day. Gran had been: there had been no change. Until the evening . . .

Her screams rang out, high and curdled. We heard Ram Milan shout and Shanti cry. There were sounds of struggle.

And all together, Bumpy, Inder Uncle and I sprang out of our chairs on the verandah and ran for the servants' quarters.

A crowd had already begun to form. Inder Uncle began shooing them away.

Munnia was inside the front room. Shanti was holding her hands and Ram Milan had pinned her legs down. Munnia's head rolled and jerked. Spittle ran out of her mouth and she screamed continuously. She looked utterly wild.

Instinctively, I shrank back.

Gran came bustling in with a bottle of tranquillizers and got two down Munnia's throat. Bumpy tried pouring water into her mouth, but she thrashed around too much.

'I should wipe her face with a wet cloth,' Gran said.

'Here let me do it,' I said, wanting to be helpful. I wrung out a small towel in water from their water pot and handed it to Gran who wiped Munnia's forehead.

Gradually Munnia quietened, still dry-eyed, and finally fell asleep.

'She needs a doctor,' Inder Uncle said from the doorway.

'The kind she needs you won't find in Rampur,' Gran said. 'Anyway, even if you did find a psychiatrist, he'd probably just dose her with tranquillizers too.'

'I don't think she should have too many of these,' I said doubtfully.

'Until she's over the worst, it's probably all we can do,' Gran said. She gave Shanti instructions to give Munnia two more the moment she began to stir. It was best if Munnia was just knocked out for a while.

We left, feeling useless and depressed.


In the middle of the night we were woken by unearthly yowls and yells.

Munnia had woken up and found everyone asleep. She had poured a tin of kerosene over her clothes and set herself on fire.

Ram Milan, sleeping lightly, feeling restless, had woken up just as her sari caught and had had the sense to knock her down, roll her on the ground and stamp out the flames with his feet which were now burnt and blistered.

We gave Munnia more tranquillizers, thankful she'd not burnt herself too badly. Only a few blisters around her ankles.

And Gran, looking at my face, insisted I take one too. I'd managed all my own problems without them. But I was grateful for one that night.

The next morning Munnia started weeping in earnest, and everyone sighed, with relief. Women began trickling in from the ahir village and the ritual wailing was begun again. They cried, beat their heads, bewailed Munnia's fate and Ram Prasad's. They repeated the story of Munnia's life, her marriage, her love and her hopes and dreams and losses over and over. They kept Munnia crying, beating her breast, tearing her hair, purging herself until she was exhausted.

They kept it up for three days. No psychiatrist, I thought, could have done a more complete job of getting Munnia to cry it all out.

But every day my own feelings became more confused. My thoughts more bitter. Nothing had made sense in London. I'd thought I'd find sense here, with tradition; safety, and surety.

I had been envious of Munnia! I had begun to find in her life, some reason and sanity! Look at Munnia now! Wasn't her breakdown more complete because she'd been so certain? Was uncertainty, doubt, fear, shock all one could expect from life? I felt I was clinging to a frail boat on a wild, rough sea with no place to dock.

Finally one morning Ram Milan and Shanti decided Munnia could stand a trip to Jagalkond, to drive home her loss. Grandpa let Hariram drive them all over in the jeep.

And peace returned to the farm.

Bringing with it a silence in which my own clamourous thoughts grew louder by the minute.

I realized I hadn't told anyone about Jimmy. Not even Janey or Barb back in London, though I'm sure they'd guessed.

Why? Was it shame? Shame at having put my trust in an English boy, and having been let down? Or perhaps it was more? But what? I couldn't see it.

Perhaps that's what I needed to do: tell someone, cry openly, purge myself.

I felt empty and lonely: I had no tradition to help me release my feelings the way Munnia had. Dad was always joking, never able to talk seriously for too long. Mum seemed always a bit awkward. She didn't really invite confidences at all. We simply weren't as open to emotion as the peasants were here. We were more . . . civilized! How my lip curled as I thought that . . . sneering almost. Perhaps yelling and wailing was the way to be sane. Emotionally stable.

I thought of Dr Able's exercises. That I usually cried to myself after I did them. I hadn't shared my feelings at all.

With anyone! Was *this* what it meant to be middle class, and suburban. How direct Munnia's people were. They weren't educated, but they were so much more in touch with the basics of life. But *we* were educated. *We* were *civilized*!

# 19

I caught up with Grandpa as he set off on his evening rounds in the fields the next day.

'Clearing your head in the fresh air, eh beti?' he said with a faint smile, as I fell in step with him.

I wanted to tell him about Jimmy, Sunaina, Rachna. To say how shattered I felt about Ram Prasad's death and Munnia's breakdown. I wanted to put my head on his shoulder and weep. Instead I said, trying to sound casual: 'Grandpa, you remember I told Lilavati we were chamars, and she said we couldn't be, because our karma was too good?'

'I remember,' Grandpa said sombrely. 'I enjoyed that.'

'Well,' I said, 'the priest at the Sharda Devi temple said . . . said . . .' I faltered, 'Munnia had *bad* karma!'

Grandpa grunted and frowned and tapped the earth with his cane a little harder.

'Grandpa,' I said, beginning to lose my thin layer of control almost immediately, 'I don't understand this karma business. You said it had to do with our past lives. But how does that follow? What has Ram Prasad's past life to do with his getting killed by mistake like that?' I stopped and bit my lip unhappily. 'Or Munnia's past life. What has that to do with Ram Prasad getting killed, and her cracking up? I feel so . . . wiped out by all this, Grandpa. Why should *I* be affected by Ram Prasad's past life, for God's sake! What has it to do with *my* past life?' I heard my voice getting louder and I stopped and tried to control it. 'It just sounds like a load of horse manure, Gramps,' I cried. 'A way to justify what's happening and do nothing. I bet the police said: "Well, it's Munnia's karma that Ram Prasad was killed. So we don't have to do anything about it!"' I was breathing hard, all wound up. 'It's fatalistic, Gramps! How can any religion allow this!'

Grandpa glanced at me and after a small silence, he put his arm around my shoulder and patted my arm as we walked.

'It's very confusing, isn't it, beti?' he said a little sadly.

'Make it make sense, Gramps,' I said tightly. 'I want to understand. My head feels like it's got a thousand knots in it.' I unclenched my fists and drew slow hard breaths to calm myself.

Grandpa took his arm off my shoulder, passed a finger over his moustache, and thoughtfully rubbed his nose, looking at me speculatively as we walked side by side. Then he grunted and sighed noisily. 'The older I get and the more I learn, the less I think I know,' he said eventually. 'I don't know whether I can give you any final answers, beti, or whether what I have to say will satisfy you. But, I'll try . . .'

We walked on in silence for a bit, while he gathered his thoughts. Then he said: 'It's a very misused word, karma. Misinterpreted, misunderstood. Even mispronounced. It's really "karm", not "kaarmaa".' He flashed a quick look at me and went on: 'There's nothing really fatalistic about karm.' He cleared his throat. 'There are many explanations of it. The one that makes most sense to me is a very simple one: it's an observation of natural phenomenon. Karm is the law of cause-effect. You understand cause-effect?'

I hesitated, I'd read about it somewhere, I was sure. In physics? I couldn't remember. 'You mean,' I said tentatively, 'like everything has a consequence? Like every action has a result?'

Grandpa nodded, looking at me. 'Every action has a consequence. Every thought has a consequence too. Some consequences are felt very quickly.' He looked down and prodded my foot sharply with his cane. I gave a small 'ouch', and hopped away. Grandpa's eyes twinkled momentarily. 'And some consequences take longer: the strands are more complex to follow, the issues are more involved.' Then, smiling slightly and looking away he said: 'Like the cause of your coming here, so suddenly.' I could feel my face flush, but he turned and walked on. 'And some consequences take several lifetimes to become clear. For instance take the ah . . . Hindu-Muslim ferment going on in the country. It's the consequence of the first Ghaznavid invasions in the eleventh century, and whatever caused *them* . . . plus the results of the divisive policies of the British Raj . . . plus the results of modern reactionary misinterpretations of the meaning of religion.' He glanced at me to see if I'd understood.

I said: 'Is that it? Just cause-effect?' I felt a bit let down.

Grandpa nodded.

'But, that doesn't *say* anything, Gramps,' I said. 'It doesn't help. I mean, can we say to Munnia, "It's all cause-effect, Munnia, so be brave"?'

Grandpa nodded as though he were reluctantly agreeing with me: 'No, it doesn't help,' he said, 'any more than it helps to throw a little light on your path to illuminate it. Your path is full of pot holes, anyway.'

We walked on. Grandpa said nothing while I absorbed this. Everything was very green and peaceful around us. The tractor throbbed quietly over to the left. Vaguely, I saw the little black birds swoop into the fields, the egrets stalk disdainfully along the furrows, looking for worms and insects.

'But, Gramps,' I said at last. 'I thought you said karm . . .' I couldn't get it quite right, 'karma had something to do with reincarnation . . . our *own* past lives. That means something Munnia did in her *past* life is making her suffer in *this* life, I can't believe that, Gramps. What proof is there that we *were* born before? That's just crazy.'

Grandpa grunted, and said a little drily, 'That's what's so wonderful about the Indian mind, beti. You don't have to believe in reincarnation for the law of cause-effect to work. If cause-effect is true now, then it extends logically back to the beginning of time itself, doesn't it?'

I clucked impatiently. 'Gramps, all right. Maybe cause-effect is valid. But where's the proof that *we're* born again?'

Grandpa stroked his beard contemplatively and nodded. 'It's hard to prove we're born again and again, that's true,' he said. 'Our consciousness is so shallow; we remember so little even about our past in *this* life, don't we? But there have been reports of very young children identifying people and places they'd known earlier. And because they were so young the

173

earlier time couldn't have been in their present lives. You may have read about such instances?'

I shook my head.

'It's documented though,' he said. 'Then there are people who've had near death experiences, and have come back to tell what it was like leaving their bodies, of glimpses of what it's like after death.' He glanced at me from below his brows. 'But in our scientific age, where everything has to be proved before it's believed, all this enters the realm of the paranormal, doesn't it? So, living in this rational world, we say it's all nonsense.'

Of course it's all nonsense, I thought, but I said: 'Do *you* think it's nonsense, Gramps?'

Grandpa grunted: 'To be quite honest, beti, I don't know *what* to believe any more. But – I'd say it has to be disproved before I'd completely disbelieve it. I don't think Western science has proved itself sufficiently for me to disbelieve the non-provable explanations of reality.'

I kicked a stone on the bund and watched it roll into the field, disappear into a furrow of the earth. 'But Gramps, how does it *help* to believe in reincarnation? I mean *why* believe in it? Isn't it possible to solve the problems of *this* life, *in* this life? Find the . . . uh . . . cause in *this* life? Why blame it on past lives or the stars and that?'

Grandpa stopped and looking soberly at me said: 'Then, beti, tell me, what has Munnia done to deserve her husband getting killed before she became a wife? For what sin is she being "punished" by this suffering? What had Ram Prasad done, for his life to be finished, just like that? What have you done, or I done to suffer with Munnia and Shanti? Is there a rational explanation for this?'

I stared at him and bit my lip. Then, hesitantly, I shook my head, lowered my eyes, and hunched my shoulders a little. Grandpa sighed and cleared his throat and walked on.

'It gives you a . . . longer view of things, to believe in reincarnation,' he said reflectively. 'The broader our views are, perhaps, the more able we are to make some sense of our experiences.'

We walked on in silence.

'Grandpa,' I said after a while, 'the priest said Munnia shouldn't be so upset, because only the body dies – the spirit is eternal.' I stopped, fighting the rush of anger the memory triggered. 'It's all very well to talk about the spirit, Gramps, but I can't imagine he really expects Munnia to console herself on Ram Prasad's spirit. Or her own. It's as though if I were to lose a leg in an accident I should say, "Oh well, never mind, my spirit's undamaged anyway". I mean . . .' I went on, my voice rising, 'I can't *feel* my spirit, Gramps. But I *can* feel the pain where my leg's gone. It's much more real. My spirit doesn't stop the pain . . .' I swallowed, trying to keep the tears back.

Grandpa harrumphed and thumped his cane a little harder as we walked, and then said quietly: 'Again, it's the long view, Sheila, the long view. Let's see if I can make it clearer.' He paused. 'Can you answer the question "What am I?" – or "Who am I?" '

'What am I?' I said, surprised.

Grandpa nodded: 'Or who?'

'Are you serious, Gramps?'

He nodded again.

I was sure there was a catch to it. After a bit I said, hesitating: 'I'm Sheila Mehta, Gramps.'

And Grandpa smiled: 'But that's just a name, Sheila beti, a label, isn't it?' Ah! there *was* a catch! He looked at the ground and frowned. 'Let's see if I can remember that quote. Ah! "A rose by any other name would still be a rose." You have heard it?'

I nodded doubtfully. But I said: 'All right, I agree. I could have been called Usha or Asha and still be me.' I smiled a little.

'So, who or what are you?' Grandpa said.

This was going to be a bit of a game, obviously. I could do with a bit of distraction, I thought, just to stop thinking about Munnia. And later I realized that's just what Grandpa intended. 'All right then, I'm my body.' I looked at my hands. 'I'm my body, all right!'

Grandpa nodded. 'And is that all you are? Are you sure?'

'Of course I'm sure,' I said, spreading my arms, looking down at my legs. 'Here I stand. Sheila Mehta in person.'

Grandpa glanced at me, raised an eyebrow and tapped the earth below him with his cane. 'Would you agree that your body is made of matter? Like water and salts and minerals and cellulose, and chemicals. Tissue, muscle, bones, water . . . all matter?'

'Ye-e-es,' I said slowly, 'stuff like that.'

Grandpa waved his stick at the fields. 'Like the trees and birds, and rocks and earth?'

'Yes,' I said, again, doubtfully, 'different kinds of matter: feathers and leaves and pebbles . . . but neutrons and protons and cells and that, way underneath.' All that biology and chemistry and physics were of some use after all, I thought.

'What makes you different to, say, a tree or a dog?'

'Oh,' I said at once, 'that's easy. Trees and dogs don't think. Man is a thinking animal.' This was junior school stuff!

Grandpa grunted: 'Or so we believe. But yes, we humans have a unique capacity for thought. So, are you your thoughts?'

'Oh yes! Gramps, absolutely,' I said, beginning to enter into the spirit of the thing, forgetting Munnia momentarily. 'My thoughts are my very own all right!'

'And where do your thoughts come from?'

'Come from?' I said blankly.

'Yes.'

Where *did* my thoughts come from? My head? I said tentatively: 'From uh – my mind?' I tapped my head, feeling I was a little more on sure ground. 'Here, Gramps.'

'Oh,' Grandpa said, smiling, his eyebrows going up in a arch. 'But that's your *brain*, isn't it, Sheila beti? Also part of your body, made of matter.'

'Oh,' I said, feeling a bit stumped. 'Aren't the mind and the brain the same thing?'

And Grandpa said gently: 'If they were, beti, would they have different names?'

That stopped me flat! I'd never even thought about it. 'I suppose not,' I said slowly.

'They say your brain is a receptor for the mind. *The* mind. The thoughts *you* think, are *your* mind. And the thoughts I think are *mine*. So we have Sheila's mind, and Grandpa's mind. But we exchange thoughts all the time, don't we? They say all minds are connected. So we have an Indian mind and a European mind. There's also a World mind, perhaps. And so, logically, a Universal mind. Does that make sense?'

It was hard keeping up with him, but I nodded hesitantly. 'But what's that to do with the spirit, Gramps?'

'We'll get to that,' he said. 'So far you've agreed you are your body. And also your thoughts, your mind? Yes?'

'Ye-e-s,' I said. 'But if my mind's not in my brain, where is it?'

Grandpa looked at my puzzled face and smiled faintly: 'I can't say this with any great certainty, beti, but some say your mind is intertwined in your body. Every cell inside you holds a thought. Your body is made up of memories. I've read of massage and exercise therapies which release thoughts from your body.'

And I remembered Dr Able saying almost the same thing: 'We can go through analysis, talking it out, or we can go through exercises to release hidden problems.' And the early morning exercises he'd given me began to make sense. Every time I breathed deeply into my stretched muscles, I *thought* of things, saw pictures behind my eyes, had feelings!

'Some say the mind is everywhere.' Grandpa pointed his stick. 'In trees and birds and rocks. It's hard to visualize a thought in a rock, isn't it?'

I nodded. *I'll* say! A thought in a rock!!

'Certainly everything man makes is solidified thought, isn't it?' Grandpa said, almost contemplatively, glancing at me, his eyes sparkling a little. 'Someone *thinks* up a building, its plan and design, and then, it's constructed. From mind to matter.'

'Oh! I see!' And I did. What Grandpa was saying was really very simple. I began to feel excited: things weren't so complicated after all.

Grandpa looked off over the fields. 'And what were you before you were in this body, with this mind, and what will you be after you leave it?' he said, almost as though he were talking to someone else.

'You mean before I was born and after I die?'

'Yes.'

'Cor, Gramps,' I said. 'How should I know? I'll be dead, I expect.'

Grandpa frowned and nodded. 'Yet that's the question that has engaged some of the best minds through history.' He paused and coughed a little. 'And where did the very first thought come from, have you ever thought, Sheila?'

'The *first* thought?' I said vaguely.

'Well?'

'You mean *my* first thought?'

Grandpa said: 'Yours, your father's, mine, my mother's, back and back and back to the beginning. Where did the first thought come from?'

I said nothing for a bit. Then I drew a deep, shaky breath. 'I don't know,' I said finally.

'Hah!' Grandpa said, stepping over an irrigation ditch.

I hopped after him. 'If I knew the answer to that I'd know what my spirit is, Gramps?'

Grandpa's eyes twinkled as he said: 'Maybe. Now if we go back, effect-cause, effect-cause, effect-cause, we'd come eventually to "I don't know" isn't it, beti? What caused all this?' He waved his stick around at the fields and trees. 'All logic, all science, the most sophisticated reasoning in physics and philosophy, everything comes to that eventually. The answer is ultimately beyond our capacity to think.'

'Beyond our capacity to think!' I repeated. Well, *that* certainly was a new thought!

'So,' Grandpa said, looking up at the sky: 'We don't know what caused the first thought to be. And how that first thought created matter. Science leads to mysticism. Philosophy leads to faith. Everything we can grasp with the best tools we have, our minds, becomes eventually ungraspable, unknowable.'

'Oh,' I said.

178

Grandpa looked at me, his eyes amused. 'You see what I mean when I say empirical proof doesn't give you any final or right answer?'

I nodded reluctantly.

'Matter is born and matter dies, or is transformed to other matter,' Grandpa went on. 'Thoughts are born and thoughts die. Or join a higher mind perhaps. But all is change. What is it that's unchanging and eternal, Sheila beti?'

I faltered, feeling suddenly, very, very tired: 'Nothing?' My steps slowed.

Grandpa didn't reply, just waited, looking at me. I wished I were back in my room, in bed. Nothing. Nothing. Nothing. It was all change. No certainty about anything. *Nothing* to hold on to. 'Nothing,' I said drearily. 'Nothing's unchanging and eternal.'

Grandpa nodded and said, musingly: 'Yes, nothing, you could call it nothing. The Great Void as some call it. Yet, from this Nothing has come Something, some creative power. Something which caused the first thought which caused all this matter being born, living and dying. Some Ultimate Cause which is beyond our comprehension.'

I began to feel peculiar then. Somehow so tired that my body began to feel light and expanded. As though something inside me was reaching out, connecting. A little bit like I'd felt when I was with Jimmy. Or opening the gate that day to go to Munnia's house; or out in the fields when I'd met that little boy; or up at the Sharda Devi temple . . . I shivered. The first thought. The first word. Phil's Bible-bashing echoed in my head. In the beginning there was the word. And the word was God!

I stopped walking, feeling I was about to float away.

Grandpa stopped and turned: 'We call this Ultimate Cause "God",' Grandpa said softly. And down I came with a thump.

'Or, Ishawar. Or Allah. Or any of the hundreds of names we've given the idea,' Grandpa said.

'Oh,' I said, very flat. And I was only just tired again.

'It's really that simple,' Grandpa said. 'Below all this mumbo-jumbo of rituals and religions and temples, that's what God is. The Creative Force, unknowable, infinite, eternal. And if this Ultimate Cause creates thoughts, which create matter, then surely this Creator lives, in a sense, in *all* matter.' His cane touched the little pink flowering weed on the bund.

I looked at the little weed with no name. The tiny stones on the earth of the bund. 'Ah,' I said, the points connecting, hesitantly. 'I . . . see.'

'Yes?' Grandpa said, looking at me keenly. He turned and walked on.

I stepped out to follow him. Then stopped again. 'Is that what they mean when they say the body is the House of God, Gramps?' I said slowly, my spirits lifting. Phil had said that once when he'd been trying to get Barb to go to church with him. 'Barb, you're the House of God. God lives within you. You must worship him, thank him for your life!' And Barb had said: 'Well, if *I'm* the House of God, Phil, old son, I don't need to go to church, do I?'

Grandpa turned, came back two steps and patted my cheek. 'Bright child,' he said, and smiled, his cheeks like small, round pumpkins under his eyes. 'If you assume that God's thought created all matter, then there are thoughts even in pebbles and rocks, aren't there?'

'So . . .' I went on, encouraged, 'if God isn't matter, he must be . . .'

Grandpa nodded and waited.

'. . . spirit?' I said, feeling surprised that it was really so simple. I wasn't feeling tired any more.

'Hah!' Grandpa said approvingly. 'The Ultimate Cause. That Nothing which created Something, Everything. And not necessarily a "he" either, eh?'

'God's a she?' I said excitedly.

And Grandpa said sweetly: 'But we don't *know*, do we, beti? The Buddhists don't even *believe* there is a Creator.'

'What do Buddhists believe then?' I said, puzzled.

'They say we are self-created, each individual spirit recreates itself. There is no one Ultimate Cause, just the Great Void. Nothingness.'

'Oh!' I said.

'But it doesn't mean we're not, as you say, "The House of God", eh?'

Then after *all* of that, what I did next was groan. 'But Gramps! How does all this help Munnia? I just don't see that she's going to get *any*thing at all being told she's the House of God, for God's sake, Gramps!'

# 20

Slowly Grandpa sat down on an upturned stone below the fence, facing the house, his hands resting on his walking-stick. The sun, setting in an ostentatious display of orange and purple and pink streaks across the sky, threw a faint glow on his white muslin shirt and his white beard falling over his chest. His brown face shone a little. His eyes had tiny dancing lights in them.

'Life does seem to be all body and feelings, needs and desires, doesn't it?' he said slowly. 'But the material *is* only one level of reality, remember that, Sheila beti. We live at many levels at the same time. The material is a very pervasive reality, very strong, and most of us are never aware of much beyond it. But you've just seen your mind at work. Your spirit – well, that's even harder to see . . .' He looked up at me, still standing. 'You've heard the saying: "Things are not what they seem."?'

I nodded hesitantly.

'And that we have to look below the surface of things to find the truth?'

I nodded again.

'Answers to our problems in this constantly changing material world are so limited, Sheila, so we try to find them in our minds, our spirits, beyond our short, uncertain, material lives.' He shook his head ruefully and patted the stone next to him. I sat down. 'Just think . . . this back-slid Marxist is now going to try to explain dharm to his grand-daugher!' He looked off into the distance and I said nothing. Dharma, Gran had said something about dharma, too.

'You know, I don't really believe there is anything called Hinduism,' Grandpa said after a while. 'Hindu was a name given to people who lived east of the Indus river. All groups had had different faiths . . . connected by the concept of dharm.' He paused, then went on slowly, 'The term

Hinduism arose as a reaction to large breakaway movements, like Buddhism and Jainism. And to the coming of other religions like Christianity and Islam. We're stuck with it today, however.' And he shook his head sadly and sighed. Then, after a bit he said: 'I think the greatest contribution the people of this subcontinent have made to the world is the concept of dharm, and we don't even know it. We've forgotten it in misinterpretations. Dharm is the foundation stone of the Indian mind. Dharm isn't religion. Religion, you see, calls for beliefs. Established religions have a central revelation: the word of God revealed to a human: a guru, a prophet, a son of God, which is then written down in a holy book and followed by believers.'

I said: 'Uh huh,' trying to sound intelligent.

'The Indian mind doesn't ask you to believe, it asks you to *see*. And through seeing, *know*. There is no one prophet or guru to whom God's words are revealed. No one book to follow. There are many books written by many people over a long period of time, all asking questions, trying to find explanations. It's wholly scientific with a large helping of reverence for the unknowable Creator.' He stopped and coughed slightly: '*And* therefore a reverence for the creations of the Creator – the environment we live in and for the natural order in things; the relationships things have with each other; the – ah, you might say – the balance of things: how one thing relates to another. The Indian mind suggests possible ways of seeing things. It never says "I know". It says "Who knows, who knows? We can but try to see."'

'Uh huh,' I said again, faint, faint glimmerings of light beginning to flicker in my head. In Science class the teachers always said: 'Let's see now . . . Shall we try . . . What if we did . . .'

'Let's see now . . .' Grandpa continued. 'People mix up karm with dharm. Karm is the consequence of your past lives, your load, you might say. Dharm has three components. First, dharm is the *acceptance* of the load of karm; second it is action without undue *attachment*, and third, dharm is action in *alignment* with the natural order. When you hear people say resignedly: "It's my karm, so what can I do!" they're forgetting dharm. Dharm is acceptance. It's not resignation or fatalism. If you didn't have the concept of dharm, yes, karm would certainly inspire resignation.' He looked at me to see if I'd understood.

'Acceptance!' I turned the word over in my tongue. It didn't taste too bad. Well, better than resignation anyway.

'Indian thinking is very practical,' Grandpa said.

'How do you mean?' I said, excited. Way, way, far away, things were beginning to make sense.

Grandpa pointed his cane at the hut in the middle of the fields. 'Say if you want to get there, where would you start from?' Grandpa really enjoyed making me think. And . . . I must say, I was beginning to enjoy it.

'So?' Grandpa repeated, 'where would you start from?'

I hesitated. 'Where I am?' I said finally. 'Here.' Could the answer be that simple? Was there a catch? One of those trick questions?

'That's right,' Grandpa said, pleased. 'And so simple you would think everyone would know that, wouldn't you?'

I nodded and suddenly, after what seemed like a lifetime of gloom, I grinned: Easy! This was easy!

'What if you wanted to get to the hut and tried to start from, say, *there*,' Grandpa pointed to the house, 'while you were standing *here*?'

I looked at him, puzzled. 'I'd be dead stupid to do that, Grandpa!'

'You'd be amazed,' Grandpa said, 'how many people try to get somewhere before they accept where they *are*. You'd be amazed how many people try to get there from anywhere *but* here. So, just try and imagine it. You're standing here. You want to get to the hut. So you try and start from the house. What would happen?'

'I'd fall flat on my face!' I said slowly.

Grandpa beamed: 'Quite right. So first you have to accept being *here*, before you can get *there*. Agreed?'

'Yes,' I said readily.

184

'Also there is the question of time. If you want to get there, how long will it take you to get there from here?'

'Well,' I said, considering, 'it would depend on which route I took.'

'That's right. And could you start before you start?'

I said, surprised: 'No, of course not.'

'Don't look so surprised,' Grandpa said. 'Most people are already imagining what it's like *being* there before they *get* there. Or else they think they ought to be there as soon as they've thought of it, so they resent being *here*. There's a lot of moaning and groaning about the way things are here, isn't there?'

'Like Tinkoo,' I said out of the blue, my gloom flying right away into clouds. 'He thinks everything about the way things are, is all wrong.'

Grandpa chuckled: 'So the first thing is to accept being here, accept the way things are. When?'

'When?' I said tentatively, again thinking the answer was so simple, it had to be wrong. 'When you're here? Now?'

'Yes, simple, isn't it? *Now.* You have to accept being here *now*,' Grandpa thumped the earth near his feet with his cane again, 'before you can get there.'

'Right,' I said lightly.

Grandpa laughed. 'Oho! you're not going to get off so easily, Sheila. Can you accept *everything* about being here now?'

'Everything?' I said, 'all right. I accept you here. And me here. And the farm and the fields.'

'. . . and Munnia, and dacoits, and the police, and . . .'

'Oh,' I said in a small voice.

Grandpa smiled. 'Not so easy, is it?'

'No, Gramps. Not so easy.'

'If you were *resigned* about it, how would you express it?'

I thought a bit about that and said: 'I suppose I'd say: "Oh well! It's too bad. But what can you do about it? It's fate, it's destiny . . ."'

'. . . It's just too bad. There's nothing we can do. Haré Ram, Haré Ram. We're victims of circumstance,' Grandpa finished.

185

I stared at him: Victims!

'But my little daughter refuses to be a victim, isn't it?' Grandpa's eyes twinkled. 'She wants to be in-charge of her life. She wants everyone to be in *control* of their lives. Victorious! Already *there*!'

I nodded bleakly.

'So does Tinkoo,' Grandpa said.

And I felt so relieved when he said that, I laughed: 'Tinkoo doesn't accept *anything*, Grandpa!'

'Nor does Bijli,' Grandpa said sombrely. 'Nor does Munnia.'

I breathed in sharply. Nor did I really, nor did Rachna.

'Nor do politicians, or the electorate, or the reformers,' Grandpa chuckled again. 'So on one end there is: "I *won't* accept: I'll fight".' He drew a line on the earth with a stick. 'And on the other is resignation: "Haré Ram, what to do, it's my fate." And here, in the middle,' Grandpa stabbed with his stick, 'is acceptance!'

A light went on in my head.

'Acceptance is *responsibility* for being here now. That's the beginning of dharm,' Grandpa said.

And that little light in my head simply switched itself off. Responsibility! I suppose it showed on my face, because Grandpa said: 'I don't think you have exactly understood, beti.'

I felt that old familiar churning in my gut.

Responsibility!

Grandpa said: 'Karm is your load, dharm is accepting it. If you want to get from *here* to *there*, you must accept everything about being here, now, and not make *desperate* efforts to get there. You shouldn't *want* being there too much, *need* it too much; you must keep your desires under control. Keep your mind from running away with you like a wild horse. Stop it chattering inside you like a mad monkey.'

He paused, looked at me directly, and said: 'If you want to get there, you will, without strain, if you first accept fully being *here*. Dharm is full acceptance . . . and,' he sighed, 'detached action. Detached action in alignment with the natural order.' He shook his head and said, almost ruefully:

'So the second component of dharm is detachment. Not to be attached to your mind: your thoughts, hopes and desires. Your mad monkey. Our minds are mad monkeys, eh? Sheila beti?'

I looked confusedly away. My mind chattering like a mad monkey! That was exactly right, I thought. Running away with me like a wild horse! Sheila has problems in England, and off she goes in an aeroplane. Running away like a wild horse! But how was I to get away from my thoughts? They went with me wherever I went. They were *inside* me! My mind entwined in my body! For a moment I was so upset I couldn't speak. And Grandpa didn't say anything either. I was thankful for that.

We looked in silence for a while at the overturned fields, the long furrows made by the plough hooked behind the tractor. Hariram drove by on the tractor looking morose. A troop of those shining little black birds with the long double-pointed tails sat on the barbed wire of the fence, over to the right.

'Grandpa, what's that bird called?' I said.

Grandpa looked at the birds blankly, taken aback by my abrupt change of subject. Finally, he said: 'They call it a chirkutiya around here. In English it's called Drongo.'

'Drongo,' I said, 'that's sort of sweet.'

'Why, are you interested in birds?'

I nodded. 'There's a bird I see here occasionally which I really love. It's a big bird with lovely turquoise and ultramarine on its wings. It's got sort of browny grey on the top.'

And just then, like a burst of multi-coloured energy, one of those birds swooped over the field, rolling, calling, and settled in a smudge of brown on a fence to the right of us.

'*That's* the one, Grandpa . . . what's that?' I pointed excitedly.

'That's a neelkanth, a Roller Bird,' Grandpa said promptly. 'Lovely, isn't it?'

'Roller Bird?' I said, trying out the name.

'It seems to roll as it flies,' Grandpa said. 'Maybe that's why.'

'It's lovely, Gramps,' I said. 'It's a bit . . . uh . . . like this country . . . you know?'

Grandpa laughed, and put his arm around my shoulder. 'Large and generally dull when resting, but sometimes brilliantly coloured, sudden . . . and noisy?'

I nodded, feeling happier. That seemed about right.

'Or,' Grandpa said, looking into the fields, 'like a time of life, when you come out of the safety of childhood, fly around in exotic clothes thinking outrageous thoughts, crying raucously and brilliantly as you roll around trying to accept the complexities of life, before you settle into adult routine.'

I felt my face flush.

Grandpa went on meditatively, still looking away, 'Like Tinkoo, for example.'

'Oh yes, *Tinkoo*!' I said, relieved. 'Yes, Tinkoo is a bit like that, isn't he, Gramps?'

Grandpa turned and looked at me quizzically, smiled and nodded.


I looked at the Roller Bird sitting majestically on the fence. It sat quite still, looking curiously around, turning its large head from side to side. It was about as big as a crow, but a lot . . . gentler-looking. Not quite so brash. Did it have a mind too?

'Grandpa,' I said finally, trying not to let it sound like a wail, 'how can I detach my mind from my body, for God's sake?'

Grandpa's laugh sounded a bit like a bark then, mixed with a snort and a harrumph. 'You can't, obviously, without getting yourself lobotomized,' he said drily. 'If you could switch your mind off there'd be no game to play, would there? No "lila". No game of life. The best we can do is learn to quieten our minds. To be superior to the chatter. Listen to it, acknowledge it, and carry on doing whatever were doing.'

I thought of Baredi then, working with such total concentration, and Gran saying: 'His work is dharma, it's worship.' I said: 'How do you quieten your mind, Gramps?'

Grandpa turned and smiled: 'Not so easy, Sheila. Meditation is one way. Exercise is another. A third is work.

Working without thought of reward.' He looked off across the fields again. 'Working with devotion, doing what you have to do without expecting a reward.'

- I grunted. 'Without expecting a reward! *Very* idealistic, Gramps.' I truly tried not to sound too sarcastic. 'I bet Baredi wouldn't work for you if you didn't pay him!'

Grandpa turned to look at me again. 'You noticed Baredi? You see? When work is done with dharm, everyone is affected by it.'

'But he *has* to be paid, right? Or he wouldn't work,' I said stubbornly.

Grandpa stroked his beard slowly: 'You know if I went into debt, had hard times, Baredi is the one man I could depend on to come here every day till he drops dead. But . . . Sheila, if I didn't pay him, if I expected him to make sacrifices – that would be *adharm* on my part, do you see? I could not face him if I were exploiting him. Dharm is a context for behaviour.

'Baredi works with detachment, without any thought of manipulating me for his own ends. When you're detached you have peace, quiet, harmony: when you're attached, you have strain, stress, and melodrama.'

I picked up a stick and began doodling on the ground. Munnia was attached to Ram Prasad . . . I was attached to Jimmy . . . Dad was attached to being a pillar of the Indian community . . . Grandpa was attached to his farm . . . or was he? Inder Uncle certainly was. We were all looking for rewards. Results. Exam results. My A-levels!

And I felt wiped out again. 'But Grandpa,' I said, slowly turning to look at him. 'All we're ever taught at school is the importance of getting *results*. What we'll do when we grow up . . . what we'll study, which college or university we'll go to . . . how quickly we'll be successful, famous, wealthy . . . We aren't taught to be where we are right now. We're always thinking of tomorrow, Gramps.'

Grandpa smiled and shook his head: 'Attached to achievement, attached to tomorrow.'

'But we *have* to achieve, Gramps. We *have* to get results,' I said despairingly.

'Of course you do,' Grandpa said gently. 'But you can do it with stress and strain; with attachment. Or you *can* do it without stress and strain; with detachment. It's a matter of attitude,' Grandpa said.

'Attitude,' I said slowly.

Grandpa nodded. 'It's a very important word. It's the cup which holds all your thoughts and actions. Dharm is an attitude. Adharm is an attitude.

'Dharm says: Be here now, flowing with what is so, doing your work with devotion.' He paused. 'If we sacrifice today for tomorrow, then when tomorrow becomes today, we sacrifice that for another illusion called tomorrow, all we'll get is effort and strain – confusion between what *is* and what *should be*.' His voice filled with amusement. 'Between being and becoming.'

I'd been looking at the ground, and I looked up at him, startled, when he said this. I remembered him saying that when I'd told him about the little buffalo boy. And I'd thought it sounded very complicated and impossible to understand. Now it didn't sound like some heavy German tome. And seeing the look on my face, Grandpa patted my back, and I looked down again.

'Getting *there* from here. Going to *should be* from what *is*, *that's* the game.' He stood up and brushed the back of his kurta. 'Shall we start back?'

I looked up, my attention drawn by a flock of egrets flying away from the setting sun, in close formation, their wings beating the air in rhythmic waves. How purposeful they looked . . . how sure of their destination. They seemed to be getting from here to there with no trouble at all!

Because their minds weren't as developed as ours?

Oh lucky birds!

A row of cows trudged on their way home silhouetted against the evening sky.

Oh lucky cows, with no great minds to produce great thoughts! Lucky cows just chewing the cud, looking at the world with great, dopey, accepting eyes!

And with the egrets and cows, Munnia's face came lurching back to the front of my mind.

I stood up, and we started back to the house.

'So Munnia has to accept being here now,' I said drearily, feeling bitter again, 'that she's a widow before she's been properly married. That's her karma.' I was, I realized, as I said that, actually thinking about me and Jimmy. It was my karma that I should fall in love with Jimmy. It was my karma that he should be so . . . stupid. Yes, stupid! Narrow-minded and stupid not to accept me. *I* had accepted him. Mum and Dad had accepted him. We hadn't made a thing about his being yellow or green or blue, had we? I hadn't gone on about his bloody background. His rejecting me was . . . unnatural!

For a while I was so infuriated, I couldn't speak.

'She has no choice,' Grandpa said seriously. 'It *is* her karm. It is what is *so* in her life. She must accept it or she'll go mad.' He sighed. 'And she will be for a while, mad with grief and loss *and* not being able to accept it. What life throws at us is not easy to accept. We can spend a lifetime learning just to do that. And then, acting without attachment to our desires, or thinking about rewards – well, *that* can take several lifetimes!' He thumped his cane. 'Thank heaven for reincarnation – so we can learn this terrible lesson, and finally be at peace! *That's* the real reason to believe in reincarnation, beti. It's hard to learn acceptance and detachment and alignment in *one* lifetime. So when we see how little we have managed in *this* life, we can console ourselves that we might achieve it in the next. Dharm is *hard*. Especially when we're not even taught to understand it.'

We walked on in silence for a while, me seeing Munnia's stricken face at the temple, the way she said so wonderingly: 'He's dead?'

Then stumblingly I said: 'If Munnia can accept her loss she'll live her life with *dharma*? And if she doesn't, she'll be resigned or bitter?'

Grandpa nodded. 'Like Shanti's resigned. Like Bijli's bitter. In fact, as most people are, in varying degrees. You don't see much detachment in the world, do you, beti?'

I said slowly: 'It's hard, isn't it, Grandpa?'

'It's the hardest thing in the world,' Grandpa said agreeably, but with sadness. 'I can assure you. Most of us are trying to get rid of our load. Somehow. "It's *not* mine", "I'm *not* responsible for it", "I *didn't* ask for it", "I don't deserve it", "Poor me. Why me?" We generally *don't* accept our karm: We generally resist it. And if some of us *do* accept it, then we're faced with action without attachment . . . We're all of us usually thinking: "I want", "I need", "I deserve . . ." '

I simply jumped when he said 'Poor me. Why me?'. It was as though he'd been listening to my most private thoughts. I said, hesitantly, wishing I hadn't ever started this conversation: 'Grandpa, why *is* the load so heavy? Is it heavy for everyone? I mean, I often think I'm being punished for something I didn't do. It seems so . . . unfair.'

'It *is* unfair,' Grandpa said mildly: 'It's the game of life. "Lila", the game of life. We'd be bored if everything were calm and peaceful and fair and we had no games to play. No rules to make up, no shoulds we wanted to achieve.'

I looked at him, startled. 'Game, Grandpa? Game?' I said acidly. 'Oh just great! A game!' Then bitterly: 'That's all we need, a game like *this*!'

Grandpa smiled: 'The stakes are high, beti. We can lose our minds, we can lose our lives. We can also gain, with dharm, some real peace, pleasure and joy.'

'Oh sure!' I said, very drily.

Then Grandpa said: 'It's hard to accept that life is unjust, isn't it, beti. Yet there *is* a natural justice. A natural balance, an order. But that can take several lifetimes to achieve. So, another reason to believe in reincarnation: if our spirits get several chances to achieve this balance of body and mind and environment – this alignment with the natural order – we can ultimately achieve moksha.'

'Moksha?' I said.

'To evolve through many lives, so we find this balance and our spirits which are small, separated parts of the Creator, are reunited in peace. Then we don't have to be born again. The Buddhists call this "nirvana", blowing out, becoming nothing.'

As we reached the house, and Raja came bounding up, I

said: 'But *why* did the Creator *separate* itself, Gramps? Into all of this?' I waved my arms in a circle, at the trees, the fields, Raja, Grandpa.

And Gramps said, smiling: 'Because, beti, God got bored being the One, the Only, Eternal, Infinite, Unknown . . . God recreated itself into all of us, because God wanted . . . recreation . . . a game to play!'

And he ruffled my hair, wiped his feet on the mat, and beaming, disappeared into the house.

# 21

After breakfast the next morning I dragged Gran into my room and told her about Jimmy. Then I told her about Sunaina and Rachna and about why Munnia's letter had suddenly become important to me, and about why I'd come. I poured it all out, like an overful sack of flour finally burst open, the words and feelings like maggots festering inside, vanishing in the light.

Gran listened without once interrupting me, and I realized as I ran on like the waters of a dam burst out of its retaining wall, how rare it is that anyone just listens to you. Really listens to you. No advice, no comments, no opinions. None of their own experiences which might parallel yours. She just listened until I'd talked myself out.

'Gran,' I said at one point while I was describing the din, the mad chattering monkeys in my head, 'I want to tell you about something that's really been bothering me. But . . .' I hesitated: I was so ashamed.

'But?' Gran said.

'But Gran, don't think badly of me for it . . .'

She smiled. 'Is it so bad?'

I nodded dumbly.

'Well, then all I can say is I'll make all attempts to pardon this terrible sin,' Gran said, her eyes twinkling.

'Oh Gran!' But then I could tell her about how relieved I'd felt in Rampur that day we were buying vegetables, to see no white faces. How I'd suddenly realized that Jimmy in white jackboots in my dreams probably also meant that I was as resentful about Jimmy being white as he was that I wasn't.

'Isn't that racist too, Gran,' I said miserably. 'Aren't I just as bad as white racists then?'

And Gran, dear Gran said: 'I don't think that's racist, beti. I think your dream says that racism in England was oppressing you, and Jimmy in white jackboots was a symbol of that oppression. I think, under the circumstances, being away from the environment that oppressed you, being glad to see brown faces, was natural. But,' she took my hand, 'I don't think that's a permanent condition, do you, Sheila? I think you are too intelligent and too big for that.'

I stared at her in utter gratitude for that.

She looked at me intently then and said, 'I'm glad you got it all out, beti.' That's all. She put her arm around my shoulder and hugged me. 'Now what about a cup of coffee to wet that throat of yours all parched from talking.'

I grinned, feeling so light I could have floated out of the window. 'I'm so glad you understand, Gran,' I said.

She mussed my hair fondly. 'What's to understand, beti? It's more important I accept. Life is a mad business, always throwing you shocks and surprises and disillusionments. Everyone has their own stories about the shocks they've had, and how they fell under them, and how they picked themselves up – or didn't.' She got up. 'After you've got a grip on your story, what's important is that you do what is really useful in the world. That's all.'

'Gran,' I said eagerly, 'I've decided I'm going to become a social worker. I'll read Social Studies at Delhi University and work in the villages afterward.'

'Good,' she said, 'I like that better than you turning yourself into an international politician trying to understand people.' She laughed, and left to get me some coffee.


Then I went to see Munnia. She was inside the quarter, refusing the daylight, refusing to see anyone. But she agreed to see me. She was just squatting on the floor, her back against the wall, staring into space. She was puffy-eyed and her face looked haggard. But she seemed calmer and managed to give me a weak smile. There wasn't anything to say that wouldn't sound clichéd, so I simply sat with her and held her hand while Shanti gabbled on about the price of vegetables, the tyre that had blown on the jeep, Hariram's fantastic abilities as Mr Fixit, about ahir children keeping rabbits as pets and that

Babuji better watch out for his next crop the way rabbits bred.

She gave me tea.

'Well, Munnia,' I said tentatively when Shanti had talked herself out and gone off, 'my holiday is over. I have to finish school in England. But I'll be going to Delhi University later so I'll be coming to see you often.'

'Sheila Bai,' Munnia said then, in a harsh, bitter voice. 'Study. Study hard and make a life for yourself. Get a good job and make a living for yourself. Never get married. Forget about children. All this is rubbish. Make a fortress of strength for yourself so you won't be dependent on anyone. Don't fool yourself that anyone will help you.' She paused, and then spat out: 'This life is a shithouse!' She used the Hindi word which was ugly to the extreme. It was shocking coming from her; it was terrible to see her placid face so contorted with bitterness.

'Do you know what they want?' she grated, her jaw clenched, eyes glittering. 'They want me to marry Mulloo!'

'Mulloo!' I cried before I could stop myself. 'Mulloo!' And my disgust and astonishment came right through. 'Have they *told* you that?'

She shook her head. 'But I heard them talking. He offered to marry me! My own uncle! And Ma and Bapu took the offer seriously.'

'Oh Munnia!' I whispered.

'That fool!' she said harshly. Then, her voice cracking. 'They're throwing me away, Sheila Bai. A girl at home is useless. A burden. A widow is even more useless. She is bad luck, because her husband died. Give her away to any lout that comes along!' She pulled her hand away from mine and rubbed it against her knee.

'Munnia,' I said bleakly, 'what will you do?'

'What can I do?' she said, her eyes flashing angrily at me. 'What can I do? I'm only an uneducated woman . . .'

'But you *can't* let them do that!' I said desperately. 'You can't throw yourself away . . .'

And I saw on her face that same complexed, troubled look

I'd seen on Sunaina's on the day she'd told me they were leaving London, and she would be married off.

'Don't say anything, please,' Munnia said, 'don't tell them I told you. They hate me so much already . . .' and she began crying, great ugly wracking sobs.

Shanti came bustling in and hustled me out. 'Leave her be now, Sheila Bai, let her sob herself out.'

She walked me to the side gate.

'Oh Baiji,' she whispered when we were out of Munnia's hearing, 'our hearts are broken. No gauna for our Munnia. All her dowry lying unused. Where shall we find her another husband? It will be so hard to marry off a widow.' She sighed deeply and unhappily: 'A grown girl is such an expense.'

Without thinking I whipped around. 'What about a grown boy?' I said, my tongue lashing out, hard and cutting.

'Oh, Hariram earns,' Shanti said, oblivious of the sting in my voice. 'Boys are good. He earns money. One day he will bring a good dowry and a hard-working daughter-in-law and in our old age he will support us. But Munnia? She will only eat.' Tears of self-pity rose in her eyes and dribbled down her broad, coarse, foolish face. She pulled her sari around her head and wiped her eyes ostentatiously.

I tried to hold my anger in check. 'You could have given her some training,' I hissed. 'You could have educated her to stand on her own feet instead of filling her with illusions about the wonders and satisfactions of marriage.'

Shanti sighed dramatically. 'It's true, Baiji, everything you say is so true. But I was not educated myself, so I didn't think to educate Munnia.' Then she looked at me and smiled tremulously. 'But we did educate her better than I was educated. She's studied to the sixth. I didn't study at all.'

'But it's not enough, is it?' I almost shouted.

'No,' she agreed. 'Now I can see that. But Ram Prasad was such a good man. Not like *him* (she meant Ram Milan, her husband). We thought Munnia would be well off with him. He would protect her. He wouldn't beat her.' Her eyes filled again. 'Baiji, you don't know how *he* used to beat me, Baiji.

Every day he used to get drunk and beat me. Hai! Hai!' she wept into her sari some more, remembering.

'He beat you?' I cried.

'Yes, Baiji,' she sniffed. 'But not now. Now I am like his mother. But when I was young, I wanted to run away.' She straightened up. 'But where could I go? My parents would not take me back. And I had children to look after. So I stayed.'

'Didn't you think,' I spat at her, 'didn't you think, that if you had been educated you could have earned your own living, you could have left Ram Milan until he came to his senses?'

Shanti began to wring her hands. She looked at me imploringly. 'No, Baiji. At first I didn't understand such a thing. A woman's place is with her man. You never leave your man. He is your god. No, I didn't think I could really leave – I only wished it.'

'But didn't you think that Munnia should have had an education which would have let her stand on her own feet in case the same thing happened to her?' I clenched my fists, wishing I could put my hands around her stupid throat.

Then Shanti said: 'Ah! Baiji. If you educate a woman she will think she's superior to her man. The man doesn't like it. And when he beats her, she will run away. Then who would look after the children and make a home and a family?'

I stared at her, sheer outrage bubbling inside me. 'You mean if a woman is educated, not only can she bear the children, she can also earn her own living. Then what *use* is a man? Isn't that what men are afraid of?'

Shanti looked at me, completely confused. 'They are so frail,' she said slowly. 'You're right, they have to feel important somehow. No, no, Baiji, we cannot educate women to earn their own living.'

At that my control snapped.

'Shanti! You idiot!' I yelled. 'Just look at what's happening around you. The men gambling, drunk, not working. Women doing all the work anyway, as well as raising their children and keeping a home. And . . . and . . . now,' I almost said: 'You want to throw her away on Mulloo . . .' but I managed to check myself. 'So now you can feed her for the rest of your life. It's all you deserve!'

And trembling, I went through the gate and clanged it shut. I turned. Shanti stood there, her face in the end of her sari, weeping.

'Oh cry!' I screamed, 'Go on, cry your guts out, you stupid woman!' and I marched into the house. I sat shaking like a eucalyptus leaf on my bed, feeling ill. I'd shouted at Shanti. When I'd been a child I'd respected her because she was older. I laughed drily at the thought. Traditionally the older were the wiser. Yet, the lower classes expected to be shouted at by the upper . . . but then my English years had taught me not to shout at anyone. Oh, God! What was right and what was wrong? I just didn't know any more.

And then, with something of a jolt I realized I'd never thought of Munnia as a dependent. It had shaken me when she'd advised me so bitterly to be independent. I'd never thought of myself as dependent on my parents. It hadn't so much as crossed my mind that my parents fed me, clothed me, fed my friends when they came; that my parents earned the money and I spent it.

Here Grandpa and Inder Uncle were feeding and sheltering me while I thrashed around wondering where I belonged. It simply hadn't penetrated my mind that it could have been otherwise, that I was ever, could ever be, a burden on Dad and Mum or Grandpa and Inder Uncle.

Never once had Dad alluded to our home as being *his* home, so Rach and I better do what *he* wanted. Not once had Mum made any reference to what they spent on our education, to our pocket money. In fact, while Janey and Barb had part-time jobs to earn pocket money, there was no question that Rach and I should follow their example. There was an implicit understanding that our role was to study, find a direction in life, a career, get married. Money never seriously came into conversations.

Dad, even though he hadn't understood what my problem was – or at least now that I thought about it, had never *appeared* to understand, had nevertheless, promptly shelled out for my plane ticket. He'd listened to my halting explanations about wanting to study in India, and had encouraged me to look into it. He hadn't even lectured me about not being ready for my A-levels.

I began to see that it was really important that I start to think of ways to support myself, to be responsible for myself. Although it wasn't spoken of, money was the bottom line. I also knew that Mum and Dad would give me the time I needed to get on my own feet.

How lucky I was! I had opportunities.

Poor Munnia!

But then, I thought good for Munnia. She was angry! In such a short time, she was angry. Look how long it had taken me. And now that she was angry, she'd begin to heal. The killer really was silence, despair and depression.

And, then, I thought about Sunaina. Poor Sunaina! How much better off, after all, I was than Sunaina. All Sunaina had been allowed to do was her GCSEs. By now she'd be married off, and Sunaina'd herself used the term, 'married off' to some yokel in Amritsar she'd never met before!

Poor Mr Raghbans Singh! He'd lived twenty years in England without changing his ideas in the slightest. How could he have understood Teji, his son, wanting to go off on his own? No wonder they'd packed up and run back to India . . . imagine Sunaina falling for an English boy! What would they have done?

Poor, poor Sunaina!

Even Munnia was better off than Sunaina, really. Munnia hadn't been taught to suppress her feelings, and control her emotions in the way Sunaina and I had, with our British upbringing. Munnia was closer to the basics, than either Sunaina or I.

I drew in a long shuddering breath. Thank God for Mum and Dad letting me try myself out, for letting me fall on my face with Jimmy, to pick myself up and try to make sense of my life myself. To be responsible for myself. Find out who I really was. To get closer to the basics myself.

Responsibility!

I tried the word out on my tongue.

It was a hard word. But it was a good word. It tasted clean and tough.

# 22

That night after dinner Grandpa and I sat out on the verandah and talked late into the night after everyone had gone to bed.

There was a soft, warm breeze. No lights twinkled in the horizon – all the threshers were silent. A dog howled in Samli Village. Crickets chirped in the bushes bordering the lawn. A night bird flapped overhead calling harshly. The sky was like a wedding veil of sparkling little mirrors, bits of tinsel and sequins sewn tightly together.

'Grandpa,' I began, 'you said Hind . . . I mean Indian thought is very scientific. But then why are there so many gods and goddesses?'

Grandpa grunted: 'Questions, questions. No end to this child's questions now!' He shifted in his chair, leaned out and patted my cheek. I was sitting on the floor almost facing him, a little to the front, my back against the portico pillar.

I grinned up at him. His chair creaked as he sat back, frowning, composing his thoughts: 'Let's see,' he said finally, 'if Hinduism is taken to be – ah – low religion then yes you can say there are gods. But if we use the term "god" to explain the inexplicable, Indian thought is monotheistic, which means there is only one creative force, Ishwar. The one and only. That something that comes from nothing . . .' he began to sound amused, 'eternal, the infinite, unknowable,' he laughed. 'All that we talked about yesterday.' He paused: 'Do you know the Sanskrit word for universe?'

I shook my head.

'It's brahman,' he said, sounding pleased. 'Indian thinking is very, very straightforward. Brahman is the universe – Brahma is the Creator of this universe. Out of the unknowable Ishwara came Brahma, whose creations we can see. Very simple.' Then his voice became dry as he said: 'But not all people are able to deal with abstract ideas, are they? So those who'd grasped the concept of creation turned Brahma into a human figure with eight arms and four heads, to symbolize the infinity of creation, the many powers of the Creator.' He snorted.

I giggled: 'It's a wonder all those arms don't get tangled up!'

Grandpa harrumphed and said: 'Clever child!' And then went on: 'The next thing to be explained was the changing world of matter. You observe change everywhere. Things are born – they live for a while – and they die. We just have to look around to see the truth of this. So Brahma created Vishnu the Preserver and Shiva the Destroyer. A very straightforward account of the reality we see around, isn't it?' He sounded pleased. And I began to feel excited, it really wasn't all that complicated! It seemed very logical: Creation, preservation, destruction.

'And Vishnu and Shiva were given human forms to make *them* easier for people to understand,' he paused. 'You think I'm simplifying this for you. But underneath the mumbo-jumbo it is really this simple. But then those who'd grasped these ideas began calling themselves brahmins, sons of Brahma. And almost immediately turned what they'd understood into rituals and demons and godlets and magic incantations to hold the masses in their power.'

He laughed drily, like a sand-scraper. 'Ending up with Brahmin, turning the Indian mind into Hinduism. Every time we humans make a little sense of reality, we mess it up with manipulation and power play. Why, no sooner do we have the concepts of Shiva and Vishnu, than we have some people saying Shiva is the most powerful, and some saying Vishnu is the most powerful. And we get Shaivites and Vaishnavites. And the Buddha, who was something of a revolutionary, said there was no Brahma, no Ishwar, only the Great Void – I suppose because the brahmins were corrupt. But,' he smiled, 'it *is* possible to see the essential ideas through the maze, isn't it? So it makes sense to you? This Brahma-Vishnu-Shiva triad who are all, really, only Ishwar?'

I nodded slowly. 'But what about all those other gods? Krishna and Ram and Hanuman, the monkey one. And that elephant one . . . whats-is-name?'

'Ganesh?'

'Yes, that one, and all the rest, Gramps?'

Grandpa said: 'Well the earlier gods were the elements: the dawn, the wind, the sun and so on. Concepts of creation, preservation and destruction are later gods. Krishna and Ram are avatars, reincarnations, of Vishnu the Preserver who comes to earth as dharm incarnate to rescue the world from adharm when times get bad.'

'Like now?' I said. 'Times are pretty bad now, aren't they?'

Grandpa said: 'Hum hum hum. Yes. We are expecting the tenth avatar of Vishnu. He's called Kalki. To save the world from the ills of the industrial age. There have been nine reincarnations of Vishnu already.' He snorted. 'Hinduism is *most* encompassing . . . The Buddha is also considered an avatar of Vishnu . . . So is Christ, did you know that?' He laughed drily and shook his head in a sort of mock wonder.

'Incredible,' I breathed, 'Christ too?'

'He was the son of God, wasn't he?' Grandpa chuckled. 'Hindus believe that if you *live* you are Hindu. People got deflected to other so-called religions, but someday they'll all realize they're Hindus.'

'Wow!' I said admiringly. I wondered what Phil would say about *that*!

'And if you understand that what passes for Hinduism is really dharm, then they're not really all that wrong, are they?' Grandpa said. 'After all, all religions come down to right behaviour, isn't it?'

Well, *that* stopped me flat, I must say.

'And what about female gods, Grandpa? Kali and that?'

Grandpa cleared his throat and hummed a little, and then told me that all the male gods have wives, who are actually concepts. Saraswati, the wife of Brahma is Learning and Knowledge; Laxmi, the wife of Vishnu is Beauty, Love and Wealth; and Parvati the wife of Shiva, has several forms; one is Durga, the Goddess of War, and of Protection; the other is Kali the Demon-slayer and Earth Mother, the Keeper of the Harvest. Sharda Devi, who was a real live human being, the saintly wife of Sri Ramakrishna Paramahamsa – himself the great saint, was awarded an aspect of Kali, whom Sri Ramakrishna worshipped. They did that a lot, gave people attributes of gods. Hanuman is the son of Vayu, the wind, and he symbolizes loyalty. And Ganesh is the son of Shiva and Parvati, and he's the symbol of reverence for one's parents.'

'God, Gramps,' I said when he paused, 'it's all very confusing, isn't it?'

'Not if you accept everything is Ishwar eventually,' Grandpa chuckled. 'The Ultimate Cause, up there beyond the brahman!' He pointed his cane at a wedding veil in the sky. 'And if you want an experience of how immense the natural order in the universe, just look up there.'

I looked up at the wedding veil in the sky: at all the planets, asteroids, black holes and goodness knows what else! – all travelling in their orderly processions out there.

And Grandpa said, quoting:

*'Who knows from whence this vast creation rose*
*No gods therein were born who can this truth disclose.*
*Whence sprang this world, framed by divine hand or no?*
*The Creator alone in heaven would tell, if even he could show.'*

He stopped, still looking at the sky.

After a little silence, he said: 'You know, Sheila, modern physicists, working on the roots of matter have come to the same conclusion: they can't tell where it all begins!' and he looked at me and smiled. 'The third component of dharm, the natural order. Can you imagine what arrogance it takes for humans to act against this mysterious, organizing force? To disrespect any part of creation is *adharm*.'

He stopped, and we sat silently, watching the stars in the black vastness above. There was a feeling of elation at the pit of my stomach, as though pieces of a jigsaw were beginning to fall into place.

'Gramps,' I said slowly, 'this *self* you talked about – you know, at lunch that day, when you said you must know yourself to understand the true meaning of religion?'

'Ishwar,' Grandpa said promptly, 'inside us all. They say our *selves* are all connected at all times, to each other and to Ishwar.' Then very gently, he said: 'Which is why we suffer the sufferings of others, beti. Why when one person does something which is adharm, against the natural order of things, against respect for the environment and other living beings, everyone suffers. And when we feel this connectedness to everything, then we have a true experience of religion.'

I nodded slowly, thinking of the few odd inexplicable moments when I'd felt melted into everything: so peaceful and clear. I said hesitantly, hoping I didn't sound silly. It really *couldn't* be this simple: 'Gramps, do we feel this connectedness sometimes in our lives?'

And Grandpa nodded!

'Yes,' he said, 'it's a sort of oceanic feeling. You have it strongly when you're a child. A feeling of union with everything, when the adharm of the world hasn't yet begun to warp you. But as you get older, and you become aware of the terrible things that can happen, this feeling gradually fades, and you feel the pain of separation more and more.

'When people fall in love they feel united again for a little while.' He coughed and laughed drily. 'That's why some people make a career of falling in love. Sex is a similar, more intense feeling of union, so many people keep looking for union in sex, and are disappointed when it's so short-lived.' He stopped, and then said very sombrely: 'Especially if they don't feel a union in mind and spirit. A union of just the body is very degrading to the spirit . . .'

I shifted uncomfortably, relieved Jimmy and I had never got that far. Just a little union of the mind, and maybe of the spirit. And remembering the really good times we'd had together, I thought that maybe we'd had *quite* a union of spirits. Well . . . then, I'd got *something* anyway, with Jimmy. And I felt so much better thinking that.

'Does anyone feel this union with the whole world permanently, Gramps?'

Grandpa chuckled. 'Some say madmen are permanently in union with God,' he said, 'because they don't feel pain. It's also what yoga and meditation are about. Your body and mind become more balanced and aligned with the natural order and you feel uplifted. It's what all those sombre hymns in majestic churches are about. Some say that saints achieve this feeling of bliss through spiritual discipline. But . . .' he laughed a little bleakly, 'this is rare. Most ordinary people just have a few passing feelings they often don't recognize and unconsciously they keep doing the same thing again and again, hoping to feel the same way again. Many people take drugs to achieve this. Don't your hippies say: "We're blissed out, man," or something like that?'

I glanced at him: Hippies!!! He really was out of date!

His eyes were pools of amusement. 'Bliss is what we all want. Freedom from pain. Moksha!'

Moksha, reunion. Back to where we all once came from!

A great sigh escaped me. It was all beginning to make sense. This incredible feeling of separation I'd been feeling, that seemed more than Jimmy or Sunaina or Munnia could have caused. The moments of feeling melted into everything which seemed to have no connection to anything outside myself.

'Leaving childhood behind is the beginning of the experience of separation,' Grandpa said quietly then.

I said nothing: it was really too close to home. I shifted, feeling very uncomfortable.

Then Grandpa told me sombrely: that this feeling of union is more common amongst people who live in what we call 'less advanced' societies. As we become more 'developed', and his voice became very dry as he said this, we feel more separated. The feeling of childhood union and innocence is strong amongst people living in tight communities with binding traditions. And they lose their innocence with education and wider horizons.

And as he talked, more pieces fell into place. Munnia's life, I'd thought, was more . . . *unified*; traditions giving her continuity and common sense. And my life was *all* separated: Jimmy, Sunaina, separating from me. Me feeling separated from England . . . and India. Rachna going a separate way from Dad and Mum. What I'd been searching for was union. The feeling of innocence I'd begun losing when Jimmy'd chucked me. I thought I'd find it back here, in Rampur, where life as I'd remembered it was . . . simpler, less complex, more united.

Grandpa was saying gravely: 'There's a sort of simplicity, Sheila, to less . . . technologically advanced societies, isn't it?' He cleared his throat and continued with a little embarrassment: 'I have to admit that I too was . . . looking for a less complex life when I decided to become a farmer. But . . .' he shifted heavily in his chair, 'there is simplicity and there is simplicity . . . a difference between, well, let's call it the *simplistic*: those with narrow horizons, blind traditions, ignorance; and the, let's say, *simple*: those like the . . . er . . . sage, the wise man, the guru.'

'Oh?' I said. I seemed to say 'oh' a lot around Grandpa.

'In between the simplistic and the simple are the complex. The complex run over the simplistic. But the simple know how to step aside,' Grandpa beamed. Then, seeing the frown on my face he relented.

'I'll tell you a story about that and perhaps you'll understand better.'

'All right,' I said readily. Understanding Grandpa sometimes felt like being at university, and I certainly wasn't ready for that! I hadn't even done my A-levels yet! Stories. Yes, stories were definitely better!

An old man got on a ferry one day to cross a river. Behind him came a young man, who said boastfully that he was the disciple of Master So and So, the greatest in the martial arts and I'm his star pupil, he finished.

The boatman told the young man that the old gentleman was also a martial arts master.

'Aha!' the young man said, 'then you won't mind demonstrating your skill against me?'

When the old man smiled and declined, the young man said: 'Are you frightened that I will beat you?'

The old man smiled and shook his head.

But the young man said to the boatman: 'Tie up at that island there, this master is going to demonstrate his skills.'

The boat came up to the island, and the old man said: 'After you, young sir.' And the young man stepped off the boat with a swagger.

'And,' said Grandpa, 'the old man, using his staff like a pole, simply pushed the boat away from the island and sailed off, leaving the young man alone, there on the island.'

He stopped, and I waited for him to go on. He didn't.

'Is that it?' I said.

'You don't understand?'

I shook my head. 'Why was the old man afraid to fight if he was such a great master?'

Grandpa shook his head and smiled. 'Was he afraid, Sheila beti, or was he wise?'

Then, with excrutiating hesitation, the tumblers began to click together: Munnia and Ram Prasad getting run over by Bijli; me getting run over by Jimmy . . . or really racism . . . Tinkoo, just waiting to run over the world with his revolutionary righteousness!

'You mean . . .' I said, 'that the old master took the simple road? He knew enough not to get involved? He knew how not to get run over?'

Grandpa chuckled.

'And the young man's was the . . . er . . . complex way? Running over others with his pride?'

Grandpa beamed.

'And the old master could not have got where he was if he hadn't – ah – been like the young man once? Arrogant and stupid and . . . complex?'

'There you are! There you are!' Grandpa nearly crowed. 'Avoiding the confrontation, the complexity, not needing to prove yourself. *That's* true simplicity. *That's* what truly makes revolutions.'

'Aaaaah!' I said, all kinds of lights going off in my head. 'Tinkoo's out to save the world, Gramps, isn't he? He thinks he's right and everyone else is wrong.'

Grandpa guffawed. 'And what do you think, Sheila? Is there anything *he* can do that's right?'

I looked up at Grandpa, and my eyes widened as his words sank in.

'Really, Sheila,' he said, 'this right and wrong, what is it? People go to war to prove themselves right and others wrong.

But does anyone really win a war? If someone's right and someone's wrong, everyone loses. The only way to win is if everyone wins.'

I stared at him. 'Are you saying there isn't any good or bad, no winning or losing, nothing right or wrong, Gramps?'

Grandpa nodded agreeably. 'Only thinking makes it so. And people agreeing to call this wrong and that right. They're called social values, agreements, norms, traditions. And if you're born into one society you have no choice . . . you grow up with its values. They're very, very strong, social agreements. Very binding. And very hard to change. Revolutionaries have seen over and over again how hard agreements are to change. You *become* what you fight against. Those that make the revolutions against oppressors, become oppressors themselves.'

I said glumly: 'Tinkoo's a daft idiot, Gramps.'

Grandpa chuckled. 'Like I was, until I learned you can't change society from the outside, by rejecting its agreements. You can only change it from the inside by first accepting them. Being *here* before trying to get *there*, working *through* its agreements, cleaning them up. More – you have to start, not with other people, but with yourself.'

I suddenly sat up. 'Grandpa! I think my problem is that I'm stuck between two sets of agreements!' I really was pleased with myself – now everything seemed to slot bang into place.

Grandpa's eyebrows went up. He slapped his thigh.

'You sound as though you have a choice to make between two societies!' he said, very amused.

That stopped me flat! Confused, I frowned. 'But I have to choose between staying on in England or coming here!'

He leaned forward, tousled my hair. 'My clever little grand-daughter,' he said affectionately. 'Your body might be Indian, but your mind is already part English. Now you'll do what is in your karm. So why don't you just relax? You're like an athlete jumping hurdles before you come to them.'

'But . . .' I began.

'Did you really have a choice about coming here, Sheila?' he interrupted me. 'When it was time to come, circumstances evolved in such a way that you came. Did you plan it? Could you have stopped yourself then? Were you in control?' He smiled gently. 'Life just led you here by the nose. You accepted the push life gave you,' his smile broadened, 'with as much dharm as you were capable of, so you aren't going too crazy about whatever it was that made you come.'

I swallowed, unable to say anything. It was just what Dr Able had said: 'Act it out. Do what you have to do and observe whatever goes on. The pieces will fit together by themselves.' Observe. Be detached!

'Could you have not come? Did you have a choice?'

I said reluctantly: 'I suppose not.'

'So if it's in your karm to go to Delhi University, you will. And if it's not, you won't. If it's your karm to try to become Indian again, you will, and if it's your karm to try to become like the British, you will. Or it could be your karm to be yourself – a new kind of person, big enough to be both Indian and British. Big enough to be *you*, Sheila.' His moustaches and beard wobbled as he laughed. 'So since you have no choice in the matter, you may just as well enjoy being right *here*, right *now*.' He tapped the floor with his foot.

'Oh! but I *am*, Grandpa,' I said, suddenly feeling very elated. 'I *am* enjoying being here right now.'

He harrumphed. 'Good then. Just stop thinking so much.'

'But,' I giggled, 'thinking is in my karma, Gramps!'

He laughed and got up and stretched: 'Quite right,' he said, 'my clever little beti. Quite right!' He yawned. 'Full circle, little girl. So it took you coming half-way around the world to realize you're a puppet on Ishwar's string, eh?'

I laughed lightly, feeling somehow relieved and expanded, even a little . . . unified! 'Seems like it, Grandpa.'

'And that yet you're entirely responsible for your life?' Grandpa chuckled, looking at me with a wry, rueful expression, one eyebrow up.

Responsible!

There it was. The final word. The word that kept coming back at me. But this time there was no churning in my gut. I stood up and stretched too.

'Yes, Grandpa, responsible,' I said.

'I wish you'd call me Pitaji,' he said grumpily.

I kissed his cheek. 'Seems to be your karma – you have a grand-daughter who's sort of English, Gramps,' I said.

# 23

Bumpy insisted on escorting me back to Delhi, and there was no way to dissuade him. 'I've got some things to buy for the farm, anyway,' he said firmly.

I was feeling strangely detached: the farm, the villages, the trees, fields, birds, plateau all seemed like a fading dream as the day advanced, and the time came to leave for the station.

I went to say goodbye to Munnia. Shanti was squatting in their front yard, dolefully stirring something over the fire. I pressed some money into her hand, saying it was for Munnia . . . I knew Munnia would accept nothing even though a parting gift was normal. Shanti thanked me profusely for the money. I wondered if Munnia would ever see it; it would probably go towards an unspoken 'board and lodging' now.

Munnia was squatting, as before, inside the quarter. She seemed hardly to notice me.

'I came to say goodbye, Munnia,' I said awkwardly. She glanced at me as though I were a stranger and went back to staring moodily at the floor on which she was drawing repetitive unformed doodles with her finger.

'I'll come back to see you soon,' I said, feeling hopeless. She didn't even look up.

'Munnia!' I said desperately, squatting beside her. 'Munnia, I must tell you something. Please listen . . .'

She looked up briefly, at the tone of my voice and dropped her eyes again.

'Listen, Munnia,' I said urgently, 'listen. I *know* how you feel . . . I . . . I . . . went through something just like this. Similar, not so . . . so terrible as your experience but . . .'

There was a thick silence, and I gazed blindly out of the narrow door of the room, at the bright light outside. How could Munnia possibly understand! She probably didn't even know where England was. But then . . . we were both human,

I thought. We may not have had exactly the same experience, but they were in a way parallel.

They were both losses, separations. Mine was a loss as much as hers. Mine was a confusion as great, perhaps even greater than hers, because . . . death was so . . . final. It didn't leave such greyness . . . Oh! what did it *matter*! Surely she could understand some of my experience. Surely she would.

'Yes, Baiji?' Munnia said suddenly.

I brightened.

'Munnia, perhaps you won't approve,' I said slowly, 'because this boy I was with . . . well, we went around together and we weren't married. Like in the movies. But I cared for him . . . and I thought we would get married . . . but he didn't think I was . . . good enough for him . . . and well . . .' I looked at the floor, squatting there, miserably beside Munnia.

I heard Munnia sigh, a long, wavering sound. 'Baiji,' she said, 'we are all foolish in our own way. It's the way to learn. . . .'

I grabbed her hand.

'I just wanted you to know I feel for you . . .'

She nodded.

'What are you going to do now?' I said. 'You're not going to . . . I mean you can't . . .'

She took her hand from mine, stood up and brushed down her sari. 'Baiji came to see me yesterday,' she began with a slow, shuddering breath. 'I'm going to the Mahila Samiti and I'm going to learn sewing,' she was trying to sound firm, but her voice wavered. 'I'm going to become a tailor, and I'm going to make my own living.'

I stood up and absolutely threw my arms around her. 'Munnia! That's brilliant!' I was so carried away I said it in English, I didn't need to translate.

'Baiji suggested it,' Munnia mumbled. 'I think it's a good idea.' She pulled away. 'Babuji said he'd pay my fees.' Her chin went up. 'I will be all right,' she said.

She looked terribly defiant, but her chin trembled, and her eyes were too bright.

'And you won't marry Mulloo?' I said.

She hesitated. Then she shook her head. It was a very small shake, but it was a shake.

'Have you told Shanti and Ram Milan?'

She shook her head again.

I sat on her cot. 'You'll have a hard fight,' I said slowly.

She nodded, looking very bleak.

I pulled her down next to me. She sat, looking at her hands.

'Will you fight, Munnia?' I said urgently.

She nodded slowly.

I grabbed her hands fiercely. 'Munnia!' I said. 'You *must* fight. Don't let them make you feel useless. You must stand on your own feet, Munnia!'

She looked up and smiled at me wanly. 'Baiji, I am so frightened,' she said.

I looked at the splotched dirty wall on the far side of the room. 'Munnia, life is terrifying. It really is,' I said. 'And I think it's good to be afraid.'

I looked at her. There were tears in her eyes. 'For you,' she said, 'it couldn't be so frightening. You have everything. Your parents have money . . .'

'Oh Munnia,' I said, 'don't you believe that! Parents having a little money doesn't make anything less frightening.'

She shook her head disbelievingly: 'You can study. You'll be a big person.'

'A big person?' I said with a dry, startled laugh. 'A big person! I don't feel very big inside, Munnia. I feel like a mouse. Having money doesn't make you a big person . . . and anyway, it's my parents' money, not mine.'

'But their money is your money,' Munnia protested.

'Oh Munnia!' I said, 'just *listen* to you! Is your parents' money yours?'

She shook her head: 'But we're poor . . . your parents will give you all you need.'

I said: 'They may want to, up to point. Yes. But you see, Munnia, I've got to stand on my own two feet . . . earn my own living.'

214

'But why?' she said. 'You're a girl, and you have parents with money. Only girls who are in trouble like me, have to earn their own money. And people look down on them.'

I flared up at that: 'Oh, sod them, Munnia! There's a thousand ways to make girls feel wrong. Whatever we do is wrong. If we do earn money, it's wrong. If we don't it's wrong. If we study it's wrong. If we don't it's wrong. It's enough to drive you crazy! Look, it's *not* wrong that you're going to stand on your own feet. It's *not* wrong, whatever people say.' I shook her by the shoulders. 'Munnia, don't you *ever* believe that! Earning your own living gives you . . . gives you self respect!' I dropped my hands. 'And . . . in a way you're lucky you know: you're going to start right away. It will take me a while – I have to go to university.'

Munnia's shoulders hunched up, and she rubbed her arms. She looked at me miserably. 'That's what I mean,' she said. 'You have money to study. You will be a big person . . .'

I shook my head. 'Munnia, having more opportunities can be . . . a bigger problem. You have more . . .' I was groping with the ideas, unsure of what I meant, 'expectations, plans . . . which never work out the way you think they should. It . . . it just takes that much longer to realize that . . . ah . . . you're going to do what you're going to do . . . er, anyway.' I faded out, my mind blank. Then I said, suddenly, without thinking: 'I really don't know what's better, Munnia. Your way, or my way. It's all just different. I think . . . not better or worse.'

But she didn't look at all convinced.

'Munnia,' I said lightly, trying to dispel the gloom, 'now you just become the best tailor in Rampur, you understand? And when I come back here next year, you'll have to stitch all my clothes.'

She smiled a little at that, uncertainly, disbelievingly.

'Munnia!' I said urgently, 'please don't marry Mulloo. Promise me that!'

And she sighed. A long, unhappy sigh. 'Pray for me, Sheila Bai. Pray for me that my mother and father don't throw me out of the house.' She looked at me desperately. 'If they do, then what will I do?' she whispered, her eyes wide.

'You just go straight to Baiji,' I said firmly, standing up, hands on my hips, glaring down at her. 'You just go to her and shout at the top of your voice. You just yell your head off, Munnia. Make a lot of noise. Don't end up like Laxmi . . .'

She stared at me and then brightened a little. 'Yes, I'll do that,' she faltered, 'I'll shout and shout and shout . . .'

'And Baiji will listen. And so will Babuji. And Bhaiyya. You know that, don't you. If you shout people will hear you. You *have* to yell: "Don't take me for granted. Don't walk all over me."'

'Like B-Bijli,' Munnia said faintly, and shivered and rubbed her arms.

I said: 'No, *not* like Bijli, Munnia. *Not* like Bijli at all. Shout like Munnia.'

Her face cleared for an instant, and she simply beamed. It was terrific to see her smile again.

And it was easier to say goodbye after that.

But as I left, I saw her sit down again on the cot, her head in her hands, her shoulders shaking as she wept.

I gave money and a sari to Laxmi, and pieces of cloth for her to stitch for her daughters. Gran had got her to make parathas, and potato curry, boiled eggs, cheese sandwiches and to pack biscuits and fruit and a thermos of tea, for dinner and breakfast on the train, making sure there was extra for travelling companions.

I hugged and kissed Grandma on the verandah as Laxmi piled the luggage on to the jeep.

'When will you come back, Sheila beti?' Grandma said.

'In a couple of months,' I answered confidently, 'before I join Delhi University in July.'

Inder Uncle and Grandpa hopped on the jeep. They were coming to see me and Bumpy off.

Laxmi's daughters waved to us as we passed the servants'

quarters: four skinny, shabby, pretty, unwanted girls, with hopeful eyes. No one came out of Ram Milan's house. How little we can really do for each other, I thought, as I imagined Munnia sitting inside trying to make sense of her life.

The sun setting in the west lit the sky so the villages to the east seemed like cardboard cut-outs against the sky. Smoke from cooking fires curled silently above the tall eucalyptus and spreading mango and banyan trees.

A trail of buffaloes plodded towards the Ahiran-ka-tolla over the open fields. A piping, child's voice cried out in dialect Hindi: 'Come on, you old whore! Get a move on!'

There were several women squatting singly and in groups in the field on either side of the rutted road. Several rose as we passed by, covering their faces or turning away. Brass pots glinted at their feet.

'Inder Uncle,' I said, 'I meant to ask you – what are those women doing?'

Inder Uncle looked at me uncomfortably and said nothing.

Bumpy said from the back between the luggage: 'They're having a social gathering – their evening crap.'

'What?'

Bumpy said calmly: 'Don't you remember, Sheila, seeing them the last few times you were here? It's the great Indian ritual.'

No, I didn't. Well, perhaps I did and didn't want to remember. I was seeing things, even those which were familiar, as though I'd never been here before! I wondered fleetingly if somehow the seven-year-old Sheila had gone to sleep when we moved to London and had woken up when Jimmy walked out on her. In between another Sheila had taken over trying to be English enough to live in London.

'No,' I said to Bumpy, 'and I suppose, yes. But out in the open like that? I thought they went behind the bushes?'

'So what's wrong with crapping in the open?' Bumpy said, amusement in his voice. 'It's quite healthy.'

'Oh Bumpy!' I wailed. 'How can it be healthy?'

Grandpa said: 'It's more complicated than you think, Sheila. The thing is, only certain castes clean toilets and they don't live out in the villages where they're not needed.'

'But doesn't the government educate the people on sanitation?' I asked, remembering the health worker teaching the women at the Malahan-ka-tolla.

'Yes,' Inder Uncle said slowly. 'They have tried popularizing bore-hole toilets – but the question of cleaners is still there. They have education campaigns, to try to get them at least to dig a hole and cover it afterwards. Some of the chamars have toilets attached to their new brick houses. The chamars are less fussy about cleaning their own toilets: being of a lower caste has *some* advantages after all. The other castes will not even have these. The low class, high caste people are the worst for blind tradition.'

'But why do they do it out in the open?' I said. 'Don't they feel shy?'

Inder Uncle laughed. 'Bibiji asked one of the women that question once,' he said. 'You know what the reply was? "Baiji, I cover my face – who will recognize my bottom?"'

I burst out laughing. That really was good! Who would indeed recognize a row of bums!

'Besides,' Grandpa said, 'you notice it's only the women and children in the open – very seldom a man? It's because if women did go behind bushes they could be assaulted. This way they're safe.'

'Oh God!' I cried, laughing fit to die, 'hazards in the bogs!'

We were out of Samli Village now, headed towards the railway crossing and Rampur town.

Grandpa said: 'Sheila, you must remember, before you criticize, that indoor flushing toilets are a very recent invention in human history. Europe and America too defecated in the open or in outhouses until only a century or so ago. And look at the toll it's taken on the environment, getting the standard of living of a small percentage of humanity on this earth to the point where they can have indoor flushing toilets.'

'What do you mean?' I said.

'Industrial pollution and waste disposal,' Grandpa said gently. 'Indoor flushing toilets are an adjunct of industrialization. Right now perhaps fifteen to twenty per cent of all humans in the world can afford them. I think that if we were to decide that our signature of progress is indoor flushing toilets for everyone, the world would choke to death on the effluents of the industrial structure which would be necessary to provide the required standard of living.'

'And,' Bumpy put in, 'think of the waste of water. A flush uses a whole tank. These people use one mug to wash themselves.'

Inder Uncle said: 'And think of the paper. Think of entire forests in Canada decimated so Americans can wipe their bottoms!'

'So,' I said. 'You don't think indoor sanitation is necessary?' I wondered what Tinkoo the communist, all for hyper-industrialization, would have to say about that.

'It's a difficult question to answer simply,' Grandpa said. 'There is a health hazard in defecating in the open. But there are also health hazards in incompletely treated sewage and in industrial effluents which flow into rivers. There are other health hazards from industries which support a high standard of living.'

And again, I said, 'Oh!' Sheila Oh Mehta! That was me.

Once again he'd given a mind boggling turn to a seemingly ordinary event: what villagers taking a crap had to do with the international economic order! It frazzled my mind, the way he thought. It excited me, and tired me out at the same time. It was like seeing how the tiny bits fit into the whole scheme of things. It was like seeing patterns. But I saw them only for small moments before they disappeared. I wondered when, if ever, I'd be able to see the whole thing clearly.

We'd arrived in the all pervasive environment-destroying din of Rampur anyway now, and I could hardly hear myself think.

We unloaded on to the head of an unwilling coolie in the din and rush and clamour of Rampur station, garishly bright under harsh neon lights. There was the waiting, the unbearable pushing and shoving as the train came in and moments of suspense as we lost Inder Uncle in the convulsive lurch towards the guard to confirm our compartment and seats.

Just getting on and off a train was a major project in India! We stashed our luggage under shouted suggestions, and the whine of the inevitably short-changed coolie. Grandpa and Inder Uncle gave me great bear-hugs and stood outside the window peering in, shouting advice and cheers as the train began its clank and rumble at the green signal.

# 24

Tinkoo, after a 'Hi, yaa', a brief clap on Bumpy's back and a nod in my direction, hurried us off the platform at Nizamuddin Station.

'You didn't have to meet us,' Bumpy said.

'Arré, yaa, I'd never have heard the end of it from Mummy if I hadn't,' Tinkoo said generously. 'Anyway I was free this morning.'

The station was clean and modern with pretty tubs of geraniums at regular intervals, but the crush at the exit gate was as manic as at Rampur.

We loaded ourselves into a run-down black and yellow taxi, fighting off three-wheeler scooter-taxi drivers and the coolie who inevitably demanded more; and rattled, banged, clanked and honked our way down Nizamuddin East, south on the Mathura Road, right on the Ring Road at Ashram towards Nina Maasi's at Green Park.

'So, Sheila *Bai*, how was the shoot-out at the O.K. Corral? Freaky scene, I hear?' Tinkoo said.

The Sharda Devi temple shooting had made the national press.

I just looked out of the window while Bumpy filled Tinkoo in. My attempt to be part of the village India was obviously going to become a family legend. Tinkoo hooted and yowled through it all, except – thankfully – about Ram Prasad and Munnia.

At eleven-thirty in the morning it was a scorching May day, threatening dust storms and grit in your eye. In the white heat Delhi looked oppressively drab. There was really nothing attractive about the houses grouped in successive colonies: Lajpat Nagar, Defence Colony, South Extension. All the houses were modern, functional, box-like.

Some of the new houses were unbelievably large; not many people in England could have afforded so much space. But on the whole, I preferred English houses, which although more modest, had definite architectural styles. Our house in Chigwell for instance, went back at least to the 1930s, and even if it *was* only mock-Tudor, it was really pretty.

The cars, the buses, taxis, scooters, the markets, houses, hospitals, everything looked dusty and shabby. The only colour came from great splashes of bougainvillea: purple, white, red, orange, which clambered over garden walls and houses giving the dusty flyaway city a sense of permanence.

Nina Maasi and Ashok Uncle (I should call him Massar, but it's such a tongue-twister) rented a three-roomed flat on the ground floor of one of the more modest houses in Green Park. There was a small patch of grass in front and a tiny yard behind, full of clothes drying on a line.

Tinkoo took me into the guest room. Bumpy would sleep in Tinkoo's room for his four or five day visit.

'Sorry yaa, got to get back to the Univ,' Tinkoo said as soon as we'd got settled. 'Mummy'll be back at three and Dad around six or seven. Bahadur will give you lunch and you should take a rest in the afternoon. There's a solid agro scene on tonight. Mummy's invited a whole bunch of weirdos for dinner to meet our phoren guest.' He meant relatives, of course! 'Got a class after lunch. Be back after that. 'Bye! Got to catch my bus.'

And he sloped off, chappals slapping, jhola swinging, his white kurta flapping behind him like a tail.

Aargh! A wonderful dose of Tinkoo for the next few days. Just what the doctor ordered!


Bahadur, the servant, a small, skinny Nepalese man gave us lunch after we'd bathed and changed our clothes. Bumpy left immediately afterward to shop. And I lounged about the house.

The living/dining area was one large central room and all the others simply opened off it. Mum didn't have the greatest taste in furniture – she went for over-stuffed velour sofas, but Nina Maasi's taste was even more slap-dash. All her furniture was square and functional with stiff foam cushions. And everything stood in almost military precision around the room.

There wasn't much British influence here and there wasn't much Indian influence either – but that the house was in India and they ate Indian food all the time except at breakfast, which was eggs and toast. They didn't even have the odd piece of Indian sculpture or even a coffee-table book on India. It was, Nina Maasi had said, a very average urban India home. You could, I suppose, call it international-middle-class-tasteless-modern.

Nina Maasi and Tinkoo arrived almost simultaneously. Nina Maasi is younger than Mum. She's quite lovely: big, heavy lidded eyes, trim little nose, high cheek-bones. But she's such a bouncing, cheerful, hurrying, scurrying, extrovert person, you forget she's so beautiful. And so intelligent.

She fired off questions about the farm, the harvest, the shooting, as she bustled about getting tea, exclaiming exaggeratedly: 'Ah Sheels! What an adventure you had!' she said thoughtlessly. 'Tinkoo should have been there . . . to look after you.' Then, after a moment's pause, realizing what she'd said: 'Just as well he wasn't. Silly fool would have got himself killed, playing hero sheero.'

'What d'you mean, Mummy!' Tinkoo flared. 'I would have stopped the goddam riot, yaa!'

Both Nina Maasi and I snorted together and smiled.

Over tea, Nina Maasi said: 'Tinkoo, better make sure Sheila gets her registration forms and prospectuses and all from Delhi U. Politics Honours, isn't it, Sheila?'

I shook my head. 'No. I've changed my mind. I'll read Social Science Honours.'

'Ho, ho, ho,' Tinkoo said immediately. 'Not going to become the great political scientist. What're you going to do with Soc Sci?'

He actually said Sock Sy, the wally!

'Social work,' I said briefly.

'Ho, ho, ho,' he said again, the bleedin' Santa Claus, 'the

despo scene in the great Indian countryside has brought out the bleedin' heart liberal in our phoren visitor!'

Nina Maasi said mildly: 'Oh shut up, Tinkoo.' And turning to me said: 'So which college? St Stephens doesn't have Social Science Honours, does it, Tinkoo? I think it will have to be Hindu College, or maybe Lady Sri Ram. Does Lady Sri Ram have Social Science Honours? That's not bad. It's all women though.'

Tinkoo said: 'Thank God she doesn't want to study languages or I'd have her in my hair all the time at JNU. Better she goes to LSR. Lock her up with the dames where she belongs.'

I ignored him. 'I'd rather go to the University, Nina Maasi.'

'Well,' Nina Maasi said. 'Why don't you go to the University and LSR and talk to some people, Sheila. You take her Tinkoo.'

And Tinkoo almost snarled: 'Oh but at your *service*, madam, of course!'

After tea I asked Tinkoo if he'd take me to a good bookshop. 'What! Now?'

I said yes, now.

'To get a book on Soc Sci? Or on Indian dacoits?' he sneered.

'Neither,' I said levelly, 'just a book.'

'Go to Khan Market,' Nina Maasi said, bustling into the kitchen. 'KD has the best books.'

Tinkoo sighed dramatically, but I knew he was ready to leave the house on any pretext.

'Don't forget to buy salami shalami and ham sham and all while you're there, Tinkoo,' Nina Maasi yelled from the kitchen.

Tinkoo wanted to catch a bus, so I insisted on a taxi. We compromised on a three-wheeler scooter-taxi.

We roared up the road, heading north away from the rush-hour traffic which seemed even worse than that of London, because there were black fumes coming out of the buses, and about a hundred different forms of transport, all zigzagging and outracing each other: cycles, scooters, mopeds, cars, buses, tempos . . . and even a few bullock carts! Going for a ride on a three-wheeler scooter-taxi is hair-raising . . . even on the wide avenues of the shady and very lovely British parts of New Delhi. The drivers seem to think they have demons sitting on their tails . . . and they all seem to know each other, the way they shout and wave at passing three-wheelers while they take corners on one wheel!

Khan Market was several notches up from Rampur, but still far short of even Ilford High Road.

I found what I wanted almost immediately at The Bookshop: *The Collins Handguide to the Birds of the Indian Subcontinent*. I leafed through it while Tinkoo went off on his obviously unpleasant errand, buying ham sham and salami shalami and all that!

I looked at the illustrations of the Roller Bird. *Coriacias Bengalensis*, it said, also known as the Blue Jay. Blue Jay? that sounded familiar. I looked up Blue Jay in the *Bird Guide to the Birds of Britain and Europe*. No Blue Jay. On the offchance I looked up Roller Bird, thinking it would be far too exotic for Europe. But there it was! Not as handsome as the Indian Roller, *Coriacias Garrulus*, it said, found in Spain, Italy and East Europe.

Garrulus – garrulous! It certainly was that, I thought, smiling. Then I looked up Jay, which wasn't half as gorgeous as the Roller. *Garrulus glandarius*! Garrulous again. I was idiotically delighted at this convoluted connection: Coriacias Bengalensis, Coriacias Garrulus, Garrulus Glandarius. Flipping through the book on Indian birds again I saw all kinds of familiar birds: hoopoes, herons, buntings, blackbirds, thrushes, finches, robins . . . God, I thought, what a *lot* we have in common. And there was so much to learn! I picked up a children's *Maharabhata* and a copy of the *Ramayana*. Grandpa had me hooked – I wanted to find out more! There was a huge collection of picture books on India in the shop: on cities, monuments, mountains, communities, states, wildlife . . . And I was looking through them, feeling more and more overawed at what had been documented, and overwhelmed by all I didn't know, when Tinkoo walked in smelling strongly of salami.

I went to the till to pay for my books. I bought both the bird books; I wanted to correlate them to find those common in England and India.

'What's so great about birds?' Tinkoo said, looking over my shoulder.

'Many birds are the same in England and India,' I said.

'So what?'

Yes, so what?

But it meant something to me. How could he possibly understand.

'Oh, nothing. It's not important.'

'God, yaa!' he said disgustedly. 'Buying books on Indian birds just like a goddam tourist. It's not enough you go and get yourself all tied up with bandits in the Indian backwoods . . .'

'Aah, Tinkoo!' I snapped. 'Forget it, all right? If you don't understand, don't criticize. Now we'd better get back or we'll stink up the place with salami.'


Ashok Uncle was back when we got in. He was sitting with Bumpy in the living room, slugging back a whisky soda, swearing loudly. He was hardly even aware of Tinkoo and I coming in. 'Damn corruption!' he was saying, when he saw us. His greeting was almost perfunctory. 'Oh! So you've returned, Sheels?'

Tinkoo and I sat down a bit gingerly.

'This is the most goddam corrupt country!' Ashok Uncle went on, 'Black money everywhere! You know the General Manager was sacked today, Tinkoo? You know why? He had built, on the side, mind you, while working for Fleet Offset, an entire printing works of his own. Can you imagine that? He was side-tracking work to his own factory from Fleet. Mr Seth! The General Manager!' He shook his large, thatched head like a stupified bull.

Then he said heavily: 'This corruption is making this country sick. And electing a new party isn't going to change it. It's deep in our own psychology, that's what it is.'

I told Ashok Uncle about Harish, the police Inspector. 'Is it *all* like that, Ashok Uncle?'

Ashok Uncle swung his huge head up and down: 'The government peon takes ten rupees to let you see his boss. The clerk takes twenty-five to move your file. The telephone repairman takes fifty rupees to fix your phone. And you better give it or the next time he won't come. The same with the electricity wallah. The bank manager won't give you a loan unless he gets a cut from it. You can get your income tax fixed for a bottle of foreign scotch . . .'

'But why do you allow this?' I cried. 'Why doesn't somebody do something about it?'

Ashok Uncle said: 'Sheila, we discuss this thing about corruption to death every day. No one seems to know what to do about it. We are all powerless it seems. We say: "But everyone else does it, how can we earn a living if we don't?"'

Tinkoo said: 'This is India, yaa, what can you expect?'

'It's like there are two ways of thinking. *All* of us hate this corruption. We say it should stop. It makes us feel bad about ourselves and puts us into endless troubles. But we say: "What can we do?"' Ashok Uncle said, disgruntled.

Bumpy sighed heavily. 'Everywhere you hear the same thing. "This is India, what to do!" You know, I think we don't respect ourselves. If we respected ourselves we would respect others, and we would have decent relationships.'

Bumpy continued: 'It's because we have two economies: the organized sector – which is Westernized and industrial. And the unorganized which is everything else, most of India. And we have two Indias, India of the cities, two hundred million Westernized consumers, and the India of the country; Bharat, which is all the rest. There are such disparities that we have people hoarding things and money just to be secure.'

'But the corruption is *everywhere*, yaa,' Tinkoo said. 'From the PM, down to the village pradhan. Never mind which country. Never mind organized/disorganized. I think it's because the tax structure is so bad.'

I snickered: 'There speaks a member of the establishment who pays his taxes regularly!'

Tinkoo looked at me with murder in his eyes. 'Aah! shut up, yaa. What do you know!'

Nina Maasi, scurrying by, table cloth in hand, Bahadur in tow, said: 'Very complex this corruption shurruption business, Sheila. Not so easy that moaning and complaining will change anything. It has long historical roots. You want to know?'

I nodded.

She hurried over to the dining table. 'Before the British, the kings gave government officials a small salary to administer their regions,' she said as she flapped the table cloth, laid it and smoothed it down. 'The officials had to give the king a sum they agreed on, and what they made over and above that, they could keep for themselves. The British before the Raj, in the East India Company, they fell in with the local system, and made quite a packet for themselves, I can tell you.' She came towards us and leaning on Bumpy's shoulder finished her sermon. 'But when the British Empire was established after 1857, they sent out professional administrators, who were not supposed to take cuts shuts and all that. They managed on their salaries only. So,' she flung out her arms, shrugged dramatically and said: 'what we think of as corruption today was normal before the British Raj. We're only confused about which rules we want to follow.'

She began her normal canter back towards the kitchen but stopped and said: 'Truth to tell, we haven't even thought about these things. We're just going on blindly with the institutions and values the British left behind. What we need is a lot of discussion on our own way of thinking and to choose our values and structures intelligently.'

Tinkoo said, surprised: 'What have you been reading, Mummy?'

Nina Maasi said primly: 'Remember I teach history, Tinkoo, eh?' and as she passed him she tweaked his nose playfully, leaving a mysterious smudge of devilled egg on it. 'So what we call bribery is only in relation to British Raj values. No point moaning and groaning about what terrible people we are and each political party blaming the other about taking kickbacks and all this black money shunny. We have to decide if we are still feudal or are we fit for modern democracy.' And she disappeared into the kitchen.

'That really is pretty awful,' I wailed, seeing not just me, but an entire nation, caught between conflicting values. 'I must say, I can't see that corruption and black money can be justified at all.'

'That's because you're basically English,' Tinkoo said, as usual completely contradictorily, for effect, the stupid oaf!

I got up to help Nina Maasi in the kitchen. But she called out from the kitchen: 'No, no. Why should you help, just because you're female. Here, Tinkoo, you give me a hand. Put the plates shlates and glasses and all. And Shokiji, when you have recovered from your hard day at the office, you look after the drinks shrinks, okay?'

Tinkoo heaved himself up with bad grace. Placing napkins between the dishes, he said righteously: 'The revolution will bring us self-respect, and new ways to relate . . .'

'Oh shut up, Tinkoo,' Nina Maasi said briskly. 'We can't even relate to ourselves without blackmailing our own hearts and minds. Where will the revolution come from?' I thought Nina Maasi was an absolute heroine, in the way she handled Tinkoo.

'Try to relate in some new way, right here, Tinkoo,' Ashok Uncle grumbled. 'Charity begins at home, isn't it? We need two crates of beer, two of Campa, two of soda. We have all the hard stuff. Here,' he threw Tinkoo a bunch of keys. 'You just drive off in my nice bourgeois Ambassador and get what we need like a good boy . . .' He chuckled hugely. 'And don't get your damn jhola caught in the door.'

Tinkoo flashed angry eyes at him, but pocketed the keys.

The dinner that night was something else! Nina Maasi had invited at least thirty relatives. And since it was in my honour, I had to circulate all evening answering those interminable questions on life in London, how I liked Delhi, how were

Grandpa and Bibiji, and Mum and Dad and Rachna. And what was I going to be when I grew up!

A cousin of Dad's and two of Mum's also lived in London, and Mum had do's like this when relatives from India visited. They were all the same. Pretty soon all the women would form a congregation of magpies and chatter on . . . in London it was about the price of air tickets, and children and washing machines . . . here it was inflation and children and servants. The men would go into a huddle and discuss politics. Endlessly. Everywhere.

There were four of Ashok Uncle's brothers, tonight, their wives, and between them, eleven children, many girls of my age, and two grandchildren: a three-year-old who got into everything, and a wailing baby with attendant ayah. There was Ashok Uncle's ancient aunt, and Prem Uncle, Mum's brother and his wife Bindu Maasi, and my other gran, Mum's mother, who lived with them and one of my other gran's sisters!

And there was a girl who glided in momentarily; standard kurta, jeans, jhola and chappals, a spiky hairdo, and a supercilious look. She gestured to Tinkoo who was sulkily passing around the small eats with Bahadur. He slipped out with her to the front garden, and after a bit, the girl vanished.

Bumpy, sitting flopped on a chair next to me against the wall for a moment, murmured: 'Tinkoo's flame. Name's Pinky. They're on, what in his crowd is called, a khufiya love trip!'

Tinkoo sauntered over. 'Freaky party scene on tomorrow night, man, at Pinky's. She's given you an invite.'

Bumpy raised an eyebrow: 'Is it okay if I bring Vijay?' And as an aside to me: 'That'll make it bearable.'

'Yah sure,' Tinkoo said. 'So he's landed up?'

Bumpy nodded. 'I called him today.' He said to me: 'That's Raja Vinay Singh's brother. He's here from London.'

Tinkoo said witheringly: 'Thinks he's a real intel type.'

Bumpy whispered in my ear: ' "Intelligent" or "intellectual". I can't remember which.'

'Aaah!' I said with an exaggerated show of understanding. 'Aaargh!!'

Tinkoo wandered off and gloomily picked up a tray of drinks. And a couple of diamond studded, chiffon clad aunts descended on Bumpy and me. I thought of Mum mimicking the ladies in London: 'Yes, ji, Haanji. Our Bunny will marry a girl brought up in India, ji. They make better wives, ji.' Here were the mothers of those very good-wives-to-be. I watched Tinkoo's many cousins, very decorously dressed in sober salwar-kameezes, making polite conversation with their elders, sitting on Nina Maasi's not so polite, military-order chairs.

'Ooh!' one of them had said to me, 'what a lovely English accent you have, my!'

Nina Maasi announced dinner at ten-thirty, and there was a general rush to the table, laid buffet style.

Tinkoo passed by, muttering: 'Everything I save, my parents spend on stupid splurges like this!'

I said gleefully: 'You're basically middle class, Tinklebell.'

I just kept getting nastier all the time, and it felt great, this Tinkoo-baiting.

A large lady in mauve, who'd arrived just in time for dinner, crying: 'Darling Nina, please do forgive, I had cocktails at the Sainis', now floated up to Bumpy like a majestic battleship. She sat down waggling her bum comfortably on the seat next to Bumpy. Bumpy leaped up doing a fast namasté, and stood before her respectfully. It was like a bloody seesaw! She down – inevitably, and he up!

Her eyelids were mauve, and her lips were mauve, and her nail polish was mauve. Mauve amethyst earrings, and rings and necklace too. Colour matched, Punjabi style. She had a well-filled plate, and shovelled the food in fast as she spoke.

'Ah, Brijinder, my dearest (munch, munch), I'm so-o-o glad you're here. I've found just the girl for you (chomp, chomp). Now I can ask them to meet you tomorrow afternoon. Are you free for tea?'

Bumpy suddenly began looking very hunted. 'Ah sure, Rano Maasi,' he said.

'And this is Sheila from London?' she cooed. 'My, Sheila, how you've grown! Why the last time I was in London . . .'

'Hello, Rano Auntie,' I said, trying desperately to place her . . . ah yes, Bumpy's mum's cousin or something . . . I vaguely remembered her visit. . . .

But she lost interest in me immediately. After all, *I* wasn't the one looking for a match! She launched into a description of Bumpy's intended's family. Father a Brigadier, good connections. Mother from a good business family. Girl educated at Lady Irwin College . . . where they were taught to be good wives, isn't it? She could cook and loved children.

Money, status, clubs, looks . . . nothing. Nothing about the people they were at all.

Bumpy listened politely, but his eyes became more and more glazed. I stood up to give Bumpy moral support. When it looked as though he wasn't going to be able to stand much more, I nudged him: 'Bumpy, Rano Auntie's plate is empty.'

'Oh,' he started. 'Can I get you another helping, Rano Maasi?'

She passed him her plate and dimpled.

I followed after him.

'Bumpy!' I said at the now scaveneged table. 'How *could* you?'

He glanced at me, and said sombrely: 'It's part of the process, Sheels. What to do?'

'There are all these girls, Bumps,' I said, indicating the rows of cousins, demurely pecking at their puddings.

His eyes followed over them. 'Between them and me, Sheels, there's a wall this thick. Getting to know any of them, with me living in Rampur . . .' he shrugged. 'Anyway, it's all luck if it works out. One shouldn't expect heavenly marriages, isn't it? Decent is enough.'

'Oh Bumps,' I wailed. 'Oh Bumpy Shumpy!'

# 25

There was a dreadful commotion in the flat the next morning – the family getting ready for the day. There was the running splash of water filling buckets; doors slammed. The radio blared a morning raga.

Ashok Uncle bawled: 'Where's my vest, Ninaji, for God's sake – there are no vests in the drawer.'

And Nina Maasi replied crossly: 'Shokiji, I'm not your mother. Why don't you look after your own underwear? I've got to get to work too, you know!'

Mum would have found Dad his vest. She'd said once ruefully that Indians who lived in India were more progressive in their thinking than Indians abroad, who seemed stuck with the ideas they took away with them at the time they'd left.

Tinkoo yelled: 'Hope you're getting ready, Sheila, if you want to be dropped off at LSR. I'm leaving in five minutes, otherwise I'll be late for class.'

'No, Tinkoo, you're not! You have breakfast first,' Nina Maasi shouted, with some remnant of maternal control.

'It isn't ready. I can't wait.'

'Bahadur!' Ashok Uncle yelled, 'get breakfast on the table . . . and find me a vest.'

'Ji Sa'ab, Ji Sa'ab,' Bahadur, sounding resigned, pattered around the flat quickly.

'Breakfast, Bumpy!' Nina Maasi cried.

There was an indistinct mumble from Tinkoo's room. I could imagine Bumpy just turning over and putting a pillow over his head – the country wallah unable to take the din of the city.

Tinkoo knocked on my door. 'C'mon, c'mon, Sheila!'

Bumpy said indistinctly: 'Why should she go with you? I'll take her to LSR.'

I heaved a sigh of relief and curled up round my knees.

'Oh fine, yaa,' Tinkoo said, just as relieved.

Nina Maasi cried out: 'Bahadur, iron that sari I put on the ironing table.'

'Ji Memsa'ab.'

Tinkoo said petulantly: 'This toast is burned, Bahadur!'

'Ji Bhaiyya.'

What would the family do without Bahadur!


Bumpy called up LSR after we'd had a leisurely breakfast served by a sleepy-eyed Bahadur, in the quiet flat emptied of the family. LSR had no Social Science Honours.

Bumpy said: 'I'll take you to Delhi U. tomorrow, if you . . . er . . . promise . . . if you come with me for tea this afternoon.'

'Oooh, Bumps! To see your prospective bride?'

Bumpy, went almost purple with embarrassment. 'Arré, c'mon, yaa, I need moral support!' he mumbled. Being in Delhi seemed to have affected his vocabulary . . . or was it stress?

He went off shopping for spares and seeds and I spent the morning calling Delhi University and affiliated colleges about Social Science Honours and admissions and scholarships.

I found out that Social Science Honours wasn't the most popular course; only a few colleges offered it. What most people did was take History or Political Science Honours and then go on to the Tata Institute of Social Sciences in Bombay for an MA.

I felt overawed and out of my depth by the time I was through. Bombay! It was enough to think about Delhi.


Nina Maasi said: 'Would you like *me* to go with you, Bumpy?' But Bumpy shuffled his feet and shook his head. 'No Nina Auntie, thanks. I know you hate these things. Sheila wants to go, don't you, Sheels?' and he looked at me meaningfully. 'Except, please . . . could you lend her a salwar-kameez?' I thought Rano Auntie, who would be meeting us, was enough auntie for any occasion!

So, wearing one of Nina Maasi's salwar-kameez outfits, which was a little short and a little loose, but really snazzy – just the right thing for the occasion, she assured me – and feeling quite excited I set off with Bumpy, all slicked down and shining, to hail a scooter-taxi.

'Let me treat us to a proper taxi for this special occasion, Bumps,' I said. The pound went a long way in India and I could afford to be generous.

But he said, rather mournfully: 'Don't treat this as a special occasion, Sheels. I'll probably be doing this ten or twelve times in the next two years.'

'Have you done this before, Bumps?' I said as we bounced and bumped our way to Connaught Place.

He shook his head and swallowed, and looked straight ahead. Poor thing was as nervous as a bee hunting for a flower in an English winter.

'Did you find out anything more about her from Rano Auntie?'

He shook his head: 'Only what you heard. It's better not to know more than these superficial details. Then it depends on whether we like each other. At least that's what I've heard.'

We got off hot and sweaty after the long scooter ride, in front of Lords Restaurant in Connaught Place.

Lords was obviously *the* place for the Delhi smart set. It was really quite glamorous in an olde-world way: overstuffed chairs, damask table cloths, roses in silver bowls, silk panelled walls, chandeliers, waiters in uniforms, thick pile carpeting.

'Oh how Tinks would disapprove!' I muttered gleefully.

'Just don't tell him,' Bumpy said between his teeth . . . and added: 'Please!'

I could feel him falter by my side when we located Rano Auntie. She was all in pink this time, looking like a comfortable round teacosy, sitting prettily with two older women, just as glamorous and colour-matched as she. Diamonds flashed and bangles clanked, chiffon swirled and perfume crept out at us, like sticky tendrils as we walked towards them.

On one side sat a girl who could have been a clone of the many cousins who'd been to dinner the night before. She was dressed in beige and pale blue. Her kameez had the most intricate and involved embroidery all over it; really unbelievably beautiful. Her nails were perfect, her hair pulled back into a long plait down her back. Nice, average-to-attractive face. Her eyes were lined with khol, and she wore faint understated makeup. She looked steadfastly down at her tea-cup.

There was an enormous assortment of cucumber sandwiches, and pastries, samosas and jalebis, and of all things – crumpets! on the table, surrounding an enormous silver teapot reflecting all the auntie faces like a mad funfair mirror.

Rano Auntie looked up. 'Oh darling Brijendra,' she cooed. No, *mooed*. 'There you are!' she grabbed his hand fondly. 'This is my cousin Ritu's son, you know the one who died young, poor girl.' She sighed exaggeratedly and the opposition women clucked sympathetically.

Bumpy did a polite namasté, and I followed. Bumpy was seated strategically next to the girl, and as he sat, the opposition ladies gave him a close once-over.

Rano Auntie introduced the girl's mother and aunt, Mrs Singh and Mrs Kumar, both attractive and self satisfied-looking ladies, and to the girl, Neeta, who managed a quick glance up, a nervous smile before she went back prayerfully to gazing at her tea-cup.

'And this is Sheila,' Rano Auntie said, a bit disapprovingly, I thought, 'Bumpy's cousin sister, ji (as though they couldn't see I was female!) from London.' At which the opposition ladies perked up considerably: foreign connections were obviously very acceptable!

'Ah, London. Very fine place, ji,' said the oppositon aunt intelligently. Poor, poor Bumps! I thought.

They made a big thing of pouring tea and passing the eats, over the most tedious conversation about family and achievements and London and NRIs – Non Resident Indians, who were now, it appeared, a well developed species of Indian, spread all over the world. I was considered one, I realized with a start. NRIs never got over their Indian heritage, and were always finding ways of retaining connections, pouring their ill-gotten wealth from England and America back to India to overcome their feelings of guilt at becoming so rich outside their own country. They desperately wanted India to become like the West. 'They think we have not progressed, ji,' said the mother. She looked around at the restaurant. 'If this is not progress, what is progress, I am wondering?'

The opposition was evidently well connected, with many NRI members in their family. That *I* was one, made things *so* much better for Bumpy!

And all this while Bumpy looked discreetly at Neeta, who, poor thing, looked fixedly at her cup.

Suddenly the aunt said: 'Neeta's a very good student, ji. Isn't it, Neeta? You got very fine marks, na? And she just passed out from Lady Irwin College. She did Home Economics, ji. Isn't it, Neeta? She loves to cook and stitch, ji, and but she's also very modern. Isn't it, Neeta? She even likes Western pop music, haena, Neeta ji?'

My God! I thought, here are the clones of Mum's London friends: 'Ji, ji, ji, na, isn't it, haena?'

And poor Neeta who certainly looked as though she almost passed out of something, just nodded dumbly.

Then the aunts etcetera went back to their chatter as smoothly as though this little litany of praise had never taken place. There was a small silence between Bumpy and Neeta.

I glanced at Bumpy, my spirits falling. What a fix! Should *I* say something? I couldn't think of a thing to say!

Bumpy cleared his throat and said politely: 'I suppose you also . . . er . . . sing and love little children?' He raised his eyebrows a little and smiling conspiratorially at Neeta, glanced meaningfully at the aunts.

Oooh Bumps! I thought. Naughty, naughty Bumps! In his own quiet way he was taking the mickey out of an event, he, and probably Neeta too, were almost forced into by circumstance. Neeta's response I thought, would decide whether they met again or not.

Neeta looked up, momentarily startled and dropped her eyes. Uh oh! But then she bit her lower lip and smiled. She looked at her mother and aunt from under her lids, sideways, and shrugged a little. She was obviously holding back a giggle.

'Yes,' she whispered. 'I am a graduate of LIC, isn't it? So I should love little children.' I kicked Bumpy under the table. He glanced at me and I grinned: this one seemed to be all right. On such fragile moments do relationships depend. I thought suddenly of Jimmy's hands, and our silly conversation about frogs and toads, and earthworms.

Rano Auntie flicked a quick look at us, and seeing that the ice was broken, raised her voice and absolutely monopolized the opposition ladies with a hurricane of trivia.

'My sister Sheila,' Bumpy said sorrowfully, 'she can't cook, she can't stitch and she sings like a broken record!'

I nodded sadly, falling in with him: 'Hopeless,' I said, 'hopeless!'

Neeta relaxed. 'I don't believe it,' she said prettily. 'You're just saying that.'

Bumpy grinned: 'No, I'm warning you, it runs in the family. I too am a hopeless cook. I sew very badly. My voice sounds like a overful drain. But . . .' he paused. 'I *do* like children. And I can *knit*. I knit very well. I love to knit. I've knitted all the table cloths and curtains in our house.'

Neeta giggled, and flashed a coy look at Bumpy.

Aaah! I thought, Bumpy you old charmer! Who would have thought it? Bingo – in one go!

Or was it?

'Lila Maasi said you live out in the country? In Madhya Pradesh? You have a farm?' Neeta said, gaining a little confidence, but with a tiny frown.

Bumpy nodded: 'Have you always lived in Delhi?'

Neeta said: 'Oh no! Papa's in the army you know. He gets posted all over the place. Once we were even in Chhindwara in Madhya Pradesh. I went to boarding school in Musoorie.'

And Bumpy began to look genuinely interested.

Yes, I thought. Bingo in one go. For all the sugar froth of these old biddies, it was all really common sense. Match the families, match the socio-economic levels, match the educational levels. Bring them together with no nonsense about we'll see if it works, or as long as it lasts . . . and if they like each other . . . well . . . bingo!

Then as Neeta and Bumpy began to talk, Rano Auntie pulled me into conversation with Neeta's mother and aunt (You speak with such a nice accent, ji. Just like the English . . .) and I began to realize with an empty hollow feeling in the pit of my stomach, that no way, ever, could Neeta's life be mine. My world was so stretched: the . . . horizons were wider; Neeta's, even Bumpy's, were still narrow enough so they just about had traditions to fall back on. But then I thought of Munnia and Ram Prasad . . .

And looking around this oppulent restaurant, the wealthy, satisfied-looking customers, I saw the huts of Samli Village, Lilavati, Mulloo. And I could hardly believe they were in the same country. And yet there was so much, so much that Bumpy, Neeta, Rano Auntie, Mrs Singh and Mrs Kumar, had in common with Shanti and Ram Milan and Munnia and Ram Prasad!

As the tea ritual drew to a close, it was obvious that Bumpy and Neeta had got that rare, elusive and most sought after phenomenon – they'd 'clicked'. It was agreed they'd meet again. 'Yes, ji. Tomorrow, ji, why not, ji.' We all said affectionate goodbyes and Rano Auntie's chauffeur drove us back to Nina Maasi's to celebrate. Bumpy looked as pleased as the honeybee who'd found a flower . . . in the blazing Indian summer sun. He leaned back over the front seat. 'Thanks yaa. I couldn't have gone through it without you, Sheels.'

'Like bloody hell you couldn't, you old Romeo, you! I didn't know you had it in you, Bumps. The way you charmed her socks off!'

Rano Auntie bubbled: 'Chhupa rustom hae.' Hidden talents. Then she turned to me and said confidentially: 'Lila was saying she knows a boy who will be a good match for you, Sheila. He wants to emigrate to London.'

And Bumpy snorted: 'Watch out for those, Sheels!'

I withdrew my hand. 'Thanks, Rano Auntie. But . . .' I shook my head and looked out of the window.

'Why? You don't want to get married?'

I shook my head again.

'Tccha, tccha,' said Rano Auntie, disapproving again.

# 26

'What shall I wear, Tinks,' I said that evening.

'Oh just be casual, yaa!'

So I pulled out my baggies and my precious red silk shirt that I kept for special occasions.

'I'm going to pick up Vijay. I'll meet you at Pinky's,' Bumpy said and took the address.

So, at nine-thirty, Tinkoo and I got on a scooter, south to West End. He was wearing the most nifty fine cotton churidar pyjamas and kurta, with terrific tiny embroidery along the neck and hem. Obviously even revolutionaries dressed for parties!

We bounced along for absolutely ages, getting sweaty and grimy even in the night.

The house we unloaded in front of was a bloody mansion! It was enormous. It was huge. It was incredible. It smelt money, money, money! It was one of those with curly balconies and arched doors and fake, sloping, tiled roofs. *And* a uniformed guard at the gate!

'*Your* girlfriend lives *here*, Tinklebell?' I said feelingly.

'Aaah! Shut up, yaa,' said Tinkoo.

We walked into a gi*nor*mous hall with a gleaming black granite floor.

There were great brass pots full of gigantic plants, and dirty great stone carvings standing curvaciously in all corners. Huge glass doors opened into an enormous living room, with Persian carpets, overstuffed antique furniture, space-devouring paintings on the walls . . . the lot! No wonder Pinky had that supercilious look at Nina Maasi's.

'What's her dad do?' I said as we started up the curving staircase, wide as the one in front of the British Museum.

Tinkoo shrugged: 'Capitalist swine,' he said. 'Some industry or other in Faridabad. But Pinky has the right ideas.'

I'll bet! I thought. In this setting she can afford not only to have the *right* ideas, she can afford to have them *all*. One by one until she's up to her eyeballs in bloody ideas!

'She taking Russian with me at JNU,' Tinkoo said defensively, as we trudged up . . . and up . . . 'Some day her father will have to give all this up to the workers.'

'Oh sure!'

We got to the second floor on to a terrace the size of a football field with a bloody *lawn* growing over it, filled with pots of plants, and a few of the most revolutionary comrades who were braving, for the moment, the hot May evening. All wearing the most splendid revolutionary jeans and pyjamas and kurtas, holding great glasses of scotch and gin in their paws. I could *tell* they were revolutionaries by their very intel-looking beards and glasses and the inevitable jholas which dangled from their oh so intel-looking hunched up shoulders.

Tinkoo disappeared immediately into bear-hugs and slaps on the back, and 'Hi, yaa's' and 'Who's the lovely lady, yaa's' and 'Don't get Pinky jealous now, yaa's'.

Pinky wafted up in the most gorgeously embroidered kaftan, and flung her arms around Tinkoo. 'Why'd you take so long to land up, yaa!' she pouted. She was really quite pretty, and her spiky hair looked striking. Very fashionable, with great hooped earrings and a hundred silver bracelets. Rachna would have fainted with envy on the spot!

Tinkoo grinned, not bothering to reply, and introduced me. 'This is Sheila, from London.' And he sounded, amazingly, pleased about it.

Pinky raised her eyebrows. 'So glad you could make it,' she said coolly, every inch the social hostess, one to whom cousins from London were a dime a dozen. 'Where's your other cousin, Tinkoo?' Ah! the *male* variety were obviously more interesting. *They* didn't even have to be from London.

'He's gone to fetch Vijay.'

Pinky brightened. 'The Kunwar of Rampur?' Well, well! Princes were even *more* interesting. But she hid it immediately. 'Hey, you guys,' she cried. 'It's hot out here, why don't you all go inside?' She turned to Tinkoo. 'You introduce Sheila around, Tinkoo, I have to see about the dinner. There are drinks inside.' And she disappeared down the stairs.

My word! I thought. Up the revolution with hostesses like our Pinks in the making! Tinks and Pinks . . . just lovely!

A row of French windows gave into a suite of rooms at one end of the terrace. All carpeted in truly revolutionary tatami and cushions. There were a few people sitting cross-legged, leaning laconically on their elbows, on the floor, having the most serious intel conversations, nodding and shaking their heads at each other. A few perfectly polished low Chinese tables here and there, round rice-paper lampshades hanging from the ceiling. The airconditioners were on, to cool revolutionary ardour and fire. And bloody *house* music whoomed and oomphed and wailed from a truly revolutionary quadraphonic Bang and Olufsen set!

'This is my cousin Sheila . . . from London,' Tinkoo said dutifully, to no one in particular. Then, 'Help yourself to drinks,' and simply left me to fend for myself, the rotten pig!

A girl wearing a flashy dhoti salwar with a thousand folds at her hips said: 'Get yourself a drink, Sheila, take your shoes off, and sit here,' she patted the floor beside her.

I took off my shoes and left them with all the others by the side of the door, got myself a Campa Cola off a table to one side where a uniformed bearer served the most astonishing variety of English and European liquor (which Ashok Uncle had ruefully said he couldn't afford and besides were usually smuggled in), and thankfully joined the girl who'd invited me to sit by her.

'So you're Tinkoo's cousin?' the girl said.

I nodded.

'I'm Suman,' she said. 'I'm also at JNU, like Tinkoo.'

'Oh,' I said, 'what are you studying?'

'German,' she said.

'Why German?'

She shrugged: 'Why not? Got to do something, yaa.'

'You could read *Das Kapital* in the original,' I said drily, looking at Tinkoo waving his arms about, already deep in conversation with two very serious-looking girls who sat, chin in hand, elbow on knee, listening to him.

243

Not missing my tone Suman giggled: 'Oh, that Tinkoo! All of us are not like Tinkoo you know.'

I looked around at the animated jholawallahs deep in intellectual-sounding conversations with each other.

'US policy in El Salvador stinks, yaa,' one of them said.

'Perestroika, sherestroika,' said another darkly. 'Gorbachev will regret it.'

'Oh,' I said flatly. 'They all sound the same.'

Suman laughed prettily. 'All pseuds,' she said.

'Ah,' I said, warming up to her a bit. 'Hmmm.'

'I tell you Nietzsche's the man to read,' said a very gloomy voice, next to me, 'he had the right ideas.'

'Man! Yah, I read him. Really froke out, yaa!'

Froke! Past tense for freak. Grief!

'Nicaragua, El Salvador, Cuba, who cares! US foreign policy stinks anywhere,' said another voice. 'But so does ours, yaa – what's the IPKF doing in Sri Lanka, I ask you?'

'I'm applying for a Ford Foundation Scholarship to go to Harvard,' said the first gloomy voice.

'Tinkoo says you want to join Delhi U?' Suman said.

So he'd been talking about me!

I nodded.

'God, why? It's such a dump, yaa!'

'Why?' I said. 'Don't you like it?'

'We're all dying to get out, yaa, and you want to come here,' Suman said almost plaintively. 'The Professors are just hopeless. You won't get much education at Delhi U, I can tell you that right off.'

'Really?' I said, surprised.

'Sure,' she said. 'They hardly ever prepare their lectures. Sometimes they don't even turn up for class. They give the same lectures they've been giving for years – never do research or update their notes. It's pathetic, yaa.'

'You mean at JNU?' I said.

'It's not so bad at JNU,' Suman said, 'but it's pretty bad at Delhi U, they say.'

She went on, 'I wouldn't join any Indian university if I were

244

you, Sheila, specially not if you want to take arts courses. Sciences are okay – if you're a real swot.'

I said: 'That's an . . . interesting thing to . . . er . . .'

Suman said: 'You bet, yaa!'

'What're you going to do with this German you're studying?' I asked again for lack of anything better to say.

She shrugged again: 'I really don't know yet, yaa. Maybe translations.'

One of the beards said solemnly, 'No one knows where they're going.'

The other said: 'It's an existential dilemma. Very Sartresque.'

'Aaah!' said the first, 'have you read Proust?'

Suman and I both looked at each other and giggled.

And just then, thankfully, Bumpy came through the door, looking as wonderstruck at the surroundings Tinkoo's amour lived in, as had I. And behind him came a large, tall guy in beard and glasses, and kurta pyjamas – carrying . . . a bloody jhola! But. Big but, like Bumpy, and unlike most of the others at the party, he didn't look as though he was in some kind of revolutionary fashion parade. His clothes were sort of rough homespun cotton for a start, and his pyjamas were straight and loose. There was something indefinably – *else* – about him.

He was immediately surrounded by 'Hey, Vijay!' 'Hi, Vijay!' 'Long time no see, yaa.' And Pinky, who'd drifted in a little earlier, absolutely glowed up at him. Uh oh, Tinkoo, I thought, he-e-ere's trouble!

Bumpy shed his chappals looking bemused and came to sit by me, wedging himself between me and a beard.

He was wearing pale trousers and a shirt, and looked quite, quite square in this crowd. *He* never carried a jhola! 'Some place!' he said, pursing his lips, looking around.

I looked at Vijay, surrounded by the partying revolutionaries. 'It seems you brought in the local hero, doesn't it?' I said drily.

Bumpy went Hmmpf!

'How is it that everyone seems to know him?' I said. 'He must be your age, well past college, I should think, if he's studying in England?' I looked around. 'You're the old fogeys here.'

Bumpy patted my arm affectionately. 'Sheels, India is a village. Everyone knows everyone else in the same socio-economic class. Haven't you seen the scooterwallahs all waving to each other even in the middle of the rush-hour traffic?'

'But,' I said, thinking of Vijay's brother, the poverty stricken, jug-eared rajaling of Rampur – remembering the white stitches on the seams of the Raja's trousers – 'he's hardly in the same socio-economic bracket as Pinky, is he?'

'Raja Vinay Singh's poor,' Bumpy said. 'But he is a Raja. He's poor because he chose to remain a Raja, and doesn't do anything to earn a living. But Vijay's different. He's adapted. There's nothing rajalike about him.'

Well, he certainly didn't look in the least royal, I thought as I watched him standing talking to a very intense-looking guy. He accepted a drink from one of the girls, who was, I thought, behaving outrageously flirtatiously. He glanced around, saw Bumpy without a drink, went over to the table, poured out a glass of something and brought it over to Bumpy.

'Just let me finish my conversation, Sheila,' he said as though we'd known each other all our lives, 'and I'll be right back.'

'You been talking about me, Bumps?' I said.

'Natch, yaa,' Bumpy said, sounding quite pleased. 'I had to tell him about the Sharda Devi temple shoot-out, and about Munnia and Ram Prasad. Isn't it?'

'Of course!' I said and realized that Rampur seemed really far away now, almost in another world. A dream.

'Did you meet Vijay at your Agricultural University?'

Bumpy shook his head. 'No, Vijay's a Dilliwallah. He went to St Stephens. I met him two years ago when environ-mentalists first began to get together at a meeting against the dam the government is planning over the Narbada River.'

I turned on him. 'Why, Bumps! A closet activist! Why didn't you tell me?'

He shrugged: 'I told you about dams flooding tribal homelands,' he said.

'The only petition *I* ever signed was on the environment,' I said, sparkling.

Bumpy grinned. 'Then you're on the right track, Sheels,' he said. 'Environmental issues cross all national barriers.'

Vijay came over just then, and sat down facing us, cross-legged on the floor.

'I feel I know you already, Sheila,' he said, in a friendly way, 'Bumpy's told me all about you.' He had a sort of broad average face what you could see of it, slightly large ears and a nice smile. There was just a tang of British accent in his voice. Just the slightest aspiration, hard Ts and Ds. I was suddenly, inexplicably lonely to hear British accents again.

He grinned: 'I believe you've been to see my ancestral home?'

I nodded.

'Picturesque, huh?'

'Yes,' I said politely.

He laughed out loud, throwing his head back, one hand slapping a knee. 'You don't have to be polite, Sheila. You can say what you really want.'

I said: 'It was a . . . an eye opener.'

He hooted. 'That's for sure!' he said. 'Poor old Vinay. There are many like him, still living in the past. Like the old Rani of Awadh, who lived in the VIP suite in the New Delhi railway station, with her retainers and carpets and blood-hounds, for years, and refused to move until the government restored her palaces and lands. They finally gave her an old royal hunting lodge on the ridge in Delhi. And there are people living in Chandni Chowk who claim the Red Fort is theirs because they are descendents of the last Mughal Emperor!'

I giggled disbelievingly.

'It's true,' he said.

By then both Pinky's rooms were packed with people. Then Pinky cried: 'Dinner everyone. Out on the terrace!' And there was a general exodus into the dry heat outside. It was eleven p.m.! The Bang and Olufsen belted out an Indian raga. And Bumpy and Vijay and I talked and talked and talked as we filled our plates and went back to sit on the floor to eat. About environment and deforestation and India's development policies. About agriculture and population. Droughts and floods.

At one point Tinkoo and Pinky joined us.

'So the ABCDs have got together,' Tinkoo said in his usual kind and friendly manner.

'ABCDs?' I said.

'It stands for American Born Confused Desis,' Pinky said sweetly, and looked coyly at Vijay. 'But of course, you can't call Vijay an ABCD. He was born in India, Tinkoo. He's only studying in England.'

Vijay smiled.

'I wish I were clever enough to go to a foreign university,' Pinky sighed. 'Papa's taking us on a tour of Europe next month. Maybe I'll drop in and see you. School of African and Oriental Studies, isn't it?'

Vijay said: 'No. Nothing so grand. Just London University. But, unfortunately I won't be back in London next month, Pinky. I'm going to Rampur and then down south.'

Tinkoo said under his breath: 'Ah! all this phoren shoren, firang shirang!'

Pinky said sweetly: 'You could come with us, Tinkoo, Papa said you could, you know that.'

'I'm not into all this jaunting around the world on pleasure trips,' Tinkoo said righteously. And suddenly I was sure Pinky's dad had offered to pay for Tinkoo's ticket! Just to keep his darling daughter happy. What a blow to poor old revolutionary Tinks! Maybe *that's* why he was so revolutionary! He had an excuse not to be a courtier. Mr Pinky whatever! I felt sorry for him.

'ABCDs,' I said, 'ABCDs.' I didn't like the sound of that.

'Desi means, native,' Vijay said. 'You know that, Sheila?'

I nodded. 'Confused Desis. Is that like NRIs?'

'The children of,' Vijay said. 'Second generation Indians – children of immigrant parents who have a difficult time

248

between their parents' values and those of the local Americans.'

'Oh,' I said flatly.

'But you would be BBCD, I suppose,' Tinkoo said gleefully. 'British Born Confused Desi.'

Bumpy said: 'Oh shut up, yaa, she was born in India.'

'So,' Tinkoo crowed. 'IBBRCD! Indian Born British Resident Confused Desi.'

God, I thought with a depressing thud in my gut, they really have us sussed. There must be lots about like me, then.

'Still,' said Vijay cheerfully, 'no worse than IBPRBSs or BBPRBSs or ABPRBSs.'

'What's that?' Tinkoo said eagerly, grinning.

'Indian Born Pseudo Revolutionary Bullshitters,' said Vijay solemnly, 'or their British and American equivalents. I've met a few, I can tell you!'

Pinky frowned at that and her dimples absolutely disappeared. Tinkoo stood up and said: 'Come on, Pinky, let's get some pudding.'

And Vijay smiled sweetly up at them and said: 'Present company excepted, of course!'

'See you, Pinks and Tinks,' I mumbled under my breath and smiled gratefully at Vijay.

And we chatted on, through the array of puds, over the Indian classical ragas, and all that wonderful intel conversation floating about.

They started dancing after dinner, part break, part jive, in a corner of the room, to alternating house music and Punjabi disco bhangra which brought self-conscious giggles from the more sophisticated in the crowd, for whom obviously, local pop was a bit passé. We talked about NRIs and BBCDs, cultural schizophrenia and corruption and the criminalization of politics, and of Vijay's experiences in London University where he was taking Political Anthropology.

Then someone pulled out hash and dope and ganja, and Bumpy said it was 'time to split'.

'I'll drive you back,' Vijay said, 'I borrowed my uncle's car. You're on my way.'

'Oh,' I said, 'the uncle who . . .'

Vijay, shuffling into his chappals, grinned. 'The very same. He had the sense to cut his losses and join the army when Father decided to remain a Raja. He's a colonel. Lives in Defence Colony.'

He slung his jhola comfortably on his shoulder and rustled around in it for his keys. 'Families!' he huffed.

It took a while to dislodge Tinkoo, and say goodbye to the ravishing Pinky.

Vijay drove a ramshackle Fiat which took a while to locate in the street which was simply jammed with fancy new Marutis.

I looked back at the house as we drove away.

'Wow!' I said feelingly.

Vijay said: 'Yeah!'

Bumpy said: 'Wow indeed.'

And Tinkoo said: 'Aaah, shut up all of you!'


The next morning Bumpy said: 'Ah Sheels, er . . . Rano Maasi said I should – er – take Neeta out for lunch . . .'

I said flatly: 'Oh.' Then, quite genuinely, 'That's great!' I'd just have to make it around to Delhi U on my own, or, groan! with Tinkoo . . .

'So,' said Bumpy, 'I – er – asked Vijay to er . . .'

And I said gladly: 'That's fine, Bumps, as long as it isn't Tinklebell.'

Bumpy laughed: 'You two!' he said.


Vijay came by at ten. And he not only took me to Delhi University but he gave me a solid tour of Delhi. For the next two days, I became one of that 'despo breed', the tourist. But I had the privilege of having as my personal tour guide, a very knowledgeable Vijay. And I bet I got to know Delhi better than Tinkoo ever did – or will.

'Delhi is a conglomeration of overlapping cities,' Vijay said, 'springing up and falling into ruins from as far back as 3000 BC, some say.' And he took me around all the cities.

Sometimes in his uncle's car, sometimes by bus and sometimes on a scooter taxi.

We started at Indraprastha, and went on to the Qila Rai Pithora ruins. We had a picnic lunch at the deserted fort of Tuglaquabad. We visited Nizamuddin Village and Sri Fort and Jahanpanah. We strolled through the crowded streets of Shahjehanabad, the once gracious city of Emperor Shahjehan. We even visited one of the families who claimed descent from the Mughal kings, and now wanted the Red Fort as their own. 'Just think of the back rent, the Indian government owes us,' said an old man, sitting on his charpai inside a run down old mansion.

Later on while I was shopping for gifts for Mum and Dad, Rachna and Janey and Barb, we passed by a grocery store run by a Sikh. And my steps faltered: Sunaina! How long since I'd thought of her. Where was she? Was she married? Was he some oaf, or was it perhaps a happy choice after all? I wondered if she would ever write to me. If she didn't, I would never know. I felt my gut wrench. I couldn't believe that, 'just like that' she'd so completely vanished from my life. How stupid. How stupid . . .

And I was quiet the rest of the afternoon. Vijay said: 'Penny for them?' And somehow I found it easy to tell him all about Sunaina. And he seemed to understand.

We went to the university and Vijay helped me get all the information I needed and all the forms and brochures. We passed by the British armories destroyed during the First War of Independence in 1857 – which British History books call The Indian Mutiny. Then we wandered around the British Imperial City, south of Shahjehanabad, the seat of British Raj. We had tea with one of Vijay's aunts who lived in one of the old British colonial bungalows on Aurangzeb Road, amidst vast grounds and ancient trees. I could see where Grandpa had got the inspiration for his house in Rampur. Then we drove up to the Rashtrapati Bhavan, which was for thirty years the British Viceroy's mansion, before India's Independence in 1947. And *everywhere* of course, I took pictures.

I saw ruins and gardens and monuments and mausoleums.

But I also saw the horrible slums made of mud and tin and canvas huddled in slushy roads, beside stagnant pools of water. No sanitation or electricity or water reached them until it was time for elections.

'They're vote banks,' Vijay said. 'This is what happens when development policies are pro-industry and political power, and anti-people. This is where the rural migrants come when hydro-electric power stations are built on their lands, or their forest homelands are flooded by dams to feed power to cities. This is what happens when the land can no longer support growing populations, when money-lenders fleece the farmers and local politicians and police terrify them. Sixty per cent of Delhi's population lives in such conditions, breeding despair, disease, fatalism, and eventually crime and banditry.'

And I thought of the ahirs and malahars and chamars of Samli trying to live in these slums! I thought of Bijli's gang and Mangal Bai and her vendetta. And newspaper reports of the growing crime rate in Delhi.

'Mahatma Gandhi,' Vijay said, 'really knew what was right for this country. Pandit Nehru's vision of an industrial India has led us into an ecological disaster. The Mahatma said industry should be in service to the people, like trustees. But people thought he was against industry. We westernized Indians have been crazy to "catch up" with the West, especially in the last ten years. If we had gone the Mahatma's way, with the right dose of industrialization, we would have had small self-contained village communities governed by their own elders, producing what they needed, and only a little extra for trade. Machines would have been fitted to the needs of people, not people to the needs of the machines. Powers would have been invested upward to the centre, by self respecting co-equals, not devolved down from the Centre, like in a monarchy, from superior to inferior. We would not have rich cosmopolitan slum-ridden cities. We would not have had the Pinkys of the world. We would have been, I think, a humbler people. And we would have had more balance.'

And I thought suddenly: With dharma. Surely that's what dharma means!

'The world is headed towards small self-governing communities – away from heavy central authority,' Vijay went on, 'it's beginning in Russia and East Europe. Perhaps people are more willing to be responsible for themselves rather than look for easy answers from authoritarian Mummy or Daddy governments.' Then he said thoughtfully, 'I think poverty is more ecologically sound. I don't mean degradation. I mean not having to judge your worth by material riches. Degradation is the result of not following our own psyche. When we follow others' instead we forget ourselves. And in India we have forgotten who we are. We've followed others' paths in preference to our own.'

And I said: 'Can't we follow both, Vijay? Can't we take the best of both?'

He looked at me swiftly from under his eyelids. 'People like you and me – that's what we have to do. Balance two worlds. Two minds. Two ways of being. Maybe more. Three or four or five ways of being. And, I believe, in finding that balance, we'll find what the whole world truly wants: self respect.'

It was great to hear Vijay talk – I felt a real empathy with him. Vijay's fundas were certainly not gol!


And Tinkoo's, I decided, certainly were!

When he said: 'Aaah! the foreign tourist Mem finally got her guided tour! Got enough pictures of exotic ethnic India for your firang friends?' I just smiled coldly at this prat who was my cousin, and raised my eyebrows, deliberately. I wasn't going to give an inch to him any more. No more conciliatory gestures. We had a private war going on, and I'd fight it to the finish when I got back, to go to Delhi U, the stupid wally!

Vijay left for Rampur the next evening with a glowing Bumpy, who had gone from success to success with Neeta, and expected to be back very shortly – to buy more farm equipment! And the next evening I flew back to London, seen off by Ashok Uncle, Nina Auntie, Prem Uncle, Bindu Maasi, my other gran, and a scowling Tinkoo who obviously wished he'd rather be on the moon!

I had my college brochures and registration forms safely packed in my bag, ready to return in a couple of months to enrol in Hindu College.

# EPILOGUE

Well, I didn't go to Delhi University.

It wasn't a decision which was made snap! like that. I didn't wake up one morning in London, knowing that I wouldn't go back to India. It sort of crept upon me, day to day.

I got back to England in time to finish my A-levels. And I was still thinking about Social Science Honours at Hindu College, after I got the results. I even filled in my forms and Dad attached a bank draft and sent it off. I got admission, but when it came time to fly back to India in July, I balked.

And when I thought about applying to university in England, I couldn't bring myself to do that either, even though there'd been a lot of discussion about it at school with the Head, and with teachers who thought I had the brains and should use them.

Not the sort of heroic decisiveness you read about in novels.

Instead, with Mum and Dad nibbling their fingernails with anxiety – behind my back, of course, I went to work at Stacey's, an upmarket bookshop in Ilford, so I wouldn't have to think about university for a while. But, of course, I did!

They didn't have as terrific a collection of books on India as The Bookstore in Khan Market in New Delhi, but I managed to persuade the manager to order many new titles. Every free moment I read. I read practically all I could about India. But India seemed, in the bustle of Ilford and being back with Barb and Janey and Rach, to be simply fading away!

Rach thought my working at Stacey's was just fine! *She* was certain she didn't want to go to university. She'd realized she had no great ambitions, *she* wanted to become a hairdresser! I think Mum and Dad were quietly pulling their heads bald over Rach.

Then, one day, Mr Sydenham, my English teacher came into the bookshop, and seeing me there, took me to lunch. It wasn't as much of a coincidence as it sounds, because I found out later Dad had talked to Dr Able about me and Dr Able'd suggested he talk to the Head. And the Head had talked to some of the teachers. Over a Big Mac Mr Sydenham told me he'd been very impressed with the essay I'd written for my A-levels. I'd described the jabbah festival and the villages, leaving out Bijli and Munnia, of course. He said he thought I had an anthropologist's eye for detail – why didn't I think about going for anthropology?

It seems that's the way, really, decisions get made. Well . . . I don't really know that it was a decision at all. It just seemed like a door had quietly opened.

You don't *decide* where you belong, really, I think, or what you're going to do. You *realize* it, gradually. As Grandpa had said, you don't actually have a choice. Life leads you by the nose. It seemed somehow right that I follow Mr Sydenham's advice. Probably it was just time. I applied to Sussex University and joined in the spring. I've been here for almost nine months now. And I like it. I work part-time at the local bookshop so I feel I *am* beginning to support myself, though Dad sends me a bit of cash now and then. It isn't quite as directly down-in-the-grass-roots as social work, and you could even say it's a rather ivory-tower way of looking at the world. I sometimes, I have to admit, think it's a cop-out. But it seems to fit me. Perhaps I have to accept I'm not the most committed person in the world: all my best intentions seem to live safely in my head. And I hope that's really just for now, and some day I'll be able to implement them.

I'm going to specialize in the tribes of Madhya Pradesh. There are a lot of them: Bhils, Gonds, Madias – who will, if India continues her present development policies, soon be the lost people of town and city slums. I've been reading books by the anthropologist Verrier Elwin who worked with them all his life. And some day, I'd like to go back to India and see if I can't be of some real use there.

I was asked by Dr Sedgwick, the Anthro Professor, seven months ago to give a talk on my experiences of the Samli villages, using slides I'd taken there. After the lecture, he suggested I write down the story of my visit.

So, because Dr Able had suggested it too, I began it. It's been hard, especially the bits with Grandpa, and I stopped and started several times. Dr Sedgewick who read parts of it encouraged me to carry on because, he said, I have a novelist's eye for detail!

Well! what can I say about that? My English teacher said I should take anthropology and my Anthro Prof says I could be a novelist!

We seem to be geared up to specialize all the time, be really good at one thing – but people aren't like that really. Machines are the real specialists; people have so many sides. I have a feeling specialization makes you lopsided, and I wish our education allowed us to develop as a whole person, a whole mind instead of just parts of it.

Grandpa, I remembered one day, had said that the original Indian system of education was more holistic, but it was only available to brahmins. When you have to educate so many people, I suppose you have to make a sort of machine out of education. Partition it and segment it and give it out in bits and pieces. And then make people able to fit themselves as bits and pieces to the machine called society that makes it possible for them to have a standard of living high enough to make it possible to have an education in the first place!

We're brought up to believe we ought to know what we want. Which to me means which part of our minds we want to develop, and I have a feeling most of us aren't able to do that at all. We want all of us there is . . . that's how I feel anyway. So I've stumbled about trying to figure out what part of me I ought to want. Which seems to me a pretty strange thing to do. Still, most of us do finally blunder into something we're better at than other things – and there we are – specializing.

Except, as Mr Sydenham and Dr Sedgwick showed me, we never really can be sure we've developed the best side we have. And I'm not sure most of us should even try, unless we're natural Mozarts, or Margot Fonteyns!

For the longest time, although my memories of India came and faded in waves as I wrote and tore up and rewrote, I'd keep remembering snaches of conversations I'd had with Grandpa, about karma. Perhaps it's my karma to be an anthropologist and perhaps it's my karma to become a novelist or perhaps it's in my karma to be a bit of both. Who knows?

And as for boys . . . well . . .

I had a letter from Vijay not long after I came to Sussex. He'd been back in London while I'd been fretting away at Stacey's, but hadn't got in touch then . . . probably just as well. I was quite chuffed to get his letter. I hadn't thought much about him after returning to London: after all, I was going back to India, wasn't I? And he'd be coming back to London. But, when I heard from him, I remembered how much I'd enjoyed our few days together in Delhi, and how easily we had talked and talked, and how much we'd agreed on. I've met him in London a couple of times, and we've gone to concerts and exhibitions and to an environmentalist's meeting, and he's been down to Sussex on long weekends. He's coming to Chigwell for Christmas and I have to say I'm really looking forward to that. But Vijay's an Indian, and I'm an . . . NRI . . . and an IBBRCD . . . so I'm cool, very cool. What'll happen? Who knows! My karma knows, I suppose.

Bumpy and I have started writing regularly. He keeps me up to date with all the news!

Laxmi's husband finally came and took her away: no wife of a thakur was going to wash dishes!

Munnia's becoming a seamstress. There was quite a hullabaloo about it with Shanti and Ram Milan. And Mulloo declared he had lost his heart to Munnia – I suppose because she absolutely refused to marry him – and threatened to commit suicide: the all-time Indian movie hero! Gran keeps them all well in check.

Pinky chucked Tinkoo eventually, which has made him even more of a revolutionary. He's joined the student wing of the Communist Party, and is messing in university politics. I wonder if we'll *ever* get to finish our battle . . .

And Bumpy and Neeta got married. She likes it in Rampur, Bumpy says, she's teaching at the Government Girls High School.

Bijli was caught by the police and is in the lock-up, like her sister . . .

The other day, rushing madly to Statistics class – my least favourite subject – I suddenly saw a brownish bird with a white striped black tail. Actually I first heard it screech, as it flew heavily down from an oak tree and hopped across the lawn. I saw the slight blue on its wings, and realized it was a common jay. Of course I'd seen many before, but this was the first time I really noticed it. 'Hey Garrulous!' I said, delighted. 'Hey Garrulous, you old thing!' And mightily pleased with myself, I danced into class.

But I needn't have bothered, because I couldn't concentrate on a thing. I kept looking out of the window, and the prof's voice faded into a sort of background drone. In front of my eyes I saw, not the lawns and red brick of the buildings of Sussex University but a small, ragged, dirty boy in tattered shoes, dirty face and innocent eyes, beating his buffalo with a stick and crying: 'C'mon, you old whore, get a move on!' And then, leaning on his stick and saying: 'Why should I want to be an engine driver? I'm a buffalo boy. Why should I want to be anything else? I am what I am!'

Then I saw a Roller Bird, browny grey and indistinct, on a branch, flying rolling and calling down to the fields, its ultramarine and turquoise wings brilliant against the harvested fields, disappearing again into its simple camouflage as it perched on a fence.

And I remembered, suddenly, where I'd heard something like: 'I am what I am.' It's in the Bible. It's what God said to Moses on the mountain, when he revealed his ten commandments. 'I am that I am.'

I remembered Grandpa saying the Roller Bird is like the sudden loud, colourful events of India in a generally brown and humdrum country, or like the colour and brilliance of youth between the brown security of childhood and the brown routines of adult life. But I thought then, my Statistics class buzzing away behind me, that the sudden colourful display of wings of the Roller Bird was really like the complexity in between two kinds of simplicity. The simplicity of the little boy, who in his innocence, had the wisdom of Ishwar, the simplicity of Ishwar, the force that created this complex world for its own enjoyment.

And we were meant to enjoy, to really enjoy all the complexities that life threw at us. All the intricacies and convolutions, everything in this 'lila', this game, that Ishwar began, because it got bored with being the One and Only, the Unknown, the Unknowable, the Eternal and the Infinite.

And as I thought that, I saw Grandpa's eyes streaming with tears of laughter, and I heard his great guffaw. To enjoy it all is dharma, to roll with the punches, ride the disasters and the tragedies, the loneliness and confusion. To accept. Because acceptance is the beginning of joy. Being here right now is dharma. And dharma is joy.

Being an IBBRCD is my karma, and that I'm beginning to accept it is a little bit of dharma.

Living in England is my karma, and that it's really okay is a little bit of dharma.

Going to Sussex University is my karma, and my enjoying it so much is a little more dharma.

And when I got hauled up by the Statistics professor in front of the whole class for daydreaming, well I took that with a pinch of dharma too!